# Midnight in the Harem

### LUCY MONROE
### CAROL MARINELLI
### SUSANNA CARR

MILLS & BOON

All rights reserved including the right of reproduction in whole or in part in any form. This edition is published by arrangement with Harlequin Books S.A.

This is a work of fiction. Names, characters, places, locations and incidents are purely fictional and bear no relationship to any real life individuals, living or dead, or to any actual places, business establishments, locations, events or incidents. Any resemblance is entirely coincidental.

This book is sold subject to the condition that it shall not, by way of trade or otherwise, be lent, resold, hired out or otherwise circulated without the prior consent of the publisher in any form of binding or cover other than that in which it is published and without a similar condition including this condition being imposed on the subsequent purchaser.

® and ™ are trademarks owned and used by the trademark owner and/ or its licensee. Trademarks marked with ® are registered with the United Kingdom Patent Office and/or the Office for Harmonisation in the Internal Market and in other countries.

Published in Great Britain 2015
by Mills & Boon, an imprint of Harlequin (UK) Limited,
Eton House, 18-24 Paradise Road, Richmond, Surrey, TW9 1SR

MIDNIGHT IN THE HAREM © 2015 Harlequin Books S.A.

*For Duty's Sake* © 2011 Lucy Monroe
*Banished to the Harem* © 2012 Carol Marinelli
*The Tarnished Jewel of Jazaar* © 2012 Susanna Carr

ISBN: 978-0-263-25359-7

024-0515

Harlequin (UK) Limited's policy is to use papers that are natural, renewable and recyclable products and made from wood grown in sustainable forests. The logging and manufacturing processes conform

Printed and bound in Spain
by CPI, Barcelona

| MERTHYR TYDFIL LIBRARIES | |
| --- | --- |
| 0456402 2 | |
| **Askews & Holts** | 13-Aug-2015 |
| | £6.99 |
| | |

# For Duty's Sake

## LUCY MONROE

**Lucy Monroe** started reading at the age of four. After going through the children's books at home, her mother caught her reading adult novels pilfered from the higher shelves on the bookcase... Alas, it was nine years before she got her hands on a Mills & Boon® romance her older sister had brought home. She loves to create the strong alpha males and independent women who people Mills & Boon® books. When she's not immersed in a romance novel (whether reading or writing it), she enjoys travel with her family, having tea with the neighbours, gardening and visits from her numerous nieces and nephews. Lucy loves to hear from her readers: e-mail LucyMonroe@ LucyMonroe.com, or visit www.LucyMonroe.com.

For Abigail and Jordan, a very special niece and nephew-in-law. I'm so proud of both of you, all your accomplishments and the love you two share. May it bless you and may you live out your own HEA with true joy and a fulfilment of the dearest dreams of both your hearts.

# PROLOGUE

*Did love die?*

Angele had asked her mother that question once, after realizing her father, Cemal bin Ahmed al Jawhar—foster brother to the King of Jawhar and her own personal hero—was a serial adulterer. She'd been an extremely naive university freshman. So certain was she of her father's integrity, she had at first believed the tabloid story about him stuffed in her student mailbox was a hoax, a cruel joke played by someone who would never be called a friend again.

To this day, she did not know who had disliked her so much they'd felt the need to shred her illusions and with them, her heart.

Her first hero had tumbled from his pedestal and shattered at her feet, and he had not even known. Not to begin with.

Her still beautiful Brazilian former supermodel mother had looked at Angele in silence for several seconds. Eyes the same espresso-brown as her daughter's for once revealed her every emotion, and all of it staggering pain. "I would consider it a great blessing, but some of us are cursed to love unwisely and to do so until death."

"But why do you stay with him?"

"I do not. We live quite separate lives."

And another belief had been crushed under the pounding hammer of reality. They lived in the United States for the sake of Angele's education and the chance for her to be raised in relative anonymity. They'd made the modern country their home because Americans had plenty of their own scandal, they didn't have to go looking for it among the wealthy community from a small Middle Eastern country like Jawhar.

In a way, her mother *had* been protecting Angele. From the truth. But she'd also been protecting herself from the embarrassment of being the well-known wife of an undeniable philanderer. It had explained why their trips to Brazil and Jawhar were shorter and far less frequent than Angele had always wanted. It had also explained why her father's visits were equally brief, though far more frequent.

"Why not divorce him?"

"I love him."

"But he…"

"…is my husband." Lou-Belia had drawn herself to her full five feet eleven inches. "I will not shame my family, or his, with a divorce."

Considering the fact that Angele's father was considered a de facto member of the royal family of Jawhar, that argument carried some weight. Nevertheless, Angele had vowed never to be her mother that day. *She* would not be trapped in a marriage by duty and a helpless love that caused more grief than joy.

She had believed she was safe making the vow. After all, while no formal announcement had been made,

Angele had been promised to Crown Sheikh Zahir bin Faruq al Zohra since she was thirteen years old. Heir to the throne of Zohra, no more honorable man existed in the Middle East, or anywhere else for that matter.

Or so she had believed. But that had been before today, when she'd received a packet of pictures of Zahir in the mail.

A sense of déjà vu washed over her, bringing back old feelings and memories so clear, she could still smell the spring grass clippings that had scented the air on that other fateful day a little over four years ago. The same cold chills washed up and down her spine, leaving a strange clammy flush in their wake.

If someone had asked her even one hour ago what one certainty she had, it would have been that Zahir would never be the center of a tabloid scandal. Besides being far too aware of his duty to his family and his position, Crown Sheikh Zahir simply had too much integrity to be caught in flagrante delicto with some woman.

Right. Her other hero.

Now, staring down at the topmost picture—an almost innocent image of Zahir helping a busty blonde into the passenger side of his Mercedes, Angele choked out a strangled laugh. The barely there sound a pained constriction in her dry throat, the present took full hold with a snap.

Here, there was no smell of grass clippings, just the subtle scent of citrus her boss favored for the air ventilation system. No clatter of other students greeting one another in the common room of the University Center. Just the sound of her own breathing in the near-empty office.

The metallic taste of fear in her mouth mocked Angele and her hand shook as she pushed the topmost picture aside with her fingertip.

The next photo showed Zahir kissing the same busty blonde, though this time she was wearing a tiny bikini as they lounged beside a private pool. Angele did not recognize the couple's surroundings; the large Mediterranean-style house behind the pool could have been almost anywhere.

It was a popular architectural style for warmer climates, from Europe to South America.

She *did* recognize the passion between the two lip-locked people in the glossy eight-by-ten, though.

And it brought back a memory she would rather forget.

She'd been eighteen and in love with Zahir since she'd started having sexual feelings. She had not cared if others understood, or believed such a young girl was capable of the emotion. She'd known what she felt and it was not a simple crush, having grown deeper with each passing year.

She'd assumed Zahir had treated her with such restraint and kept his distance since the deal had been brokered because she was too young. But at eighteen she was formally an adult. At least by standards of the country she'd been raised in, the United States.

They were at a state dinner, their first time attending such an event as a couple. She'd thought it the perfect opportunity to share their first kiss and had brazenly cornered him in the courtyard. Or as brazenly as a rather shy woman who had not been blessed with her mother's stellar beauty in the gene pool could be.

Filled with trepidation that could not stand against her determination, she had gazed up into eyes that had looked almost black in the dim light, though she knew they were gray. She'd grasped both his arms, her fingers curling around strong biceps that emanated heat even through his shirt and dinner jacket.

She'd tipped her head back, letting her own eyes close, and pleaded, "Kiss me."

Certain this man who was to be her husband one day would comply, *must* comply, she had waited in silent anticipation for what had felt like hours before gentle lips brushed her forehead.

Her eyes had flown open. "Zahir?"

"This is not the time, *ya habibti*." He had gently pushed her away. "You are still a child."

Crushed, she had been able to do nothing but nod and try to blink back tears of mortification.

He'd shaken his head and patted her arm. "Shh, *ya habibti,* our time is not yet."

As he'd escorted her back to the party, she had consoled herself with the implied promise and the fact he had called her his *darling*. Twice.

A harsh laugh barked out of her as the photo of him kissing that other woman blurred before her eyes. Angele was twenty-three and *still* waiting for him to realize she was no longer a child.

Without this photographic evidence, would she have ever realized that day was *never* likely to come?

Blinking away the moisture in her eyes, she focused on the pictures again, sliding one to the side and to reveal another beneath it until they were spread across her desk in undeniable evidence. This was not the first time she'd gone through the photos, but now she refused to look away, or stack them again neatly in an attempt to hide from what they represented.

Zahir did not think *this* woman was a child. No, Elsa Bosch was everything a man was looking for in a lover. Extravagantly beautiful, voluptuous, *experienced*.

Angele winced at her own assessment, knowing she was none of those things.

She was not sure Zahir's honor was besmirched by his liaison with the German actress. Not yet. After all, *their* betrothal had never been formally announced and he'd treated Angele like a distant cousin, not a lover. Despite her clumsy attempt at eighteen to rectify the matter.

She'd allowed her own love and the future she'd believed they were meant to share to become the foundation for fantasies that shared no touch with reality. She'd believed that, one day, he would realize she was not the young girl the marriage contract had been negotiated around.

She'd been waiting ten years. *Ten years.* A decade in which she'd never dated, not even attending her high-school prom because she'd considered herself taken. She'd had male friends in college, but none that she'd allowed to see her as anything but a study-buddy.

She'd just assumed that like her, Zahir had filled his life with family, responsibilities and friends…not a particular *woman friend*.

Unlike her own father, Zahir had been discreet in his relationship with Elsa Bosch. But the fact was: he'd had one.

These pictures could not be denied. So much like that

time when she was at university, shouldn't her pain be every bit as profound?

But she felt hollow now. Empty. Devoid of the emotions that she'd nurtured in her heart toward him for so long.

Unlike that last time, this sender was demanding money in exchange for silence. If Angele did not pay, the note accompanying the pictures promised every American and European tabloid would get the opportunity to buy a set of photos along with a very embarrassing tell-all story.

The fact Zahir was having an ongoing affair with an actress who had starred in a skin flick was scandalous enough to cause considerable upset in the royal families of both Jawhar and Zohra. Angele shuddered when she considered their response to a full-on exposé. The moment she'd gotten the pictures, she'd started researching the German actress.

While the woman spent less time in the spotlight than someone might expect, she was in no way a suitable companion for the heir to a kingdom.

However, Elsa was clearly his companion of choice.

These photos showed a great deal of skin, but even more passion. And happiness. *Zahir's happiness*. Angele had never seen him smile like he did in some of these shots. Even when he wasn't smiling, he had an air of relaxation he did not have around her.

Love might keep a woman married to a philanderer, but it might give another woman, a different type of woman, the courage to set the man she loved free.

Looking at those pictures, Angele knew deep in her heart that she could not allow Zahir to be held to a contract which had been brokered by men who had never given love between the two people involved even a fleeting thought.

Her love for him demanded more.

His lack of love for her demanded freedom.

# CHAPTER ONE

HEART heavy with guilt at his envy, Zahir listened to his youngest brother speak his wedding vows.

Amir's voice came close to breaking as he promised, not just simple fidelity, but also love to his bride. Grace's eyes glistened, but her smile grew as she gazed at her groom with rapt fascination. Her own voice trembled as she returned the promise of love.

Love.

Both his brothers had found it with women not altogether suitable. But as neither were heir to the throne, their choices were hardly world-shattering. It was not the same for him.

His choice of bride had been set by an agreement between Zohra and Jawhar a decade past. His gaze skimmed the guests nearest the bridal party, gliding past his beaming father, king of their small Middle Eastern country, and his teary-eyed mother, to the woman he would one day wed. Though they shared no blood relation, Angele bin Cemal was treated as a favored niece by his uncle, the King of Jawhar.

Their eyes met, but she broke the gaze immediately, firmly fixing her gaze on the couple saying their vows.

He felt the dismissal, but was not surprised by it. Not after the past months preparing for the royal wedding.

Shocking everyone, the woman both royal families acknowledged would one day be *his* wife had refused to be a member of the bridal party or to participate in any meaningful way in the wedding. Citing her lack of close relationship to either the bride or the groom as her excuse, Angele had stood firm against every attempt by his mother and even Grace to include her.

Zahir had taken her uncustomary intransigence for what it was: a demand that he formalize an engagement between the two of them. Clearly she was done waiting patiently for her own nuptials. And, after the events of the past month, he realized the time had come to do his duty.

Besides, her father had kept his part of the bargain; he'd long since cleaned up his behavior so that he no longer courted tabloid attention.

After Zahir's mother had told him how devastated Angele was by her father's string of infidelities and the fact she had not spoken to the man in more than a year, Zahir had decided the time had come to do something about it. He wasn't close to his future bride, but Cemal would one day be a member of his family and Zahir wasn't about to stand by while the older man embarrassed *them* with his lack of discretion.

So, Zahir had laid down the law to Cemal. He'd told the older man that he would not marry a woman whose father's tabloid fame rivaled that of a European rock star.

Cemal had believed him. He'd patched things up with his wife and had not been featured in a scandal rag for almost five years, proving he took his daughter's future more seriously than his own marriage vows. Zahir kept the grimace such thoughts brought from his face.

He would never be that man—loveless marriage, or not.

He suspected that, unlike her mother, Angele would never tolerate it. Her surprising streak of stubbornness gave him hope for the years ahead. He did not want to tie his life to a doormat.

Regardless of how intriguing Zahir found this new side of Angele, his patience grew thinner by the minute as the wedding festivities marched forward. She took her stubbornness to a new, inexplicable level. She repeatedly declined to be in any of the formal wedding photos.

"Come, my little princess, I believe your point has been made." King Malik of Jawhar patted Angele's shoulder, his words showing he had put the same interpretation on her actions as Zahir had done. "Do not be the camel that tries to drink with its tail."

Angele smiled at her honorary uncle, though the expression did not reach her too serious eyes, and shook her head. "The formal shots are for family, not friends."

Stunned, and a little impressed, Zahir frowned. He had never heard her deny the king before.

"You are nearly family." *And would be soon enough,* Zahir implied, knowing she was intelligent enough to get his meaning.

She simply shook her head again and turned as if to go.

He reached out to grab her arm and then yanked his hand back, realizing what he'd almost done. They were not formally betrothed and to touch her so familiarly in this setting would be highly improper. As future king of Zohra, Zahir never acted without propriety.

At least in a public setting.

His behind-the-scenes impropriety was over as well, and he still felt a fool for pining after what he could not have.

A life of love and happiness, as his brothers were building for themselves, was not to be for him.

King Malik laughed. "You begin to see the child as a woman with her own will, do you not?"

Zahir could not deny it. He had never seen Angele dressed with such an evident intent to entice, either. It had worked. He found her quite alluring. Used to barely noticing her at all, he'd been shocked by the low burn of arousal he'd felt when she had arrived. With new highlights shining in her dark brown hair, she wore it swept up to show off the slender column of her neck and the creamy, delicate slope of her shoulders.

The soft peach color of her couture dress was the only thing demure about it. Clinging to her slight curves, it fell inches short of her knees. While she did not share her mother's supermodel stature, in the dress and matching heels that added at least four inches to her height, Angele's legs looked every bit as long as the Brazilian beauty's today. And twice as sexy.

Add to that the fact that her stubborn refusal to participate in the wedding as a member-to-be of the family had intrigued him from her first refusal three months ago, and it was a lethal combination to his recently restrained libido.

Reminding him that his future wife had not been raised in the secluded environment inhabited by the women in the royal palace of Jawhar, she had continued to stand by her first denial. He'd been more than a little stunned to realize he liked it.

While his marriage would not be the love-match his brother had made, it would not be as much of a dry connection of two overly similar lives as he had always anticipated, either.

Frankly love could go hang, as far as he was concerned. This newfound passion and interest was all that he required, or wanted.

"Wasn't the wedding beautiful?"

A bittersweet smile curving her lips, Angela looked up at her mother. "It was, but the love between Amir and Grace made it even more so."

"It reminds me of your father and my wedding." Lou-Belia sighed with a fond reminiscence that Angele found difficult to understand. "We were so much in love."

"I do not think Amir is like my father."

Lou-Belia frowned. "You know Cemal has settled down."

Angele did know. She still floundered in her feelings for a man who spent the better part of two decades flaunting his marriage vows, only to become the model of propriety in the face of his only child's betrayal-fueled rage and disapproval.

She was thrilled for her mother that the older couple's marriage seemed to be working again. The two spent a great deal more time together now, going so far as to live in the same domicile even. Her father was quite affectionate toward her mother these days, too.

But it hurt something deep inside Angele that her

father had not stopped his behavior until *she* had confronted him, and then refused to have anything to do with him for more than a year. What did that say of the strength of his love for his wife?

He'd pleaded with her mother to fix the breach between them and in the process, Cemal and Lou-Belia had found each other again.

"So, the past does not exist?" she asked helplessly.

"We let it go for the sake of the future." Lou-Belia's world-famous smile was soft but tinged with chiding. "It has been five years, *menina*."

*Little girl.* Angele hadn't been her mother's little girl for a long time, no matter what Lou-Belia, or Zahir for that matter, believed.

Still, she gave her mother a tight hug. "You are a kind and forgiving woman. I love you."

*But I don't want to be you,* she thought to herself.

With that truth burning in her mind, she went looking for the man who would one day be king.

Some minutes later, Angele slid around the partially opened door to Zahir's office. He had disappeared from the wedding feast and she'd known she would find him here.

"Shirking your duty, Prince Zahir?" Her arms crossed over the sweetheart neckline of her short-short designer original. "Tsk, tsk, tsk. What would your father say?"

The room was very much like Zahir: masculine, rich and imposing. And yet there was something in the artwork and the old world furnishings that reflected more, something special—an appreciation for beauty that she knew few were aware of.

But while Zahir didn't pay her any particular attention,

she had watched him closely and probably knew more about the real man than most. She still wondered at her ignorance of the secret revealed short months ago.

She'd decided it was willful blindness on her part, but that had not made her feel any better. Only mind-numbingly stupid.

She was a twenty-three-year-old virgin with no prospects and she knew she was to blame for that fact. She had clung to hopes and fairy tales that would never come true in the real world. Her parents' marriage should have made her realize that.

Zahir looked up from some papers on his desk, his gray eyes widening a fraction at the sight of her. He quickly stood to his full, impressive six feet four inches. He wore the traditional robes and head covering of a crown sheikh over a tailored suit that made him look mouthwateringly attractive to her.

Not that he was even remotely aware of the effect he had on her. She would have to be on his radar as an actual woman for that to happen.

"Princess Angele, what are you doing here?" He had always called her *Princess,* though she was not one.

But her godfather, King Malik, had nicknamed her such and the nickname had stuck. She'd always thought it sweet, but now realized it was one more barrier that Zahir kept between them.

His refusal to call her simply by her first name, as any man intent on marrying a woman might do.

He looked past her, no doubt expecting some kind of chaperone. But she'd left her mother and all other potential protectors of her virtue at the feast. She pressed the door closed, the snick of the catch mechanism engaging loud in the silent room.

"Have I forgotten we were to meet?" he asked, sounding perplexed, but not wary. "Did you expect me to escort you to the table?"

"I'm perfectly capable of walking to my own table." At her request, they had not been seated next to one other. "I know about Elsa Bosch."

She hadn't meant for that to be her opening salvo, but it would have to do. She'd paid the blackmailer, not once, but twice. After this weekend, Zahir's reputation would no longer be her concern. The picture taker would have to find another cash cow.

Distaste flicked over Zahir's features, at what she was not sure. Was he disgusted by the gossip rag that had printed a picture of him and his lover at a tête-à-tête in Paris the week before last?

Compared to the pictures Angele had seen, the two sitting at an intimate table for two was a boringly tame image. But as she'd suspected, the very fact Zahir was "friends" with the actress was cause for speculation and scandal.

Or was he disappointed in his prim and proper almost-fiancée bringing the subject up? She'd worked so hard for so many years to be the perfect image of his future queen.

Little did he know it, but *that* Angele was in ashes on the floor of her office back in America.

"That is not something you need concern yourself with."

Those words shocked her, hurting her when she thought no more wounds could be made. She had expected his anger. Disdain. Frustration, maybe. But not dismissal. She'd not expected him to believe that she had nothing to say about the women he shared himself with while leaving her untouched. Unclaimed. And achingly unfulfilled.

She wasn't ignorant. She knew that sex could and should be wonderful for a woman, but she was entirely inexperienced and she intended for that to change. Tonight.

The realization that Zahir had more in common with her father than she had ever believed almost derailed her determination but, in some strange way, it made it okay for her to make her bargain.

"The picture was rather flattering, to you both."

He stood up, "Listen, Princess—"

"My name is Angele."

"I am aware."

"I prefer you use it." If only for this one night, he would see her as a person in her own right. "I am not a princess."

And never would be now. Nor was she the starry-eyed child who had reacted with delirious joy upon the announcement of their future marriage. The past ten years had finally brought her not only adulthood, but a definitive check with reality.

The man she had loved for too long and if her mother was to be believed, would probably love until the day she died, had no more desire to marry her than he wanted to dance naked at the next royal ball. Perhaps even less.

"*Angele,*" he said, as if making a great concession. "Ms. Bosch is not an issue between us."

He was so wrong. On so many levels, but her plan

did not include enumerating them, so she didn't. "You were smiling in the picture. You looked happy."

Certainly he had never given Angele the affection filled gaze he'd given the German actress even in that single, oh so tame, picture in the tabloid.

Zahir looked at Angele as if she had spoken something other than one of the five languages he conversed in with extreme fluency.

"I read that you broke things off with her." Angele had gone from supremely ignorant of her fiancé's social activities to an expert on the gossip surrounding him.

"I did."

"Because you were photographed together."

He frowned, but gave a quick jerk of his head in acknowledgment. "Yes."

She found that sad. For Zahir. For herself. For Elsa Bosch even. Had the woman realized she was so expendable? Then again, she might well have been the person who had extorted money for silence from Angele.

Regardless, Elsa was not the real issue here. And Angele needed to remember that, no matter how hot her retinas burned with the images of the other woman in Zahir's arms.

She pushed away from the wall and went to look at the statuary displayed in a dark mahogany case. Her favorite was a Bedouin rider on a horse, carved from dark wood. They looked like they would race off into the desert.

But she noticed a new piece. It was another Bedouin, but this figure was only the man, in the traditional garb of the nomadic people. He looked off into the distance with an expression of longing on his features so profound her heart squeezed in her chest. "When did you get this?"

"It was a gift."

"From whom?"

He did not answer.

She turned to face him. "It was Elsa, wasn't it?"

His jaw locked and she knew he would not reply.

She refused to let that hurt her. "She knows you well."

"I will not lie. Our association was measured in years, not days." His tone had an edge to it that Angele had no hope of interpreting.

And his use of the past tense did nothing to assuage Angele's feelings.

"Yes, I gathered." The photos she had been sent spanned a timeline that could not have possibly been anything less. Someone who did not know and watch him so closely would not have noticed perhaps, but it had been obvious to Angele.

"The tabloids print trash. I'm surprised you read it."

She did not react to the taunt. Nor did she answer the implied question of where her information had come from. She said the one thing that needed saying. "You don't want to marry me."

"I will do my duty by my father's house." Which was more a confirmation of his lack of desire than she was sure he meant it to be.

"You'll make a great king one day." He was already an accomplished politician. "But that is not a direct answer and you neglected to note, I wasn't asking a question."

"If this is about Ms. Bosch and our now defunct association, please remember that you and I are not officially engaged."

"I am to take comfort in the inference you would not be unfaithful if we were?" she asked carefully.

His brows drew together and for the first time since the discussion started, she saw anger make its way to the forefront. "Naturally."

"I don't."

"Don't be ridiculous, Prin—Angele, I am not your father."

"No, you aren't." And she would never give him the opportunity to prove them both wrong, either. "This isn't about Elsa Bosch, not really."

Ultimately it was about love. It was about loving someone enough to let them go. Only that sounded so cheesy, she'd never speak the words aloud. And it was about knowing she deserved to be loved, fully and completely, by the man she would spend the rest of her life with.

He did not look like he believed her claim and she could practically see the thoughts zinging around in his facile brain. He was trying to figure out the right words to reassure, when in fact none existed.

None that he could say anyway.

Again it was time for truth. "Your brothers have both found wonderful happiness while you have been stuck in a promise made on your behalf by two men with too much power and too little comprehension of the cost of their dynastic plans."

"I do not consider myself stuck. I was an adult when that agreement was made." Yes, he'd been all of twenty-four and as bound by duty as any young adult male could be. "I chose my future."

An alpha male like Zahir would have to convince himself of that, or he could not accept the limitations imposed on him by others. It simply was not in his nature. He had the heart of a Bedouin, if also the responsibilities of a landed royal.

"You do not wish to marry me," she repeated, refusing to be sidetracked. "And I won't let you be forced into doing so by duty."

Nor would she allow herself to be railroaded into a marriage with the potential to be every bit as miserable as her parents were for so many years.

His eyes narrowed, his expression turning even more grim than usual. "You are not making any sense."

"We've been promised for ten years, Zahir. If you had wanted to marry me, we would already be living in wedded harmony here in your family's palace." They would definitely at least be formally engaged.

"It has not been the right time."

She'd heard that argument before. And believed it. First, she'd been too young. Then, his father's health had been precarious. The idea of announcing an engagement during such a time was not appropriate, or so Zahir had claimed. Then, Khalil had gotten engaged and stealing his spotlight during the preparations for, celebration of and immediate time after Khalil and Jade's wedding would have been wrong. The same excuse came convenient to hand when Amir and Grace became engaged.

For ten years, five—if you only counted the years since she became an adult—they had not found the right time to announce their engagement, much less actually get married. And they never would, if it meant finding a time when Zahir *wanted* the nuptials to take place.

Though Crown Sheikh Zahir bin Faruq al Zohra would no doubt eventually allow duty to force him into following through on a marriage he did not desire.

Since she would be the other half of that marriage, she wasn't going to let it happen. Realizing that had meant giving up her dreams. And that had hurt, even more than seeing the photos of Zahir kissing Elsa.

But then who was Angele kidding? Certainly not herself. Seeing the unfamiliar happiness on Zahir's face had lacerated her heart far more than the passion. The numbness having long since given way to a devastation she would have happily avoided for the rest of her life. And her heart was still bleeding.

Better that, than a lifetime of pricks from the knife edge of the constant knowledge that she was not the woman her husband wanted to be with however. When she'd conceived her current plan, a steel band had formed around her chest, and that constriction was still there. Sometimes, she felt like it was the only thing stopping her from falling apart.

But that, too, would fade. Eventually. It had to.

How much worse would it be to live the rest of her life married to a man who did not love her and never would? Who did not even like her enough to spend any time with her not dictated by their roles and responsibilities?

To watch Zahir find joy in the arms of other women as her father had done over and over again? Angele wasn't about to go that route.

Even after receiving the packet of pictures, funnily enough it had been the announcement of Amir's marriage that had settled the issue for her. Amir had been meant to marry another member of a powerful sheikh's family, but Lina had refused the match and Amir had ended up married today to the woman who held his heart instead.

As Angele had told her mother, Amir and Grace's very real love had made the wedding ceremony beautiful.

What she had not told her mother was that she had seen the envy in Zahir's expression when he had looked at Amir as he stood up with him. No one else had noticed, of course, but Angele had spent a lifetime watching Zahir with more attention than research scientists gave their life's work.

Lina's courage had given Angele the courage to come up with her plan. And Amir's happiness today had cemented her determination to follow through with it. If there was any chance Zahir could know his brother's happiness, he deserved to have it.

She could do no less for the man she loved with her whole heart.

And she would accept nothing less than that, either, even if it meant spending the rest of her life alone.

"Zahir, I have always found you to be honest. A man of deep integrity." His liaison with Elsa had not changed that.

As he'd pointed out, Angele and Zahir were not actually engaged. And he had never once lied about it. She'd simply never thought to ask point-blank if he had sex with other women. However, she was no longer rock-solid in her belief he would not take mistresses after their marriage. In fact, that certainty had died a pretty painful death.

No matter what he'd said today.

"I am."

"Are you in love with me?" One of those point-blank questions she could not avoid asking. Not now.

He did not even blink, his handsome features set in an emotionless mask. "Our association is not a matter of love."

"No, I know it isn't, but please, this once, just answer my question with a simple yes or no."

His jaw tightened.

"Please."

"I do not see why you would ask."

"I'm not asking you to understand, simply to answer."

"No."

She almost asked if his negative was a refusal to answer, but then she looked into his gray eyes and saw the smallest glimmer of pity. He knew she had feelings for him he did not return.

The pain his answer caused wasn't mitigated by the fact she'd been expecting it. Though she really wished it had worked like that. Knowing he did not love her and hearing it from his lips were apparently in totally different realms of experience.

She managed to nod. "That is what I thought."

"Love is not necessary in a marriage such as ours."

"I don't agree. I will not marry a man who has no hope of loving me."

"I—"

"Have not found something worthy of love in my person in ten years—you are not likely to find it now." In fact, she was so certain of that impossibility, she was ready to take desperate action.

"You are all that is admirable in a future princess and eventual queen."

*But not as a woman he could love.* She left the words unsaid as he did. "You deserve the happiness your brothers have found."

"It is not in my stars." His tacit agreement sent another javelin of pain straight through her, but she refused to buckle under the fresh wound.

She had a plan and in the end, it would be best for both of them. "It can be."

"I will not turn my back on my duty." And his tone censured her for suggesting he try.

"I will."

# CHAPTER TWO

ZAHIR felt those two small words like they were blows from the strongest of sparring partners. Part of him had always expected some kind of betrayal from Elsa Bosch, though not to the extent she had gone to. He had never been able to give her what she craved: commitment for the future.

However, he had believed Angele a woman of supreme honor and understanding of her duty.

"You are not serious." He looked closely, trying to see evidence of too much champagne, but her pupils were not dilated.

Her cheeks were flushed, but the topic of their conversation could easily account for that.

"I am." She looked down at the Bedouin figure and reached out to touch it almost wistfully. "I will not allow you to be locked into a marriage with a woman you cannot love."

"And you expect to be loved by your husband." Where had she gotten her romantic notions of marriage? Certainly not from her parents.

"Yes."

"You appear to forget the importance of duty and family obligation."

A deep, burning anger flickered briefly in Angele's dark eyes. "My mother's adherence to duty is one of the primary reasons I am so determined not to follow through on this farce of a marriage."

"There is no farce in joining the royal houses of Zohra and Jawhar."

"I am not of the royal house of Jawhar, no matter how indulgent King Malik is toward me and my father."

It was true. From one of the most influential families in Jawhar, Cemal had been fostered in the royal household when his parents died. He'd been raised like a brother to Malik, but they shared no blood relation. Which had actually played in favor to the agreement drawn up ten years before as Zahir and Angele had no blood common between them.

"I did not think this bothered you."

"It doesn't."

"You cite it as reason for not keeping your commitment."

"I never made a commitment. When I was thirteen I was informed that one day we would marry."

A mere girl. He had felt compassion for her. "But you never complained. Why now?"

"I spun fairy castles in the air, dreams that took me too long to realize they had no basis in reality."

Dreams of love. Didn't she know? That commodity was not for such as them. "You need to consider this more carefully."

"Zahir, I'm giving you your freedom." Exasperation and a tinge of anger laced her tone. "Instead of trying to talk me out of it, you could simply say thank you."

Did she really believe she was doing him a favor? He did not think so. "Our families will be shamed."

"Oh, please. Nothing official has ever been announced."

"Nevertheless, the expectation exists."

"So?" She shrugged, as if really, this did not matter. "Those who have expectations will have to be disappointed."

"Like my father. Like the man you call uncle. They will be humiliated."

The look she gave Zahir said she did not buy his calamity scenario. "Disappointed maybe but, in that regard, not as much as they would be by a divorce."

"Why divorce?" Though he admitted he did not know her as well as he could, he had never considered her a pessimist. "You are not making any sense."

"Zahir, can you honestly tell me that you are not feeling even a little niggle of hope right now? That relief isn't warring with your need to talk me out of doing what you know you want?"

Shock held him silent. Her words implied that she actually believed she was doing him some sort of favor; that somehow he would and even *should* thank her for threatening to break her word. He tried to think of what could have caused her to draw such a ridiculous conclusion, but despite his superior intellect he came up with nothing.

No possible reason for her outlandish ideas.

She sighed, her shoulders slumping just enough that he knew she was not as calm about this as she was pretending to be. "Your silence speaks better than your words could. I will take full responsibility for the aborted engagement with our families and the media."

"No." He surged up from his desk, realizing that perhaps now was not the time to intimidate with that barrier between them.

"I have only one request."

He halted on his way around the desk. "What is it?"

"I want one night in your bed, the wedding night I will not now have."

If she had shocked him with her threat to break their agreement, this request practically had him catatonic. What in blue blazes was she *thinking*?

"Why?" he ground out while trying to somehow make sense of his prim and proper princess-to-be offering him, no, *demanding* from him, something that should not be indulged in until after their marriage.

The next heir could not be conceived under a cloud.

"I want you to be my first."

Well, naturally. "But you do not wish to marry me."

Did she truly believe there was any sense, even the smallest modicum of logic in such a scenario?

"Did you want to marry Elsa Bosch?"

He'd indulged in fantasies at one time. He'd believed himself in love. More fool him. But even then he'd known it was pure fantasy to even consider such a thing. He'd soon realized that more than her career made her the wrong choice as future queen of Zohra.

Even in his most youthful exuberance of untried emotion, he had not been a fool. "It was not a consideration."

"But you had sex with her." The blunt words falling from Angele's usually prim mouth added to his sense of falling down the rabbit hole.

It was time to put a stop to this conversation. "That is not something I will discuss with you."

"I'm not asking you to—I'm simply making an observation."

"This entire conversation is insane."

"No, what *is* insane is two people prepared to marry for the sake of nothing but family obligation in the twenty-first century."

Her American upbringing had much to answer for.

"I will one day be king. The woman who rules Zohra by my side must be a suitable match." Angele knew this. He should not have to repeat it for her. "*Love* has nothing to do with the obligations you and I must uphold."

"You say it like it's a dirty word."

It was his turn to shrug. In his life? That particular emotion had caused more pain than pleasure.

"Your brothers have both found love."

"They do not have the responsibilities of the crown to uphold." And neither man had had a particularly smooth road to *true love*, either.

Zahir had no desire to follow in their footsteps in that regard. He had enough of his own challenges in life to face as ultimate leader and servant to his people.

"Your father doesn't wear a crown."

"Don't play semantics with me—this is too important." He could not believe she was saying these things. "I believed you understood the importance of your obligations."

"My greatest obligation is to myself. I know you

don't see it that way." She quoted an Arabic proverb he often used that was strangely apt to their situation. "I'm not that person. I don't believe countries will topple if their leaders seek personal happiness in a manner of integrity."

"What is honorable about breaking our engagement?"

"We aren't engaged."

"As good as."

"Really? You truly believe that?" she asked as if his answer carried great import.

"Yes."

Unutterable sadness came over her features and the light in her eyes dimmed. "I'm sorry."

"You will give up this idea of backing away from our wedding?"

"No." Her voice was laced with determination, but there was a flicker of fear in her expression.

And suddenly, he thought he understood. Things that made no sense began to fall into a picture he could comprehend. *She was concerned about their compatibility in the bedroom. As well she might be.*

In one respect, she was spot-on. They were not a nineteenth-century couple where the bride and groom had been expected to go to the marriage bed untouched. Or, at the very least, the bride.

She'd spent her life in the United States, surrounded by a culture that had demystified sex and frequently glorified it. He had never made improper advances because, despite his claim, they were not actually engaged.

At first, Angele had been too young, and later he'd had his liaison with Elsa. A relationship doomed from the beginning, but one that allowed him to come as close to escaping the stranglehold of his everyday responsibilities as he ever would, if only for the brief moments they'd had together.

He had foolishly allowed his emotions to get involved. So, when he'd discovered he was not her only lover, he had been hurt. And he was still angry with himself for being that vulnerable.

In the midst of his own self-allowed turmoil and the growing crush of his responsibilities without outlet, he had neglected to notice the impatient discontent in the woman he was slated to marry. Yet another casualty to the folly of allowing emotions to reign in one's life.

Angele shook her head and glared at him. "Stop it."

"Stop what exactly?"

"Thinking so hard. I just know you're trying to figure out a way to guilt me into maintaining the status quo. And that is not going to happen."

"No, I can see it is not." Angele needed reassurance that their marriage would not be devoid of passion.

Something he had done nothing to convince her of in the intervening years since the original contract was negotiated. Considering how his member stirred in his trousers at the sight of her in the sexy dress, he knew he would have no problem reassuring her now, however.

"You want to have sex with me."

She flinched, but squared her shoulders and nodded. "I'm offering you your freedom. I do not think a single night of lovemaking too high a price to pay for that."

The words were just noise to cover her sexual fears

and insecurities. He understood that, but one thing stood clear. She considered a night in his bed a gift.

He looked deep into her eyes and made another realization—one that both inexplicably pleased him and stirred pity in his heart. "You are in love with me."

Zahir had always known Angele fancied him something rotten, but he'd considered it a mere girlish crush. However this woman before him was no child and the feelings so apparent on her features had a depth that shocked him. Love was not a comfortable or safe emotion. From this point forward, it would not hurt her to love him, but she did not know that. He would never betray her as Elsa had betrayed him.

"What was your first clue? My clumsy attempt at a kiss at eighteen, or my slavish devotion and refusal to date other men despite the fact we are not formally engaged?"

If he expected shock from her at his revelation, or horror, he would clearly receive neither.

He did not point out that her love for him made no sense in light of her demands and threats to back out of their families' arrangements. He had already decided she had no real desire to do that, she was simply looking for reassurances.

The need for which made even more sense in the light of her feelings for him.

Nor did he point out that her love was based on a distant relationship. How could she know him well enough to love him? But she believed herself in love and that was enough to cause her pain and worry in their current situation.

"I apologize for not realizing your feelings sooner."

Acknowledging the hurt she must have experienced over the years of their pseudoengagement, was not comfortable, but he was not a man to shirk from his responsibilities. "Love is a painful emotion."

"You're telling me?" she asked with disbelief and then the horror came. The color drained from her face as her eyes registered a mortal wound. "You *are telling me*...that you loved her."

For the first time in his life, he was tempted to outright lie. He had learned the art of misdirection and when it was most politic to withhold information at an early age, but he made it a practice never to tell a direct falsehood. Even for the sake of politics.

His honor would not stand for it.

"It does not matter. Ms. Bosch and I are finished."

"But you loved her, didn't you?"

"That is not something I'm ever going to discuss with you." The past was over. He and Angele had a future to build.

His youthful feelings embarrassed him and they were over regardless.

"You don't need to. The photos show the truth, if you look for it. I didn't...I don't think I wanted to believe it was possible. It was painful enough to accept you were so much more relaxed and happy with her."

"You gleaned all this from a single photo?"

"No, but that's not something *I* want to discuss right now."

No, right now, she wanted reassurances he was more than happy to give. Nevertheless... "We can hardly disappear from my brother's wedding feast."

"Why not? You did."

"I had business to attend to if my father was to remain free to preside over the festivities."

"You often sacrifice for your family."

"It is my privilege to do so."

"I believe you mean that."

"I do."

"You're an amazing man."

"And you love me." He had no intention of opening himself to that depth of emotion again, but he would protect hers. It was his duty to do so.

And he always did his duty.

"The wedding festivities will last into the wee hours of the morning. Tonight is not the ideal time for us to share our bodies for the first time."

"What do you suggest?"

"You are in the country for the next three days?"

"Yes, we're staying for the full wedding celebration."

Despite Angele's refusal to play a role in the wedding, her family had been at the palace since the prewedding festivities began. He had seen very little of her because he had been busy with state business. He had believed she was busy with the bridal party, even if she wasn't an official member of it.

"I will make arrangements for your last night here. There are no official events after the final breakfast that day."

He put his arm out. "Now, I believe it is time we returned to the feast."

She laid her small hand in the crook of his arm and let him lead her from his study, the stress this discus-

sion had caused her evident in the fine tremors of her
delicate fingers against his jacket sleeve.

Two nights hence, he would show her she had nothing
to fear from him in any way.

Despite the sun having set an hour before, the tile floor
on the balcony off Angele's room warmed her bare feet.
She'd long since discarded the expensive but uncomfortable glittery heels she'd worn for the final celebratory
feast of Amir and Grace's nuptials.

She still wore the figure hugging silk sheath. By an
as yet undiscovered New York designer, its subtle com-
position made the most of her figure, hinting at bedroom
seductions while having no single element that could be
pointed to as anything other than proper.

Her father had been angry she'd foregone the traditional dress the women of the Jawharian royal family
had opted to don for the evening feast. Only Angele
*wasn't* a Jawharian princess, no matter how much her
father might wish otherwise.

Her mother had stood up for her. Looking like
American royalty in a beautiful European-designed
gown, Lou-Belia had told Cemal to take a chill pill.
The look on Angele's father's face had been worth the
price of admission and then some.

But the expression that flashed over Zahir's features
when he'd seen Angele's dress had been even better.
His gray eyes had heated to molten metal and his lids
had dropped in a look of pure sexual predatory interest
before he'd schooled his features into diplomatic blank-
ness. It hadn't been just the once, either.

She'd caught that heated stare directed her way more

than once over the course of the evening. Each time, it increased her desire for the feast to be over, for her one night with Crown Sheikh Zahir bin Faruq al Zohra to begin.

The celebration *was* over now and she could go to Zahir as soon as she wanted. The only thing stopping her was the garment lying so innocently on her bed.

She'd discovered the *galabeya* upon returning to her room. The traditional wedding dress in this part of the world, the white silk gown embroidered with gold thread looked like it belonged in an *Arabian Nights* fantasy. The Arabic lettering in the intricate embroidery told the story of the first Sheikh's marriage to the wife that helped him found the house of Zohra.

A note from Zahir lay atop the *galabya*.

My dear Angele,
You indicated a wish to have a wedding night. Please do me the honor of wearing this gown, worn by my grandmother in her wedding to my grandfather.
  I look forward to seeing you in and out of it.
  Zahir

The day before, he had told her to come to him via the secret passages she'd never known for certain existed. She'd guessed, since the palaces in Jawhar all had them, but Angele had never been privileged with that information regarding the royal palace of Zohra. Until now.

Now, when she planned to leave the palace of Zohra tomorrow and never return to it.

With a deep sigh, she turned from the darkness toward the warm light emanating from her bedroom. The *galabeya* shimmered under the glow, calling to and repelling her with equal fascination.

He wanted her to wear a wedding dress on their single night together. It was mind-boggling, but not nearly as shocking as it should have been. Part of her wanted the fantasy. Her subconscious at least was on the same page as her soon to be former almost-fiancé.

So, why balk at his request? The *galabeya* was easily the most beautiful one she had ever seen, the needlework making the Arabic letters look like art and perfect in each stitch. The matching slippers were beyond elegant. And looking at them, she knew they were exactly her size.

How had Zahir managed that?

A tiny voice warned against the cost tomorrow to that kind of indulgence tonight. But it was her *one night,* the only time for her to be with the man of her dreams. Perhaps it would make the morrow harder, but she would not balk at letting it fulfill every fantasy possible.

She changed into the *galabeya,* shivering with a sensuality she'd kept locked deep inside since her first sexual feeling, as the silk whispered against her skin. She'd opted to wear a modern bra and panties in matching white silk and lace, rather than the traditional underclothes Zahir had left with the dress. After all, this wasn't a wedding, but a seduction.

Though she was not at all sure any longer who was seducing whom. Certainly Zahir showed none of the reticence about bedding her that he always had done before.

Perhaps it was because his relationship with Elsa had ended. The one and only time their picture together had featured in the media, it had quickly been followed by a discreet announcement that any liaison there might have been between the two had ended.

In addition, Angele could not let herself forget the offered price for this night was ultimately Zahir's freedom. Perhaps that, if not she directly, accounted for his increased ardor in her regard. Whether or not he was willing to admit it, he clearly wanted out of their pseudoengagement.

Or had he always been attracted to her in some fashion, but unwilling to act on it because to do so would force the issue of their marriage?

She preferred that scenario to the one where he found the prospect of freedom so appealing, it alone birthed lust in him over her body.

Refusing to analyze the confusing situation any further, she brushed out her hair and changed her makeup to a neutral palette with eyes that were rimmed in kohl.

If not for the highlights in her hair and barely there underclothes, she could have been a bride of Zohra from a hundred years ago. She saw no one in the secret passageways, but heard a peal of feminine laughter as she passed the access to what must have been Amir's rooms.

It sounded much too close to be muffled by walls. Having no desire to be caught on her way to Zahir's room, Angele scooted into a crevice as the sound of bare feet padded down the passage she had just passed.

"Shh…the operative word here is secret," Amir said in a loud whisper to his still giggling wife.

"How did I not know they existed all the times I stayed in this palace?"

"You were not yet my wife."

"I am now." Grace sounded both awed and very pleased by that fact.

"Indeed." Amir's voice was laced with pure possession, however.

"So, are we going to explore?"

"Would you rather do that, or return to our rooms and celebrate our marriage?"

"Guess." Silence filled only with the sound of kissing and increasingly heavy breathing followed. Then, Grace said in a husky voice, "This week-long wedding thing is pretty neat, I must say. Western brides only get one wedding night."

Their voices faded as the footsteps returned the way they had come and Angele released a pent-up breath. She did not know how Zahir had stood maintaining a hidden affair for so long.

One night was enough to stretch Angele's nerves tighter than a model's corset....

# CHAPTER THREE

SHE made it to Zahir's room without further incident. Then she stood in front of the lever that would swing an ancient wardrobe within the room open like a door, and gathered her courage. This was it. The moment she'd craved far longer than anyone else would ever know.

She reached out to pull the lever, but the "door" was already opening. It swung inward to a room lit by numerous candles.

Clad in the traditional wedding garments of the Zohra royal family, Zahir looked at her with an expression so serious, it made her breath catch. "I began to think you had changed your mind."

Unable to speak, she shook her head.

"Your wedding night awaits." He stepped back. "Come."

Her heart hammering, she followed him into the candlelit room, but jerked when he reached behind her, and then blushed at her jumpiness.

"Be at peace. I am only closing the access to the corridor."

"Can just anyone come in through it?" she asked, another worry finding its place in her maelstrom of emotions.

"Only the family knows of its existence, and a select few of our security detail, those whose families have served the royal house for generations."

"But still." What if his brother, or father, or something, decided to make a late night visit?

"I have locked it from this side. The lever on the other side of the wall will not move."

Relief washed over her. "Amir and Grace were in the corridor."

Zahir's entire body tensed. "Did they see you?"

"No."

He nodded, relaxing a little. "It would not have been a total tragedy, but I would prefer you not to be made the object of speculation."

She begged to differ. If she'd been seen, dressed as she was, it *would* have been both humiliating and a huge and total tragedy. Nothing would stop her uncle from forcing the marriage if she were caught in such a circumstance.

Thank goodness, only the royal family of Zohra knew of the passages. And her.

"How did you know I was in the corridor? Is there some kind of alarm?"

Zahir merely shrugged, but there was an odd expression in his eyes, the soft light of the candles giving his angular cheeks a burnished glow that almost looked like a blush.

He reached out and cupped her cheek. "You look beautiful."

"You didn't like my dress earlier?"

"You know I did."

"Do I?"

"Oh, yes." His hand slipped around her head and settled against her nape. He used the hold to gently tug her forward until their bodies were a mere breath apart. "You are a minx. How did I not realize this before?"

"Minx is such an old-fashioned word."

"I am an old-fashioned guy."

"You think?"

"In some ways, I am very traditional."

Then, before she could answer, he lowered his head and she finally got the kiss she'd always wanted.

And it was every bit as tender and romantic as she could ever have hoped. Letting out a little sigh of pleasure, she let her lips part slightly.

Zahir's tongue swept inside, claiming her mouth with unhesitating, if gentle, demand. Her arms moved of their own volition, her hands clasping behind his neck as she melted into him. His big body shuddered at the full-on contact and she could feel the evidence of a tightly leashed desire pressing impressively against her stomach.

The evidence that he did indeed want her made her bold and she tangled her tongue with his, responding to his kiss with an abandon she'd never known she was capable of.

She'd spent so many years repressing her sexual desires, they rushed through her now with the power of a California wildfire.

She moaned, moving against him, needing more than the kiss, but too involved in it to do anything about that.

As if he could read her mind, Zahir's hands began exploring her body through the thin silk of the wedding *galabeya.* He traced the embroidery along her spine, sending raptures through her body.

When his hands cupped her bottom, she could not suppress a needy whimper. An approving growl came from deep in his chest as he lifted her to press the apex of her thighs against his hardness.

Her legs spread of their own volition, but the skirt of the long Arabic gown constricted how far she could do so. He didn't seem to mind, making another sound of approval as he intimately thrust against her. The contact between them, even through the layers of silk of their clothing, sent electric sparks exploding along her nerve endings. His thrusts became more urgent as she felt warm moisture develop between her legs.

How could this feel so good? How could she feel so out of control already? They weren't even naked yet.

He tilted her pelvis just so and suddenly sensation unlike anything she'd ever known was making her womb clench. She mashed her mouth against his, needing to be closer.

He gave her what she needed, taking their kiss into something wildly carnal.

Unfamiliar tension built inside her, pleasure tinged by almost panic at the unfamiliarity of it, made her body shake even as she pressed against him in wanton need for something she couldn't give name to.

And then it came, that nameless something, a supernova of sensation that made her body go rigid as she cried out against his mouth. A sob built in her throat as the pleasure burst, and ebbed, and burst again.

She couldn't breathe. She couldn't think. She could

only feel and that was too much. Too intense and yet she never wanted it to end.

But something this immense had to end, or kill her. She was sure of it.

Her heart felt ready to explode from her chest. If this is what he could do to her with a kiss, she was never going to survive what was to come.

The jolts of pleasure grew farther apart as her body ebbed toward relaxation more and more until she was completely limp against him. Her grasp on his neck nothing more than a caress, really, as her muscles certainly weren't supporting her.

Finally, breaking the kiss, he swung her high against his chest and smiled down at her. "You are amazing."

She could not speak to respond, merely shook her head. He was the incredible one, playing her boldly like a sitar's strings.

"Making love to you will be my greatest pleasure." She forgave him the smug tones edging his voice.

They were well-earned. Besides, his words weren't smug at all. He could have said it would be *her* greatest pleasure, and they both knew that would be the case.

She was a virgin after all.

Making the other claim was a sop to her feelings that she could not help loving him for. Tonight would definitely not be the beginning of her learning to suppress that love like she always had her feminine sensuality.

That would come later, when she was not in his arms, experiencing feelings and emotions beyond comprehension.

Even so, she wanted to ask if he meant it, but knew that would be a very stupid thing to do in the circumstances. A negative answer was so not what she wanted to hear right now. Still, she could not help giving him a doubtful look.

His expression turned intensely serious as he carefully laid her on the huge bed. "You are the only woman I have ever touched that has been mine alone. You cannot know what satisfaction that gives me."

She wanted to call him a chauvinist. Tell him he was arrogant beyond belief. But most of all, she wanted to ask what he meant. Of course, Elsa would not have been untouched when Zahir began seeing her; his former mistress would have had liaisons with other men.

Angele didn't do any of that, though, because for the first time in all the years she had known this man, a glimmer of vulnerability showed through his super-controlled exterior.

"All yours." For tonight.

His teeth flashed in another sensual smile. "All mine."

If he sounded like he was making a permanent claim, she convinced herself it was simply her ears hearing what they craved. Not a truth that resonated in her heart.

"You will make love to me now?" she asked softly.

"I have been making love to you since you stepped into my room."

She did not question it. She certainly could not deny it.

He began to undress, pulling back the layers that named him crown sheikh of his people until he stood before her in the soft glow of a hundred candles, his perfect body completely open to her gaze.

Skin a shade darker than hers covered bulging muscles she would not have expected in a man who spent his days playing politician. She'd always known he was strong, but now she believed the rumors that none of the security force in the palace could best him on the sparring mat.

"You look like an ancient Bedouin warrior."

"A man cannot be weak and lead his people."

"I have never questioned your mental stamina."

"You mean you *have* questioned my physical prowess?" he asked and then laughed, the sound free and full of genuine amusement.

That laugh was as much a gift as the pleasure he drew so unnervingly from her body.

She choked on her own amusement. "Of course not, I just…"

Her eyes could not help devouring him with hungry need. He was so incredibly masculine, his hardened sex standing out from his body in impressive splendor.

"I think you like looking."

"I think I do, too."

"You sound surprised."

"I don't make it a habit of looking at naked men."

There was that laughter again and she could not even mind it was at her expense. "I should hope not."

"It suddenly occurs to me that I'm debilitatingly naive for a woman from my adopted country." She doubted there was a single woman who worked on the fashion magazine that employed her as an editorial assistant that was as innocent to sexual things as Angele.

"You are exactly as you should be."

She knew he meant it, but she could not help thinking

that if she'd been a bit more experienced, perhaps he would not have found Elsa such a fascination.

She dismissed the thought as unnecessary and destructive. Elsa Bosch was not here, was not even in Zahir's life any longer. Angele was. For now. And at this moment in time, that was all that mattered.

"I think I could stand here and let you look and you would come from that alone."

"Arrogant."

He shrugged. "Perhaps, but you cannot know what a pleasure it is to have those doe-soft brown eyes eating me up like the tastiest dessert at the feast."

"I doubt there is another man alive who I would find more appealing." She didn't mind telling him the truth.

Tonight was not for self-protection. That started tomorrow. When she flew back to the States, no longer a virgin and no longer the promised future bride to the heir to the throne of Zohra.

"Naturally."

She laughed again, her heart tripping in her chest at his obvious desire to be seen as the best in her eyes. "Naturally."

"No other woman can compare to you lying on my bed as you are."

Wearing his grandmother's *galabeya,* he meant, looking like the bride she would never be. But surprisingly the thought did not make her sad, but rather brought a smile to her face. "You've never brought another woman in here, have you?"

"Of course not."

"You're living out your teen fantasies, aren't you?" she teased.

He shook his head. "They're much more recent than that."

She opened her mouth to say something else, but he reached down and caressed his shaft with a sure hand. She gasped. She wanted to be doing that.

"All in good time," he said as if reading her mind.

Then he stepped forward until he stood against the bed. "It's time to undress my bride."

It wasn't a real wedding night, but he was going to make it as close to one as possible for her. And she was going to let him.

She wasn't surprised when his first action was to remove the slippers on her feet, but it shocked her speechless when he leaned down to take each foot into his hand and place a soft, sensuous kiss on the arch. He didn't stop there, either, but caressed her feet, pressing points that seemed directly linked to the empty ache inside her.

She was moaning and clenching her thighs by the time he'd moved his attention to her calves.

"Such soft, silky skin, but I know a place you will be softer."

Her breath came in harsh pants and she shook her head.

"I assure you, you are. Soft, delicious and wet."

Delicious? Did he mean...but her thoughts splintered as he pushed her gown up to expose her thighs to his gaze and that talented mouth.

Words gasped out of her without meanings as she

discovered that her inner thighs were far more sensitive than she'd ever realized.

He chuckled, the sound wicked and delicious. "Are you sure it is the right time to be praying, *ya habibti*?"

"I…what? It…"

That smile that told her he was about to do something naughty creased his sensual mouth. Then, he pushed her *galabeya* higher and suddenly stopped, letting out a deep sigh of clear approval. "Oh, this is nice."

"You like my panties."

"Oh, yes, *ya habibti,* very much." He stroked a single finger right over her clitoris and pressed down into the silk.

She jolted, arching her body toward that teasing touch.

"I do like these, but I am going to adore what is underneath them."

"You are so much earthier than I ever expected."

"I told you, I am a traditional man of my people. We celebrate the delight of pleasure."

"Your Bedouin tribes, perhaps."

"You would be surprised."

Maybe she would be. Like Jawhar, Zohra was one of the few Arabic countries whose outlook and culture had always suffered less religious oppressions than their surrounding neighbors or the rest of Eastern Europe.

"I'll take your word for it."

"You should not have to." It was the first time he had outright criticized her upbringing in America rather than Jawhar.

"So, show me now." She wasn't about to get into a discussion on that particular topic right now.

"Oh, I fully intend to." And he did, caressing her until she was in a fever pitch of desire.

She wasn't sure how it happened, but she lost the *galabeya*. Finally. He took a moment to admire her in her lacy bra before removing it. He paid the kind of homage to her breasts that felt almost spiritual, but at the same time was very, very carnal.

Her nipples were aching and her panties literally soaked before he pulled back to ask, "Are you ready for me?"

"I've been ready." She'd meant to yell it out, but her voice was gone it was a barely there croak.

"I also."

But still, he took his time removing her wet panties. And then, instead of covering her with his body like she expected, he pressed her thighs wide apart and began to touch her with careful, knowing fingers.

"Zahir," she pleaded.

"It will be easier for you if I deal with your maiden-head with my fingers."

"What?" she gasped in a shocked whisper. And then shook her head frantically. "No. I… That's…"

But his forefinger and middle finger were already pressing inside, pushing against the barrier that stood between her virginity and their ultimate connection. He rubbed gently, making circles with his fingertips, pressing, pressing…always pressing.

It was a dull ache, not a stabbing sting. The small pain helped bring her to a more alert awareness as Zahir started his preparation of her body for his penetration.

"You are so careful with me," she breathed.

He gave her that smug half smile that she found more endearing than annoying. "Naturally."

"Is it a learned trait, or bred into you, I wonder?"

"What?" he asked, but his knowing gray gaze said he had the answer already.

"Your arrogance."

"You have met my father. It is genetic."

Yes, she knew the king of Zohra as well as the King of her father's country, Jawhar, and she would have to concede the point. Supreme confidence was definitely a family trait.

"Khalil and Amir do not seem quite so over the top with it."

"I am not sure Grace or Jade would agree with you but, *aziz,* you should not be thinking of other men while I am doing this." He pressed against her clitoris with his thumb and all thoughts of arrogance and his family flew from her brain.

A long, low moan snaked out of her throat as pleasure intensified in that one spot and then radiated outward. He continued the pressure massage against the thin barrier while caressing her sweet spot with his thumb in a way guaranteed to make her forget her own name.

She felt the stunning ecstasy begin to build again, this time all the more intense for knowing what it would lead to. Her body went rigid with tension, the dull ache inside her drowned in the hurricane of desire.

As the pleasure exploded he pressed through the barrier, her pleasure muting the sting of pain. She still felt it, but somehow it was natural, a moment meant only for them.

He looked into her eyes, his own so dark they appeared black. "Now, I make you mine."

She didn't reply. Could not form words to deny the claim and refused to face the truth of its temporary nature.

There was no need for her to respond as he moved between her legs, his engorged, steel-like hardness pushing inside her.

She could feel the stretch as her most intimate flesh strained to accommodate his. His member was much thicker than his fingers had been inside her. The sensation of not only being joined to him, but completely filled by him washed over her.

Neither spoke as he rocked gently with his hips, pressing deeper with each small thrust. Their gazes remained locked, the connection something so much more than physical. But then, she'd never expected anything else.

She loved this man with her whole heart and sharing her body with him was both spiritual and highly emotional.

Despite the obvious need making his muscles bulge from the tension of holding back, Zahir leaned down and placed the gentlest of kisses on her lips.

Tears washed her eyes, but she wasn't ashamed of them. They seemed an appropriate reaction to this moment. He did not seemed fazed by them, either, merely tilting his lips at one corner as he brushed the moisture away with his thumb.

"Are you ready?"

She almost asked for what, but he shifted just that much and she felt a new type of pleasure. Something so intimate and primal that she could do nothing but nod.

He did not smile, though she could sense his satisfaction at her agreement. He did begin to move, starting a careful, steady rhythm that was at once wonderful and not enough.

"More, please, Zahir."

He shook his head; the strain around his eyes the only indication that holding back was taking its toll on him. "Not this time. You are too new to this. You will have nothing but pleasure from me this night."

"It *does* feel good," she said somewhere between pleading and affirmation.

And they didn't have a *some other time* between them.

Rather than answer, he kissed her again, but this time with an unrestrained carnality that revealed how close to losing his control he really was. She responded, losing herself in the joy of their connection.

His movements grew jerky, though he did not let himself go as she was craving. A small voice in the back of her head told her she would thank him for his control later, but right now, she was once again reaching for the pinnacle of pleasure.

When it came, it washed over her in a warm wave unlike the frantic convulsions of the first time. However, his body seized, muscles straining, his neck corded as he threw his head back and let out a primal shout of completion.

A sense of accomplishment washed over her, adding to her happiness. She had given him this, just as he had given her unimaginable pleasure.

"It is done." His voice held a profundity that touched her deeply.

No matter the cause, she and Zahir had been one for this moment in time.

She wanted to say something, but tiredness overtook her and she felt the room fading even as Zahir whispered words of praise next to her ear, their bodies still joined.

# CHAPTER FOUR

ZAHIR lowered himself and Angele into the steaming, fragrant water of the bath. Worthy of communal baths anywhere in Zohra, the traditional mosaic tiled rectangular bath could easily accommodate four adults. It would only ever serve him and Angele however.

As her toes touched the water, she began to stir.

The soft lighting was brighter than the candlelight in the bedroom, but not so bright it should hurt her eyes. Nevertheless, he bent protectively over her as she wakened. He'd never had a lover fall into dozing like she had, a picture of perfect peace and contentment.

It had stirred something inside him he did not want to examine too closely.

"It smells so good," she whispered as she snuggled her head into the joint of his shoulder and neck.

A small bag of fragrant herbs floated on the surface near them. He had added the vial of specially prepared oils to the steaming water as well. "It is the traditional bathing treatment for after the wedding night."

"For all of Zohra, or for your family?"

"These herbs and spices are mixed only for the royal family." He brushed his hands down her stomach, tempted to go lower, but refrained. She needed time to recover before he made love to her again. "They are supposed to help assuage the aches and pains post coitus."

"They're doing a bang-up job." The husky tone of her voice challenged his intentions further.

"I am glad you find it so."

"Don't you?" she asked, as if daring him to deny the lovemaking had not been impacting for him as well.

He had no desire to attempt such a falsehood. "I do."

Though he suspected he found the bath slightly more reinvigorating than she did. He could not imagine a more pleasing wedding night. The marriage would have to be organized and dignitaries from all over the world invited, but he had no intention of maintaining chastity with her between times.

He could even be grateful they had this time to explore their sensual relationship without concern of the next heir's conception. He wondered what form of birth control she had decided on, but did not feel tonight was the one to discuss such mundane matters.

Tomorrow would be soon enough.

Angele was intelligent and highly organized. He had no doubt whatever option she'd chosen it was the best and most reliable on the market. When she planned something, she did it with a thoroughness that impressed even his father, or so the king had told Zahir.

He felt honored she had planned this time for them, no matter what nerves had prompted it.

"Your en suite is huge. Is that a royal thing or a rich thing?"

"It is a Zahir thing." He spent his life serving his

people. When he got an opportunity to relax, he wanted to be able to do so in absolute comfort.

"I suspected, but well…it's not as if I've ever gone into my parents' en suite or my uncle's, for that matter."

"You have refused to live in your parents' home since their reconciliation."

"It happened when I was an adult." She paused as if thinking of the past. "It was time for me to get my own place anyway."

"Had you been raised in Jawhar, you would have remained with your parents until our marriage."

She tensed, but her tone was even as she said, "But I was not raised in Jawhar."

"No, you were not."

"Does that bother you?"

"No." While he found her independence somewhat disconcerting, he found he liked the woman floating in his arms.

"You've made a couple of comments that implied it did."

"Mere observations on differences are not an accusation of unacceptability."

"Sometimes, they feel like they are."

"Feelings are not fact."

"True."

"Emotions cannot be trusted." That reality had been drilled into him from childhood as he trained from his earliest memory to take over leadership of the kingdom of Zohra.

"Perhaps that is true sometimes, Zahir, but the lack of emotion can be just as bad."

"To control one's emotions is to control the negotiation."

She sat up, unexpectedly sliding away from him in the water. "All of life is not a political negotiation." She settled on the underwater bench opposite, her gaze searching, her expression earnest. "Don't tell me you use those tactics when dealing with your family?"

"Not telling you would not make it any less true."

Her lovely brown eyes widened and then narrowed. "You mean that."

"I do not make it habit to lie."

"You hid your relationship with Elsa Bosch for years." An expression of chagrin came over Angele's features before she bit her lip, clearly wishing she had not said that.

Nevertheless, he would answer the implication. "I kept it private. This is a necessary survival tactic for those of us who spend the majority of our lives in the public eye."

"Discretion is minimal, subterfuge preferred," she said quoting something he knew his uncle often said.

"Sometimes subterfuge is necessary, but that does not make me a liar."

She looked away, her brows drawn together, but then she sighed. "So, you treat your parents like competing world leaders?"

While it was hardly a subtle way for her to change the subject, he did not call her on it. He had no desire to discuss one of the major mistakes of his life.

"My father especially. I successfully negotiated for my first horse." He smiled at the memory. "I lost the negotiation for a private family-only birthday party when I was ten, though."

"You were shy?"

"Timidity is not an acceptable trait in a world leader."

"You were ten."

"Nevertheless, I was not shy."

"Then why no other children?"

"That option was not on the table for negotiation."

Her brow wrinkled charmingly. "I don't understand."

"I lobbied for a party with my siblings. My father insisted on a state dinner."

Her gasp was far too adorable. Perhaps even he could be influenced by the emotion of the moment the first night with his bride.

"You mean you weren't allowed to have a children's party at all?"

He shrugged and admitted, "I was seven when I had my last children's party."

He had continued to try to negotiate for one until his twelfth year, when his father had informed him he was a man and had to put away childish things. It was the way of things for someone in his position. He knew his cousin in Jawhar had been raised with a similar set of ideals.

"That is terrible."

He shook his head. "You are too softhearted."

"No child of mine would be forced to have a state dinner for his birthday celebration." She sounded like she was discussing some form of torture.

And he could not help chuckling. "I learned the importance of my role and responsibilities."

It had been an effective lesson in putting the needs of his people before his personal desires.

"You learned that you were not allowed to be a child." Her tone implied she had just discovered something of importance about him. "It wasn't the same for your brothers."

"Naturally not."

She glided back toward him through the water. "Tonight, no one else is here. This is not about duty and obligation."

Suddenly a stricken expression took over her features. So, she remembered she had made this night a condition of the ridiculous "offer" she had made to let him out of their families' agreement.

He was tempted to let her flounder simply because the entire premise to this night was so very ludicrous.

However, she was right. "Making love to you in no way feels like a duty."

Her gaze searched his, as if trying to ascertain the truth of his statement. He knew she would find what she sought. For he spoke the truth.

Which was something of a relief for him, though he would never admit it.

The brilliance of her smile was worth his admission. "Tonight you are simply Zahir, not Crown Sheikh."

He was never anything less than what he was, leader and servant to his people. Not even during his time with Elsa, though for those stolen hours he had come closest to being simply a man than any other.

It was not a thing Angele could comprehend. Even

had she been raised among their people. To know from birth that an entire country depended on you for its well-being was a circumstance known by only a handful in the entire world. And from those he had met, he knew not all were raised from infancy with the sense of responsibility to their people that his father and mentors had instilled in Zahir.

He would not shatter Angele's beliefs however and they were not entirely false. While not the entire truth, either. This night, he *was* as far removed from his position as dutiful sheikh as he could allow himself to be.

Fully cognizant he needed to make the night special so Angele would lose her fear of intimacy between them, there was still no denying that making love to her in this way—without the benefit of an official wedding—was not the action of a dutiful, responsible sheikh of his people. An internal voice, that sounded suspiciously like one of his mentors, chided him. Telling him there were other ways he could have allayed Angele's fears.

The simple truth, as unexpected as it had been to realize, was that Zahir *wanted* Angele. He found her more sexually desirable than he'd ever allowed himself to realize. The years they had waited to formalize their engagement, much less marry, had taken a toll on him as well. Though he had not known it.

He had forced himself never to think of her sexually. At first, because she had been so young and later because that part of his psyche was reserved for Elsa.

He now accepted that Angele was the ideal woman to share his bed and had been all along.

He pulled her back into his arms. "Are you ready to continue this night out of time?"

Her doe-soft eyes darkened with desire and she nodded before angling her head in a clear invitation to kiss.

It was an invitation he would never reject again.

Angele woke to pleasurable, never before experienced aches in her body. No doubt the pain would be acute but for the two soaking baths Zahir had insisted she share with him the night before.

A night filled with more passion and pleasure than she had ever thought possible.

The temptation to ask him to maintain their status quo as promised for future marriage was so strong, she'd literally had to bite her tongue to keep it back as they said their goodbyes in the wee hours of morning.

Though she would have much preferred waking in Zahir's arms at least one time in her life, she understood his concern with the possibility their tryst would be discovered if she did not leave while all but the security men on duty slept. So, she had gone, her body sated and her heart filled with longing for what would never be.

Although she had showered with Zahir before leaving his rooms, she took another bracing one in semi-cool water now. She needed every trick to maintain her resolve.

She packed quickly, leaving out the four envelopes she had prepared before stepping foot in Zohra.

One held a letter to her pseudouncle, the King of Jawhar telling him she was backing out of the agreement to marry Zahir sometime in the distant future. She apologized, pleaded with him not to hold her father accountable for her choices and told him she would understand if he no longer recognized her as part of his family. Her heart would have broken at the prospect, but it had shattered all those months ago when she'd first seen evidence of Zahir's affection for Elsa Bosch and there wasn't anything left to break.

Or so she told herself.

The second envelope was similar to the first, only the letter inside was written to Zahir's father. In this one she once again apologized and begged the king to consider her actions her own and in no way a reflection on her pseudouncle or her own parents—as none were aware of her growing discontent with the agreement as it stood.

The third envelope was thicker. It contained a letter to Zahir, this one the only one she had written this morning. She thanked him for their one special night and told him she would never forget it.

She also explained about the enclosed pictures, detailing when she had first received them and how. She gave him as much information regarding the blackmail as she could, including a list of payments she had made and how she had done so. She assured him she had told no one, not even her parents of the pictures or the blackmail monies she had paid.

She hoped he would discover how best to keep them out of circulation, for his sake as well as his family's. But come tomorrow, or perhaps even tonight, the blackmailer would know that Angele was no longer a pony in this race.

Her eyes flicked to the final envelope, the one that would ensure there would be no turning back. Though, really, it was only symbolic. It held a press release, scotching any "rumors" of a suspected permanent connection between the house of Jawhar and the house of Zohra vis-à-vis a marriage between her and Zahir. She had included a couple of personal quotes. One to the effect that she had no desire to live her life in the public eye as a royal and the other her absolute refusal to make a permanent home outside of her adopted country, America.

After reading it, her father might disown her and her mother would undoubtedly be furious, but Angele wasn't going to live the rest of her life without love. She just wasn't.

She might not be American by birth, but she'd been raised around an entirely different set of ideals to the duty-bound royals that led Jawhar and Zohra. While she loved the country of her birth and Zohra as well, at heart? She was a modern American woman.

She wasn't about to allow Zahir to be forced into a marriage he so clearly had never really wanted, either.

She was under no illusions. He would probably enter another arranged contract, but this time he was older. Zahir would have more input into who his chosen bride was to be. Angele could only hope, for his sake, that it was someone he *could* develop real feelings for.

She snuck down the secret passageways for the last time and left Zahir's packet in his room while she knew he was busy with his father. She left each of the letters to the kings with their respective secretarial staff. And finally she dropped the press release off with the PR department.

She had prepared a timed email with a duplicate release to be sent to the major news distribution agencies in a few hours. She would be in flight back to the United States when news hit.

Cowardly? Perhaps, but she preferred to think of it as politic.

Back in the U.S., her denial of a connection to the House of Zohra would constitute little more than a blip in the plethora of social news about drunk-driving celebrities and irresponsible megaconglomerates destroying ecosystems.

Once she was in the car headed to the airport, she pulled out her phone to make the most difficult call of her life. Her parents would not be pleased.

Refusing to take the easy route, she called her father first. That conversation went much as expected, but when he blamed her mother for insisting Angele be raised in the United States, she'd had enough.

"Had you managed to keep it in your pants, I would have grown up in Jawhar. Don't you dare blame Mom for this."

His outraged gasp at her crassness had no problem translating across the cellular connection.

"In point of fact, it was your ongoing infidelity that convinced me marriage to Zahir would never work," Angele added. "I will not put myself in the position of living as Mom did."

"She never wanted for anything."

"If you really believe that, then you've learned nothing despite your change in behavior."

"You do not speak to me with such disrespect, Angele."

"The truth is not disrespect." He couldn't even accuse

her of a snarky tone, because her voice was as devoid of emotion as her heart right now.

She preferred the dead feeling to the pain that was sure to come as her final separation from Zahir sank in completely.

"Your mother and my relationship is not your business."

"I agree, but that does not change the fact that your example is one I absolutely refuse to follow."

"Zahir is not a hot-blooded man." The words *like myself* were implied but not said.

Angele wasn't about to tell her father just how wrong he was. After the previous night, though, Angele knew the truth. And the certainty that Zahir had spent similar nights with Elsa Bosch managed to pierce her numbness with a hurt that Angele chose to ignore.

So much for a decimated heart having no capacity for further pain.

"You cannot do this, Angele."

"It's done."

"We will discuss this further later." The royals of Zohra and Jawhar had nothing on her father for arrogance. "Right now, I am to meet Malik and Faruq. I am sure you and I both can guess the planned topic of our conversation."

"You are not listening, though why that should surprise me, I have no idea."

"Angele!" The shocked way he said her name spoke volumes.

"Please, Father. I love you, but I don't want to live my mother's life. I simply won't. I delivered letters to both kings with my stated intentions and apologies before leaving the palace."

"Leaving the…where are you?" For the first time, her father's voice sounded worried rather than angry.

The car pulled up outside the airport. She got out without answering her father, or waiting for the driver to open her door.

Once her luggage was on the curb, she said, "I'm on my way home."

"Your home is here."

"It never has been and it never will be." She sighed, ignoring the twinge in her heart the words caused her. "Please listen to me, Father. I included a copy of the press release I sent out to the major news agencies with the letters I delivered to the kings. Your meeting would be best spent deciding how to deal with the PR ramifications of my decision than trying to determine how to change my mind."

"Of course we will change your mind."

"No, you won't."

"Damn it, I changed my whole lifestyle to ensure this wedding would one day take place. You will not derail that in a fit of feminine pique."

"What are you talking about?"

"Surely Zahir told you about the little talk we had several years ago. He's always been your hero." Her father's tone implied he'd neither enjoyed the *little talk* nor the fact he'd lost his place as Angele's hero.

Tough. He was entirely responsible for both she was sure. And yet, she heard herself saying, "I'm sorry."

Though why he should think Zahir would have told her about the discussion was beyond her. Before this wedding feast, the time she and Zahir had spent together alone could be measured in minutes, not hours.

It was her father's turn to sigh. "Zahir informed me that he would not marry a woman whose father made headlines in the scandal rags on a regular basis."

She had no problem believing that. Zahir's near rabid protection of the family name and reputation of the royal house was well-known.

"So, you turned faithful..." She paused, swallowing down bile. She'd thought he'd done it to save their relationship and that had hurt enough, as she'd so wanted him to do it for her mother's sake. To learn he'd done it to earn a more entrenched place in the royal house just made her sick. "Or at least *circumspect,* in order to make sure your daughter married into the Royal House of Zohra."

"Faithful," her father bit out. "I realized my actions were doing all harm and no good. Certainly they never had the effect I had hoped."

"You hoped sleeping around would have some kind of positive impact?" she asked with patent disbelief.

"Your mother refused to get pregnant again. I accused her of becoming pregnant with you only to trap me into marriage to begin with." A long drawn-out pause followed. "She never denied it."

"Was this before, or after you had your first affair?" What was she asking? Her brain and mouth were connected without a filter in there somewhere.

"It does not matter."

"I'm sure it did to Mom."

"She would not even try to give me a son."

"I am sorry to have been such a disappointment to you." And she'd never even known she had been.

"That is not what I meant."

Strangely she believed him. Her father hadn't ever done anything to make her feel like he had wished she'd been a boy. "I thought you didn't care if you had an heir since you aren't actual royalty."

"You know our people, though you were not raised full-time among them."

And in the culture of his homeland, to have no son to leave his name and worldly possessions was a great tragedy.

"I'm sorry," she said again, feeling her father's pain across the distance between them.

She understood the dynamics of her parents' marriage a little better, but she still had no desire to emulate it. "Mom loves you. She always has."

"I know that now." For the first time since their initial greeting, her father's voice held a measure of contentment. "I say again, Zahir is not me. He will not make my mistakes."

Memories of the photos she had left in Zahir's room rose to taunt Angele as she pulled her rolling case to the private plane security checkpoint. Even so, she did not reveal to her father that Zahir was no lily-white duty-bound sheikh, no matter what everyone else believed.

"I can't marry him, Father."

"You must."

"No."

"These are just prewedding jitters."

"We aren't even officially engaged." *Sheesh.* "This

is me being smart enough to avoid a future that holds no appeal for me."

"It's a future you are imagining, not the one that will be."

"Have you always loved Mom?" she asked instead of answering.

The answer was immediate and without doubt. "Yes."

"And still you hurt her for years, as she apparently hurt you as well." Angele understood now it had gone both ways, but that certainly did not give her more hope for her own future. "If you two, loving each other, could do so much emotional damage, how much worse in a marriage that only one person feels love?"

"Zahir is not a man to love." Her father's instant answer without even pausing for thought to consider which of them felt that love was another brick in the wall Angele was trying so hard to build around her heart.

"My flight is leaving in a few minutes."

"You are not leaving Zohra."

She heard the threat in her father's voice, but she ignored it. She'd taken precautions to make sure she could and would leave today. She'd finagled a spot on a private plane headed to the States. So, even if the commercial flights were grounded while the royal guard searched for her, she would be going. Even so, she had timed her call to her father so that it would take a miracle for her flight to be discovered and stopped in time.

"Please, accept it. The press release has already gone out."

"We can say it is a hoax."

"I'll do a live interview."

"You will not."

She would do whatever it took to stand by her decision and let her silence tell him so.

Her father cursed fluently in Arabic. "Malik will disown our friendship."

"He's not that vindictive."

"It is a matter of pride."

"Yours. If it was all that important to either of the kings, one, or both of them, would have pressed for an official date before now. The agreement has been in place for a decade."

"You have only been an adult for five of those years."

"Half a decade."

"They are pressing for it now," he said, rather than argue the point.

Very typical for her father. Focus on the now, on the positive and ignore everything else.

She wasn't so sanguine and never had been. "It's too late."

Her father cursed again and she winced. She had known this conversation would be hard, but had foolishly thought herself immune to her father's disapproval.

"I love you, Father. I hope you'll be able to forgive me one day."

She hung up before he could say anything more.

She went through VIP customs, barely registering the words spoken to her or those she used in reply. Her heart ached. Whoever said emotions are felt in the head had never been in love. Her chest felt tight, like any second her heart was just going to give up and stop beating.

No matter what she'd said in her letters or on the

phone to her father, walking away from Zahir was the hardest, most painful thing she'd ever done.

Last night had been the most amazing experience of her life, but then she'd looked at those pictures again and she knew. No matter how good a lover Zahir might be, he didn't love her. Only right now, she almost thought living with him without his love would be better than living without him at all.

She forced her feet to move forward, to climb the stairs to the private jet. The owner said something to her. She replied, but couldn't remember what either said as she buckled herself into her seat. She did remember pleading a headache, glad when that seemed to buy her the silence and privacy she needed.

She didn't know the retired statesman or his wife very well and they appeared content to keep themselves to themselves. As far as they knew, they were doing a favor for the Royal House of Zohra, but they clearly didn't expect conversation.

For which she was grateful, rather than offended. She wasn't up to it. It was taking all her strength to stay in her seat and not return to the palace and a passel of angry royals.

The captain had just announced he would be taxiing into position for takeoff shortly when Angele's mother's number showed on the screen of her phone. She turned it off as the engines warmed up.

Nothing productive could come from her talking to her mom right now. And her call with her father had been difficult enough.

Angele's mother's love and approval had always been

freely given. The prospect that breaking the contract with the royal family of Zohra might change that was not an outcome she felt emotionally ready to deal with.

# CHAPTER FIVE

His body beneath his robes of state rigid with shock, Zahir stared at his father. Replaying the words Faruq had spoken in his mind did not aid in making sense of them.

Angele would not have done this. She could not have done this. Not after their *very* successful night together.

"You did not expect this," Faruq said with some censure.

No, Zahir had bloody well not expected anything like this. Not after last night. Especially after last night. But betrayal and shock were choking him, anger their close bedfellow, so he merely shook his head.

"Her leave taking, these letters…" Faruq wasn't sounding like a father, but a disappointed king. "It all implies forethought and planning."

"It's one of her talents." Zahir allowed with heavy irony to mask his growing fury.

His gazed jumped from his father's grave expression to matching looks on the two other men in the king's private study. King Malik's frown was two parts anger, one part confusion. Cemal appeared resigned, though clearly not happy.

That attitude of resignation bothered Zahir more than he wanted to admit, feeding the anger he was doing his best to keep under control. "Did you know about this?" he asked the older man.

"No." Cemal did not elaborate, but King Malik was more than willing to fill in the gaps. "She called him on her way to the airport."

"And we were unable to stop her flight?" Zahir asked, knowing full well how feudal he sounded and really, not caring.

"She cut the timing too fine and left on the private jet owned by one of the wedding guests."

Zahir cursed.

"She outwitted us," King Malik said with some admiration.

Zahir did not comment, but reached out in a silent demand to see the letter his father still held. He was not so impressed right now by Angele's superb attention to detail.

Faruq passed the papers over. "She included a copy of her press release as well—it denies rumors of your possible betrothal."

"You're serious?" Zahir asked in an angry disbelief he was unable to entirely quash.

There was being thorough and there was being outrageously stubborn.

Faruq nodded grimly. "According to her letter, it won't go live for a few hours."

"She did not want us blindsided by the announcement," King Malik said.

*Blindsided*? After the night they had spent in his bed, how could Zahir be anything but? He scanned the pages in his hand. "Like hell she does not wish to live in Zohra. She loves it here."

Both kings nodded their agreement, though it was King Malik that spoke. "That has always been my understanding."

"She chose the excuse most likely to lose her favor with the people of Zohra and Jawhar while increasing Zahir's sympathy with them." It was the first time since Zahir had entered his father's study that Cemal had offered anything more than a monosyllabic answer to a question. "It is the equivalent of her falling on her sword."

The words conjured up Angele's claims she would not allow herself or Zahir to be railroaded into marriage, and her subsequent promise to take the blame in the media and with the royal families. He'd convinced himself she didn't mean it. Clearly he'd been spectacularly wrong regarding her motives for their "wedding night."

Not in the least comfortable with an image of himself as being so weak he needed such protections, the fury inside Zahir went from simmer to full boil. He was not that man. That she could not see that truth infuriated him, but like always, he kept his emotions under tight control.

"The fact she broke the engagement was enough of a sympathy vote for me," Zahir said with cold sarcasm.

Cemal shook his head. "Not if she gave her true reason for doing so, which I've no doubt she did to you."

Zahir remembered the conversation he'd had with his intended only three nights ago, words he had dismissed as nerves. "You believe she spoke to me of this?" He shook the papers in his hand, his grip so tight they wrinkled.

He wasn't denying it, but he wasn't admitting anything, either.

"I know my daughter. She does not take the easy way out."

"That is why she called our engagement off with a letter," Zahir mocked.

How had she considered it unnecessary to speak to him personally? Had she thought her illogical claims in his study that night to be sufficient final word on their future?

If she did, it only showed how very little she truly understood the man who she would one day marry.

Cemal wasn't buying it. "She called me and I'm confident she spoke directly to you."

"Did she?" Faruq demanded of his son.

Zahir gave a jerk of his head. Regardless of whether he accepted that conversation as definitive word on the subject, obviously Angele had seen things differently. He ignored a curiously sharp pain in the vicinity of his heart at her easy dismissal.

"And you did not feel it politic to warn me, or her uncle?" Zahir's father demanded, his own anger blatant and no distant relation to the emotionless facade he had always demanded of Zahir.

"*Adopted* uncle," Cemal stressed, once again entering the discussion. "And it's not an *engagement*. Their relationship was never formalized. Not in ten years."

"We all know the reasons behind that," Zahir said.

"Camel dung." Cemal made no attempt to hide his

disgust. "You could have announced the formal engagement anytime, but you chose not to and my daughter got tired of waiting."

"So, she thought to force my son's hand with this?" Faruq asked in a deadly quiet voice.

Zahir's father had taught him to negotiate, to manipulate and to retaliate. The man hated being on the receiving end of circumstances and manipulations out of his control.

Cemal's expression turned even stonier than it had been as he'd voiced his accusation of Zahir's neglect over his duty. No, he hadn't labeled it as such, but each man in this room knew who was responsible for the ten-year-long "understanding."

"On the contrary," Cemal said, his voice just as cold as Zahir's father's had been. "This is my daughter making sure nothing can force her into honoring a contract she believes would sow nothing but unhappiness for her future."

"That is ridiculous, *my brother*," King Malik said, laying his own stress on the family claim along with a conciliatory hand on Cemal's shoulder. "The girl is in love with Zahir and always has been. It's as easy to read every time she is near him as the most basic of primary books."

Zahir grimaced. "A woman in love does not break off an engage—" At Cemal's narrowed eyes, Zahir amended his words to, "a *contractual promise* for future marriage."

"She does if she believes her love will never be returned."

Zahir wasn't going there. "She is no starry-eyed

teenager to expect flowers and poetry from a marriage such as ours."

"I think you are missing the point here," Cemal said. *"There isn't going to be any marriage."*

"And this pleases you?" Zahir accused, stunned by the possibility. He was no man's idea of a poor son-in-law choice.

"Not at all, but I know my daughter well enough to know that once she sets a course of action, she sticks to it."

Zahir didn't disagree. Cemal and Lou-Belia had wanted Angele to attend finishing school in Paris rather than university in the States. Angele had gotten her degree from Cornell. Neither had approved her decision to get her own apartment, but Angele had lived on her own since her sophomore year at university.

Zahir had never given much thought to what he considered Angele's minor rebellions, particularly when he had approved her choices both times. He had not wanted her to marry him without having had a chance to live at least something of a normal life.

Now, he thought he'd been a fool to encourage the blatant independence. Had he spent more time getting to know her, he would have realized what such choices might wrought.

"We can put out our own press release saying hers was a hoax, perpetrated by our enemies," King Malik suggested.

Cemal shook his head. "She threatened to do a live interview if we did that."

So, Cemal had tried to dissuade his daughter from her intended path.

And all Zahir could concentrate on was the truth that such persuasion should not have been necessary after the previous night. Those hours out of time fed Zahir's anger and an unfamiliar tightness in his chest.

"So, we have no choice," Faruq said with a worried glance at his son.

Zahir was no object of pity or concern and never would be. "There is always a choice. We will release our own statement."

"And what will it say?" King Malik asked, hope gleaming in eyes reflecting a lifetime of power and even less tolerance for not getting his own way as Zahir's father.

"That I recognize waiting so long to announce our formal engagement was a mistake. I will woo my bride-to-be. The country can expect announcement of my formal betrothal by the end of the year."

If hearts and flowers were what she wanted, then they were what he would give his errant bride-to-be.

His father's bark of laughter was tinged with no less disbelief than Angele's actions had sparked. King Malik and Cemal merely stared at Zahir as if he'd taken leave of his senses.

"You doubt my ability to woo one innocent woman after witnessing my skills at negotiations with world leaders?" he demanded.

Cemal coughed. "A woman is not a world power."

"No, but one day your daughter will be married to one." Zahir bowed his leave-taking to his father and King Malik, inclining his head to Cemal. "If you will excuse me, I have a campaign to plan."

If fury drove him more than desire, that was his own business.

His father frowned, but said, "If you are sure this is the course of action you want to take, I will have the press release with your apology and intentions drawn up and disseminated."

"Do you have another suggestion?"

"You could let her go."

"I cannot. In waiting too long to finalize our engagement, I failed Angele. I will not do so again through inaction." Besides, they had already had their wedding night.

There would damn well be a wedding.

"Good luck," Cemal said, sounding like he meant it.

King Malik nodded. "My staff and family are at your disposal. I will have my wife create a dossier most likely to help you in your cause." King Malik turned to Cemal. "She will draw upon Lou-Belia's knowledge of her daughter as well."

Cemal nodded. "Good. Her mother knows Angele better than anyone else."

"Thank you." Not that Zahir doubted his ability to convince Angele to marry him.

However he would take what help was offered. After all, he had been certain that after the previous night she would never have gone through with this farce of denying him to begin with.

He understood his intended's motivations a thousandfold better several hours later. He'd finally returned to his rooms only to find a thick envelope with his name on it and stamped with a red Private prominently in several places.

The letter was somewhat illuminating, but coupled with the pictures, Zahir realized he was damn lucky Angele had handled breaking the contract the way she had. Acknowledging that did nothing to improve his black mood.

The fury he'd felt at her defection was nothing compared to the incendiary rage he experienced knowing she had been subjected to blackmail.

Looking through the pictures, he had no doubts about who had taken them and used them for monetary gain, either. There could only be one person. Only Zahir had thought Elsa too smart to risk something like this. She stood to lose far more than she could ever hope to gain.

Regardless of who the culprit was, though, Angele should have brought the problem directly to him. Instead she had paid the money.

They were not close, but she had to have known that he would deal with the problem.

The fact Angele had paid money to keep his name out of the tabloids boggled his mind. It simply was not the way things were done. She had to have known he would have safeguards in place in just such an event.

She certainly expected him to be able to take care of it now, or so her letter suggested.

Nevertheless, her loyal, if foolish, actions were further indication that she was indeed in love with him. Or believed herself to be. He gave very little credence to love and all it entailed, but her feelings for him should make his wooing a simple matter.

A little voice amidst all his anger reminded him that he'd thought his seduction and lovemaking would have prevented her leaving in the first place. His father wanted to know why not just let her go?

It was simple really. Zahir didn't lose. Ever.

Equally as important, Zahir accepted that he owed his future bride a courtship. He was furious with her, but his own inaction in regard to their betrothal and ill-advised relationship with Elsa had driven Angele to her recent actions.

Zahir had failed in his duty to her and that was worse than losing. That was a blow to his integrity he simply would not accept.

First, he had to handle Elsa and her threats. She must be made to understand that Angele was and forever would be off-limits.

Then Zahir would go after his reluctant bride.

Sitting at her desk at the magazine, Angele read the article her mother had sent her the link for. Confusion slowly morphed to sheer, unadulterated anger.

That arrogant idiot.

Even after seeing the pictures she'd been sent, Zahir thought he could convince her to go through with the wedding contract. Did he have no idea how hopeless that belief should be?

Apparently not.

He was quoted as saying he'd been neglectful and planned to rectify that. Really? When? After all, she'd been home for two weeks and he'd not so much as called her in all that time.

Typical.

A couple of days ago, she'd received a short note, in his own handwriting. It had stated that the "picture problem" had been taken care of and that he hoped to see her soon. Like that made everything better. The excitement she'd felt at seeing the return address on the stationery, quickly followed by her disappointment there hadn't been anything more personal in the short missive, and then the tiny curl of hope at his professed desire to see her soon had made her mad.

And disgusted with herself.

Almost as disgusted as she was with him right now.

What really had her blood pressure rising was his statement his countrymen could expect announcement of a wedding date by the end of the year.

Not merely the formal engagement, but the actual *wedding date*.

If she'd been reading a printed newspaper she could have thrown it down. Would have thrown it right into the garbage. As it was, all she could do was glare at her computer monitor while a growingly familiar nausea rolled over her in a clammy wave.

She was sprinting for the bathroom moments later, anger at Zahir vying for supremacy at upset at her own colossal stupidity.

Zahir arrived at the magazine's offices late Friday afternoon, six weeks after Angele had left Zohra. He was in search of the woman he had spent far too many sleepless nights thinking about over the past weeks.

It was his guilt at putting his duty off that kept him

awake. He wasn't happy that his inaction had led to the need for this dramatic wooing.

He liked the fact his and her names had featured prominently in the media since she'd felt the need to back out of the contract even less. First, speculation on her motives and then his reaction had kept the gossips busy. Then reaction to his own press release had been flurried and florid.

Finally the long-distance wooing he'd done while preparing his offices for his absence had sparked several articles and numerous requests for interviews. He'd turned them all down—well, all but one. However, he'd allowed details of the gifts he'd showered his fiancée-to-be with to leak.

A woman deserved others to know she was appreciated and Zahir was doing his best to express that appreciation for Angele. It had taken a while, a couple of weeks in fact, for his fury at her defection to simmer down to the point he could focus on wooing rather than reading his errant bride-to-be the riot act. He was proud that none of the short notes accompanying his gifts and flowers held any sort of recriminations in them.

He'd even agreed to do an interview and photo spread for her magazine. He'd allowed the magazine's photographer into his offices at the palace in Zohra and agreed to pictures both in his robes of state and wearing designer suits custom tailored to his tall frame for the fashion magazine's feature article.

His every overture, including that one, had been met with a frustrating silence.

Now that his schedule was cleared, the time had come to step up his game.

Accompanied by his personal bodyguard and security detail and dressed in his best Armani and over robes of his office, Zahir carried a bouquet of yellow jasmine into Angele's office building. The receptionist looked up, her eyes going wide as he approached the large half-moon shaped desk in the center of the large lobby.

Giving one of his practiced political smiles, he asked, "Can you direct me to Angele bin Cemal al Jawhar's office?"

The young woman's eyes went even wider as she scrambled for some papers she nearly knocked from her desk, without looking away from Zahir and his security men. "Um...I don't...let me just make a call."

She scrabbled for her phone, her cheeks going a rosy-pink. She dialed and then started speaking rapidly almost immediately.

"Yes, there's a...I mean I think he's a sheikh, or something. I don't think he's dangerous, but he's got these scary-looking men with him. He's looked for Angele. I think it's Angele anyway. He called her Bin-something, but we've only got one Angele, right? I mean, there's an Angie in accounting, but no one else called Angele..."

He could hear the sound of someone speaking on the other end of the line, the deep tones indicated a male, but Zahir could not be sure.

"Yes. Oh, probably. He's carrying a bouquet of those exotic flowers Angele's been passing out to whoever would take them over the past few weeks."

Zahir's brows drew together as the implications of the receptionists words sank in. Angele had been disposing of the flowers he sent her by giving them away to all and sundry? What had she done with the jewelry, then? Pawned it?

His annoyance must have shown on his face because the receptionist flinched and the papers she'd managed to save went sweeping to the floor. It was probably a good thing she wore an earpiece for the phone, or the receiver probably would have gotten dropped as well.

Zahir took a step back from the desk as he schooled his features into impassivity.

The receptionist was nodding at whatever she was hearing over the phone, though she hadn't said anything for several seconds.

She jumped. "Um…yes, of course I was listening. I'll call her extension. Right now, sir."

The flustered woman pressed a button and then three more. "Um…Angele? Well, yes, I did mean to dial your extension. It's just there's a man down here that looks like, well he could be dangerous, or something, but he's got flowers." The woman turned away, making some effort to whisper, though her words were still clear. "You're sure he's not dangerous?"

Zahir managed to keep the scowl he felt off his features, but it was a close thing.

"All right. I'll tell him you'll be down shortly. It will be shortly, won't it?"

Apparently even Angele's patience had worn thin with the young woman because there was clearly no reply. The receptionist looked up and then flinched, her face blanching as she must have realized he could hear every word she'd spoken.

"Uh…Angele said she'll be down soon. You can… you should probably wait for her over there." The young woman waved toward some chairs by the window on the far side of the large lobby. Zahir nodded stiffly and led his security detail to the other side of the lobby.

"Hello, Zahir."

He turned at the sound of Angele's voice, his smile of greeting sliding right into a concerned frown.

Her usually honey-gold skin was wan and she had circles under her eyes not hidden by her makeup. She also looked like she'd lost weight; her pale cheeks were hollow.

"Are you well?" he asked and then could have bitten his own tongue. He knew better than to make queries of this type in a public place.

"I'm fine." She smoothed her hand down the front of her sheath dress.

The color of eggplant, the dark purple was usually a complimentary color for her, but today it only served to enhance the washed-out tone of her skin. Nevertheless, she wore it with stylish élan, her accessories and hair as well put together as any of the models her magazine photographed.

Regardless, she really had no business being at work if she was not feeling well. She needed to be home in bed, being pampered and coddled. His plans for the evening took a sudden shift.

"It is good to see you." Bowing slightly, he offered her the bouquet of yellow jasmine.

She simply shook her head, making no effort to take the flowers. "I'm cleared to leave. Did you have a destination in mind for this conversation?"

There was something off about Angele's attitude, but he had no time to ponder it as she turned and began

PROPERTY OF MERTHYR TYDFIL PUBLIC LIBRARY

walking toward the front doors. He handed the flowers off to one of the security guards to deal with. And then, he caught up to Angele with his longer strides and they exited the building together.

His limousine waited by the curb. She headed toward it without hesitation. Bemused by her assertive and frankly, unexpectedly cooperative behavior, he followed.

They were in the limo when she turned to him and asked, "Where are we going?"

"We have reservations at Chez Alene." But he did not think they should keep them.

"My favorite restaurant."

"I am aware."

"My mother?" she asked.

"Ultimately, yes."

*"Ultimately?"*

"Uncle Malik believed I needed assistance in my plan to woo you."

"Let me guess, he had the queen compile a dossier." There was nothing in Angele's tone to indicate how she felt about that, one way or the other.

"Yes."

She nodded, making no comment on the fact they had known each other their whole lives and a dossier of that type should not be necessary.

"You gave away the flowers I sent you?" he asked.

"Yes."

"Might I inquire why?" He wasn't sure he wanted to know what she had done with the jewelry, or the designer bags and shoes he'd had her mother pick out for her.

"Why did you send them?"

"You deserved a proper wooing after my years of neglect."

"Duty then."

He opened his mouth to deny it, but could he without dishonesty? Not completely. "Perhaps, to an extent. However, they were also a reminder that you were in my thoughts even separated by the miles."

"Poetic."

He shrugged. "What can I say? I am a man of my culture."

"You're a pragmatist with a terrifying ability to gauge human nature and use your observations to best effect."

"You do not believe me sincere?"

"I believe you were thinking of me, but we both know the reason for that, and it didn't have a thing to do with some romantic longing to see me."

"Define romance. Our last night together was not so forgettable."

Her hand settled against her stomach and she frowned. "No, it really wasn't."

"That bothers you."

She sighed, looking out the tinted windows at the traffic surrounding them. "It doesn't matter."

"I assure you, it does."

"No, it really doesn't."

"I know you think—"

"Look, let's just stop this politically motivated seduction, all right?" Despite her confident words—if possible, she looked even more fragile and out of sorts than before. "It's a waste of both our time and your efforts."

"You are so certain I cannot sway your mind?"

"You don't need to. If you agree to certain conditions, I will marry you."

# CHAPTER SIX

ZAHIR waited for Angele to take the words back, or at the very least, enumerate these said conditions. But she simply stared off into space, breathing shallowly.

"This is unexpected," he said finally when it became apparent she had nothing else to add.

In fact, he was so stunned his usually facile brain had the speed of cold honey in processing her immediate capitulation.

"Disappointed?"

Oddly he was. And not a little bit wary as well.

"I am aware you love me," he said, feeling his way in a blind negotiation he had not expected in any form at this stage. "I still believed your pride too wounded to make our reconciliation an easy one."

She laughed humorlessly. "You believe I'm agreeing to marry you because I love you?"

"Why else?" The prospect she had suddenly decided to submit to duty was not the comfortable thought it should be.

"We didn't use condoms that night."

His brow wrinkled as he tried to catch her point. "So?"

"So." She rolled her eyes and waved at her stomach as if that was answer enough.

His brain had no trouble catching up this time and the implication stole all the air from his lungs.

"Surely you were on the pill, or some other form of birth control. You planned the night well ahead of time." He'd been certain of that during their night together and even more convinced after seeing her letters to the kings and polished press release she'd left behind.

"Yes, I planned it. No, I didn't go on the pill as part of my preparations." Self-loathing laced her voice. "I should have...I realize that now."

"Why the hell not?" he demanded, his voice raised in a way he never allowed.

"I don't know. It wasn't rational. I know that, but I thought...one night. I was a virgin, disgustingly naive. I wouldn't get pregnant." She frowned. "I thought you'd use condoms."

He ignored the last statement and concentrated on the ones that came before it. "You are too smart for that."

She glared at him and then seemed to deflate. "Yes, I am. There's no excuse. I really just thought...I don't know. I've tried to understand why I didn't say anything when you didn't use a condom, but my excuses are feeble and stupid. Even to me."

"You expected me to use condoms?" He couldn't dismiss the claim a second time.

Her brow furrowed as if she didn't understand his question. "Well, yes."

"Why?"

"Why not? We weren't lovers. For all intents and purposes, what we had was a one-night stand."

"What we had was a premature wedding night," he practically shouted and then took a deep breath in shock at himself.

She waved her hand in dismissal, apparently unmoved by his loss of cool. "Call it what you like, but I expected you to use condoms and when you didn't... Well, that first time, I was just so lost to the moment and afterward, I thought the damage was already done."

"Damage is right."

That brought the glare back, but there was something else in her expression, something he couldn't quite name. "What is your problem? You're getting your way."

"You think this is me getting my way? My first child has been conceived without the benefit of a wedding ceremony. I have spent my entire life protecting my family from scandal and now it will visit itself on my child. He or she will forever carry the stigma."

"Please. This isn't the Middle Ages."

"If this child is my heir, his throne could be called into question." He cursed, using more than one language and feeling like that still was not enough to express his fury at the current development.

"Do a DNA test."

He drew himself up and scowled. "I do not doubt his paternity."

"I know that." She rolled her eyes. "I meant so there could be no question of the baby's parentage to others. Anyway, it might be a girl."

"Yes, because the men in my family are so good at fathering female offspring." They hadn't done so in five generations that he knew of, not in his direct lineage anyway.

She turned an interesting shade of green and started taking more rapid shallow breaths.

"Are you well?" What the hell was he asking? She was pregnant. Of course she was not well.

"Morning sickness," she gasped between breaths.

"It is nowhere near morning."

"The baby doesn't seem to care."

"This is not acceptable."

She cringed, her expression filling with too many emotions to name. "You don't want the baby?"

"Of course, I want this child. How could you ask such a thing?"

"Well, you're acting like it's the end of the world, or something."

"Are you that naive?"

"I am not naive. Not anymore."

"I disagree. You have not considered the complications this pregnancy will cause. It will be all over the press. After a lifetime of protecting my privacy and behaving with circumspection, I will make a bigger tabloid splash than your father and my brother combined."

"You don't want me to have this child? You think I should terminate my pregnancy?"

"Have you lost your mind?" How had she gone from what he had said to something so reprehensible? "Do not ever suggest such a thing to me again."

"I wasn't suggesting it. I'm not the one having a temperamental fit."

The accusation snapped the last thread of his control.

"Did you do this on purpose?" he leaned forward and asked, memories of Elsa's betrayals freshly branded in his brain. "Was this your way of getting back at me for my relationship with Elsa?"

"Now, who's making insane accusations?"

"Women scorned have been known to do worse."

"You never scorned me, you arrogant ass!" Then she swallowed convulsively and scrabbled for the button that would open the sunroof.

He reached up and pressed it when she seemed unable to make the stretch. "When you were eighteen, and I refused your kiss."

"That was five years ago."

"Revenge is a dish best served cold."

She took several deep breaths before saying, "I can't believe this."

"Join my world."

"Oh, get over yourself."

Fresh air came in through the opening in the roof and Angele leaned back in her seat, seemingly breathing easier. Good.

He mentally ran through a list of things needed doing. Consulting an eminent obstetrician was top of the list. "You are not taking this seriously, what this pregnancy means."

"Oh, I'm taking it seriously all right. I know exactly what it means."

"Oh?" She certainly had not shown proper understanding so far.

"Yes." She shot daggers with her usually doe-soft eyes. "It means I'm agreeing to a marriage I don't want."

"Why?"

"Why what?" she asked, sounding genuinely confused.

"Why agree to the marriage?"

"Because I'm not a stone-cold bitch."

"I never said you were."

"My mother told me something a few years ago. It was after I found out about my father's infidelities. I apologized to her for having to live in the States where I could know relative anonymity, instead of her home country of Brazil where she was better known. She'd done it to protect me."

"I am aware."

"Well, she told me I had nothing to apologize for, that from the moment a baby is conceived, his or her needs must come first."

"You are willing to marry me for the sake of our child."

"Under certain conditions, yes."

The limo pulled to a stop.

She looked at him with that same sick expression she'd had before opening the sunroof. "We're not at the restaurant. We're hours too early for dinner."

She swallowed convulsively on the word dinner.

"No, we are at your apartment building. I originally had planned to give you time to get ready for our date."

"More like, you intended to seduce me before dinner and hoped to cement the romantic proposal over dessert." The words should have been mocking, but she merely sounded resigned.

"You think you know me." She was wrong. On the proposal over dessert part.

He'd planned to woo her in person for two weeks before popping the question, so to speak.

"What?" she asked. "It would have been a good plan, if unsuccessful."

"You do not think I could seduce you?"

"I'm positive you could. Even feeling like my stomach is a jumping board for little green men right now, but I still wouldn't have said yes to your proposal."

"But you will now, because of the pregnancy."

"Neither of us has a choice. This baby deserves better than to be shunted to the side as the unacknowledged offspring to a future king."

"I would never refuse to acknowledge my child."

"You know what I mean."

"No, in fact, I do not."

"Never mind. This arguing is making me even more nauseated than usual."

The sickly pallor to her skin lent truth to her claim. He mentally shook himself. Now was not the time for recriminations. What was done, was done.

He had been right earlier; she clearly needed taking care of.

"Then we will not argue."

"Thank you." She sighed again, letting her eyes close as she seemed to concentrate on her breathing.

When the driver opened the door, Zahir wasted no time exiting and then leaning back inside to help Angele alight from the car. Once she'd cleared the vehicle, he bent and lifted her into his arms.

She gasped. "What are you doing?"

Flashbulbs went off and he knew this picture would show up in the media sooner than later.

"I am caring for you. You clearly need looking after."

"The papers are going to have a field day with speculation accompanying those shots."

"They'll have more than enough juicy tidbits of truth to publish over the next weeks."

"We're not going public with the…" She looked around and closed her mouth.

He carried her toward the building allowing his bodyguard to go inside first and the rest of the detail to bring up their rear. "These things have a way of making it to the light. Better to announce the happy event than scramble to respond when some tabloid does."

She let her head fall onto his shoulder. "I don't want to."

"We will talk about it later," he said in his newly formed determination not to cause her stress with further disagreements.

Angele sat at the bistro-style table in her kitchen and watched with bemusement as Zahir efficiently prepared a pot of peppermint tea.

"You are awfully comfortable in the kitchen for a Crown Prince," she observed, happy to focus on anything but recent revelations.

She'd done a lot of facing reality and growing up over the past weeks. Realizing she was pregnant at all, but much less with the probable heir to the Zohrian throne, was all the catalyst she'd needed to shed the last of her naiveté. She'd been shocked by her own joy, even in the face of all this pregnancy would mean.

Like she'd told Zahir, the baby came first, but more than that, she already loved her child and always would.

Angele would do what needed doing to make sure her child's life was all it should be, but that didn't mean she wanted to talk about it right then. She was just starting to feel something other than nauseated.

Zahir shrugged as he finished pouring the boiling water through the infuser into the teapot. "According to my mother, the inability to do something as basic as make a cup of tea is the mark of laziness rather than wealth."

"I'm sure Lou-Belia would agree with her."

"Your mother is an imminently sensible woman."

"You think it sensible to stay with a man who chose infidelity over argument in the attempt to convince her to have another child?" she asked, curiosity rather than bitterness in her voice.

Between discovering she was pregnant and accepting the inevitable consequences that would have for her life, Angele had come to terms with a lot of things. Her present required all her energy; she didn't have any left over to dwell on her family's past.

Zahir carried the teapot and two mugs to the small wrought-iron table. "Life is what it is."

"I think I'm finally learning what that really means."

"She chose what she considered the lesser of two evils." Zahir's tone said he knew what that felt like.

In his position, she would be surprised if he didn't. Nevertheless, Angele warned, "It's not a choice I would make."

"You cannot doubt that things are completely over between Elsa and me."

"No, but there are other Elsas in this world."

"I have no interest in them."

"I hope that's true."

"You doubt my word?" Zahir's shock was almost comical.

She poured the tea, adding a scant teaspoon of sugar to hers. "Not exactly."

"Then what, *exactly*?"

"The future. I doubt the future."

"Well, don't."

She wanted to laugh, but simply shook her head. "If only it were that easy."

"It can be."

"Certain safeguards would make it easier."

"The conditions."

"Yes, my conditions."

"For you to marry me, despite the fact you carry my child." He stirred not one, but three teaspoons of sugar into his tea.

She'd always found his sweet tooth endearing, something she knew about him that few people noticed. Because he didn't eat desserts. But he did drink cocoa and put lots of sugar in his coffee and tea. Seeing evidence of that sweet tooth now brought a measure of comfort, a reminder that not everything had changed.

He was still the same man she'd fallen in love with from afar, the same man she'd planned for most of her adult life to marry.

"Yes."

"I'm not going to like them, am I?"

"No." There was no point in sugarcoating it—no matter how much he might like sweet things, but she wasn't going to feel guilty for trying for some semblance of assurance for her future, either.

She might not be that naive, year on from university woman who believed she could have a one-night stand with the man she loved and come out of it relatively unscathed, but she still had to have some level of hope for her future. His agreement to her conditions would give her that.

He sat back, his mug in one hand, his eyes fixed on her with that patented intensity of his. "I am all ears."

She took a deep breath and went for broke. "I want a prenup that guarantees me the right to raise our children in the United States in the event you take a lover."

She waited for the explosion, but none came. He simply sat, sipping his tea in silence and looking completely unperturbed.

"Nothing to say?"

"I assume there is more since you said *conditions* plural, not condition in the singular."

"Yes." Was he really as sanguine as he appeared? "I mean it."

"I assumed you did."

"You aren't angry."

"Considering your past, such a condition is hardly a shock."

"But…" He would never countenance his children being raised outside of Zohra. She finally stuttered as much out loud.

"Naturally not, but since it won't happen, I fail to see why I should become upset over your need for the reassurance on that score."

He was right, it *was* a reassurance. He might not

maintain fidelity for her sake. However, she was wholly convinced that he would for the good of their children and the sake of the throne he protected so carefully.

Feeling light-headed with relief he'd accepted the first and she would have thought the *hardest* hurdle to overcome, she said, "I am glad you are not offended."

"I would be, if I believed your request was based on a lack of trust in me personally."

"You don't?"

"It's obvious that your past has a great deal of bearing on this, as I have said."

"And you do not think your ongoing relationship with Elsa figures into it all?"

"That was before we were formally engaged."

"You said you considered us as good as."

"In one respect that is true, just as in the same respect, a part of me already considers the throne of Zohra mine. However, it will not in actuality be until my father abdicates in my favor or sees his final days on earth."

"So, you did make a distinction." She was more thankful to hear that than she would ever admit to him.

"Do you not know me even that well?" he asked, sounding like he was finally feeling the offense she'd expected him to take earlier.

"I thought I did and then I got those pictures."

He winced. "Point taken."

"I realize now, I was hopelessly naive in my expectations, but those photos devastated me," she admitted.

She had no trouble reading his expression for once, it was pure dismay. "You believed I would be celibate once the contract was signed?"

"Yes." She felt foolish for that belief now. It had been a teen girl's fantasy she'd never reconsidered in the light of adulthood. At least, not until she'd been forced to. "You see, *I was*."

"When I signed that contract, I was a twenty-four-year-old man. You were a thirteen-year-old girl."

"Are you saying it would not bother you if I had taken a lover since becoming an adult?"

He opened his mouth and then shut it again, no words emerging.

"Smart choice."

He frowned. "My initial response does not paint me in a favorable light."

"No doubt."

"Your other conditions," he prompted, clearly not wishing to dwell on his unpalatable double standard.

"There are only two more."

"They are?"

"Your heir is allowed to have a childhood."

"I had a childhood."

"Until you were seven, yes I got that."

"I was not an unhappy child."

She was convinced that a man of Zahir's strength would have bloomed under any conditions, but she refused to allow her own children to face the same exact sort of childhood he'd been raised with. "This is not a negotiable point."

"You do realize that saying something like that to me is like waving the red flag to the bull?"

"I didn't—now I do."

"You wish to rephrase it?"

"No."

His brow rose in clear surprise.

"I am willing to marry you despite major personal misgivings for the sake of our unborn child. There is no point in doing so if being raised amidst the royal family of Zohra will be a source of unacceptable sacrifice and potential unhappiness for him."

"I told you, I was not unhappy."

"And I'm telling you, that heir to the throne, or a youngest daughter, it doesn't matter to me. My children will have the chance at a true childhood."

"As defined by you?"

"Ultimately, yes, but I am open to discussion on issues of importance to you."

"I will enjoy the challenge."

"Of course you will."

"Your final condition?"

This should be an easy one for him to accept, considering his own circumstances. "None of our children will have their marriages arranged for them."

"I acknowledge you are not as pleased with our arrangement as you were in the past, but that is no reason to dismiss centuries of tradition." A full measure of offense laced his voice and drew his spine ramrod straight.

"It's a tradition that should have disappeared with the Dark Ages."

"I disagree." If anything, his tone became more clipped. "The practice of arranging marriages is still common in the Middle East, parts of Asia and Eastern Europe. Just because you were raised in a different culture does not mean one is superior to the other."

"Your brothers are both happier because their

marriages came about because of love rather than a contract."

"And my parents fell deeply in love after marrying because *their* parents arranged it."

"The risk of it not working out is too big."

"Love is no guarantee of happiness." He sighed. "Surely your parents' own marriage is enough to prove that to you, but if not—merely consider the divorce rate of your adopted country."

"I'm really surprised this is such a sticking point for you." This was the one condition she had believed he would accept without argument. "I would have thought that your own present circumstance enough to convince you."

"You were wrong." He said nothing more, simply staring at her with a bone-deep determination that she had no doubt carried sway at any table of negotiation.

But she couldn't back down about this. Zahir would never have been forced into marriage with her if not for that stupid contract. He would never have shown any interest in her and she would never have demanded that night in his bed.

The guilt she felt for doing so now was a big enough burden to carry. She couldn't bear to think of her own children having to submit to those kinds of circumstances.

She took a fortifying sip of tea, but he spoke before she got a chance to further her case. "I will offer this compromise."

She looked at him expectantly, waiting to hear what his supreme skills at negotiations would come up with.

"We will not force our children into an agreement."

"That's hardly a compromise. No one forced, or even cajoled you, for that matter. You signed that stupid contract out of duty and a sense of personal obligation."

"And I am not the one regretting that choice."

"You would be if Elsa hadn't slept around. You'd be wishing you could marry her right now."

"And if I had married her, even if she had been sexually faithful, I would have tied myself to a callous gold digger." He sounded like he considered that salvation from a fate worse than death. "The contract has been nothing but a boon in my life."

"That's why you looked at Amir with such envy at his wedding."

The shock on Zahir's features lasted less than two seconds, but it was enough for Angele to know he had not believed anyone had realized he harbored those feelings. "I expect to enjoy a relationship as fulfilling with you."

"I thought you made it a practice never to tell an outright falsehood."

"Eventually," he added, as if the word were pulled from him with rusty pliers.

She almost smiled. He was so intent on doing his duty, he would even create a hope for the future that had no basis in their current reality.

"But you do not believe love has any place in an agreement such as ours."

"We are getting off topic."

"Yes, we are. No arranged marriages for our children."

"I will agree not to press an arrangement on our

children, but will not refuse to exercise my authority in conducting a negotiation on their behalf should they wish for me to do so."

She had a feeling that was as good as she was going to get on this point. "You absolutely promise to abide by the spirit, not simply the outlined terms on this point?"

"You are not a competing business or political interest. Believe it, or not, I do know the difference when it comes to family." Which was not a yes, but might actually be something even better.

It was acknowledgment that she, and their children, fell in a different category than other entities in his life. She might not have his love, but she would have a unique place in his life.

That would have to be enough.

# CHAPTER SEVEN

ANGELE woke to the sound of Zahir talking in rapid-fire Arabic in the other room. He'd insisted she lie down while he took care of having dinner delivered.

A glance at the alarm clock beside her bed showed that a little over two hours had passed, startling her. She hadn't been sleeping well since returning from Zohra and had been positive she would not fall asleep when she'd acquiesced to Zahir's concern.

The man was far more adept at hovering than she would ever have suspected.

He didn't sound like a concerned husband-to-be right now, though; he sounded like a man who was brain-storming spin on the announcement of her pregnancy.

She surged to her feet, thankful the dizziness that had plagued her off and on for the past weeks was not showing itself. The need to pee, however, was. And no matter how urgently she wanted to speak with Zahir, it took precedence. She made a quick trip to the bathroom before going to find her stubborn fiancé.

His robes of office nowhere to be seen, his suit jacket and tie lying over the back of a nearby chair, Zahir sat on the sofa. An open laptop was on the coffee table in front of him, the screen showing a website dedicated to the care and feeding of pregnant women.

The indulgent smile that caused slipped right off her face as his words registered. He was still discussing how best to announce Angele's pregnancy, but now she knew who he was talking to. His father.

*He'd told his father.* Which meant her parents would know soon, if they didn't know already.

Her knees going weak, she stumbled to sit on the sofa.

Zahir jerked to face her, his expression going concerned in a moment. He hung up faster than she'd ever heard him end a conversation with the man who was both father and king.

"Are you well?" He leaned toward her, examining her with all the intent of doctor on a house call. "I thought you would be better after a rest, but you are looking peaked."

"Thank you," she said with pure sarcasm. "Every woman wants to hear she looks like death warmed over."

"But I am concerned."

"Not so worried you hesitated to tell your father about my pregnancy though you knew I didn't want you to."

"It is a blessed event. Naturally I told him."

"That's not the way you reacted in the car." He hadn't seemed even remotely blessed then.

"I saw the potential problems first. It is in my nature." His tone was pure shrug even though his shoulders remained immobile.

She used to tease him about that trait. Right now, she found it more frustrating than funny. "We also agreed in the car that we would wait to announce my pregnancy."

"Actually we were out of the limo when you expressed your opinion in that direction."

She made a sound of pure frustration at his attempt to tease around the issue. "You didn't argue with me." She took a deep breath and released it slowly, praying her earlier nausea would not return. "Silence is an implication of agreement."

"Clearly it is not."

"You knew I would assume you would wait to tell our families until we had spoken further about it."

"I did not tell your family."

"You think your father hesitated to share the news with King Malik and my father?"

Zahir shrugged, looking far from repentant. "It is good news worth sharing."

"You are a manipulator."

"I prefer master of circumstances."

"Call it what you like, I won't be tricked that way again."

"I did not trick you. I avoided unnecessary conflict so as to prevent further upset."

"I am upset now."

"Why?"

"I wanted to wait to tell *anyone*." She glared. "And I heard you—it's not just your family. You want to tell the world."

"I explained my viewpoint earlier."

"And that's it? We disagree and you do whatever you please?"

"Would it make you feel better if I claimed other-wise?"

"It would make me feel better if you said it and meant it."

"It will not always be as I wish it."

"Oh, really?"

"You left Zohra, did you not?"

"You're saying you would not have prevented me if you had been able to?" She made no attempt to temper her skepticism.

"You gave me no such opportunity."

"So?"

"So, you are intelligent and resourceful. I will not always get my way."

"I need to know that you won't act without thought to my feelings. I don't want a marriage based on a series of one-upmanship competitions."

"We are not children."

"Agreed."

"I did consider your feelings."

"And yet you still called your father with the news."

"Waiting to do so would only cause you further stress and upset. Prolonging a thing of this magnitude only invites more complications as it becomes more likely the opportunity to act on your own timetable will be taken away."

"No one knew I was pregnant until I told you."

"You have not been examined by a doctor?" he asked with clear censure.

She rolled her eyes. "Yes, of course, I have and everything is normal and as it should be."

"Good. I will expect the family physician to conduct his own exam however."

"I wouldn't expect anything else."

"So, this doctor knows that you carry my child."

"She knows I am pregnant, not who the father is and she is bound by laws of confidentiality."

"And you claim you are not naive."

"This isn't Zohra, Zahir. Dr. Shirley has no reason to believe the father of my child is a person of interest to the media. I'm hardly one of the glitterati myself."

"Perhaps that was once true, but things have changed since Amir's wedding."

That was putting it mildly. "You mean the very public courtship you were supposedly engaged in?"

*"Supposedly?"* he prompted, sounding none-too-pleased.

"I left Zohra six weeks ago. Today is the first time I have heard from you."

"I sent daily gifts for the past few weeks."

"Without a single phone call."

"This did not please you."

"Of course it didn't, but it didn't surprise me, either."

"I cannot claim the same. Your actions after our single night together astounded me."

"I told you my plans."

"I thought you were doubting the existence of passion between us."

"And when you gave me proof it existed, you assumed I would go forward with the plans to marry?" she asked, unable to hide her disbelief at his assumptions.

"Yes."

"You only hear what you want to hear."

"It is a failing."

"But not one you are often accused of."

"This is true."

"Yet, you don't deny it."

"How can I? Clearly, in this instance, I did hear what I deemed probable and acceptable."

"Lina walked away from the marriage arranged for her with your brother. What's improbable about that?"

"You are not Lina."

"No, I am not. She was raised with a much stricter sense of responsibility to her family's position."

"Lina was not in love with my brother."

Angele could not argue that point. Lina and Amir had barely known each other, despite growing up in the same circles.

"I see you do not deny loving me."

"What would be the point?"

"In the car, you intimated your feelings were not involved with your decision to marry me. It is only natural then to question if they have changed."

"My feelings for you were not a deciding factor in my decision to marry you. Our child's future was."

"Do you still love me?" he asked bluntly.

"Does it matter?"

"I prefer to know."

He'd been honest with her to this point, she could offer no less. "Yes, but I consider my love a detriment to this situation, if you must know."

"But of course it is not. Surely our life together will be eased because of it."

"You think I'll let you have your way because I love you?" she asked suspiciously.

"I am not that foolish, but it is my hope you will be content in our marriage because of it."

More likely it would cause her nothing but pain, but admitting that was just one step on the open and honest communication highway, her pride wasn't about to let her take.

The buzzer sounded and Angele gave Zahir a look meant to maim. "Two guesses who that is and the first one does not count."

"Dinner," he said with smug assurance.

She hoped he was right, because she was so not up to playing happy families with her parents right now. She was still annoyed with her father for not giving her a heads-up on Zahir's plan to publicly court her. Angele had zero doubts Cemal had been in the know on that score, if not a major instigator.

And while her mother had said she'd forgiven Angele for breaking the contract, initially Lou-Belia had been hurt and very angry. They were talking again, but things were still a little stilted between them.

Zahir's bodyguard answered the summons from the doorman and then dispatched one of the security detail to retrieve their dinner.

One brow raised, Zahir smiled.

"Don't be so smug. They'll show up sooner than later."

"And you do not wish to see them? To share the happy news in person?"

"What part of *I don't want to tell anyone* isn't sticking with you, Zahir?"

He frowned, his eyes dark with disapproval. "It seems to me, you are the one regretting the advent of our child."

She opened her mouth to reply that of course she regretted becoming pregnant, but snapped it shut again on the words. Words, once spoken, could never be unsaid.

And she would never say such a thing about her baby, no matter the change in circumstances it brought to her life. The truth was, Angele had spent more years believing she would one day marry Zahir than the few months determined not to do so.

It was time to put her big girl panties on and deal with it. She was going to be Princess Angele bin Faruq al Zohra, and one day—God willing far into the future—she would be queen.

"No matter what the complications, I do not regret this baby." She pressed a hand to her stomach. "But I'm not up to presenting pure joy and celebration for my parents' sake, either. At the very least, I'm fighting a constant battle with nausea and an on-again-off-again vertigo that is truly disturbing."

He nodded, his handsome face set in lines of concentration. "I have been researching how best to treat morning sickness that has the poor manners not to confine itself to mornings."

"I've tried ginger and soda crackers. It helps a little, but I'm still not holding my food down."

"There are other options I read about. And according to our family physician, Vitamin B6 apparently helps a large percentage of women who suffer morning sickness.

He also recommends acupressure wristbands used for antinausea as the result of motion sickness."

"I'm not sure I can hold a vitamin down long enough to do any good."

"There is also a combination medication that can be administered orally, or in a prepared hypodermic, but it can make you tired."

While that wouldn't thrill her, it had to be better than being sick. "I'll survive."

"It would make it difficult for you to do your job."

"Today was my last day." She'd given a month's notice soon after confirmation she was pregnant.

Shock widened his eyes. "You've already worked out your notice?"

"Yes."

"I expected argument about the need for you to leave your job."

"No."

"I see."

There would have been no point. It would be ridiculous for an editorial assistant to come to work with a bodyguard detail and she wasn't kidding herself. Angele knew that as soon as Zahir was made aware that she carried his child, security around her was going to be a 24/7 reality.

Besides, once they were married, she'd no doubt they could and would visit the States often, but no way could she continue to live here.

"You reconciled yourself quickly to your changed circumstances," he mused.

"I had a lot of years to plan what our eventual marriage would require."

"This is true." He looked lost in thought for several moments and then asked, "So, you do not refuse to live in Zohra?"

"I only said that for the press release. While I will not pretend to have been raised there, or stifle who I am for the sake of conformity, I love Zohra. But I told you I wouldn't allow you to be blamed."

"I was very angry when I read that press release. I do not think I have ever been angrier in all my life." He said it so dispassionately that it would have been easy to dismiss his words as overkill.

Except for the look in his eyes. The color of molten metal, they shimmered with remembered rage at odds with the rest of his calm exterior. She was beginning to realize that for all her hero worship of the man, she didn't know Zahir as well as she thought she had.

Seeing even a remnant of that furious reaction shocked her to her core and something told her it shouldn't. That she should have realized he would never see her defection the way she intended it to be taken.

Regardless, she wasn't completely buying the story he'd never been so mad. "Not even when you realized your former lover with a seriously questionable reputation was threatening to out your liaison to the press?"

The slightest movement that could have been a wince showed on his features when Angele said the words *seriously questionable reputation*, but other than that, Zahir didn't show any further emotion to the words. Certainly he didn't exhibit that latent anger he had in regard to Angele's actions.

"You knew it was Elsa?" he asked with just a

tinge of surprise. "Your letter was careful not to point fingers."

"I didn't know if you still cared for her." And she hadn't wanted him hurt any more than he would be by knowledge of the pictures and blackmail itself.

"She'll never attempt to hurt you again." The flat truth in his voice didn't allow Angele to doubt it.

She nodded. "I assumed you neutralized the threat to your good name."

"My name and reputation were a secondary consideration in this instance."

She found that hard to believe, but didn't call him on it. They had more important things to discuss. "So, when are we getting married?"

He didn't blink at the change in topic. "Since you are already six weeks along, there is no hope of a quick marriage stifling future rumors."

"Hence your insistence on announcing my pregnancy before our official engagement?"

"The announcement will be a joint affair."

"How lovely." The entire world would think he was marrying her because she carried his child and potential future heir.

But then, was that any different than the knowledge they were marrying as the result of a political contract between two kings? Probably not. It was her own fault that she'd always considered the other as less important because of her feelings for Zahir.

Talk about burying her head in the sand. "I'd make a fine ostrich," Angele muttered.

Zahir gave her a quizzical look, but she waved it

off and said, "We could do something small fairly quickly."

Lou-Belia was going to pitch the fit of a lifetime when she realized her only child's wedding plans had to be rushed *and* scaled back.

"Small?" Zahir said the word as if doing so pained him. "For the Crown Sheikh of Zohra? I think not."

"Everything doesn't have to be done on a world leader scale." Really, really, it didn't.

Only the look on his face said it did. "Learn to accept the inevitability of it. We are political leaders, not celebrities to indulge in a secret ceremony on some private island. Our people will expect and deserve the opportunity to celebrate our joy with us."

"Not to mention assorted world leaders and their hangers-on," she grumbled as the reality of her change in circumstance began to make itself felt.

"It is inevitable."

"So, what do you suggest? I would prefer not to waddle down the aisle nine months pregnant."

"Be assured, it will not be that bad."

"How bad are you proposing it be?"

"You would be best past this nausea."

"Agreed." Fainting on her walk down the aisle was not the impression she wanted to leave with dignitaries and world leaders, much less her future family.

"We are in luck. Usually trying for any event of this magnitude with any less than an entire year of planning would be impossible. Two years would be preferable, but my father is hosting a summit to discuss world oil reserves in two months time. Were we to coordinate the wedding celebrations to coincide with the summit, the important political guests would already be in Zohra."

There was no room for sentimentality in that scenario, but she accepted that was her own fault. She couldn't help wondering if they had followed the contract and a regular schedule of engagement and marriage, if it would not have been the same, though.

"Our wedding is a political event." Which she'd known somewhere in the back of her mind, but had not really given thought to what that meant in the grand scheme of things.

She'd always looked at the Zohra-Jawhar connecting, never considering the further implications to her life.

Zahir was not one of his brothers. He was in fact a Crown Sheikh, uncontested heir to the throne of both an oil and mineral rich country.

"I've really messed up, haven't I?"

He didn't deny it, but quoted another favorite Arabic proverb. One that was pretty much the equivalent of, *it is what it is.*

"For all my fantasies and daydreams, I never really considered what being married to *you* meant," she admitted.

"Had you attended finishing school rather than university, you would have had training in that regard."

She forced herself to remember what he'd said on their night together, that an observation was not a criticism. "But you supported my decision to go to university."

"I knew what marrying me would mean to you." Again, the shrug was in his voice rather than his shoulders.

"Wouldn't that make you even more determined I learn my future role?"

"I wanted you to have a chance at a normal life before we wed."

"But…" Unsure what she wanted to say, she let her voice trail off.

"My mother and aunt have both promised to mentor you in your new role."

"You've accomplished an awful lot in the two hours I slept." Not that she was surprised by that.

She did know him well enough to know how efficient he was and how very adept at making things work, whether it be a property rights negotiation or a family dinner. It had always been a pleasure to watch him finesse those around him.

She could hardly complain he was doing it to her now.

But he shook his head. "I made the request years ago, when you decided to go to university in America."

"It's no coincidence that every trip to Zohra and Jawhar in the past several years has included significant time with the queens." She'd been flattered, a little nervous and ultimately happy to spend time entertaining others with the respective women.

Though she would have traded that time for time with him in a heartbeat. That wasn't something she needed to admit to right now, though.

"No coincidence," he confirmed.

"I thought your mother was just getting to know me."

"She was, but she was also teaching by example

and trying to share knowledge of your future life with you."

"Sneaky."

"I prefer subtle. I did not want you overwhelmed by the realities of what your life would be, though I wonder now if we were too subtle." His expression had gone contemplative. "You have too little understanding of what the role should and will mean for you."

She couldn't deny it, but it was still uncomfortable acknowledging that truth. "Maybe you didn't want me getting cold feet and backing out of the contract."

"Interestingly enough, I never once considered you would break the contract." He shrugged and said a word she was pretty sure meant *fool* in French.

"You are not a fool."

"I misjudged the character of two important women in my life."

# CHAPTER EIGHT

"ARE you comparing me to Elsa?" Angele asked in a deceptively calm voice, while her temper stirred.

She'd made mistakes, but she was so coldhearted that she would cheat on Zahir and then blithely try her hand at blackmail.

"Only in my false perceptions of you both, not your respective characters."

Still, Angele felt the need to say, "I did not betray you like she did."

He quoted another proverb, this one about seeing two sides of the same mountain leading to different impressions of the same thing. So, he read her attempt to walk away as a betrayal. She knew it had made him angry, because he'd admitted it. Understanding the source of that anger, only made it harder to know about.

Horrifically naive, maybe, but she hadn't meant to let him down.

She turned her head away, looking at the painting over her small fireplace. It was a cheerful impression of jazz musicians on the streets of New Orleans, done after the rebuild of the city. It always infused her with hope. Right now, all she felt was malaise.

Knowing how very deeply she had disappointed

Zahir hurt. "I was protecting myself from a marriage without love, but I thought I was giving you your freedom, too."

"I accept that."

"But you don't accept it was a gift intended to benefit you." She had not been motivated entirely by beneficence, but she had wanted him to have a better chance at happiness, too.

She hadn't realized she'd been capable of hurting Zahir, but obviously, she'd been wrong. While his heart might not have been touched, she had dealt a serious blow to his pride and to his sense of honor.

Not to mention his trust in *her* integrity.

She sighed when he did not answer. "So, we somehow organize a momentous wedding while the world watches in two months time."

"Just so."

Apparently he was as willing to move their discussion forward as she was. There was simply no point in rehashing old arguments. Somehow, she would prove to him that she had his best interests at heart. And maybe, in the same space, she would learn to accept that he felt the same.

He'd certainly done his best to protect her and allow her what he thought she needed for happiness. Perhaps, in his mind, the years'-long wait had been as much for her benefit as his.

Moreover, he'd said repeatedly that he believed in fidelity in marriage. Making their engagement official would have required him breaking things off with Elsa. And while it hurt that he had not wanted to do so, Angele thought that Zahir had deserved his slice of happiness not related to his duty or role as future king.

Unfortunately for him, things had ended badly and unquestionably painfully.

If Angele could not be that moment out of time for him, she would show him she could be more. That she, Angele bin Cemal al Jawhar, could be a source of joy in his everyday life.

She would start now, by helping to plan the wedding with grace and as much enthusiasm as she could muster. "I think we need to call in the experts."

"A wedding planner? The PR department? Our palace event coordinator?" he asked while making notes on his phone.

"All of the above, I'm sure. But I was thinking the queens and my mother. Nobody throws a party like Lou-Belia."

Zahir paused and looked up, his gray gaze fixed on her. "I thought you did not wish to speak with your parents this evening."

"There's no point in putting it off." And some very good reasons not to, the chief among that Angele was not a naturally selfish person. "Mom will be hurt if I don't call her tonight, but we'll want to coordinate a conference call with her and the queens for tomorrow."

The buzzer sounded again.

"Impeccable timing," she said, putting on her game face and getting up to answer the summons, sure it was her parents showing up to share in the happy news.

Zahir's bodyguard beat her to it and Zahir asked, "Why do you always assume it is your mother when the buzzer sounds?"

"You honestly think King Malik has not already called my father?" she asked in response.

"Most assuredly, but are your parents not on the list of approved visitors for the doorman?"

"Of course, but it's policy for the doorman to buzz me to let me know I have visitors even if he doesn't need my approval to let them on the elevators."

"I see. It is very different than living in a royal palace."

"Yes, it is, but you've stayed in hotels."

"No one gets to me until they've been through at least two layers of security. There are no buzzers in my life."

Not sure he had been joking, Angele laughed anyway. They might have been raised as close as family, but their lives were entirely unrelated in so many ways.

A few moments later the door opened to reveal her obstetrician, not her parents.

Angele gasped as the older woman with salt-and-pepper hair cut in a short stylish look came into the living room. "You make house calls?"

Dr. Shirley gave Zahir a measured look before turning back to Angele. "In your case, I do, apparently."

"What did you do?" Angele demanded of Zahir.

"I did not conscript her, I assure you."

Dr. Shirley gave him another strange look. "No, he merely had someone in the White House give me a call and make the request."

"The White House?" Angele asked in a voice that nearly failed her.

"Yep, it even came up on my caller ID that way. Pretty crazy." Dr. Shirley sounded somewhere between annoyed and awed. "I've never been contacted by my local congressman, much less a White House lackey."

"What did he say?" Angele asked with unconcealed fascination. She'd never spoken to anyone from the White House, either, though she knew Zahir had attended State dinners there.

"That in the interest of Foreign Relations, I should consider making a personal call on you this evening."

"That's wild."

The other woman laughed. "I thought so, too. Apparently the father of your baby is quite worried about your ongoing nausea."

Worried enough to make a Federal case out of it, literally.

Angele stored away the warmth that made her feel and said, "I thought we would look into the nausea medication tomorrow."

"Why wait?" Dr. Shirley said, tongue so obviously firmly in cheek. "I've got a prepared hypodermic in my bag."

"You're getting a kick out of this," Angele accused.

"Yes, I think I am."

Angele shook her head and then asked, "It won't hurt the baby? You're sure?"

"Absolutely not. I wouldn't give you anything that might harm your baby, but I'd like to try the acupressure band to begin with. If that doesn't work, there is an *acustimulation* device that is a step up, but it can cause minor skin irritation. And of course, I'd like to give you a shot of Vitamin B6 right now."

"Will that make me tired?" Angele asked, remembering her conversation with Zahir.

"No, though I recommend taking these sleeping pills in conjunction with Vitamin B6 at night before going to bed." Dr. Shirley handed Angele a familiar box. "They're approved for use during pregnancy and enhance the antinausea effects of the B6."

"When my mom takes those, she's usually pretty tired for a good part of the next day."

Dr. Shirley shrugged. "It happens. Depending on the dosage and your response to it, daytime sleepiness can result."

"I've got a lot of planning to do. I can't afford to be sleepy all day."

"Your health is of utmost importance." Zahir's tone brooked no argument.

Angele smiled at him. "Thank you for your concern." She turned back to the doctor. "I'd really prefer to try the other options first."

Right then, her stomach roiled and she had to turn away and swallow convulsively. Sometime soon would be good.

"I doubt it's much of a stretch to assume it's been a pretty hectic day for you," Dr. Shirley said. "I'd actually recommend you take the sleep aid tonight, and be grateful for the extra rest if it helps you nap tomorrow, too. From what you told me in my office at your last appointment, you haven't been getting much rest lately."

"I've had a lot on my mind."

"Considering who the father of your child is, I'm not surprised." The older woman reached out and squeezed Angele's shoulder comfortingly. "It isn't every day a woman finds herself making a family with an honest-to-goodness future king."

"I'm very honored." And she was, but overwhelmed was a word that fit as well.

"I'm sure you are, but you're also tired. And that's not good for you or baby."

"I had a nap earlier."

"You've still got a full set of luggage under those eyes," the doctor unapologetically pronounced.

Angele frowned at Zahir. "Why didn't you tell me I looked like a fright?"

"You do not look a fright, but I do recall telling you that you did not look rested."

Oh, right. "So, bags, huh?" she asked the doctor with a wince.

"Steamer trunks."

She gave a short laugh and sighed. "In the arm or the bum?"

"Let's go into the other room."

A stick in the bum then.

For the first time in weeks, Angele woke up feeling pretty good. No flulike symptoms, no urgent need to rush to the bathroom and throw up. She was still a little tired, but Angele would take that feeling over extreme nausea any day.

The bed beside her was empty. However, the rumpled pillow on the other side gave testament to the fact she hadn't spent the night alone.

Considering her ambivalent feelings toward their up-coming marriage, she should not enjoy that knowledge so much. But she did. Even though they had not woken together, knowing she and Zahir had spent the night in the same bed felt right.

Too right.

She'd been deluding herself to think she could really walk away from Zahir if he was determined to marry her. The baby made giving in easier, but the truth was, he would have eventually worn down her resistance. Because he had made it clear, he'd had no intention of giving up the future they planned together.

She just hoped neither of them would learn to regret that stubbornness.

Angele followed the scent of coffee to the kitchen and found Zahir and a dapperly dressed elderly gentleman with kind eyes sitting at the small table.

Both men rose as she came in.

Feeling better than she had in days, even with the smell of coffee and freshly cooked bacon in the air, she smiled. "Good morning, gentlemen."

Zahir introduced the older man as Dr. bin Habib, the physician to the royal family of Zohra.

"My O.B. was just here last night." She looked at Zahir. "How many doctors do I need?"

"Technically Dr. bin Habib is acting on behalf of the baby at this point. Though he will coordinate care with your obstetrician both here and when we return to Zohra."

"Please tell me you haven't tried to strong-arm Dr. Shirley into traveling to Zohra with me. I'm not her only patient."

"I have made no attempt to strong arm the honorable doctor."

There was something in his tone that made Angele look at Zahir askance.

The Crown Sheikh shrugged, doing a pretty poor job

at casual regardless. "If I perhaps offered her a very per-suasive remuneration package for doing so, that cannot be considered an attempt at coercion."

"Zahir!"

"What? You expect me to ignore your needs in favor of strangers."

"I'm sure there are perfectly competent O.B.s in Zohra." Though a small part of her was more than a little relieved she wouldn't be changing doctors.

"It is best to maintain continuity of care."

"She passed your background checks, then?" Angele couldn't help teasing.

She had no doubts that if Zahir had not considered Dr. Shirley the best of the best, no generous remunera-tion would have been offered.

"She is without equal."

"Did she accept your offer?"

"She did. She will travel with us to Zohra and then, barring any unforeseen complications, return monthly until your seventh month, at which time she will make her temporary home in the palace for the remaining duration of your pregnancy."

"You promise you did nothing to force her deci-sion?"

"Such as?"

"Such as having the White House call her…again. Or her congressman or anything like that at all."

"I did not."

Angele nodded. As long as the choice had been Dr. Shirley's, Angele wasn't about to complain about something she wanted. "Any decaffeinated coffee on hand?"

"Naturally." Zahir poured her a cup from the carafe on the counter rather than the one on the table.

Dr. bin Habib bowed slightly. "I will remove to the living room while the princess partakes of her breakfast."

Angele didn't bother to argue that she wasn't actually in fact a princess. Yet. Instead she said, "I won't be long. I don't eat much in the mornings right now."

"I am sure you will find the nutritionally balanced menu to your liking," Zahir interjected.

She refrained from rolling her eyes and gave him a tight smile. "I'll do my best."

But she wasn't going to risk the debilitating nausea returning by eating too much, or something that might trigger it—no matter how good it was for her.

Zahir pulled out her chair and she sat down with a quiet, "Thank you," as the older doctor left the room.

Breakfast was, in fact both palatable and not over-whelming. Zahir kept the conversation light while she ate, waiting until she was finished to broach the subject of the wedding again. "I have arranged a conference call with our mothers and the queen of Jawhar, as well as the event coordinator for the royal palace."

Angele bit her tongue on the slightly sarcastic retort that first popped into her mind and said, "Great. What time?"

"Eleven this morning."

"Won't the event coordinator have gone home for the day at that point?"

"He will make himself available."

She supposed that for a man who considered himself on call to his position 24/7, asking an employee to stay late of an evening did not seem like an unreasonable request. "Okay. Mom will be over in about an hour."

She'd called her parents the night before, after getting the shot of Vitamin B6 and before taking the safe-for-pregnancy sleeping pill. Lou-Belia had been uncharacteristically calm when faced with the news of impending grandparenthood and the upcoming royal wedding. She'd agreed to come over in the morning, suggesting Angele get a good night's rest.

Angele couldn't help thinking that Zahir had somehow managed to contact her parents ahead of time and apprise them of his wishes to encourage her to get more sleep.

"Is your father coming also?"

"He is."

"It will be a busy day for you."

Angele didn't argue, but wondered if busy was a code for challenging, because she knew that was exactly what her day was shaping up to be. Not that Zahir's would not be equally difficult. He had to come up with a definitive plan to announce what many would say was scandalous news. He would be questioned and criticized.

The media was going to have a field day with the situation; the perfect prince had fallen from grace.

And it was her fault.

Knowing he had anticipated her being on the pill or some equally effective form of birth control added to her sense of guilt. Not that he couldn't have at least asked, but *she'd* known for a fact they weren't using anything.

"What is that look?" he asked, his brows drawn together in a concerned frown. "Do you wish to postpone these meetings?"

"That's hardly an option."

"I will make it an option if that is what you need."

"How can you be so nice to me right now?"

"How can I not?"

"It's my fault we're in this situation."

"Assigning blame is useless, but if you must do so, then assign me my portion. I was the one who waited too long to act on the intentions in the contract between our two families."

"I *knew* we weren't using birth control."

"Yes."

"Aren't you angry with me? You were furious yesterday."

"Yesterday is best left in the past."

And she knew he meant both literally the day before and their ill conceived night together.

"You're going to be a figure of public speculation and gossip for months because of this." And she knew how much that had to bother him.

"Highly doubtful. It will be a nine day's wonder. And I refuse to forget that had Elsa been more vindictive and less greedy, I would already be so."

The knowledge obviously weighed heavily on him. Angele could see it in the rigid tension of his shoulders and the haunted shadows in his gray eyes.

"That's in the past too."

He shrugged, but she knew he was too much of a perfectionist to extend the same acceptance for mistakes to himself that he seemed determined to offer her.

"My own idiocy is not something I will forget any-time soon," he said, confirming her thoughts.

"So, we've both been idiots. It's time to move forward."

He laughed, the sound as surprising as it was surprised. "I do not believe anyone has called me an *idiot* in all my adult years."

"Not to your face anyway," she said, tongue in cheek.

His dark brows rose. "Not behind my back, either."

"Your arrogance is showing again."

"It is never very far below the surface, I assure you."

"What happened to the humble servant to your people?"

"The two are not mutually exclusive."

"Not in your world, anyway, right?"

"My world is your world."

"It is now."

"I could wish you were happier about that fact."

"It is what it is," she said, using the American vernacular for one of his favorite Arabic proverbs.

His jaw went taut, though nothing else gave away the fact her reply had not made him happy. "There was a time when you were nothing but pleased to be my intended."

"It's going to sound trite, but I grew up." She smiled, hoping to take any sting the words might have for him.

She wasn't trying to slight him, merely tell him the truth.

"Those words should be bitter, but from your mouth they are not."

Good. She was determined to live by her decision to

accept her fate and stop whining, even internally. "I'm not bitter."

"Then there is great hope for our future."

"Yes, I suppose there is." They would never have the happy families fantasy she'd always dreamed of, but they could have a solid marriage and good life together.

She could do nothing but hope.

# CHAPTER NINE

ANGELE'S HOPE FOR THE future seemed to prove true over the following weeks.

Often running interference with her family and his, Zahir willingly stayed in the States with Angele long enough for her to finalize preparations for her permanent move to Zohra. While she had to give up her apartment, he promised to buy a home with proper security for their trips back to U.S. in the future.

Announcement of their forthcoming wedding and the advent of their first child was met with a surprisingly positive response in both Zohra and Jawhar. The scandal rags didn't have much to report because the legitimate press had been given all the details along with photos of the "happy" couple together in both the United States and Zohra after she had officially relocated.

Zahir offered to handle the official press conference with his father, but Angele insisted on standing by his side. Begin as you mean to go on. That's what Lou-Belia had taught her and Angele had no intention of being a shrinking violet who spent her time hiding in the royal palace. They gave an interview to a leading personality reporter and Zahir made it very clear that he considered the "miscommunications" during their "courtship" to be his fault entirely.

His hero status was growing by the minute and not just with the public. Angele found herself falling more deeply in love with the man she was about marry than she'd ever been.

Crown Sheikh Zahir bin Faruq al Zohra was everything she had ever wanted in a husband and his behavior over the weeks leading to the wedding only reinforced that truth. He continued with what she privately termed his *unnecessary* courtship. After all, they were already headed for the altar with no chance at either of them backing out.

Nevertheless, he'd taken her to dinner both in Zohra's capital and such romantic hotspots like Paris—a high speed helicopter was an amazing form of transportation. Apparently it was good to be sheikh.

In addition to his attention, he showered her with gifts and more flowers, warning her he would be less than pleased to discover she'd been giving them away to the domestic staff as she had his first offerings.

She'd kept them all, pressing the loveliest for safe-keeping. More the fool her.

It grew increasingly difficult to maintain her emotional distance, but she wasn't about to wear her heart on her sleeve like she had her whole life. Not when his was still so firmly encased behind a brick wall.

Angele saw no evidence that Zahir's feelings toward her had grown romantically. She didn't consider his courtship in that light. It was a politically expedient tactic that might be working, but wasn't fooling her where it counted.

In regard to his feelings.

In fact, with his absolute refusal to touch her with anything more than the briefest buss of his lips over hers in greeting or parting, she was fairly certain even the passion he'd briefly exhibited for her was long gone. While he'd shared her bed at the apartment, he always went to sleep long after her and was up before she opened her eyes in the morning.

Sure as certain, he never touched her intimately.

That didn't stop him from having more opinions regarding their wedding than even Lou-Belia could lay claim to. Angele didn't care what color of linens decorated the formal dining room, or how the royal crests of the Zohra and Jawhar were displayed.

Zahir cared about both and so much more. He'd even given Lou-Belia some advice concerning Angele's trousseau. Angele had no idea what that advice was, only that Lou-Belia was beside herself that he'd offered it.

"As if I do not know exactly what fashions would best suit my own daughter," her mother fumed as they traversed the high fashion district of Paris.

"I suppose it hasn't occurred to either of you that I've been choosing my own clothing for years now?" She'd been an editorial assistant on a fashion magazine, for heaven's sake.

Not that anyone seemed to remember that salient fact.

"You don't want my help shopping?" Lou-Belia asked, managing to sound both hurt and patently shocked.

"Of course, I want your company." Which was not the same thing, but she was hoping her mother would not notice.

Not that it mattered. By the end of the day, Angele had had her fill of both her mother and Zahir's advice. Not only had he taken her mother aside, but he'd called two of the couture shops they had appointments with and made recommendations for particular outfits for her try on.

His choices were rather sexy for a man who was back to treating her like a favored cousin.

When she muttered something to that effect, Lou-Belia said, "Nonsense. He's treating you with respect."

"I'd rather he treated me like a woman."

"Apparently he's already done that, or I wouldn't be looking forward to becoming a grandmother before the year is out."

Angele gave her mother a speaking glance, but shut up about Zahir's lack of interest in the physical side of their relationship.

She didn't stop thinking about it though. Every day he treated her like an ice princess instead of his princess brought back the pain of the years he'd ignored her for other pursuits. He'd promised her that he would not take a lover, but in the darkest hours of the night, Angele lay in her lonely bed and wondered.

Zahir helped Angele from the limousine, his bodyguards holding foreign reporters back. Their own people maintained a respectful distance, though their interest was just as avid.

It was not the first time he had brought his soon-to-be bride to one of the top restaurants in their capital for a romantic dinner. He was used to being stared at and talked about when he went into public. He was their future king. Naturally they would find him of interest.

And Angele handled the interest with aplomb, making him proud and not a little surprised by her perfected public persona.

Regardless, he usually preferred to keep his public profile to well-managed levels, but a ten-year-in-the-making courtship required extra efforts.

Not that they seemed to be making any impact on the woman who carried his child and would soon carry his name as well. She had retreated behind a smiling facade that irritated him beyond reason, because it was so different from the Angele he was accustomed to.

For as long as he could remember, Angele had looked at him with a big dose of hero worship and not a small dose of want. He'd done his best to ignore the want because for too many years, she'd been all too young. Still, it had been there. And he had grown used to it. Had in fact, no idea how much he enjoyed that state of affairs until it was gone.

She was never anything less than pleasant, but she was also never anything more than pleasant. She might refute the title of princess because she could not claim it by birth and could not yet claim it by marriage, but she had the attitude down. Her aura of serenity could rival his mother's at dinner of State.

The problem was, that unlike his mother, Angele did not drop the serene little smiles and even tones when she was in the private company of family.

The vulnerable, sweet princess he had always known was now hidden behind the politically polished princess who had made her apologies to their people despite his willingness to take full responsibility for their *estrangement*.

Right now, although they were supposed to be spending time cementing their bond, her attention was firmly on those around them rather than him. Angele nodded and smiled to the Zohranians while managing to ignore the paparazzi yelling questions and taking their picture. And he had no reason to believe it would be any different once they were inside the restaurant, where she would no doubt maintain this infuriating distance.

Suddenly she dropped to her knees. He leaped forward, his body hovering over hers protectively while he looked around for some threat, even as he put his hand out to help her back to her feet. Which she ignored. It was only then that he realized a small child had managed to get away from his parents and through the small throng of reporters.

In her designer original gown, her face and hair perfectly coiffed, Angele opened her arms to the clearly frightened child. The little boy threw himself at what he obviously saw as safety.

She scooped him up, whispering something to the child that made him respond with a nod. All the while cameras flashed and Zahir had no problem imagining the front cover story of the social pages tomorrow.

Standing, Angele turned to him. "It appears we've made a friend."

Zahir smiled at the child giving him a shy sideways glance. "Hello, little man. Where are your parents?"

"Wanted to see the princess," the boy said instead of answering.

"I see. She is very special, is she not?"

The little boy nodded and Angele gave the child the first genuine smile he'd seen from her in days. "What is your name?"

Zahir didn't catch the muffled answer over a commotion going on to his right. The young girl his bodyguards allowed to come forward looking two parts terrified and one part awed, resembled the boy too much to be anything other than an older sister.

She confirmed Zahir's guess with her first words. "My brother didn't mean anything. I'm supposed to be watching him in the car while our parents run an errand, but we wanted to see the new princess."

"Please don't be upset." Angele gave another one of her genuine smiles to the girl. "He hasn't caused any trouble."

The girl did not look appreciably mollified. "My parents are going to be very angry."

"Perhaps they will not be so upset if they join us for dinner," Angele said.

The young girl stared as if she could not believe what Angele had said. The maître d', who had joined them outside, was looking at Angele with much the same expression on his usually unflappable face.

It was a politically brilliant move that would do much to shore up his princess' popularity with his people. And considering the lack of success of Zahir's attempts to romantically woo his bride-to-be, he didn't mind the extra company tonight.

Angele gave him a pleading look that had nothing in common with her new persona of serenity ice princess, and there was no chance he would kibosh the invitation. He turned to his bodyguard with instructions to find the parents and have them join the royal couple and their children in the restaurant for dinner.

He would have done far more for the genuine and warm gratitude now glowing in Angele's espresso-brown gaze.

Angele stood outside the secret passageway door to Zahir's rooms. Her hands were clammy and the nausea that had for the most part abated, was back in response to her jumping nerves.

This evening, she and Zahir had connected in a way they had not since she'd first seen the hurtful photos. She hoped they could connect in other ways tonight as well.

Before she could allow herself to change her mind, she lifted her hand and knocked on the panel. Then, without waiting for an answer, she pulled on the lever. It wasn't locked from the other side and the door swung inward.

A quick glance revealed that Zahir wasn't in the bedroom, so she crossed to the sitting room. His expression inquiring, he was standing up from a desk with an open laptop on its surface when she came in.

He'd discarded his robes of State and his suit jacket, as well as his tie. His shirt was unbuttoned at the neck, giving her a glimpse of the dark hair that covered his chest and the sleeves were rolled up to reveal his muscular forearms.

It was an intimate look, few would be privileged to see.

His eyes widened fractionally as they focused on her. "*Princess*, what are you doing here?"

"I wanted to thank you for allowing that family to have dinner with us." Angele had other plans as well, but she had enough diplomacy not to mention them right off the start.

"It was surprisingly enjoyable." He bent down and pressed a button on the laptop, sending it into hibernate.

So, he wasn't going to try to rush her out of there. Good. "Surprisingly?" she asked.

"I do not usually enjoy dining with strangers."

"You do it often enough in your official capacity."

"Exactly."

"Yet, you didn't hesitate to extend the invitation for them to join us when I asked." And that made her feel warm and gooey inside.

Was that pathetic? Did it matter? It was her life, after all. Not someone else's. She needed to live it for her happiness, or what she could grasp of it.

Which was why she was here, instead of chewing on all sorts of unpleasant possibilities for the future in her lonely bed.

He reached out and touched the corner of her softly curved lips, an unreadable expression on his face. "I will always try to give you what you desire, when I can."

"I appreciate that." Did she need his love when she had his commitment?

She'd certainly felt cherished over the past weeks, even if his actions had not been driven by more tender feelings.

"We will be content together." He winced as if unhappy with his own choice of words.

"Contentment is not bad."

"No, there are far worse fates."

That there were better possible fates hung between them, unsaid, but not unappreciated. By them both, she felt. And she was not sure that meant what it once did.

Hope sparked a tiny light deep in her heart.

Taking her courage in her hands, she stepped firmly into his personal space. "You said you would always give me what I want."

"If it is within my power."

She nodded, pretty confident that what she wanted was definitely within his power. Reaching out, she laid her hands on his biceps and then curled her fingers around the hard muscles there. She smoothed her thumbs along his arms and he made no move to stop her. The knowledge she was allowed to do this shuddered through her.

He was hers, as she was his.

One day this man would be King of all Zohra, but from the day she had agreed to marry him, he had been *her man*. And always would be. All man, all hers. Even if his birthright made him larger than life in every other way.

"Angele?" he asked in a strangled voice.

He wanted her. And it wasn't just his voice that gave him away. All sorts of little indicators showed she affected him powerfully, if she was looking for them. And she was looking. His nostrils flared, his pupils were dilated and the muscles beneath her fingers were rigid with tension.

The passion was not gone, merely banked. Relief strengthened her resolve. "You want me."

"Yes."

"Make love to me."

"I cannot."

She let her gaze drift down the front of him. His tailored suit trousers did nothing to hide the rigid length behind his placket.

She smiled, her nerves settling just a bit. "I think, in fact, that you can."

He laughed, the sound warm and filled with real humor. "Physically I am more than able. I am aching, *Aziz*."

Her breath caught. Did he realize he'd called her beloved? But then, men in this part of the world often called their wives such. It did not mean that he loved her.

Still, it did mean he saw her as his to treasure.

"Then, let me assuage that ache."

"I would like nothing more."

"What is stopping you?"

"I gave my word to your father that I would not take advantage of you prior to our official wedding."

She latched onto the word *official*. She'd suspected something since that night, now she would confirm it. "You already consider me your wife."

He said nothing.

She challenged him with her gaze. "Tell the truth."

"I do," he gritted out. "You are my wife."

It was romantic really, though she wasn't about to admit it. "Possessive."

"Yes."

"I came to you in a wedding gown and you made me promises you never spoke out loud," she guessed.

"It was the only way you would accept the gift of my virginity."

"Yes."

She smiled.

He growled. "I am an old-fashioned man, but I am not naff."

Angele suppressed the desire to giggle. He sounded so put-upon. "No, I'd never accuse you of being sappy." But she couldn't deny the old-fashioned label.

Even Elsa had been an example of that. Zahir had been a man in his sexual prime when he signed the agreement for their eventual marriage. He needed a sexual outlet and he'd looked for one.

Angele had no doubt he hadn't expected to feel anything real for Elsa, or for the affair to last as long as it did. Knowing he had cared so much, that Elsa had been able to hurt him, hurt Angele. However, it was over and he was truly hers now, in every way.

"Does the future king of Zahir allow another man to determine the parameters of his life?" she challenged.

"I made a promise."

"Not to take advantage, but how is it taking advantage when in your heart, I'm already your wife?"

"And in your heart?" it was his turn to challenge.

She could give him nothing less than the truth. "I'm yours, Zahir. I always have been."

"That's not what you said in your letter, or that press release."

"I wanted to give you your freedom."

"So I could find *true love*."

She was sure he meant to say the words true love with

more sarcasm, but his tone carried more confusion than cynicism.

And suddenly, she realized something very important. Just because he was not in love with her did not mean Zahir did not need her love. In fact, she was no longer fully convinced he did not love her, either. After some fashion anyway. There was something there, something she did not yet understand, but she was determined to.

"You hold yourself back from me," she said, not as an accusation but as bait.

She needed to understand this complicated man. Angele would be the first to admit, she'd been so blinded by her own emotions, she had all but ignored his.

One thing had remained true for ten years, though. This man had always intended to marry her and by his own admission, he had intended to bring his formidable honor to bear in remaining faithful to her.

"I would say you are the one that has put up walls between us." He frowned, though he did not move away from her.

If she didn't know better, she would think he was no more capable of doing so than she was.

"You think?" she asked, wanting…maybe even needing to hear this from his mouth.

"You used to love me."

"I still do." And denying it to both of them was doing nothing but hurting the man she had no desire to hurt and herself.

She hadn't shocked him with her request they make love, but her words of love made him jerk back as if struck. "No, you do not."

She moved closer again, so their bodies were less than a breath apart. "I do."

"You do not smile at me as you used to."

"The last few weeks have been stressful." And she'd thought they would be better off if she buried her deeper emotions, so they came to each other on a level playing field. But hiding her feelings was not natural to her, not like it was for him.

In order to do so, she'd had to cut off her emotions completely, hiding behind what she called her political female figure facade. She'd had plenty of examples growing up, but it was only tonight she'd realized how much the constant facade had been smothering her.

She needed to be herself sometimes, but most particularly with him.

"Love is not required in a marriage such as ours is to be, but both parties should like each other, I think." He sounded like he was trying to convince himself as much as her.

Instead of allowing herself to get upset at this further evidence he didn't love her, she listened to what he *wasn't* saying. She heard his need, a need she doubted he allowed anyone else to glimpse.

"I do like you, Zahir, and I love you." It was easier to admit now that she'd already said it. "I never stopped."

He reversed their hold so that it was his hands holding her close, with no hope of moving away. "You are mine. I will never let you leave me again."

"I'm not going anywhere." She needed him and was coming to accept that on some very important level he needed her, too. "I want you to make love to me."

"And my promise to your father?"

"Is nullified if making love is an act of caring rather than slaking mere physical desire."

"Of course I care for you. You have always been as important to me as any of my family. That has not changed."

It wasn't the romantic declaration of the century, but for Zahir those words were a promise of commitment deeper than most men were even capable of making.

"I believe you."

Then, it was if something inside him broke. Maybe it was his self-control, because he took her mouth like an invading army intent on total conquest.

# CHAPTER TEN

SENSING he needed this as much as she did, she allowed her body to melt into him in a surrender powered by her own desire. And was that really surrender at all, or a victory?

She certainly felt like she was winning as his lips drew forth passion that even surpassed the single night they had shared together.

He swung her up in his arms and headed toward the bedroom, though his mouth never left hers. Part of her marveled that they didn't bump into walls or door-jambs, but then this was Zahir. The man could navigate the minefield of world politics, his own rooms were no challenge.

They came down onto the bed together, his heavy body covering hers, proof of his desire pressed into her stomach. Taking the kiss to the next level, he thrust against her, his essence surrounding and grounding her, blocking out everything else.

Heated moisture soaked the scrap of fabric between her legs and she spread them, seeking more stimulation. But there were too many layers in the way, her own outfit preventing her from getting as close to him as she wanted to. She whimpered, wanting it and every other bit of clothing off her.

He made a sound of satisfaction as he continued to kiss her with a masterful passion that was far beyond what he had shown her before. It was as if that night he'd been treating her like she'd been made of spun-glass. And perhaps since it had been her first time, he'd been right to do so.

But now, there was an elemental, almost primal power radiating through every kiss, every caress.

And his hands were everywhere, clever fingers that knew how to draw forth urges and sensations she hadn't even known she was capable of. Her clothes came off and so did his, though she couldn't remember the sequence or even who took off what.

But the moment when he pressed her hands upward and curled her fingers around the wrought-iron spindles on the big bed's headboard and told her not to let go was seared into her mind like his passion seared her heart.

She stared at him. "Why?"

"I want to pleasure you."

"And I need to keep my hands here for you to do that?"

"It will please me."

She didn't understand. She wanted to touch him, but she wanted to do what he asked, too. The idea of giving total control over to him both alarming and very, very alluring.

"You're kinky!" she accused with equal parts shock and desire.

"I am a man who knows what he desires." That was so not a denial.

"You like being in control."

"This surprises you?"

"No." Though maybe it should. Wouldn't a man who had to control so much, want to give a little up?

His fierce, primal expression said, *not this one.*

Not her sheikh.

He arranged her legs so that they were bent at the knee and spread apart in a wanton display that would have embarrassed her if she wasn't so excited.

"Will it always be like this?" she asked breathlessly. Would he always want this extra bit of control?

He looked up from his heated perusal of her most intimate flesh. "I do not know. I have never done this before, but it is something I have long wanted."

She moaned, the words more effective than any touch. "I'm glad this is special between us."

"Everything we share in our marriage bed is special. No woman has ever belonged to me as you do and I have never belonged to another woman as I do to you."

"What do you mean?" He was far from a virgin.

"You own my future." With that he touched her sweet spot, his fingers going on to thoroughly explore every bit of intimate flesh exposed so fully to his gaze. "You are so beautiful."

"I don't think women are beautiful there."

"You know this because you have looked?" he asked teasingly.

Even knowing he was teasing, she still jerked in shock. "Zahir! Of course not!" She'd never seen female *parts* outside of a sex education book and those were clinical diagrams.

"Then you cannot know, so I will forgive your doubt."

She turned her face away, embarrassed and pleased and even more embarrassed because she was pleased.

"Every inch of you is beautiful, including this flesh only I and your doctor will ever see."

That had her looking at him again. "You didn't used to think I was beautiful."

"You were thirteen when our contract was signed. To have looked upon you in that light would have been wrong."

"I didn't stay thirteen."

"In my mind, you did."

She almost laughed, but the seriousness in his expression could not be denied. A jolt of unexpected understanding went through her. Perhaps this, more than anything else, explained the passage of ten years since that darned contract had been signed.

She stopped wondering seconds later when his touch robbed every logical, and illogical for that matter, thought from her brain. He knew exactly how to touch her, playing with her breasts and teasing her nipples into turgid aching nubs.

But he didn't stop there; no, he seemed to know secrets about her body that had escaped her notice. Caressing her inner thigh, that spot in the center of her back, her nape, he stimulated numerous little bundles of nerve endings she'd had no idea existed on her body. Even after that first night together.

She writhed, begging him to come inside her and finish this spiral of pleasure, but she did not let go of the headboard.

He rewarded her with his mouth. First on her breasts, then the other hot spots he'd exposed on her body and then finally on that place he said was beautiful to him.

She was still screaming out her first orgasm when he surged inside, filling her beyond comprehension.

Just as the first time, it wasn't merely her body he filled, but her heart and her mind until she could not breathe without breathing him in, could not think without thinking of him, could not feel without feeling him.

Her second orgasm came over in a wave of such intense pleasure, it bordered on pain.

He wasn't done yet, though. He held himself rigid through her body's convulsions and only started moving again when her breathing had slowed down to hiccupping pants.

He brushed at the tears she hadn't even realized she'd been crying. *"Aziz."*

"I love you, Zahir."

Something moved in his gaze and then he started to move again, this time building to a rhythm that left her gasping with no sound for her scream when she reached the pinnacle of pleasure again...with him.

He insisted she sleep in his bed that night after they bathed together; she rested better than she had since returning from the States, her body, mind and heart as at peace as they could be.

She woke the next morning to gentle hands moving over her body. She went to reach for him, but her hands were stuck and it was then she realized they were bound to the headboard with something made of the softest silk.

"Zahir?" she asked as her eyes opened to the shadows of early dawn.

His look was as intent as she'd ever seen it. "Is it all right?"

Perhaps another woman would say no. Perhaps with another man, she should. But Angele knew what Zahir was asking her and it wasn't just whether or not she was willing to let him make love to her with her hands bound.

He was asking if she trusted him enough to allow it.

The only things she knew about kink were the jokes passed around the water cooler at her former job, but this was instinctive. She didn't need to know about anyone else's intimacy to know this was right between her and Zahir.

He needed to know she trusted him completely and if she was honest with herself, and she always tried to be, she needed to know the same thing. This binding was for both their sakes, a chance to undo the damage too many years between the signing of the contract and their actual wedding had wrought.

It wasn't a declaration of love, but it was one of intent.

She could accept it. "Yes. It's all right."

The tension in the lines around his eyes dissipated and he smiled, happiness glowing forth in a way she'd never seen from him. "You are so alluring this way."

And he was unbearably sexy with that look of joy in his eyes. He might not love her, but then again he might. No matter what had been said on the subject to this point. One thing was certain, though: she was able to give him something no one else could. He'd told her he'd never tried this type of thing with another woman and she believed him.

He would not trust a casual lover not to go to the tabloids with the sexual peccadilloes of the Crown Sheikh of Zohra.

He was a man who must maintain personal control at all times and had far too much responsibility on his plate for any normal man. But he was not an average guy, not even close.

He was something more and so was this. Something special and incredible.

"Will you ever let me turn the tables?" she asked, not sure she wanted to, but curious.

"If you'd like." And she knew he meant it. He was willing to trust her in ways he would *never* have trusted another.

"Maybe someday…" she said, the last word trailing off into a moan as his heated mouth made love to her body.

Rich male humor sounded even as he upped the stakes and drove her toward pleasure only he had ever been able to give her.


Zahir accompanied Angele on the walk back to her room, shrugging when she commented that if they were caught together in the secret passageway there could be no doubt what they had been up to. "You are mine."

"You're a possessive man."

"And are you any less possessive?"

She didn't even have to think about it. "No."

"Good."

"I thought men didn't like clingy women?"

He stopped them in the passageway outside her room and gave her a serious look that melted her right to her toes. "Cling, *Princess*."

She choked out a disbelieving laugh as his mouth covered hers in a kiss of unmistakable claiming.

When their mouths separated, he sighed. "I have business of State in Europe. My flight leaves later this morning and I will be in meetings until then."

"Where in Europe?"

"Germany."

Her breath caught, but she wasn't giving in to jealousy. He'd told her to cling. Had he meant it? "Berlin's Fashion Week is happening right now. I could come with you and write a freelance article. I'm sure I could get into some of the runway shows."

"If you are sure you can get away from the wedding preparations." His smile was brilliant.

His reaction left no doubt he wanted Angele to come. This was no grudging acceptance. She'd never be a whiny-clingy type, but she knew that wasn't what he meant. Zahir wanted to know that no matter how independent she was by nature, that she needed him and would make time to be with him.

"Lou-Belia and your mother have it under control."

"You have given them full control of the festivities."

She wasn't sure if that was an observation or a criticism, but she chose to take it as the former. "You may as well realize that planning social events is not my thing. I've got a great attention to detail and can coordinate my life to the Nth degree, but I don't enjoy poring over guest lists and seating charts."

He nodded, as if confirming his own thoughts. "It is not a requirement of your position. We have a more than competent event coordination team."

"I know. The palace event coordinator is pulling his hair out at both our mothers' overt interference in every detail of the wedding."

"My mother said you will not allow any one to see the dress you have planned to wear for the formal ceremony?"

"That's one thing I refuse to compromise on."

"Mother said you won't tell them anymore than that it is white."

Was he fishing? And was it for his sake, or his mother's? Angele knew both Lou-Belia and Queen Adara were frustrated by Angele's secrecy on the matter.

She wasn't giving in, though. "That's all they need to know."

"She said you told her that it would not clash with the traditional couture chosen for the rest of the family and wedding party."

Angele merely shrugged. If he thought she was giving him any more details than she'd given his mother, he was wrong. No matter how sexy she found him and his interest in their wedding.

Though if he knew her as well as she had come to realize he probably did, he would realize exactly what she planned to wear to speak her vows.

Angele napped on the flight to Germany. The night before hadn't seen either of them sleeping much, though

Zahir didn't seem affected in the least as he worked in his seat beside her on the private royal jet.

Her morning hadn't been exactly relaxing, either. Lou-Belia had come close to meltdown when Angele told her she was flying to Germany with Zahir. Angele had spent the remaining hours on wedding preparations, despite the fact someone else could easily have made the calls and decisions she ostensibly made. Ostensibly because all she did was rubber stamp approval plans already put in place by her mother or Queen Adara.

Angele had exactly twenty minutes to pack for the trip. It was a good thing she was used to travel.

They were in the limousine, driving away from the airport, before she realized there was a real possibility Zahir would take her to the chalet in the photos that had prompted her to try to break their contract. She didn't like that possibility. Not one little bit.

"Where are we staying?"

He named a posh hotel in downtown Berlin.

Stifling any sign of the abject relief she felt, she couldn't help probing. "I thought you owned a chalet you used when doing business here."

"It's been sold as have most of our business interests here in Germany." He looked at her as if challenging her to ask further.

She wasn't sure she wanted to. "Oh."

Either she trusted him, or she didn't. She chose to.

"We couldn't cut all ties—it wasn't what was best for Zohra, but they have been minimized," he added in the silence that followed.

She felt she should respond to that in some way, but

wasn't sure how. She finally settled on a quiet, "Thank you."

"No thanks needed." His words were more forceful, as if trying to impart a message he did not want to come right out and say.

And apparently, that was that, because he didn't say anything further and answered his phone when it buzzed in his pocket. However, she felt a lightness in her heart that could not be denied.

Their connecting hotel suites were both luxurious and comfortable. His comment that she could use the bedroom in hers as a dressing room put paid to any doubt she might have about where she would be sleeping over the next three days.

Despite the fact that she now traveled with a security entourage, Angele found no difficulty in getting last minute VIP seating for the main runway shows. It was past midnight when she made it back to the hotel that night. She was tired, but wired.

"You really love the world of fashion, don't you?" Zahir asked.

She shrugged as she kicked off her pumps. "What can I say? It's in my genes."

"Fashion is a lucrative industry."

"It is."

"Considering how little you like to plan events, I do not suppose you would consider coordinating a fashion week in our capital?"

Excitement made her heart rate increase. A fashion week, or even a single runway show was nowhere near as boring an event as a State dinner. "That depends. Can

I hire a team to help me? Can we designate a charity to couple with and make the event about more than just fashion?"

"Of course."

"Then, yes, absolutely. I would love to."

"Good."

"It's no longer seen as quite the thing for a political wife to be without some interests of her own," she acknowledged.

The British weren't the only country that pushed a princess to be more than her title.

"Just so."

She smiled, enjoying the fact he had thought about what sort of interest would make her happy. Because she knew Zahir was not a spontaneous guy. "You've been thinking about this for a while."

"Years."

Wow. Just, wow. "I thought so. I could have continued writing freelance fashion articles, you know. We don't have to invent an industry for me."

"I'm sure you will continue the writing. You are very good, but it is time Zohra joined the rest of the world in showcasing modern fashion."

"Right, like you really care if there is a runway show in Zohra's capital."

"What is important to you, is important to me."

She threw her arms around him and hugged him. "I just love you so much, right now."

He laughed, his eyes going hot with an expression she was coming to know very well. "That is good to hear."

She cocked her head to the side and smiled up at him. "I don't want our children raised by nannies."

"Agreed."

So, a very part-time interest. She could work with that.

"Are you ready for bed?" he asked.

"I'm tired, but not sleepy."

"I think I can fix that."

And he did.

## CHAPTER ELEVEN

THE next day, she got up early and when he left for his meetings, she accompanied him. The car dropped her and her security detail off at the main pavilion. She spent her morning focused on the German designers and boutiques, taking dozens of pictures in between miniinterviews with designers, boutique owners and other attendees of the show. It was unsurprising, but nevertheless pleasing how eager people were to be quoted in an article written by the soon-to-be wife of the Crown Sheikh of Zohra.

Her pregnancy caught up with her around lunchtime and she returned to the hotel for a nap after eating a light snack from the food stalls.

She woke up hungry and decided on a late lunch in the hotel restaurant before returning to the Fashion Week festivities.

The *hauptkellner* looked surprised to see her, but then nodded to himself as if working something out. He said something in rapid German to another waiter that she was sure Zahir would understand, but Angele's German was not up to such rapid speech. Then he turned and led her toward the back of the restaurant, where the tables afforded a lovely view of the garden out the wall of windows.

She was so intent on the view she didn't immediately see the other occupants at the table the head waiter had stopped beside. He snapped his fingers and the other waiter appeared with a third chair, since the two already at the table were occupied.

By Zahir.

*And Elsa Bosch.*

Zahir's face had gone completely blank, but Elsa looked both amused and slightly sick to her stomach.

It was an interesting reaction that Angele cataloged almost subconsciously as she took the chair the waiter held out for her. The *hauptkellner* placed her napkin in her lap while the waiter laid another place setting at the table.

He went to hand her a menu, but she waved it away. "I'll just have a chicken Caesar salad."

She didn't know if they had it on the menu, but was confident the chef could come up with something. It was taking all her concentration to maintain an air of calm and casual demeanor while seated at the table with her soon-to-be husband and his former mistress.

The waiters left and Angele released a breath she hadn't realized she'd been holding. "Well, this is awkward."

Neither of her companions had an answer for that, so she turned to Zahir. "Not to be rude, but I believe you told me this particular problem had been taken care of."

Elsa made a sound of annoyance, but didn't say anything.

"I believed it had, but then further developments arose."

"She's trying to blackmail you now?" Angele asked in Arabic, fairly confident none of their fellow diners could overhear to quote her for the gossip rags.

She made no attempt to hide either her disgust or her shock. Only an idiot risked making an absolute enemy of a man like Zahir.

"No."

"I am not sure if that makes me more relieved or worried." Perhaps a week ago, her reaction to this situation would have been much different. Okay, there was no maybe about it, but she'd decided to trust him. Totally and completely.

And she was going to keep doing so, unless she was given a whole lot more than a public lunch as evidence she shouldn't.

"Elsa was not the blackmailer."

Angele's gaze flicked to the other woman, who seemed to be listening with interest. "No? You confirmed she was."

"She did not deny it when I confronted her and threatened to bankrupt and dismantle her personal production company if so much as a single picture from that envelope ever found its way into the press."

"I imagine a tell-all article would have paid her well enough to tempt her regardless."

"I was more than generous in our parting. She signed a contract stipulating absolute media silence in exchange and would have to pay back every penny I ever gave her or spent on her if she broke it."

"So, how could she think she would get away with blackmail?"

"She didn't."

"It was my brother," Elsa spoke in English, but made it clear she had enough understanding of Arabic to have followed the gist of their conversation.

"Your brother?" Angele asked in the same language, feeling shock on shock.

"He hadn't signed anything." Elsa shrugged. "He's an idiot. He did not realize that the way the contract was worded that I had signed, it wouldn't matter. I would still have to pay the price."

"Elsa is here to pass over all the printed copies of the pictures as well as her brother's hard drive and backup thumb drive."

"He could still have other copies."

"He doesn't," Elsa said.

"I'm supposed to take your word for it?" Angele asked, maintaining a tone of slightly bored interest for which she was rather proud, considering the maelstrom of emotions roiling inside her.

Elsa's shoulders gave an elegant roll, sort of a shrug and sort of something else.

Angele's gaze flicked to Zahir to see his reaction, but his eyes were fixed intently on her and her alone.

"Do you believe her?" Angele asked him.

"It does not matter if I do, or not."

"Because you will not leave it to chance."

"No. Even as we speak, he is on his way to Zohra to face blackmail charges."

"What?" Elsa demanded a lot louder than was probably wise.

Zahir finally settled his gaze on her and Angele shivered. She wouldn't want that look fixed on her. Ever.

"I am not convinced you were unaware of your brother's schemes. In fact, I can almost guarantee he's too stupid to have considered Angele the better target."

Elsa blanched.

"If he names you as accomplice, expect extradition proceedings."

"But you can't do this. I brought you the pictures."

"Thank you. They and your brother's hard drive will be used as evidence in his trial."

Elsa looked stunned. "But that's not fair."

Angele wondered at the other woman's lack of understanding of the way that Zahir thought and the type of action that thought process would lead to.

"And you think blackmail is fair?" he asked, not sounding like he really cared if she did, or not.

"But you said you would not prosecute if I ceased and desisted."

Had Zahir ever really fallen for that damsel in distress act? Angele could barely suppress the need to roll her eyes.

Looking as unimpressed as she could hope, Zahir said, "That was when I believed you to be the culprit. I owed you some level of protection, regardless of how things ended between us."

He *was* an old-fashioned guy. He'd said so on more than one occasion. Zahir would not have sent Elsa to prison, unless she forced him to it. Her brother, on the other hand, was another matter. Being a man, being someone willing to trade on his sister's former relationship, in Zahir's eyes, Mr. Bosch was fair game.

"But Hans wasn't going to do anything more."

"Really?"

"Of course."

Zahir looked intently at the other woman, as if weighing her veracity. Angele, for one, believed her or at least that Elsa believed what she'd said.

"Then, explain the blackmail letter Angele's father received last week."

"My father?" Angele asked in shock as Elsa's perfectly painted mouth opened and closed like a landed carp.

Zahir returned his gaze to Angele. "Yes. Cemal came to me immediately with the demand."

"Oh, stop harping." Elsa frowned at him. "You make Hans sound like a criminal when he was just trying his luck."

"I did not say it was Hans, *Aziz*."

Elsa gasped and then glared at them both. "So, that's it. You've tricked me into naming my brother and providing you with evidence against him."

"Would you prefer to face the charges on your own?" Zahir asked pitilessly.

Once again, the other woman went pale, this time her hands shaking as she went for a sip of her white wine. "No."

"I thought not."

"I could still go to the tabloids with my story."

"You've tied all your money up in your productions company. You can't afford to pay me back."

"So sue me for the money, the story will be out there for all the world to see."

"I have already released an official statement admitting a past liaison with you that I deeply regret along with the news that your brother will be tried for blackmail in my country." He was speaking to Elsa, but looking at Angele, as if her reaction was the only one that mattered.

"That sounds like the smartest move you could make." He'd shown her with news of the baby that in some cases transparency circumvented a media frenzy.

Once again Elsa did her carp impression and this time it was even less attractive than the last. "I..."

Zahir turned back to her. "Would do well to keep your media silence. Or you will pay the price for your poor judgment just as your brother must pay the price for his."

"But that's all it was, it was poor judgment. He can't go to prison for that."

"Poor judgment that leads to breaking the law also leads to jail." Zahir shrugged and stood. "It is the way of things."

He put his hand out to Angele. "Come, *ya habibti*."

She stood without hesitation. She still had plenty of questions for Zahir, but they could wait for privacy. She turned to Elsa before leaving. "You have a choice right now."

Elsa said nothing, but cocked her head as if inviting Angele to continue.

"Zahir forgave your betrayal and was willing to overlook even worse in his eyes because of your shared past. Don't make him an enemy now."

"Isn't he already?"

"If he was, you would be on the plane with Hans right now."

"He's my brother."

"I understand that, but he broke the law and my guess is this isn't the first time."

Elsa's flinch confirmed Angele's supposition.

"It's just the first time he's had to pay for it. Believe it, or not, Zahir is doing Hans a favor."

"How do you work that out?"

"The next time, your brother could have attempted to blackmail the wrong person. That person might not take legal recourse, but something far more permanent than a few years in prison."

"But prison in Zohra."

"*Isn't* a third-world hellhole. It's prison. With family visitation and guards who face far stricter reprisal for corruption than most other developed nations."

Elsa's eyes filled with tears, but she nodded. "I'm not stupid. I'm not going to the media with a tell-all."

"I appreciate it."

"He was always yours."

"I've come to realize that."

"I deserved a chance at happiness." Elsa meant the man she'd betrayed Zahir with.

"Yes, you did. But so do we."

"Can he serve his time in a German prison?" Elsa asked Zahir without looking at him. "At least then, I could visit him often."

Zahir did not answer, but Angele gave the other woman a look meant to convey her intention of discussing the matter with him. Elsa must have gotten it because she nodded slightly.

The waiter was coming with Angele's salad as she and Zahir walked away from the table. Zahir instructed the clearly confused man to have her food delivered to his suite.

Neither Zahir nor Angele spoke on the elevator ride up to their floor. Once they were in his room, he let out a deep sigh, but didn't say anything, either.

"Was this the State business you had to take care of?"

"No, but the other business made a good cover for handling this issue." Zahir looked like he was waiting for something.

An explosion perhaps? Only Angele didn't feel like exploding.

"Do you have any more work you have to do today?" she asked him.

"No."

"Would you like to come to the Fashion Week with me?"

She didn't think she'd ever seen Zahir looking so nonplussed.

And then he frowned. "No. And I would prefer you did not leave, either."

"Why is that?"

"You know why."

"Spell it out for me."

"We need to talk."

"About?"

"About what happened in the dining room, damn it." Zahir rarely cursed in her presence.

She took heart in it. He was upset. And while maybe she should feel badly about that, she was actually pleased. "What exactly did you want to talk about?"

"You caught me having a meal with my former mistress."

"You were gathering evidence for the court case against her brother."

"You would expect me to have told you my plans prior to meeting him. I'm sure you are further angered by the fact I did not tell you about the attempt to blackmail your father."

"Nope." She thought about it to make sure and then shook her head. "Not angry."

He opened his mouth, but then closed it again without speaking.

"You wanted to protect me from upset while I was pregnant."

"I cannot guarantee I would behave differently if you were not pregnant," he said, as if admitting some deep dark secret.

"I get that."

"You do?"

"What do you think I mean when I tell you that I love you, Zahir?"

"I do not know."

"That's becoming more than a little apparent. I don't just love the bits about you I find comfortable. I know you see the world through eyes influenced by generations of responsibility that comes with your role. You protect your family, you protect your people, you protect me. It's in your DNA."

"That does not bother you?"

"I'm not promising never to get angry, or call you out over it, but for the most part? It makes me feel safe. Cherished."

"I do cherish you."

"I believe you."

"You do?" his voice was tinged with wonder.

She smiled. Nodded. "I do."

"I did not want you under more stress than you already are."

"I understand."

"You do?"

"Yes. I would do the same for you."

For once, it was easy to read her world leader love's facial expression. Utter shock and a shade of disbelief.

She laughed. "Don't you think your mother has ever protected your father from stress when she could?"

"Yes, but…"

"No buts, we'll both protect each other."

"Do you think I am being too harsh on Elsa's brother?"

"No, but if you can work it out so he serves his time closer to his sister, I think that would be good."

Zahir nodded. "It will be done."

"For me, but not for her?" she asked, curious that he had shown no indication of even hearing the other woman's request.

"Yes."

"She said you've always been mine."

"You said you believed her."

"I do. I didn't for a while," Angele admitted. "I do now, though."

"What changed?"

"I figured out that you love me."

"What?"

"I'm not even sure you haven't always loved me, but you wouldn't let yourself consider such a thing because I stayed thirteen in your mind. You transferred your feelings for me onto Elsa, but not enough to allow you to even consider marrying her instead of me."

"How...I..." He went silent for several long moments, took a deep breath and let it out. "You're right."

"Say it."

"I will on our wedding day."

"Yes, you will, but you'll say it now, too."

"Now who is being bossy?"

"You'd be bored silly with a pushover."

"I love you."

She started to cry, but he didn't say anything. How could he? His own eyes were just as wet.

He made her eat the salad before taking her into the bedroom and laying her gently on the bed.

"Another wedding night?" she asked softly as he divested them both of their clothes.

"A night of affirmation. I love you beyond reason. It is not an emotion I ever thought to experience. I know now what I felt in the past was lust mixed with relief at being just a man, for a few short hours. But I realized something, I've never been able to leave my role behind...not even when I was with her. Only with you, can I be what I am and still be free to be just a man."

"You are the man I love, the man I have always

loved." Her words came out breathless as he touched her in places that made her quiver, squirm and moan.

"And you are the woman I love, will always love." And then he proved it with his body, making gentle, long love to her, repeating the words in every language he spoke fluently and a few he did not.

When he yelled out *Aziz* when he climaxed, she knew she really was his beloved.

# EPILOGUE

ANGELE wore the dress Zahir had given her on their first night together for their wedding, making his mother cry and his father beam with unadulterated joy. Their wedding celebration lasted a full week before he took her on a honeymoon to Paris, telling her it was appropriate for them.

It was the City of Lovers after all.

They were at the top of the Eiffel Tower when he wrapped his arms around her, pulling her into his body as they looked out over the City of Light. "Beautiful."

"It is." She snuggled back against him. "I want to hold this moment in my heart forever."

"We can get my bodyguard to take a picture."

She smiled. He was a crown sheikh; they went nowhere without security, but sometimes that came in handy. Like when getting snapshots of their honeymoon highlights.

At least the security detail didn't share their suite, just had rooms on either side of them.

"Let's," she said, in answer to his suggestion.

He made the request in Arabic and then bent down to kiss her as their guard pressed the button for their picture with Paris at night in the background.

She was breathless and bemused when Zahir lifted his head.

"You are in all the pictures of my future that my heart can see."

She accepted his words for truth. She understood... she'd never seen a future for herself without him in it, no matter how hard she'd tried to for that brief time.

No wonder he refused to dismiss the idea of an arranged marriage for their child.

It had certainly worked out for them.

# Banished to the Harem

## CAROL MARINELLI

**Carol Marinelli** recently filled in a form where she was asked for her job title and was thrilled, after all these years, to be able to put down her answer as 'writer'.

Then it asked what Carol did for relaxation and, after chewing her pen for a moment, Carol put down the truth—'writing'. The third question asked, 'What are your hobbies?' Well, not wanting to look obsessed or, worse still, boring, she crossed the fingers on her free hand and answered 'swimming and tennis'. But, given that the chlorine in the pool does terrible things to her highlights, and the closest she's got to a tennis racket in the last couple of years is watching the Australian Open, I'm sure you can guess the real answer!

# PROLOGUE

'I SHALL return on Monday.' Crown Prince Sheikh Rakhal Alzirz would not be swayed. 'Now, onto other matters.'

'But the King has requested that you leave London immediately.'

Rakhal's jaw tightened as Abdul pressed on. It was rare indeed for Abdul to persist when Rakhal had made his feelings clear on a subject, for Rakhal was not a man who changed his mind often—nor did he take orders from an aide—even his most senior one. But in this case Abdul was relaying orders that came directly from the King, which forced him to be bold.

'The King is most insistent that you return to Alzirz by tomorrow. He will not hear otherwise.'

'I shall speak with my father myself,' Rakhal said. 'I am not simply going to walk away at his bidding.'

'The King is unwell, though....' Abdul closed his eyes for a moment, grief and worry evident on his face.

'Which is why I shall be married before the month's end,' Rakhal interrupted. 'I accept that it is important for our people to have the security of knowing the

Crown Prince is married, especially with the King now ill, however...'

Rakhal did not finish his sentence. He did not need to explain himself to Abdul, so again he changed the subject, his black eyes daring Abdul not join him this time.

'Now, onto other matters.' He did not wait for his aide's nod. 'We need to discuss a suitable gift to celebrate this morning's news from Alzan. I want to express my delight to Sheikh King Emir Alzan.' A dark smile twisted at the edge of Rakhal's full lips, for despite the news about his father's health, despite the summons for him to return to Alzirz and choose a bride, the week had at least brought one piece of good news.

In fact two pieces of good news!

'Something very pink,' Rakhal said, and for the first time that morning Abdul smiled too, for it was good news indeed. The birth of female twins in Alzan gave the Kingdom of Alzirz some much-needed breathing space. Not much, for undoubtedly Emir and his wife would soon produce a son, but for now there was reason to smile.

Long ago Alzirz and Alzan had been one country—Alzanirz—but there had been much unrest and the Sultan at the time had sought a solution. A mix-up at the birth of his identical twin sons had provided him with one, and on his death the Kingdom of Alzanirz had been divided between his sons.

It was a temporary solution—at least temporary in desert terms—for the mathematicians and predictors of the time had all agreed that in years, or even hundreds of years, the two countries would again become one. It could be no other way, because a special law had been designed for each country that meant one day they would be reunited. Each country had been given one law by which they must abide, and only the opposing ruler could revoke it.

In Alzirz, where Rakhal would soon be King, the ruler could take but one wedded partner in their lifetime, and his firstborn, whether boy or girl, would be heir.

Rakhal's mother, Layla, weak and thin and grieving her Bedouin life, had died birthing Rakhal, her only child, and the country had held its breath as the tiny, premature infant struggled to hold on to life. For a while it had seemed that the predictions of old were coming true, and that the Kingdom of Alzirz would be handed over to Alzan's rule—for how could a baby born so early, a baby so tiny, possibly survive?

But Rakhal had not only survived. Out of the starvation of his mother's womb he had thrived.

In Alzan the one rule was different—there the King could marry again on the death of his wife, but the ruler of Alzan must always be male. And now, as of this morning, Emir was the father of two little girls. Oh, there would be much celebrating and dancing in Alzirz tonight—their country was safe.

For now.

Having entered his third decade, Rakhal could no longer put it off. He had rowed frequently about this with his father, but now accepted that it was time for him to choose his bride. A wife he would bed at her fertile times only, for she would be rested at other times. A wife he would see only for copulation and at formal functions or special occasions. She would live a luxurious, pampered life in her own area of the palace, and guide the raising of children he would barely see.

Emir would see *his* children.... Rakhal recognised the darkness that dwelled within him as he thought of his rival, but it did not enter his head that jealousy might reside there too—for Rakhal knew that he had everything.

'Do you have any ideas as to a gift?' Abdul broke into Rakhal's thoughts.

'Two pink diamonds, perhaps?' Rakhal mused. 'No.' He changed his mind. 'I need to think about this. I want something more subtle than diamonds— something that will make him churn as he receives it.' Of course he and Emir were polite when they met, but there was a deep rivalry between them—a rivalry that had existed before either was born and would be passed on for generations to come. 'For once I will enjoy choosing a gift.'

'Very well,' Abdul said, gathering up his papers and preparing to leave the study in Rakhal's luxurious hotel suite. But as he got to the door he could not help himself from asking, 'You *will* speak with the King?'

Rakhal dismissed him with a wave of his hand. He did not answer to his aide—he had said that he would speak to the King, and that was enough.

Rakhal did speak with his father. He was the only person in Alzirz who was not intimidated by the King.

'You are to return this instant,' the King demanded. 'The people are becoming unsettled and need to know that you have chosen your bride. I wish to go to my grave knowing you shall produce an heir. You are to return and marry.'

'Of course,' Rakhal responded calmly, because there was no debating that point. But he refused to dance to his father's tune—they were two strong and proud men and often clashed. Both had been born natural leaders, and neither liked to be told what to do, yet there was another reason that Rakhal stood his ground and told his father he would not return till Monday. If he boarded a plane immediately, if he gave in without protest, then his father would really know that he was dying.

And he *was* dying.

Hanging up the phone, Rakhal closed his eyes and rested his head on his hands for a moment. He had spoken at length yesterday with the royal doctor and he knew more than the King did. His father had but a few months to live.

Conversations with his father were always difficult, always stilted. As a child Rakhal had been brought up by the maidens, and had seen his father only on special occasions. Once, as a teenager, he had joined his father in the desert and learnt the teachings of old. Now, though, as leadership approached for Rakhal, his father seemed to want to discuss his every move.

It was one of the reasons Rakhal liked London. He liked the freedom of this strange land, where women talked about making love and demanded things from their partner that were not necessary in Alzirz. He wanted to linger just a little longer.

Rakhal had a deep affinity for the city that was, of course, never discussed. Only by chance had Rakhal found out that it was here in this hotel that he had been conceived—a break with desert rules that had not only cost his mother her life, but also threatened the very country he would soon rule.

He stood and headed to the window and looked at the grey view, at the misty rain and the cluttered streets. He could not wholly fathom this country's appeal, for he knew it was the desert where he belonged, the desert he must return to.

The desert that was summoning him home.

# CHAPTER ONE

THE policewoman could not have been more bored as she instructed Natasha to fill out the necessary forms.

And, yes, in the scheme of things it wasn't exactly riveting that her car had been stolen, and neither was it a disaster, but on the back of everything else that she was dealing with, today of all days, Natasha could very easily have put her head on the desk and wept.

She didn't, of course. Natasha just got on with what she had to—it was how this year had been. Her long, thick red hair was wet from the rain and dripped on the counter as she bent her head. She pushed it out of her eyes. Her fingers were white from the cold. If her car *had* to have been stolen, Natasha almost wished it could have been in a couple of days' time, when she would have known nothing about it.

Natasha was supposed to be spending this gruelling day planning a holiday. It was the anniversary of her parents' death, and she had wanted to mark it somehow. She had been determined to push on with her life, but had finally listened when her friends had said that she needed a break—a proper one—and it didn't need to be expensive.

As a substitute teacher it had been easy for her to arrange a fortnight off, and today she had been planning to visit the cemetery and then go to a friend's house to book the cheapest, hottest place on the planet she could afford. Instead she was standing in a draughty police station, politely trying not to listen as the woman beside her reported a domestic incident.

The policewoman's voice suddenly trailed off midsentence. In fact the whole room seemed to stop, even the argument breaking out between a father and son paused, and Natasha looked up as a door beside the counter opened.

She watched the policewoman's cheeks redden, and as Natasha followed her gaze she could certainly see why. Walking into the foyer was possibly the most beautiful man she had ever seen.

*Definitely* the most beautiful, she amended, as he walked past the counter and came into full view. He was tall, with exotic dark looks, his elegance so effortless that he wore even a torn shirt and a black eye well.

He was tousled and unshaven, and the torn shirt allowed for more than a glimpse of one broad coffee-coloured shoulder. As he gave up trying to fasten the broken buttons on his shirt he moved to tuck it in, and even though Natasha looked away the image of a flat stomach with a snake of jet hair danced before her eyes. She struggled to remember the registration number of the car she'd owned for more than five years.

'Maybe you should go and sit down to fill it in?' the policewoman suggested.

Natasha was quite sure she was only being helpful because, now he had moved, Natasha was blocking her view of the exotic prisoner. Still, it was rather nice to sit in a front row seat and every now and then look up from the form to witness him sliding in his belt and buckling it, and then, a moment later, when they were handed to him, slipping on his shoes.

'Are you sure we can't offer you a ride home?' a sergeant asked.

'That won't be necessary.'

His voice was deep and low and richly accented, and despite the circumstances he was very much the one in command—there was an air of haughtiness to him as he took his jacket from the sergeant and brushed it down before putting it on. The gesture, as some dust fell to the floor, was curiously insolent, as if telling all present that he was better than this.

'We really are sorry for the mix-up...' the sergeant continued.

Natasha quickly looked back to her paperwork as *he* made his way over to the bench where she sat, raised a foot and placed it beside her, and proceeded to lace up his shoe. There was a delicious waft that reached her nostrils, the last traces of cologne combined with the essence of male, and though she resisted, though she tried terribly hard not to, her body did what it had to and despite Natasha's best intentions she looked up.

Looked up into a face that was exquisite, into eyes that were at first black but, as she stared, became the indigo of a midnight sky. He let her explore the vastness, let her deep into the reaches of his gaze, then he withdrew that pleasure, his concentration moved back to his footwear and Natasha was for a second lost. So lost that she did not turn her face away, still watched, mouth slightly gaping, as his dark red lips tightened when the sergeant spoke on.

'As I said before, Your Highness...'

Natasha's mouth gaped fully open. No wonder the sergeant was groveling. There was a diplomatic incident unfolding right here in the room.

'...I can only apologise.'

'You were doing your job.' Shoes laced, he stood to his impressive height. 'I should not have been there in the first place. I understand that now. I did not at the time.' He looked down at the policeman and gave a brief nod—a nod that was final, that somehow confirmed he was giving his word. 'It is forgotten.' Relief flooded over the sergeant's face even as His Highness snapped his fingers. 'I need my phone.'

'Of course.'

Natasha was dying to know what had happened, what the mistake had been, but unfortunately she couldn't drag out filling in the form any longer, so she went up to the counter and handed it in. She could feel his dark eyes on her shoulders as she spoke with the policewoman, and as Natasha turned to go their eyes met briefly for the second time. Briefly because Natasha tore hers away, for there was a strange suggestion in his eyes that she could not logically explain.

'Good morning.'

His words were very deliberate and very much aimed at her. They forced her gaze to dart back to him as he greeted her in circumstances where it would be more customary to ignore another person. It was almost inappropriate to initiate a conversation here, and Natasha flushed as she returned his greeting.

'Morning...'

There was the slightest upturn to his mouth—imperceptible, almost, but there—as if he found her voice pleasing, as if somehow he had won, for still he stared. There was a bizarre feeling of danger. Her heart was racing and her breathing was shallow and fast. Instinct told her to run—especially as that haughty mouth now shifted a little further, moved to almost a smile. There was a beckoning in it, and she understood now the danger. For her body still told her to run—except *to* him.

'Thank you.' Natasha turned to the policewoman, thanked her for her assistance, and then, because she had no choice, she walked past him to reach the exit.

It was an almost impossible task, for never had she been so aware—not just of him, but of her own body: the sound of her boots as she clipped past him, the relief in her nostrils as they once again detected him, the burn of his eyes as they unashamedly followed her progress. And, though she could not know, she was certain of the turn of his head as she passed him, and knew he was watching as she walked out through the door.

It was a relief to be out in the rain—never had she had a man so potent linger in his attention on her— and Natasha walked quickly from the police station,

crossing at the lights and then breaking into a run
when she saw her bus. It drove off as she approached
it and she felt like banging on the door as it passed,
even chased it for a futile few seconds, knowing what
she would see now.

She tried not to look—tried to disappear in the
empty bus shelter—but of course she could not. He
walked out of the police station and down the steps
in his slightly muddied tuxedo, and instead of turning up his collar, as most would, he lifted his face to
the rain, closed his eyes and ran a hand over his face
as if he were showering. He made a wet winter morning suddenly beautiful. He made the whole wretched
day somehow worth it for that image alone. Natasha
watched as he lifted his phone to his ear and then
turned around. She realised he was disorientated as
to his location, but he walked on a little farther and
located the name of the suburb from the sign on the
police station's wall.

No, he did not belong here.

He pocketed his phone and leant against the wall. It
was then that he caught her watching. She tried to pretend that she hadn't been. Deliberately Natasha didn't
jerk her head away. Instead she let her gaze travel past
him and then out into the street, willing another bus to
appear, but she could see him in her peripheral vision.
She knew that he had moved from the wall and, ignoring the pedestrian crossing, was walking very directly
towards her. There were angry hoots from drivers as
he halted the traffic and calmly took his time—it was
Natasha's heart that was racing as he joined her in

what once had been *her* shelter. Except it wasn't the rain Natasha needed sheltering from.

He stood just a little nearer to her than was polite. Natasha couldn't really explain why she felt that, because soon the shelter would fill up, and on a rainy morning like this one soon she and any number of strangers would be crammed in like sardines. But for now, while it was just the two of them, he was too close—especially when she knew, was quite sure, that he didn't need to be here. *His people* hadn't told His Highness that perhaps he should get the bus.

What was he doing here? her mind begged to know the answer to the question. What had the mistake been?

'The husband came home.'

His rich voice answered her unspoken question, and despite her best intentions to ignore him Natasha let out a small, almost nervous laugh, then turned her head to him. Immediate was the wish that she hadn't, that she had chosen simply to ignore him, because those eyes were waiting for her again—that face, that body, even his scent; he was almost too beautiful for conversation—better, perhaps, that he remain in her head as an image, a memory, rather than become tainted by truth.

Something deep inside warned Natasha that she should not engage with him, that it would be far safer to ignore him, but she couldn't, and her eyes found his mouth as he spoke on.

'He thought that I was in his house stealing.'

Rakhal looked into green eyes, saw a blush flood her face as it had when last their eyes had met—

only this time there was a parting of her lips as she smiled. But that initial response was brief, for quickly, he noted, she changed her mind. The smile vanished and her words were terse.

'Technically, you were!'

She went back to looking out into the road and Rakhal fought with a rare need to explain himself. He knew what had happened last night did not put him in a flattering light, but given where they had met he felt it important that she knew the reason he had been locked up if he were to get to know her some more.

And of that Rakhal had every intention.

There was a very rare beauty to her. Redheads had never appealed to him, but this morning he found the colouring intriguing. Darkened by the rain, her hair ran in trails along her trenchcoat. He wanted to take a towel and rub it dry, to watch the golds and oranges emerge. He liked too the paleness of her skin that so readily displayed her passions; it was pinking now around her ears. He wanted her to turn again and face him—Rakhal wanted another glimpse of her green eyes.

'I did not know.' He watched her ears redden as he carried on the conversation. 'Of course that is no excuse.'

It was the reason he had assured the policemen he would not be taking things any further—because she was right: technically he had been stealing, and that did not sit well with Rakhal. He could surely live and die a hundred times trying to work out the rules of this land—there were wedding rings, but some chose not to wear them; there were titles, but some chose not to use them; there were, of course, women who chose to lie. And, in fairness to him, it was particularly confusing for Rakhal—for his heartbreaking looks assured that many a ring or a diamond were slipped into a purse when he entered a room. But instead of working out the rules, this morning he chose to work out this woman.

Direct was his approach.

'What were you at the police station for?'

She was tempted just to ignore him, but that would only serve to show him the impact he'd had on her, so she attempted to answer as if he were just another person at a bus stop, making idle conversation. 'My car was stolen.'

'That must be inconvenient,' Rakhal responded, watching her shoulders stiffen.

'Just a bit.' Natasha bristled, because it was far more than *inconvenient*, but then if he was royal, if he was as well off as his appearance indicated, perhaps having his car stolen *would* be a mere inconvenience. But maybe she was being a bit rude. He had done nothing wrong, after all. It was her private response to him that was inappropriate. 'I was supposed to be going on holiday…'

'A driving holiday?'

She laughed. Perish the thought! 'No.' She turned just a little towards him. It seemed rude to keep talking over her shoulder. 'Overseas.'

Those gorgeous eyes narrowed into a frown as he

attempted to perceive the problem. 'Did you need your car to get you to the airport?'

It was easier just to nod and say yes, to turn away from him again and will the bus to hurry up.

They stood in silence as grumpy morning commuters forced him a little closer to her. She caught the scent of him again, and then, after a stretch of interminable silence, when it felt as if he were counting every hair on the back of her head, he resumed their conversation and very unexpectedly made her laugh.

'Couldn't you get a taxi?'

Now she turned and fully faced him. Now she accepted the conversation. Rakhal enjoyed the victory as much as he had enjoyed the small battle, for rarely was a woman unwilling, and never was there one he could not get to unbend.

'It's a little bit more complicated than that.'

It was *so* much more complicated than simply getting a taxi to the airport. Truth be told, she couldn't really afford a holiday anyway; she had lent her brother Mark so much money to help with his gambling debts. She had been hoping to take a break for her sanity more than anything else, because her brother's problems weren't going away any time soon. Still, this dashing stranger didn't need to know all about that— except he did not allow her to leave it there.

'In what way?'

He dragged out a conversation, Natasha recognised. He persisted when others would not. 'It just is.'

Still he frowned. Still he clearly expected her to tell.

Tell a man she had never met? Tell a man she knew nothing about other than that he ignored social norms?

And he was ignoring them again now—as the lengthening bus queue jostled to fit beneath the shelter he placed a hand on her elbow, instead of keeping a respectable shred of distance as the crowd surged behind him, forming a shield around her. And if it appeared manly, it felt impolite.

As impolite as her own thoughts as his fingers wrapped around the sleeve of her coat. For there was a fleeting thought that if the queue were to surge again he might kiss her—a thought too dangerous to follow as her body pressed into him. She moved her arm, turned away from him, and was it regret or relief when she saw her bus?

Natasha put her arm out to hail it and so too did he. Except she quickly realised it wasn't the bus he was summoning—it was a black limousine, with all its windows darkened. The car indicated and started to slow down.

'Can I offer you a lift home?'

'No!' Her voice was panicked, though not from his offer. If the car stopped now then the bus wouldn't. 'It can't park there...'

He didn't understand her urgency, or was incapable of opening a car door himself, because he stood waiting till a man in robes climbed out and opened it for him. 'I insist,' he said.

'Just go,' Natasha begged, but it was already too late. The bus sailed happily past the stop blocked by his vehicle and Natasha heard the moans and protests

from the angry queue behind her—not that it per-
turbed *him* in the least. 'You made me miss my bus!'

'Then I must give you a lift.'

And, yes, she knew she should not accept lifts from
strangers—knew that this man had the strangest effect
on her. She knew of many things in that instant—like
the angry commuters she'd be left with, and the cold
and the wet. Yes, there were reasons both to accept
and to decline, and Natasha could justify either one.

She could never justify the real reason she stepped
into the car, though—a need to prolong this chance
meeting, a desire for her time with this exotic stranger
not to end.

It was terribly warm inside, and there was Arabic
music playing. The seat was sumptuous as she sank
into it, and she felt as if she had entered another
world—especially when a robed man handed her a
small cup that had no handle. She could almost hear
her mother warning her that she would be a fool to
accept.

'It is tea,' she was informed by His Highness.

Yes, her mother might once have warned her, but
she was twenty-four now, and after a slight hesitation she accepted the drink. It was sweet and fragrant,
and it was much nicer to sit in luxurious comfort than
to shiver at the bus stop. She certainly didn't relax,
though—how could she with him sitting opposite her?
With those black eyes waiting for her to look at him?

'Where do you live?'

She gave him her address—she had no choice but
to do so; she had accepted a ride home after all.

'Forgive me,' he said. 'A few hours in a cell and I forget my manners.' His English, though good, was the only part of him that was less than perfect, and yet it made him more so somehow. 'I have not properly introduced myself. I am Sheikh Rakhal, Crown Prince of Alzirz.'

'Natasha Winters.' There was not much she could add to that, but his haughty, beautiful face did yield a small smile when she said, 'Of London.'

Their conversation was somewhat awkward. He asked her where she had been intending to go on holiday, and seemed somewhat bemused by the concept of a travel agent or booking a holiday online. In turn he told her that he was in London for business, and that though he came here often soon he would be returning to his home.

'And now I return you to yours,' he said, as the car turned into her street and slowed down.

Somehow she knew things would not be left there.

'Would you care to join me for dinner tonight?' Rakhal asked. He did not await a response—after all the answer was inevitable. 'I'll pick you up at seven.'

'I'm sorry.' She shook her head. 'I've already got plans.' She flushed a little. She was clearly lying. She had no plans. She was supposed to be jetting off for two weeks and had told him as much. And she was tempted, but they had met in a police station and he was wearing a black eye from an aggrieved husband. It didn't take much to work out that he would want more than dinner.

And so too would she.

She was stunned at her reaction to him; never had a man affected her so. It was as if a pulse beat in the air between them—a tangible pulse that somehow connected them. There was a raw sexual energy to him, a restless prowess, and she dared not lower her guard for this man was far more of a man than she was used to, more male than she had ever encountered before. She reached for the door.

'Wait,' Rakhal said, reaching out his hand and capturing her wrist.

There was a flutter of panic that rose from her stomach to her throat at the thought that he might not let her out—or was that just the effect of contact, for his fingers were warm on her skin?

'You do not open the door.'

Neither, it would seem, did he, for the robed man who had served them tea was the one who climbed out. Rakhal's hand was still on her wrist and she waited. For what, she wasn't quite sure. Another offer of dinner? Or perhaps it was he who was waiting? Maybe he thought she would ask him inside?

She looked at that handsome face, at the mouth that was so sorely tempting, and then at his come-to-bed eyes. She could almost see them reflected there—could envisage them tumbling in her bed. It was a dangerous vision to have, so she pulled her wrist away. 'Thank you for the lift.'

He watched her almost run to her house, saw her safely inside and then gestured to his driver to move on. They rode in silence.

Abdul knew better than to question why Rakhal

had been at a police station, where the bruises were from—it was not an aide's place to question the Crown Prince. He would bring him a poultice later, and again over the next few days, in the hope that the bruises would be gone by his return to Alzirz.

Right now Rakhal had more than bruises and several hours in a prison cell on his mind. He had never been said no to before; quite simply it had never happened—but he did not grace the markets and had no need to barter. Rakhal knew she was not like the women he usually played with but, oh, the heaven of getting her to unbend. It was a shame he was leaving on Monday. She might be worth pursuing otherwise. Still, maybe the next time he visited London... Except he would be a married man by then, and something told him that Natasha would be even more disapproving.

He wished she had said yes.

Natasha thought the same almost as soon as she stepped inside. Away from him she was far more logical—she had just turned down a dinner invitation from surely the most gorgeous man alive. The loss of her holiday and her car seemed like minor inconveniences compared to what she had just denied herself. She moved to the window and watched his car glide off. Her hand moved to her wrist, where his fingers had been. She replayed their conversations again.

He had been nothing but polite, she told herself. It was her mind that was depraved.

She kicked herself all day as she dealt with the car insurance company, and then tried to sound cheerful

when one of her friends rang to tell her they had se-
cured an amazing deal for ten nights in Tenerife. They
would be leaving tonight, and was Natasha quite sure
that she didn't want to change her mind and join them?

Natasha almost did, but then she looked down at the
figure that had been quoted as the excess on her insurance and regretfully turned down her second amazing
offer in one day.

Her brother's debts were not Natasha's responsibility, all her friends said, but actually they were. Natasha
had not told anyone about the loan she had taken out
for him—which was why her friends were unable to
understand why she didn't want to come away on holiday with them, especially after such a hellish year.

To Mark's credit, since she had taken the loan he
had always paid her back on time, and Natasha was
starting to feel as if she could breathe, that maybe he
was finally working things out. A payment was due
tomorrow, and she pulled up her bank account online.
Her emerging confidence in her brother vanished as
she realised that his payment to her hadn't gone in,
and immediately she rang him.

'You'll have it next week.'

Natasha closed her eyes as he reeled off excuses.
'It's not good enough, Mark, the payment's due tomorrow.' She cursed at the near miss—she might have
been *en route* to Tenerife, not knowing that she had
defaulted on a loan payment. 'I can't afford to cover
it, Mark. I had my car stolen last night.' She would not
cry, she was tougher than that, but for so many reasons

today was especially hard. 'When I agreed to get this loan you promised you would never miss a payment.'

'I said you'll have it next week. There's nothing else I can do. Look,' he said, 'how soon till you get the car insurance payout?'

'Sorry?'

'You said your car had been stolen,' Mark said. 'You'll get that payment soon. That will cover it.'

'It might be found,' Natasha said. 'And if it isn't the payout will buy me another car.' But, even though there was so much to be addressed, she was tired of talking about cars and money on today of all days. 'Are you going to the cemetery?'

'Cemetery?'

She heard the bemusement in her brother's voice and anger burnt inside her as she responded. 'It's their one-year anniversary, Mark.'

'I know.'

Natasha was quite sure he'd forgotten. 'Well?' she pushed. 'Are you going?'

As he reeled off yet more excuses Natasha simply hung up the phone and headed to her bedroom. But instead of getting on with tidying up, for a moment or two she sat on her bed, wondering how everything could have gone so wrong. This time last year her life had been pretty close to perfect—she'd just qualified as a teacher and had been doing a job she loved; she had been dating a guy she was starting to if not love then really care for; she'd been saving towards moving out of her parents' house. She had also been looking forward to being a bridesmaid at her brother's wedding.

Now, in the space of a year, all she had known, all she had loved, had been taken. Even her job. As an infant school teacher she had been on a temporary placement and about to be offered a permanent position when the car crash had happened. Knowing she simply couldn't be the teacher she wanted to be while deeply grieving, she had declined the job offer, and the last year had been filled with temporary placements as she waded through her parents' estate.

Their will had been very specific—the family home was to be sold and the profits divided equally between their two children.

How she had hated that—how much harder it had made things having to deal with estate agents and home inspections. And going through all the contents had been agony. It was a job she felt should have been done in stages; she had wanted to linger more in the process of letting go. But Mark had wanted his share and had pushed things along. Her boyfriend, Jason, had been no help either. He'd been uncomfortable with her grief and uncomfortable providing comfort—it had been a relief for Natasha to end things.

And now, one year on, she sat in the small home she had bought that still felt unfamiliar, living a life that didn't feel like her own.

Tears wouldn't change anything; sitting on her bed crying wasn't going to help. She headed downstairs and, one cup of coffee later, unable to face a bus, she called for a taxi, asking him to stop and wait as she went into a florist and bought some flowers.

She hated coming here.

Wasn't it supposed to bring her peace?

It didn't.

She looked at the headstone and all Natasha felt was anger that her parents had been taken far too soon.

'Maybe it's too soon for peace?' Natasha said aloud to them, except her heart craved it.

No, there was no peace to be had at the cemetery, so she took a bus home and had a long bath to warm up.

Anticipating packing for her holiday, Natasha had pulled out all her clothes, and late that afternoon she tackled the mountain strewn over her bedroom. But Rakhal and their brief encounter was still there at the back of her mind, and he was so much nicer to think about than her problems closer to home that she allowed herself a tiny dream...

What if she *had* said yes to him?

What, Natasha wondered, did you wear for dinner with the Crown Prince Sheikh of Alzirz?

Nothing that was in Natasha's wardrobe, that was for sure. Except as she hung up her clothes there it was—still wrapped in its cover. She had never really known what to do with it. It was to have been her bridesmaid's dress for Mark and Louise's wedding, but Louise had called the wedding off a week before the date, which had left Mark devastated. It was then he had started gambling—or rather that was what he had told Natasha when he'd come to her for help. Now she wondered if it had been the reason for Louise calling things off.

She had been so angry with Louise for destroying her brother. The car accident resulting in the death of their parents had been devastating, but the upcoming wedding, though hard to look forward to at first, had been the one shining light—Mark and Louise had been together for years, and her calling it off had had the most terrible effect on Mark.

Yet now Natasha was starting to wonder if Mark had been the one who had destroyed himself—if his gambling problems were in fact not so recent.

She hadn't spoken with Louise since the break-up. Louise had always been lovely, and for the first time Natasha allowed herself to miss her almost-sister-in-law. She resisted the urge to call her, because Louise didn't need to be worried with Mark's problems now.

Instead, Natasha slid open the zip and pulled the dress from its cover. As she gazed at it she wished again that things had turned out differently.

It was gold and very simple, with a slightly fluted hem that was cut on the bias, and thin spaghetti straps that fell into a cowl neck. It would be wrong to pull it on with wet hair and an unmade-up face, for if ever there was a dress that deserved the full effect it was this one.

So Natasha dried hair and then smoothed it with straighteners. Louise had wanted her to wear her hair up. It was the only thing they had disagreed on, but of course it was to have been Louise's day, and so she would have won. Natasha took her thick red hair and twisted it, securing it on the top of the head with a clasp, then put on make-up as best she could. She took out her mother's earrings and necklace, holding the cool pearls in her hand for a moment. Natasha rarely wore jewellery for the same reason she didn't wear perfume: it irritated her skin. But today she made an exception and put the jewels on. It should still be her mother wearing them. How Natasha wished that she could rewind a year, because things had been so much simpler then.

But if she started crying she might never stop, so Natasha looked in the mirror instead. The dress was stunning and Louise had been right—with her hair up it was even more so. The necklace and earrings were the perfect final touch and, again as Louise had assured her, she didn't look like a traditional bridesmaid. More…Natasha looked again and gave a smile. Had she said yes to Rakhal, this was what she would have worn, for now she was fit for a prince.

Still he played on her mind—but then why wouldn't he? He had been the one saving grace in a pretty miserable day. And then she heard a knock at her door.

Perhaps it was Mark bringing over the money? Or an aunt dropping round to mark the one-year anniversary of her parents' passing?

While normally she would have run down the stairs to answer, given how she was dressed Natasha held back and went to the window. She peeked through a gap in the curtain. Peering down into the street, she saw a limousine—but even before that she knew it was him.

Had known at some level that she had been dressing for him.

That this morning their attraction, or whatever it was that had occurred, hadn't all been in her imagination, that he had felt it too.

And now Rakhal was at her door.

# CHAPTER TWO

RAKHAL had spent the day trying to forget Natasha. He had completed the most pressing of his appointments and then peered through the impressive list of female contacts in his phone.

This evening none of them had appealed.

He could, if he'd chosen to, have returned to the exclusive London club he often frequented, where he was assured of a warm welcome from any number of young socialites who would be only too happy to spend a night in a prince's bed.

He'd chosen not to.

Instead he had headed down to the hotel bar, taken a seat in a plump leather chair. In a moment a long glass of water had been placed in front of him, for here in London, it was his drink of choice. Less than two minutes later, another option had appeared. Blonde, beautiful, her smile inviting.

With but a gesture of his hand he could have invited her to join him or have a drink sent over to her.

It was that easy for Rakhal.

Always.

Both here and at home.

He'd thought of the harem that served his every need—the harem that would still serve him even after his marriage—and suddenly he'd been weary with *easy*. He was bored with no thrill to the chase.

He'd gestured to the bartender, who had walked over ready to take his order, to serve the blonde a glass of champagne, but Rakhal had delivered other instructions.

Now the car he had summoned waited as he knocked again at her door. Rakhal did not have time to play games, and neither did he have time to take his time. And yet here he was. All day she had intrigued him. All day his first taste of rejection had gnawed. Perhaps she was already in a relationship? he had pondered. But something told him she was not. There was a shyness to her, an awkwardness he found endearing. Rarely was effort required from him with women— perhaps that was the novelty that had brought him here.

He decided that the novelty would quickly wane, but that thought faded as soon as she opened the door.

It was as though she'd been waiting for him—had somehow anticipated his surprise arrival.

Appealing before, she was exquisite now. Her hair was dry, its true colours revealed: the colours of a winter sky in Alzirz as the sun dipped lower over the desert, reds and oranges and a blaze of fire. His only qualm was that he wanted to see it worn down— *would* see it worn down, Rakhal decided, before the night's end.

'What are you doing here?' Natasha had had her

panic upstairs and was as calm as she could manage now—as casual as she could hope to be when dealing with the sudden arrival of Rakhal.

'I said that I would pick you up at seven.'

'And I told you I had plans...' Natasha started. Yet she did want time with this intoxicating man and her refusal was halted. For all day she had regretted saying no to him, all day she had wished she had said yes, and now she had her chance. 'Actually, my plans have changed...' She hoped her make-up hid her blush as she lied. 'My friend isn't feeling well.'

'Well, now that your plans have changed...' He knew she was lying, and he would not ask her to join him again. He had asked her once, had even come to her door. Now he stood silently awaiting her decision, for it was up to Natasha now—he did not beg.

The decision was an easy one. He was even more beautiful than she remembered him from this morning. He was wearing an immaculate charcoal-grey suit and his hair, messy that morning, was now swept back. The bruise on his eye had turned a deep purple, and Natasha felt her nails dig into her palms as she resisted the urge to reach out and touch it, to run her fingers over the slight swelling at his left cheekbone. It was bizarre the effect he had on her. Never had a man made her more aware of her femininity.

Natasha swallowed, for he made her aware of her sexuality too, in a way no one ever had—certainly not Jason. She was filled with a sudden desperation for the night not to end—and it would, Natasha knew, if she did not go with him now. It would end this instant if she did not simply say yes.

'I'll get my bag.' Natasha hovered a moment, unsure if she should ask him in—embarrassed to do so, but worried it would be rude not to. 'Do you want to—?'

'I will wait here,' Rakhal interrupted. He wanted their night to start, and was not sure if she lived alone. If she did—well, he did not want to ruin any tentative progress with a kiss delivered too soon. It would be hard not to kiss her. He was already growing hard.

He turned out to face the street, to look at the neat hedges and the houses. He tried to fathom her, tried to work her out just a little, surprising himself because for once he had a need to know more about the woman he would be spending the night with.

She found a bag and quickly filled it with her purse and keys, then took a moment more to steady herself than to check her make-up. She found a jacket that didn't really do justice to the dress. Even though it had stopped raining it was a cold, clear night, and she really couldn't go out with bare arms, so she slipped it on and walked down the stairs. She could see his outline in the front doorway as he waited for her to be ready.

He waited too while she locked the door, and then they headed to his car. This time it was his driver who came around and opened the door, and there was no man in robes waiting inside when she climbed in. She was nervous at being alone with him.

Yet he was the perfect gentleman. He took the seat opposite rather than next to her, making polite conversation as the car moved through the dark streets.

He did nothing and said nothing untoward—in fact he didn't even comment on how she was dressed. No doubt he was used to going out with women dressed up to the nines. She wondered how he'd have reacted if he knew just how unusual this was for her, if she'd answered the door in jeans and slippers. Would the outcome have been the same? Would he have waited while she changed...? Would the usual outfits in her wardrobe have sufficed for a night like this?

She doubted it.

Yet he had seen her dripping wet this morning, had seen her at her worst, and still there had been *want* between them. The doubt blurred as she pondered this most stunning man. She could see his hand resting on his thigh, the dark skin, the manicured nails, and then she turned her gaze away when she realised he was watching her too. Her jacket felt like a blanket. The car was too warm. Both these things she blamed for the heat that spread across her body as she admitted her desire. She wanted to press a button, wanted the window to open and the night air to blast her face cool. When they turned a corner and his stretched-out leg rolled just a little nearer to her rigid feet she wanted to lift her feet to his waiting hands, to simply be ravished.

They pulled up outside a luxurious hotel. As the door opened Natasha saw faces turning and was uncomfortable with this rare scrutiny from onlookers. She was grateful when his hand took her arm, and told herself that it was Rakhal they were looking at as they were welcomed and then led through the hotel and into a restaurant.

Again he turned heads.

Natasha knew it had nothing to do with *her*, for the place was filled with jewelled and made-up women. It was Rakhal who drew the eye, Rakhal who had forks pausing on their way to ruby-red mouths and small murmurs rippling across tables as people attempted to place him. And no wonder, Natasha thought as she took a seat, with his dark looks, his elegance, there was a poise to him that could never truly be taught.

And tonight *she* was dining with him.

The table was beautifully set with white tablecloths and candles, and the silverware and glasses gleamed, yet it was not the luxurious surroundings that unnerved her, but the company that she kept. It wasn't his title that intimidated either—well, perhaps a bit, Natasha conceded—but really it was the man himself that had her stomach folding over on itself, had her still unsure as to whether she should have said yes to his offer. Because despite the silk of his manners there was that edge to him. She knew she had taken on more than she could ever handle.

The waiters lavished attention on them, pulling out chairs and spreading napkins over their laps as Rakhal ordered champagne.

Natasha declined. 'Not for me, thank you. I'd prefer to drink water.' Oh, she knew the cost of a bottle of champagne would be nothing to him, but somehow she didn't want to feel beholden, and she was also mindful that her common sense was somewhat lacking around him. Champagne might only exacerbate the fact.

Rakhal too, it seemed, was only drinking water, for

he cancelled the champagne, ordered iced water and then turned his attention to Natasha. 'Is there anything you are allergic to?' he asked. 'Or anything you particularly do not like to eat?'

'Oh!' It was a rather unusual question. 'I'll just wait to have a look at the menu, thank you.'

'I will make the selections,' Rakhal responded.

Natasha felt her lips tighten. She certainly did not want him choosing her dinner for her, and she told him the same. 'I'd like to wait and see the menu.'

She was determined to win on this—for this was a man who didn't usually take no for an answer. Not this morning when she had declined his lift, nor tonight when he had come to her door despite her turning down his invitation to dinner. And now he thought he could choose what she ate. Well, he had chosen the wrong person if that was the case.

Her voice held a warning when she spoke again. 'I can order for myself, thank you!'

'I'm sure you can. But I have asked my chef to prepare a banquet, so he needs to know if there are foods to which you are averse.'

'Your chef?'

'I stay regularly at this hotel and so I ensure there is a chef from Alzirz. Naturally when I'm away the other guests get to sample his delightful cooking, but tonight he is preparing food exclusively for us...' He watched the movement in her throat as she swallowed. 'Of course I can have him come out and discuss your preferences, if you'd prefer...?'

'No.' Natasha shook her head, her face flushed,

more than a little embarrassed at the fuss she had made. 'That won't be necessary.'

And Rakhal watched her blush, visible even in candlelight. 'Perhaps I could have somebody write down the ingredients so you can check through them...' He was enjoying this now.

'Of course not. I'm sure it will be lovely. It is more that I thought you were choosing *for* me...'

'I am,' Rakhal said, and watched her rapid blinking. 'Tonight you are my guest, and you should not be worrying about making decisions. Say I were to come to your house tomorrow for dinner...' He watched the red darken on her cheeks as she pictured it. 'Perhaps you would ask my preferences, but you would not give me a menu.' He leaned forward a little. 'You would prepare dishes that you thought might please your guest. Well, I do not cook, but I have asked my chef to do the same...to cook with foods that are fresh and flown in from my country.'

'You have food flown in?' How spoilt *was* this man? she wondered, taking a sip of her drink.

'And water too...' Rakhal responded without a qualm. 'I am served water that is sourced from my home.'

She paused as she raised the glass to her lips. French champagne probably cost less. And then, as he had since the moment they met, he surprised her again.

'If I am to give wise counsel then I should be nourished by my land...'

A waiter topped up her glass as the first course

was brought: a selection of dips and breads and fruits. Rakhal explained his selections.

'The water is from a spring deep in the desert, and this is what I always start with.' He picked up a date and a small silver knife. 'Usually they are served quartered, but I prefer to pit my own.'

He slid the knife through the shiny fruit and exposed the stone. She felt her stomach curl as he inverted the date and popped the stone out. How, Natasha tried to fathom, could slicing a date be seductive?

Dates were something her grandmother served at Christmas.

Dates were prunes.

Dates were not sexy.

He dipped it in some oily goo and she watched his long slender fingers swirl it around. Then he lifted it to her mouth and she accepted, trying to touch only the fruit. But her lips met his fingers and she had to force her mouth not to linger, to take the fruit, not to capture his hand and taste his fingers. It scared her, the effect he had on her, the places he took her mind to. And she knew that he knew it as he pulled his hand away.

As Natasha chewed the rich fruit, she amended her thoughts.

Dates *were* sexy.

'It is called *haysa al tumreya*.'

His voice was low and for her ears only, and she tasted the hot sauce around the sweet date as she listened.

'The date tree is the most important. It provides shade around the spring...'

As they ate he told her about the oasis in the desert, about the fruits and ripe peaches for nectar and about the aubergines that made the *baba ganoush* she tried next. It held a smoky flavour that had her closing her eyes in bliss as she tasted it. He told her about the foods that grew beneath the tall date trees, and she ate and she listened and she looked, and he was intriguing rather than spoilt, and at each turn more beautiful still.

Rakhal was right. It was nice to be spoiled, not to have to make any decisions, simply to listen and to talk as they shared the sumptuous food. He told her a little about his land, about his life in Alzirz, and she told him a little about herself too—or rather he asked her about her family.

'My parents were killed last year in a motor accident,' Natasha said. She waited for the flurry of sympathy, but he simply stared and waited for her to go on. 'I have an older brother. Mark.'

'And he takes care of you?'

'I take care of *myself*,' Natasha answered. Aware her response might have been a little brittle, she softened it. 'It's been a difficult year, but I manage.'

She was relieved when they were disturbed by the waiters bringing another impressive course, and then he told her more about the land from which he came. About the palace that looked out to the ocean and the desert abode to which he escaped.

'It sounds beautiful.'

'You would love it,' Rakhal assured her, and for a moment he glimpsed her there—the jewel in his harem.

They ate more food from his country, and she could taste the sun. When he could not hear something she said he moved his chair around the table until he sat next to her. Dessert was a shared plate, and he fed her fruit from his fingers again. Sometimes Natasha forgot she was in a busy restaurant. Sometimes she forgot her own inexperience under the gaze of this very experienced man. For his voice made her ears ache to hear him, had her inching a little closer to him.

For Rakhal too this night was different. There was candour—he normally would not tell a woman such things about his home, about his life and his thoughts, but with her conversation was pleasing. Now they were speaking of traditions, and he was honest—telling her that one day he would marry, that he would return to Alzirz and select his bride. Though he was not completely honest, for he did not tell her it would be soon.

'How do you choose?' She was more than a little curious. 'Will she be wealthy? From another royal family, perhaps?'

'We do not need wealth—Alzirz is rare in that its royals choose their partners from the people. My grandmother was Sheikha Queen; my grandfather was a wise man from the desert. She chose him for his knowledge, for at times the country moves too quickly and we need to remember the ways and teachings of old. When I am King...'

'You will be *King*!' Natasha couldn't keep the surprise from her voice. 'Are you scared?'

He gave her an extremely quizzical look. 'I am never scared.'

She doubted he was. She had never met a man so assured. 'So you're the eldest?'

'I have no brothers or sisters.' He saw her slight frown and it was merited—because in his country it was expected that there would be many heirs. It was imperative to the country's survival, in fact. 'My mother died giving birth.'

'I'm sorry.'

Rakhal did not do sentiment. He had been brought up without it and, as his father had explained, he could not miss someone he had never known. But there was a twist somewhere inside him as she expressed her condolences.

'What was she like?'

'She died giving birth to me,' Rakhal said again. 'How would I know?'

It was certainly rarely discussed. In fact Rakhal could only recall a few brief conversations where his mother had been mentioned even in passing. Needing more, he had once spoken with an old man in the desert—a man who, it was rumoured, had lived for one hundred and twenty yellow moons. But tonight was the first time someone had directly asked him about his mother.

'You must know *something*?'

'She was from the desert too,' Rakhal said. 'From an ancient tribe with rare lineage.' He remembered what the old man had told him. 'She was apparently a wise and beautiful soul.'

He had revealed too much—or rather more than he was used to. He looked down and saw their hands intertwined. Rakhal was not usually a man who held hands, not in this way, and so he reverted to ways more usual for him to get the night back to where he felt safer. He pressed his thumb into her palm. The beat of pressure and the slide of his fingers around her wrist had the colour rising on her cheeks. He was tired of talking. He wanted to bed her. But when she did not return the pressure, when she rather pointedly removed her hand from his, Rakhal made no attempt to retrieve it.

'I should take you home.'

He should, for the restaurant was practically empty. And yet she was curiously disappointed and terribly conflicted as he led her through the foyer. He'd been the perfect gentleman—only she wasn't sure it was a perfect gentleman she wanted. But their night was coming to its conclusion, for she would not be asking him in.

And perhaps Rakhal realised that. Realised that this might be his last chance. For he halted her, turned her to face him.

'Have you enjoyed this evening?'

'Very much.'

'I have enjoyed talking with you.'

She did not understand how rare, how unique this compliment was—could not understand that Rakhal did not do deep conversations with the women he dated. And yet he had enjoyed talking with Natasha.

He smiled to himself as the colour rose from her neck to her ears. He saw the pearls that hung from her earlobes and his fingers moved and captured one.

'These are beautiful.'

'They were my mother's. I don't usually wear jewellery...' She moved her head away from him—just a little, but enough to signal a warning. A warning Rakhal did not heed. Instead his other hand moved to the jewel that hung on her chest, a heavier pearl, and he recognised its beauty. He was surrounded by it after all.

'Why not?'

'I don't like it...' She could hardly get the words out, could not carry on a conversation with his hands so close, with his fingers grazing her flesh. 'It irritates...' she attempted. But it didn't tonight, and neither did the fingers near her throat. Her skin almost begged for more of him. 'But I make an exception sometimes for these.'

'I can see why. The pearls are exquisite.'

She could hardly breathe. One hand was at her ear, the other near her throat, and she felt trapped, cornered—but deliciously so.

'They were actually my grandmother's...' Her voice was too high and breathy. She was sure he did not want her family history—except these were the one precious thing that remained. Oh, they weren't worth a fortune, but the antique rose-gold was precious, and there was just so much history there. 'And her mother's before that. She...'

Rakhal picked up a strand of red hair that had escaped from the clasp and ran it through his fingers, then brushed it behind her ear, his fingers trailing along her neck. His knowing eyes watched the pulse quicken. Feeling the beat of it on his warm fingers, he wanted her hair down. He wanted to taste her mouth and he wanted it *now*.

Perhaps he knew how his kiss would affect her. For before it was delivered he moved her to a wall, to a darkened alcove away from other guests and the night concierge, to a place where she was almost alone with him. And there was so much want in his dark eyes, so much sex in his gaze, it frightened her more than he could know.

'Perhaps I should…' Natasha had started to tell him she should perhaps get home, because now the moment had arrived she was both wanting and terrified, but then she could not speak for his mouth was on hers.

He had chosen his moment carefully, in the midst of a sentence, when her mind was just a touch less on him. He tasted first lipstick, and he saw her eyes widen, and then he did not look any more. He closed his eyes and felt instead—felt her momentary resistance, a brief flailing in his arms and then acceptance.

And she did accept—for how nice it was to kiss him, or rather to be kissed by such a man. Nothing came close, for when his mouth found hers quite simply it overruled.

It overruled fear, it overruled logic, it blew out logical thought processes—all it did was consume. All night she had wondered about this moment, when the skilled attack might come, and even with him so close, still when the moment had arrived it had surprised her. And the kiss surprised her too, for it surpassed all she had known, all she'd thought she knew, all she'd even dreamed. His lips were soft, yet firm, and extremely insistent. His hands were precise. They went to her shoulders and kept her still as he kissed her thoroughly, as he drowned that first futile hint of protest with his mouth, and she felt the muscle of his tongue and flared at the taste of him.

Completely instant was her response, and there, beneath the layer of cologne that had teased her since the morning, was a musky male scent that was simply a trigger, for her hands shot to his hair and her fingers knotted into the silken raven locks. It revealed more than teasing for her senses, for his hair was glossy with exotic pomade, and she inhaled the oils. Her mouth moved to his command, and when it did, when she was gone, when he knew she was ready, he toppled her a little more against him, moved her deeper into his embrace.

It was more instinct than a plan he was following now. For Rakhal, too, this kiss was different. It was a kiss that was not just about what was to follow.

Rarely did he fully indulge—when he returned to Alzirz, in the time before he chose his wife, every need of his would be met by his harem. There would be no need to kiss, no need to arouse. It would be *his* pleasure that was the mutual goal. And then he would marry— and, yes, he would kiss and arouse his wife, but with a different aim. For she would be removed from his bed after two days. And as he waited for news of a suc- cessful coupling his harem would indulge him again.

But here in this strange country there were different rules: women's demands were different. It was a place where you kissed for pleasure.

What a pleasure.

His tongue was probing, his chin rough, his mouth smooth, and his hands knowing—reading her want as if it were dotted in Braille on her dress. They were down at her waist and then at her hips, pulling her in a little more, enough for her to feel his hardness. She gasped into his mouth and forgot her surroundings, arched him. He pressed her in still further and she felt him through her clothes, felt a rare wild recklessness—*that* was what he made her feel—that a man she had met just this morning could have her cast her morals to the wind.

He would never know the struggle as she forced her body to halt.

He felt her lips pull away and could only admire her, for there was heat beneath his fingers and her breath was rapid and soft on his cheek, her eyes dilated with arousal. Another moment, Rakhal was sure, she'd have come—and not just to his room.

'I will get you home.'

She was shaking beneath his fingers and he must not rush her. She was a virgin, Rakhal was quite sure of it—which was an incredibly rare treat these days.

*Tomorrow,* Rakhal vowed.

On his last night as a single man in London he would bed her.

Rakhal was completely certain.

# CHAPTER THREE

THE ride home was not what she was expecting.

Natasha had thought, as she stepped into the limousine, that she would spend the journey fending him off—especially when this time he sat next to her. She had, after all, felt his fierce erection, had tasted the passion of his kiss. Her lips still felt bruised and swollen, and her body could not settle.

His thigh sometimes met hers as the vehicle turned a corner, but there was no repeat of the kiss, and, unlike Natasha, Rakhal seemed completely calm, perhaps even a little indifferent. She wondered if he was annoyed—if perhaps he thought she had led him on... She wasn't even sure, as they pulled up at her house, if she would see him again—but so badly she wanted to.

He did not attempt to reclaim her mouth. Just gave her a brief kiss on the cheek as the driver came round to get the door. Nor did he try to angle for an invitation to come in.

He wished her goodnight and saw the flicker of confusion in her eyes as the car door was opened and cold air climbed in. Rakhal knew exactly what he was doing. Tonight she would lie burning, recalling their kiss, wondering if he would call her, and he would keep her wondering—would time things carefully. When she was sure she had blown it, when she was sure it was over, her doorbell would ring and there would be flowers and jewels to soothe her, and…

Rakhal watched her climb out of the car, saw the feminine curves that tomorrow he would caress, and for the second time in his life thought he would enjoy choosing a gift. He had kissed her as she wore gold and he would take her when she wore silver. A dress would be included in his gift…

Not that Natasha knew that.

She should be relieved, she told herself. She had had the most wonderful night, Rakhal had been a wonderful companion, not quite the perfect gentleman, and yet she was disappointed. Her body still twitched from his touch; her heart still skipped as she reached her door.

She turned around and gave a brief wave. She certainly would not ask him in to her modest house. But as she went to push in the key she frowned as the door opened under the weight of her hand alone and she saw that the lock was broken.

The driver awaited Rakhal's instruction, and Rakhal waited for her to step inside. He frowned as she turned to him. Her eyes were urgent and he could see the fear on her face. Immediately he stepped from the car.

She didn't need to say it. One look into the hall and it was clear she had been burgled.

He walked past her, went straight inside, and saw
that it was in chaos. Drawers had been pulled out, and
the sofa had been slashed. He halted Natasha as she
went to run upstairs, caught her wrist and pulled her
down to his level.

'I will check upstairs,' Rakhal said, instantly taking control. 'You will wait in my car.'

He was relieved that he had not driven off sooner,
worried too as to what might have happened if he had
not taken her out that night. He went to climb the stairs
and check for himself if the intruder was still there.
Rakhal had no fear, his irritation was only that she did
not obey him—for as he reached the top of the stairs
Natasha came up behind him.

'Go back down,' he ordered. 'I told you to wait in
the car.'

But she brushed past him, opening her bedroom
door, and he heard her sob of horror. He was black
with fury. The mattress was slashed too, the wardrobe
emptied, boxes, bags—everything lay strewn and torn.

'You are to go down and wait in the car.' His driver
had come into the house now, and he was almost as
dark and as forbidding as his master. Rakhal spoke to
him in Arabic. 'Go with him,' Rakhal said. 'You are
safe. I will call the police…'

'Please don't.' They were the first words she had
spoken since leaving the car and he could hear the
shock and terror in her voice. 'Please, Rakhal, I don't
want you to call the police.'

'Of course I must. You must report this…'

'No!'

She'd held onto her tears for so long, scared of what she might unleash, and she held them back now. She pressed her fingers into her eyes to stop them from falling, clamped her mouth on her chattering teeth and swallowed the scream that was building.

She managed words instead, scarcely able to believe what she was saying, yet knowing in her heart that it was true. 'I think that's exactly what my brother wants me to do.'

She was incredibly grateful that Rakhal was here, that he did not ask questions, that he did not pry. Instead he held her for a moment and then led her to his car. He poured something into a small glass and then added water and ice. She watched the fluid turn milky. This time it was not tea.

'Arak,' he informed her, and she took a sip.

It was strong and sickly and she tasted anise. It burnt as it made its way down to her stomach. She sipped slowly as he made a few phone calls—though not to the police, for he spoke in his own language.

'I have people coming to the house to make sure it is safe.' He looked at her. 'Are you sure you do not want me to call the police?'

'I don't think I'll be calling to report the robbery,' Natasha said.

'You really believe that your brother would do this to you?'

'I don't know what to think at the moment,' Natasha admitted. 'But if it was him I'm not sure I'm ready to turn in my own brother.' Panic was rising within her.

Maybe she was wrong. Maybe it was a simple burglary. 'I don't know what to do—'

'I told you earlier,' Rakhal interrupted, 'you do not have to make any decisions tonight.' There was no question of him leaving her here to deal with this alone. 'You will come back to my hotel with me.'

# CHAPTER FOUR

'EVERYTHING is being taken care of.'

They were back at the hotel, in his sumptuous suite, though Natasha didn't really take in her surroundings. She sat on a chair as he made another phone call, and despite the warmth of the room she felt as cold as if she was sitting out in the street. It wasn't so much the burglary that had upset her, more the thought that Mark could stoop so low. She knew that now she was safe, and that now that things were being dealt with, Rakhal would have some questions, but when he came off the phone he told her first what he had done.

'I have a member of my staff at your home,' Rakhal explained. 'I have informed him that he is not to touch anything—that will give you some time to decide how you want to proceed. Now, I must ask you again—do you really think your brother did this?'

'Yes.' It was the most terrible admission, it actually hurt to say it, but she was tired of covering up for Mark and exhausted from the stress.

'Why would he terrify you like this?'

'Money.' Natasha's eyes briefly met Rakhal's, but

then she tore her gaze away, guilty at her admission, as if she were betraying Mark by voicing it. She still hoped that she was wrong. 'I'm going to ring him…'

'And say what?'

'I don't know,' Natasha admitted. 'Maybe I'm wrong…' Her heart lurched with hope she knew was false. 'Maybe I've just been incredibly unlucky to have my car stolen and my house broken into on the same day…' Then she closed her eyes, remembering what her brother had said about the car insurance.

'I will give you some privacy,' Rakhal said, and she was grateful for that.

She spoke with Mark for perhaps a minute at best, and then sat for a moment or two more in silence, till Rakhal came out. She gave him a pale smile.

'I'm not unlucky.'

'I'm sorry.'

So too was Natasha—more than he could know.

'Did he admit to it?' Rakhal asked.

'Of course not,' Natasha said. 'And he doesn't even suspect that I think it's him—I just knew from his voice, from the questions he asked…'

'Natasha, can you tell me what is going on?'

'It's not your concern.' She really hadn't told anybody. Oh, her friends knew in part, but she had never really revealed all of it to anyone. 'It's better that you don't get involved.'

'I became involved when you asked that I do not call the police,' Rakhal said, and then he looked at her pale features, and the unshed tears in her eyes, and in an unguarded moment he spoke from his heart. 'And you are my concern.'

She was.

Whatever had taken place today would not end as he had first planned. He knew that this was more than one of his regular one-night stands—knew that even when he flew to the desert on Monday, even when he married, still she would be on his mind.

Still he would take care of her.

'It's complicated,' Natasha said.

Rakhal doubted that it was, but he said nothing. Instead he let her talk.

'My brother was supposed to get married six months ago.' She hated talking about family things—her parents had always been so private and she was too. You dealt with things without asking for help; that was the way she had been brought up. Yet her brother didn't seem to have inherited the same resilience. 'A week before the wedding his fiancée, Louise, called it off.'

Still Rakhal said nothing, simply let her speak.

'Since then he's been going off the rails. When my parents died the family home was sold...that's when I bought my house—well, some of it. I have a mortgage...' Natasha said, uncomfortable discussing money with a man who clearly had so much of it. She was worried that he'd think she was asking for his help.

But he gave her a nod, told her to go on. And she wasn't exactly volunteering the information—his silence was dragging it out of her.

'But after he and Louise broke up Mark just burnt his money.'

'Burnt?' Rakhal frowned.

'Not literally,' she answered. 'He started gambling, bought a flash car... He owes a lot of people money. A couple of months ago I took out a loan for him. I was able to get one because I had the house...'

'Is he repaying the loan?'

'He was—but not this month.'

'One moment.' His phone was ringing. He glanced at it before answering, then took the call.

Natasha sat there as he spoke in his language, and it gave her a pause. She was embarrassed and angry that her one perfect night had turned out like this—that yet again Mark had spectacularly ruined things. She was embarrassed, too, at all she had told Rakhal, and Natasha wanted out.

'Where are you going?'

'Home,' Natasha said. 'Look, thank you for a lovely evening. I really am sorry about how it turned out.'

'You're not going home.'

She gave a tight smile—she certainly didn't need this.

'I'll be fine...'

'Natasha, that call was from my aide. Your brother has just gone to your home. It would seem he is a very angry man. He's looking for some jewels. He says that they are his...'

She knew that that was what he had been looking for—the pearls she was wearing tonight—that Mark would insist she put them down as stolen on her insurance claim and, worse than that, in her heart she knew that had she not been wearing them he would have sold them. He would have sold them and then had her claim the insurance money. She was simply too drained to cry, too exhausted to think.

'You must rest,' Rakhal said. 'I will ring and book you a suite.'

'I don't need a suite,' Natasha said. 'The sofa will be fine.'

'My guests do not sleep on a sofa.' He was in no mood to argue, and neither was he that much of a gentleman. 'And neither do I.'

'Please, don't...' She ran a worried hand over her forehead. It seemed stupid but she did not want to be alone—and if that was the price... She recalled his kiss, the bliss she had found in his arms, and knew it was a price she was only too willing to pay.

But Rakhal did not like to win by default. And then he saw her jump as her phone rang, saw tension tighten her features as she took the call.

'That's not your concern, Mark.' She screwed her eyes closed. 'There isn't much missing... *I'll* decide if I speak to the police.'

'Turn off the phone,' Rakhal instructed. He was worried for her. Her brother was out of control now that his plan was not working. 'You did not tell him where you are?' Rakhal checked.

'I just told him I had booked into a hotel. He'd never guess it's this one...'

Rakhal wasn't taking any chances. 'You will stay here tonight.' There was another bedroom in his luxurious suite and he showed it to her. 'A bath has been

run for me but you are to take it. You need some time
to wind down. I will have a shower first…'

Natasha sat in the lounge as he showered, touched
that he had not pressed her in any way, had not taken
her in his arms to comfort her, for she knew very well
how it could have turned out. She was terribly glad that
he had been there—tried not to picture how tonight
might have been had she not met Rakhal.

'I am done.'

He walked into the lounge, a white towel around his
hips, and she saw the snake of hair she had glimpsed
that morning, the bruises on his shoulder from his
battle with the police and the aggrieved husband. His
skin was wet, his hair was too, and in the middle of
one of the worst nights she glimpsed the possibility of
the best night of her life. Her throat was tight as she
looked at him and, though touched at his thoughtful-
ness, that he had not pressed, a part of her rued it too.

'I am going to bed,' Rakhal said, for he could feel
the change in her tension, could see the need for escape in her eyes, and he too was remembering their
kiss. But he would keep his word to himself. 'You take
your time. Tonight this is your home.'

She let out a breath as he closed the bedroom door,
then headed to the bathroom and undressed. She
should be in tears, or scared or something, but she
looked in the mirror and saw lust in her eyes, and she
was so very aware that he was near.

Natasha had thought that, given it had been run a
while ago, the bath would be cool when finally she

stepped into it, but of course it was scented and warm, for she was in *his* world now…and she wanted his bed.

Rakhal wanted her too. He lay awake and tried not to think of her bathing. There was no question of sleeping. He was more than used to a woman in his suite—just not in the spare room. He listened to the gurgle as the water drained, and tried and failed not to picture her climbing out. He was hard beneath the sheet but he resisted, lay there liking the rare feeling of unsated arousal, savouring his restraint, anticipating the reward—because tomorrow he knew she'd be his.

He did not regret his earlier choice of words to her. She *was* his concern now.

Except on Monday he must return to his land and time was fast running out. He thought of the harem, but perhaps she would not be receptive to that suggestion, and he thought too about keeping her as a mistress in London. It was an intensely pleasurable thought; he would grant her the gold stamp in her passport that would give her full privileges, would enable her to visit him freely. When he heard her pad past his door he had to bite on his lip so as not to summon her in and share the news.

He had promised himself tomorrow.

A prince did not break a vow.

# CHAPTER FIVE

Natasha was awoken by the sound of silence—only then did she realise the full extent of the usual background noise of a hotel. The heating whirred and then stilled; the alarm clock stopped ticking; the darkness blackened further. Natasha sat up, taking a moment to remember where she was and all that had happened. She tried the light at her bedside but it wasn't working, and then patted the end of the bed. She found the thick bathrobe, still damp from her bathing. Pulling it on, she made her way out of bed, her hands in front of her to find the window, but even as she parted the blinds there was nothing to see: the streetlights and neon signs were all out.

'It's a power cut.' Rakhal had been awake anyway, and he spoke as soon as she opened her bedroom door. 'The back-up generator should kick in soon...'

It was darker than she had ever known it, and she was grateful when he crossed the room. Then she felt awkward as she put her hand up to him and encountered skin.

'Sorry.' Even though it begged to linger she pulled

her hand away, and despite the dark she was sure he was smiling at her nervousness.

But Rakhal was not smiling. His eyes were long accustomed to the dark and he could see the parting of her lips. He was resisting the urge to kiss her, for all night the kiss they had shared had been driving him wild.

He could smell her, and it was different—for the bath had been prepared for *him*, and her feminine scent now mingled with the exotic oils of the desert. He wanted to take her, wanted to stay in the darkness and simply give in. And he could, Rakhal realised, for it was tomorrow now—midnight had long since gone. So he lowered his head and brushed her lips. She jerked her head just a bit, and then he found her mouth again.

Just a dust of his lips was all he gave her, and then again, and then once more. It was a different kiss, a tease of a kiss, because this time it was Rakhal who pulled his lips back just a little, till her hungry mouth searched for his.

And still his mouth stayed gentle. It was Natasha's lips that were insistent. But he did not return the pressure till her mouth was almost begging, raining kisses on lips that stayed loose, and then he relented, gave her the bliss of his tongue and a mouth that was slow and measured. He made sure she was frantic for his soothing and then, without warning, without even subtly checking, his hand slipped into her dressing gown and caressed a nipple that was hard and waiting. He slid his palm over the soft skin till it was essential that his other hand held her or she might sink to the floor.

But he did not hold her.

He let her become dizzy and weak, he let his towel fall, and she let her robe open so his manhood rested on her stomach. Her lips were on his shoulder now, she was leaning on him as if to regroup, but he did not let her; he kissed her ear to blot out the whispers of doubt that chained her and licked at the tender flesh beneath her lobe till she moaned on his shoulder. Her hand moved to explore what would soon be inside her. He kissed her neck and tasted the pearls, kissed the pulse that thrummed against his lips. Her unskilled fingers felt sublime as he moved his hand to slide beneath her waist, and he inwardly cursed at a knock at the door.

He ached with regret as he tied her belt and then picked up his towel, and she stood blushing and burning and wanting as he let in a frantic butler, loaded with candles and eager to ensure that their most esteemed guest was all right, explaining that the whole of London had been blacked out.

Rakhal was annoyed at the intrusion, though in the circumstance it was to be expected, and at least, he conceded, when they were alone again he'd get to start all over with Natasha and he did like her kisses. Also, the lounge room was not the most convenient of locations. He would have had to interrupt her anyway to take her to his room so that he could sheathe.

'Let us look at the view,' Rakhal suggested, for he could certainly do with some fresh air while the butler set up candles around the suite.

'What view?' Natasha asked, because all of London had been plunged into darkness. There were just a few

cars on the road giving out light, a few people stepping onto the street to see what had happened. It was
surreal, for it was more dark than she could ever have
imagined.

'This view,' Rakhal said—and then she looked up.

The sky was a blaze of stars. The more she looked
the more she saw—a swirl of masses that moved and
glittered—and there were purples and blues, and the
majesty of the sky she lived under was only now revealed.

'It's amazing.'

'It is nothing compared to the desert,' Rakhal said,
but it was an amazing sight indeed—though his eyes
had turned to her now, and he could see the white robe,
could see the glitter in her eyes.

He wanted to show her the stars in the desert. He
told her a little about it—that the roof of his desert
abode was pulled back at night so he could sleep under
the stars, as did true desert people. Not every night,
he told her, but on nights when he needed to think…

And he told her a little of the land that was beautiful. He told her ear, for her body was now against
him as they revisited their kiss. Except the pause had
Natasha thinking—had her knowing that she needed to
be brave, that there was something he needed to hear.
She was embarrassed at the thought of his reaction.

'Rakhal…' She pulled back from his kiss. 'I need
to tell you something…'

'You don't.'

He knew already.

'I was in a relationship…' He frowned but she could

not see it. 'The thing is….' She burnt as she said it.
Yes, she respected morals, but in this she had been
hurt. 'I haven't slept with anyone before—he wanted
to wait till we were married…'

He felt her skin burning beneath his fingers and the
answer for Rakhal was simple.

'Then he should have married you.'

And Natasha had thought the same—not that she
had wanted marriage to him, more that she had wanted
his desire. Had wanted him not to be able to resist her.
Had wanted an ardour that simply hadn't been there.

But it was here now.

'I know we come from different worlds…' She was
being brave again. 'I'm not expecting…' It was terribly awkward to say to a man she had known only for
one day, but Rakhal said it for her.

'I will marry someone from my land.' Rakhal was
not awkward about discussing such things. 'But for
now I can adore *you*.'

And he would adore her later too, he decided, for
she would be his mistress. But he would not dazzle her,
would not confuse her. He would tell her gently of his
ways, for he was determined to keep her.

'Tonight we get to know each other, and if you are
still sure in the morning…'

She was sure already.

They moved into his bedroom and he pulled back
every curtain and opened all the windows. The air
blew out the candles beside them until only those at
the far end of the room remained. Their light lit the

bed a little. He made no apology for the temperature; instead he peeled off her robe and led her to his bed.

And she shivered—but not from the cold—as he kissed her, and after a night spent tossing and turning it was a relief to lie down naked next to him.

He was so broad and so male. Her only regret was that she could not see him properly. But her hands searched him instead—the chest and the shoulders and the stomach that had teased.

His hands caressed her too as he spoke.

She wanted to know about him, wanted to know more of his mysterious ways, and even if the conversation seemed a strange one to be having as they touched each other's bodies there was a need to understand him, to learn all she could while she could, for she knew it would not be for ever.

They were facing each other, talking between kisses, his thigh over hers and his hand in her hair. His mouth was at her neck and then down at her breast, and how lucky was his future bride, to have this every night, Natasha thought as his lips nuzzled her skin. And maybe she said it, for somewhere deep in the darkness he told her he would be with his wife for just two nights a month.

'You'll only sleep together two times?'

Rakhal laughed, but it was more a low growl as he lifted his mouth from her breast. 'Much more than two times,' he explained, for he wanted her to learn his ways, wanted her back in Alzirz with him—which meant she needed a little of the truth. 'For two days and nights we will be together...'

'And then?' She could hardly breathe. His mouth was suckling at her breast, and she almost did not want him to answer for the feeling was sublime, but he lifted his lips and blew cold air onto her wet flesh before speaking.

'She will be taken away and hennaed, and then she will rest as we wait to see.'

'And then?'

His hand was on her stomach, moving towards her intimate curls. 'If there is no pregnancy she returns again when she is fertile.'

'You will hope she is pregnant, then?' Natasha said, for she would want to be back in his bed. 'So you can see each other again?'

'No,' he corrected. 'If she is pregnant then I do not see her till after the birth.'

'But…'

She could not understand, but he did try to explain. 'She will rest and be pampered.'

'I'm sure she'd rather be with you,' Natasha said, 'and you with her.' She blinked at the impossibility of it—to be married and kept apart. 'So you'd go for months…' she was more than a little embarrassed to voice it '…without…?'

'Without seeing her,' he confirmed.

'I meant…' She swallowed, for his hand was moving to her thigh now. 'Without sleeping together…' His warm fingers were between her thighs. 'Without sex…'

'Of course not.' His mouth was back at her breast,

his tongue stroking it to an aching peak. 'I have my harem.'

She opened her eyes, went to push his hand away from where it was gently probing, for the thought of a harem was almost repugnant—and yet her eyes met the stars and her mind was split open. There was a tightening very low in her stomach and she wanted to hear, was strangely turned on by his ways, by the impossible ways she did not understand yet wanted to hear about.

'Tell me,' she breathed, closing her eyes to the moment.

He had felt her tense, had inwardly kicked himself for saying it too soon—for in this land his ways were not understood. But time was of the essence. One night with Natasha would not suffice, so he had to tell her more truths.

'Tell me,' she said again as his fingers parted her moist butterfly. 'Won't your wife mind…?'

'She will be relieved,' Rakhal said. 'For she will not be troubled with my needs.'

'But…'

'I will sleep only with my wife unsheathed,' Rakhal explained as his fingers slipped inside her warmth, 'and I will do this only with her…it is only she I will make come… Otherwise it would be considered unfaithful.'

There was strange honour to his ways.

'And the women in the harem…?'

'They are for me, not I for them.' He lowered his

head and replaced his fingers with his mouth. 'There is none of *this*.'

And he parted her legs and gave in to himself. He would miss this. This was why he loved this land. When he went back this sweet pleasure would be only for his bride. He tasted and it felt like the last time. He probed with his tongue and felt her hands in his head and it *was* the last time, Rakhal realised, for his wife would not be so bold as to demand more from him, and nor would she weep and beg as Natasha did now.

All the tensions of the day were throbbed out into his mouth.

And afterward, she lay trying to remember how to breathe. The stars were still watching and so too were his eyes—and, no, she did not want to wait for morning.

She drank water from the carafe by the bed and could not fathom that it came from the desert. She poured some more and Rakhal drank it. She tried to rest and he tried to let her. Yet it was as though the night would not let them wait for morning; it was as though the stars had other plans for them and were willing them on.

His kiss on her shoulder made her tremble in anticipation. She could stay like this for ever, Natasha decided, as one hand played with her bottom. Still he kissed her, and then his other hand massaged her nipple. He kissed her with words while his hands were moving, stroking, assuring, telling her what she needed to hear. How, since the moment he had seen her at the police station, she had been on his mind—

which, Rakhal thought, was true. How, since the moment he had met her, he had wanted her—which again, he conceded, was true.

And he said many more things—for here in this strange country, where women made simple things complicated, where they demanded declarations and promises that could never be kept, he played by the rules, gave in to the madness of the land just one more time and said things he perhaps ought not to—like how much he wanted her. Except that, too, was true.

He told her how aroused he was as she burned beneath him. He moved his tongue along her shoulders and then down to suckle at her breast, and he kissed her nipple longer, until the taste was imprinted on his tongue.

His skin was smooth and soft, his erection both compelling and terrifying—for she knew now that they would make love.

His fingers concluded that she was ready.

'Will it hurt?'

'A little,' Rakhal said as he sheathed himself.

He was over her, his erection nudging at her entrance, and he felt her tension, felt her tight and nervous. He moved his fingers down to where she was now dry.

'We don't have to...' he whispered.

'I want to,' she said, but she was honest. 'I'm scared.'

'You guide me...' he said.

And then her hand was around him, and he was so solid it terrified her more. The sheath came away in her hand.

'I will put on another…' He did not show his impatience, knew it would not help, but Rakhal was not used to anything less than seamless lovemaking. He knew that if he interrupted things now the moment would be gone. It was for that reason—that foolish, foolish reason—that he stayed.

'Just relax,' he said, for he could feel the wanting in her body at odds with the dry desert between her legs. But now, without the barrier, she had softened a little. He could feel her moist at his tip and he kissed her calmer, perhaps just a little wilder. 'Better?' he asked.

'Much.' For her panic was easing and lust was trickling back. 'I'm sorry…' She was—and embarrassed too at her cumbersomeness.

'Natasha…' She had nothing to be sorry about. He would stretch her just a little, Rakhal decided, while she was damp and more moist. 'Just a little way,' he whispered. She moaned as he stretched her, for it hurt and yet it was sublime.

He pushed and felt only physical resistance. Her mind was with his now. Gently he moved, backwards and forwards, until she begged him to enter—and he did, tearing her virgin flesh. She bit into his shoulder and he thought then he might come, was dizzy from fighting it, but of course he must not. Rakhal knew that, for he was still unsheathed.

He would come out now, he decided. Except he slid deeper inwards.

She sobbed, for, yes, it hurt. It hurt because it was almost cruel to have a man as well endowed as Rakhal as your first lover. But it was a delicious cruel, Natasha soon realised, as her body adjusted to him.

'Just a little way more,' Rakhal said, and he thought he might die from the pleasure as he felt the beckoning of her muscles dragging him in. 'Stay still,' he warned, for the soft buck of her body brought him dangerously close.

She tried to, but she had never felt anything like it, to be so completely filled, and it killed not to move with him, not to move her hips to her body's command. She gave in then, lifted her hips, and he moved out. And then as his tip neared the exit he plunged in again, for just one more taste.

He would be careful, he told himself as he sank in deeper and then did it again.

She could never have realised all she was missing out on. She felt his golden skin beneath her fingers, felt the animal passion that fought with his restraint, and the orgasm he had brought her to in the small hours was bypassed already. She could feel tension in her thighs, and low, low in her stomach, and she felt as if she might scream.

'Rakhal,' she warned, for she was so close to the edge.

'Let go,' he said, for he wanted to feel her come around his naked length.

Rakhal would not leave her in London; he wanted her in his land—she would be in his harem. He was giddy with the thought that he might have her again and again.

Natasha was giddy too. Her hips rose to his and

their groins ground together; he was bucking within her, and her muscles were milking him, and Natasha found ecstasy there in his arms.

Always he loved the release, but as he came to her it was like nothing he had ever sampled before—he saw the stars in his head, the same stars that bathed the desert and shone on them tonight; he swept past Orion and pulsed deep into her.

And then he returned, back from the desert to his hotel room and to cold realisation.

He had done the unthinkable…

# CHAPTER SIX

NATASHA lay trying to make sense of things.

There was no excuse save insanity, which was what she felt around him. She was usually the most sensible person—reserved, some might say.

Just not with Rakhal.

His kisses, his touch, his words had taken her to places where rational thought was left behind.

After a moment he spoke.

'Natasha…what happened there…' He actually didn't know how to broach it, for this was not a conversation he had had before. This sort of thing simply did not, *could* not happen to him.

'Shouldn't have,' she finished for him. 'We didn't use anything…'

'*I* didn't,' he said. 'The mistake was mine.'

She turned and looked at him, saw the grim set of his jaw, knew what he must surely be thinking: she had trapped him somehow. Her mind whirred for possible solutions and she breathed in relief as one flew in.

'There's a pill…' Those indigo eyes turned to her, but they were black and unreadable now. She babbled

on some more, in an effort not just to reassure him but
herself, as if talking could somehow erase the madness that had taken place in this bed.

He looked in silent horror at the woman he had just
made love to. He accepted all responsibility for what
had happened. She had been a virgin; he was a royal.
He should have known better—he always knew better. Till now.

Rakhal had been raised as a leader in crisis. He
must always remain calm. It had been ingrained into
him, beaten into him at times, and he was grateful for
those teachings now. He knew that she did not understand the implications, but Natasha's talk of a pill that
could end things had adrenaline coursing through his
muscles and his heart thumping in alarm.

He knew this had not been an attempt to trap him.
There was a strength to her, a dignity that suddenly unnerved him. This was a woman independent enough to
go it alone. She might not even tell him about a baby—
perhaps with curls of gold and its father's dark skin—
and if he left now he might not even know.

Still, he did not reveal his horror. His voice was
pleasant and calm when it came. 'There is time yet before you need to worry about such things.' He pulled
her into his arms. 'I told you—you are to worry about
nothing.'

She lay there soothed as his hand stroked her, as he
told her that everything would be okay. She slept, but
it was not restful, for whenever she turned or moved it
was as if he were awake and his arms found her again.

At dawn she listened as the stranger who had become her lover moved to another room and chanted prayers she did not understand. And she said prayers of her own too, asking for forgiveness for her foolish mistake. It was a simple mistake. Of course they would get away with it… She heard him shower, then she heard him speaking on the phone, but it was in his own language so she didn't know what was being said.

Rakhal did not like what he heard.

Her brother was back and raging, demanding the jewels, demanding she call the police. Rakhal could not let her go back to that house. He issued instructions and did not repeat them. He only needed to say things once.

He returned, dressed in a bathrobe and unshaven. The bruise on his eye was more grey than purple now. He was still so impossibly beautiful as he sat on the edge of the bed and looked down to where she lay.

'Look…about what happened…' She wanted to discuss it properly—she wasn't actually sure that she could take a pill. She wanted to know what he was thinking. But Rakhal had other ideas.

'There is no point worrying about that now,' Rakhal said. 'Whatever happens we will sort something out. Get dressed.' He smiled down at her. 'I want to take your mind off things. I will take you to breakfast. Somewhere nice.'

'I haven't got anything suitable to wear. We could have breakfast here.'

'We could,' Rakhal said. And he pulled back the sheet and went to climb in. Then he changed his mind, smiling down at her, naked and warm.

She wriggled in delight as he traced his fingers down her hips and then paused, his eyes tenderly appraising her. 'Why don't we have breakfast somewhere a bit special?' He spoke the language of romance, the language women here seemed so badly to need, and he spoke it easily for he had had much practice. 'Paris!'

'Don't be...' Her voice trailed off, because this was his life, this was his world, and still she could not fathom it. 'I haven't got anything to wear...my passport...' It was all too impossible. 'We can't just...'

'Why not?' Rakhal said. 'I have a jet. We could be there in a couple of hours. Or lunch, maybe... I will have some clothes brought up for you...' He made the impossible so easy. 'I will send someone to get your documents, and I will have my people tidy your house. I don't want you being distressed...'

She thought of her house, the mess and the chaos she would have to return to, and she *wanted* the reprieve before she went back to her life, wanted the escape. Always around him she forgot to be sensible, and Natasha nodded her head. *Yes.*

She chose clothes from a selection from one of the hotel boutiques which Rakhal had had brought up to his suite. She chose a dress in the palest grey with a matching long coat. The hotel organised someone to do her hair and make-up too. It was the height of decadence.

The luxury of it all should have been making her giddy, but it was Rakhal who took care of that. The approval in his eyes as she came out of her bedroom and the kiss to her throat before they headed to the airport was a brief reminder of what had taken place last night. And it was not clothes or make-up she wanted. She would have happily stripped bare there and then— except Rakhal had other plans.

Plans which had swung into action. From car to plane it was seamless—for Natasha at least. There was not a hint from the staff who greeted them as to the chaos this rapid change in the Prince's plans had caused.

'Your Highness.' The robed man who had been in the car the morning she had first met him was there as they climbed on board. He bowed and kissed Rakhal's hand, and nodded his head to Natasha, then disappeared into an area towards the front of the plane.

'It's amazing!' It really was; there was a desk and large leather chairs, a bar and even a bed—it was beyond luxurious even for a hotel room, but the fact it was a plane had Natasha reeling. 'You have a *desk*?'

'I fly a lot,' Rakhal explained. 'And often I am working...' He gave her a smile. 'But not today. We should take our seats—we will be taking off soon.'

He held her hand as they taxied along the runway and took off into the morning. They would be in Paris within an hour, the captain explained once the plane had levelled out.

'I should get changed,' Rakhal said, and looked up as the steward came to take their order for breakfast. 'Just juice and pastries,' Rakhal said. 'We will be dining when we land.' He looked to his guest, supremely polite. 'If that is okay with you?'

'Of course.' She looked around the jet and he saw her eyes linger on the bed.

'Why not stretch out a little?' Rakhal suggested.

She would never have the chance to sample such luxury again, Natasha realised as Rakhal headed to the bathroom. And it was luxury to lie on the bed, to close her eyes and rest on soft pillows as the plane took her away.

It felt as if she had been sleeping for ever and the plane seemed darker when she awoke. The shutters were down. She stretched luxuriously, a little surprised when she looked over and saw Rakhal on his computer at the desk, speaking with Abdul his aide. He was not dressed in the suit she was used to. Instead he had changed into robes and had a *kafiya* on his head. Natasha's first thought was—to her shame—that she would be a little bit embarrassed walking around Paris with him dressed like that, for he looked so royal, so imposing. But even before that thought had been fully processed, even before Rakhal turned around, the truth of her situation was slowly dawning.

'How long till we land?' Still she tried to deny the obvious—because things like this surely couldn't happen to someone like her.

'A couple of hours,' Rakhal said, and Natasha noted that he didn't even attempt to lie.

'And how long have I been asleep?'

'For a while.'

She tried to keep calm, but fear was coursing

through her, and it was blind panic that had her racing from the bed to confront him where he sat.

'You can't do this.' She attempted to reason with him. 'You can't just *take* me!'

'You left me with no choice but to do so.' Rakhal was completely unmoved by her dramatics. She was starting to shout now, to beat him with her hands. He captured her wrists. 'This is about protecting what is mine.'

'I'm not yours to protect...'

'That is yet to be determined.'

And Natasha knew then it was not about *her*.

'With all that was going on, with the things you were suggesting, I could not leave you.' To him it was logical. 'If you are pregnant with my child then I need to be certain you are taking care of yourself and that you will do nothing to jeopardise its existence. You will stay in the palace, where you'll be well looked after by women who will take the best care of you.'

'Where will you be?'

'In the desert. Soon I am to take a wife. It is right that I go there for contemplation and meditation. We will wait to see the outcome with you. You will be well taken care of, you will be looked after, and, if you are not pregnant of course you can come back home.'

She could feel hysteria rising—wanted to slap him, wanted to run for the emergency exit. But still he held her wrists. There was nothing but nothing she could do.

'And if I am?' Natasha begged, but she already knew the answer.

'If you are pregnant—' so matter-of-fact was his voice as he said it '—then there is no question that we will marry.'

# CHAPTER SEVEN

IT WAS dark as they came in to land.

She could see the palace rising out of the desert, and it was the most terrifying feeling as the plane touched down in a country she hadn't even heard of till yesterday.

They had flown for hours, and when the fight in her had died Natasha had sat in a chair and stared silently out of the window. For a while she had thought they were flying over the ocean. She'd thought she could see white rippling waves. But she had come to realise that the near-full moon lit a desert beneath them. It had shown her all too clearly the remoteness of the land Rakhal would one day rule—the land he was taking her to now.

An assistant helped her into a robe that covered her from head to toe, only revealing her eyes, and once off the plane they were driven a short distance to the palace, which stood tall and exquisite, though it felt far from welcoming as she stepped out of the car. Natasha knew it would be hopeless to fight here—there was no point kicking and screaming. Even if she could get away there was nowhere to run; all she could do was stay calm and appear to have given in to him.

He was unfamiliar in his robes, dark, mysterious and forbidding, and she cursed again at her foolishness, rued the trust she had placed in him. Rakhal was flanked by several men who spoke in low voices, while Natasha was surrounded by a group of women. They walked swiftly through fragrant gardens, and only when they were safely inside the palace did Rakhal speak with her again.

'You will take refreshments with the maidens—my father has asked that I speak with him.'

For the first time she witnessed tension in his features, but his voice was as haughty and assured as ever. As he turned to go, perhaps he saw her fear, for he tried to comfort her.

'Natasha, I understand you are scared, that this must be overwhelming for you, but please know that I would never hurt you.'

'You already have,' she flared. 'Lies hurt too, Rakhal. You lied to get me on that plane—you didn't make a single attempt to speak to me, to discuss what we should do.'

'There could be no discussion—your words left me with no choice but to act.' He remained unmoved. 'Now I will speak with the King. It is not every day that a Crown Prince returns in circumstances such as this. For now you will wait.'

She had no choice but to wait, to sit as Rakhal swept out of the room, dark and unapproachable—a stranger.

Rakhal did not like to leave her.

He was more than aware how terrified she must be. Yet there had been no choice but to bring her here. Had it been any other time he could have waited things out in London, but festivities were already starting in Alzirz—their Crown Prince should be deep in the desert now, contemplating his country's future, asking the desert for guidance as he chose his future bride, not walking into his father's study to be chastised.

He was braced for a row, his back ramrod-straight, his features expressionless, as would be expected of any ruler about to go into battle. He was ready for anything as an aide opened his father's office door, braced for confrontation as he stepped inside, and yet nothing, *nothing*, could have prepared him for the sight that greeted him.

He was more than grateful for his brutal training, for the beatings he had taken in the desert, for the cruel lessons he had been forced to learn, for his mask did not slip as he laid eyes on the frail shadow of a man who had once been so strong. His voice did not waver as he greeted his father; his eyes did not shut as he watched the feeble King attempt to stand.

Rakhal kissed his father on both cheeks, as was their way, but it was not born of affection—it was simply the way that things were done.

He waited for admonishment, for his father to tell him he was a fool, but instead his father coughed, and then coughed again as Rakhal waited, his fury building towards the palace doctor, who had told him there was still much time, that they were talking months. But that was the trouble with staff who were loyal. Even an esteemed doctor did not want to face the truth at times.

The truth was in front of Rakhal.

The truth he could clearly see.

Soon he would rule.

'I thought you would go straight to the desert.' The King's voice was thin and reedy, and as he gratefully sat back down it was clear that he was growing weak.

'I will depart for there shortly.' Rakhal kept his sentence brief. There was a thickness to his throat that was unfamiliar, a sting in his nose as he looked at the man who had been so strong and proud and tried to address him as if he still was.

'So why the detour?' The King coughed again. 'You are wasting time.' He saw his son frown—the only emotion he had displayed since entering his office. 'There are only two days for coupling. You have wasted many hours travelling.'

'That is not why I brought Natasha here.' Rakhal instantly understood what his father meant. 'I can assure you that what happened yesterday was a mistake. If Natasha is not pregnant then I fully intend to choose a bride from Alzirz—a woman who understands our ways, who will be proud to give birth to our future leader. The people will not take this well—I am aware of that...'

'They will be appeased if there is an heir.'

'Natasha would be a poor choice.' It sounded harsh, even to Rakhal, yet it was essential that his father understood—for Natasha's sake as much as the country's. Except his father had other ideas.

'You have already made your choice,' the King interrupted. 'When you slept with her unsheathed.'

'It was once.'

'It needs to be more.' The King held his son's eyes. 'The desert must play its part in this.'

For the first time Rakhal saw fear in his father's eyes.

'We ignored its rules once—'

'Father,' Rakhal broke in. 'My mother's death had nothing to do with that.' Logic told him this, education told him too, and yet in this Rakhal's voice did waver; in this Rakhal perhaps was not so strong.

'You were conceived in London,' the King said. 'None of the rituals followed. For weeks we did not know that your mother was with child. And look what happened. You, Rakhal, know better than anyone the ways of the desert cannot always be explained. I am from a lineage that is pure royal; you are from a lineage that is both royal and from the desert. Are you so brave as to test your modern theories out with your own child?'

For the first time since their meeting the King's voice was strong and he stood to confront his son.

'I was young and bold like you once. I did things my way instead of the ways of old—and look what happened. Your mother died in childbirth; you were born so small that you were not expected to survive. The desert taught us a cruel lesson, yet it gave us one chance to redeem ourselves—*you* are that chance, Rakhal. Go now and have her oiled and prepared.'

Even as Rakhal opened his mouth to protest, the King found his voice and overruled him.

'And tomorrow she shall be hennaed and rested.'

'It is better that she stays at the palace now.'

'*No!*' The King was adamant. 'Your role is that of protector—she will be terrified here without you. She shall remain in the desert with you till we have an answer.'

Rakhal was appalled at the prospect. His time before selecting a bride was for deep contemplation. At night he could give in to his body's urges, feast with the harem, and then return to the festivities and select his bride. It was unthinkable that he should have Natasha there in the desert with him—especially if he could not be with her. For it was forbidden. Once hennaed and painted, her body was not for him.

'She does not belong in the desert.'

'She does not belong in this land.'

For the first time Rakhal glimpsed his father's anger.

'However, we shall deal with the problem, not the cause. You will do well to remember that from your teachings. Perhaps your choice was not the wisest, but the people will soon forgive if it proves fruitful. If not, the people need never know...'

'Which is why you want her hidden away in the desert?'

His father was older and wiser, and still he had more answers.

'You cannot hide in the desert,' the King responded. 'My wife—your mother—told me that. The desert will always reveal the truth. There are maidens waiting for her there—they will keep me informed, as will Abdul. There will be no more discussion.'

He looked his son in the eye and Rakhal did not like what he saw there. The once black eyes were now pale and milky. But on this point his father stood strong.

'I am still King.'

'And one day I will be,' Rakhal said, but his father refused to be swayed.

'Go now,' he ordered his son. But as Rakhal reached the door he halted him. 'You have heard the news from Alzan?'

'About his twin girls?' Rakhal had far too much on his mind to smile, for now he had to tell Natasha not just that she must join him in the desert, but that to-night she must join him in his bed.

His father had had the excuse of ignorance when he had bedded his mother, had believed then that the teachings were merely fables. Rakhal did not have that excuse—his mother's death had been a warning. And yet he could not force himself on her. And it would be force, Rakhal knew. So he had far more on his mind than to engage in idle gossip.

'About his wife.'

The King's words halted Rakhal as he went to walk out. 'His wife?' Rakhal turned around.

'Rumour has it that the Sheikha Queen was most unwell during her pregnancy. That it might prove fatal were she to try and conceive again.'

'And is this from a reliable source?' Rakhal checked.

'Of course—and it had been confirmed by the most

reliable,' the King said. 'Of course he did not say it directly—he never does.'

Rakhal knew who his father was refering to: the wizened old man from the desert.

'But he sees not just one test but two…two tests that will divide us for ever or reunite Alzanirz. Perhaps that test is the twins. Of course Emir would not waste his breath asking me to forgo the rules—to allow a princess to rule Alzan.' He looked to his son, saw despite the strong jawline, despite the unblinking gaze, that his features were just a little pale.

'We allow a princess to rule Alzirz,' Rakhal said. 'If Natasha is pregnant, if the gift is a daughter, she will one day be Queen.'

'Which is why Alzirz will go on.' The King smiled, but then it died on his lips and there was hate in his eyes. 'Did Emir's father revoke the rule when my wife died?' Bitter were his words. 'No. Instead the entire burden of our country's future fell to you, and now it is time for you to accept that burden like a man—like the Prince you are—and ensure our country continues. Which is why you will take this woman to the desert and to your bed this night.'

Rakhal walked through the palace. History lined its walls—not just portraits of the royals, but oil paintings of the desert and the people from whom he came. He walked into the lounge where Natasha sat silent, and despite prompting by Abdul she refused to stand when he entered. All eyes except hers were on him.

'You are to come to the desert with me.'

'No.'

He heard her inhale, heard the rate of her breathing increase. 'We are leaving now.' Rakhal ignored her refusal. Abdul was watching him after all. But once they were alone he would talk to her. He would reassure her. For now he had to appear to be abiding by the rules. 'The helicopter is being prepared.'

*'No!'*

This time she did bite and kick and scream, but her protests were futile.

It could, as Abdul informed her, be no other way.

# CHAPTER EIGHT

NATASHA had never been on a helicopter, and as it took off her stomach seemed to rise with it. She closed her eyes on a living nightmare. Abdul was on one side, and there was also a young veiled woman beside her. Rakhal sat opposite, speaking in Arabic to his aide, and she tried to shut out the words coming in over the headphones. But suddenly Rakhal spoke in English.

'To the left is Alzan.'

Natasha snapped open her eyes. 'I don't need a tourist guide.'

'I am simply trying to orientate you,' Rakhal said.

Realising that any information might help, Natasha looked out of the window. But all she could see was endless desert and panic rose within her. She could die here, right this minute, and no one would ever know; her friends and family didn't even know that she was here.

'There—over there,' Rakhal said some time later, 'is my desert abode.'

As it came into view she could see a collection of tents, but as the helicopter hovered she saw that it was not just tents—more a large complex. The helicopter's spotlight, as it searched for its landing spot, illuminated horses circling their enclosure as the light disturbed them, and there were camels too. But more surprising for Natasha was that there were swimming pools. She counted three of them, right there in the deep of the desert, and even without the helicopter trained on them they were lit up. Beside one there were people brightly dressed and dancing.

Even though she had nothing to compare it to, his desert abode was nothing like she had expected.

Cold air hit her cheeks as Rakhal helped her out of the helicopter. His strong arms lifted her down and they ducked under the blades, his grip tight on her hands. Within two steps her shoes were lost in the sand. She made no attempt to retrieve them. Her footwear was simply irrelevant now. Her only thought was that she wanted to run back to the helicopter, to dive in and be lifted away. But by the time they had reached one of the tents the helicopter was already taking off into the sky.

Natasha could hear the throb of sensual music from the poolside, the sound of laughter too, and the cool air was tempered with incense. It was almost irreverent. Perhaps the servants were having a party, Natasha wondered. Perhaps they had not realised Rakhal was returning tonight.

It was quieter inside, but there was no relief to be had.

'You will put on these,' Rakhal informed her.

And though she did not want the small slippers she

obliged. She wanted to be alone with him, wanted to argue away from Abdul's dark eyes that followed her every move. An argument about slippers was not high on her priorities!

'Not your robe,' Rakhal halted her as she went to take it off. 'The maidens will do that.'

Four women were approaching, their heads lowered, bowing to Rakhal and reaching out for her. Natasha flinched. He spoke to them in Arabic and they backed away.

'Come through,' Rakhal said. 'I have told them I need to speak with you first.'

He led her through to a larger area, and thankfully the maidens did not follow. It was dimly lit and had a sensual luxury. There were cushions everywhere, and low tables heavily laden with food, and perhaps they had been expecting him after all, for there was music coming from behind a screened area and incense burnt in here too. She felt as if she was stepping into somewhere forbidden.

She was almost right. It wasn't forbidden, but it was most unusual to have a woman here with him, and Rakhal was more than a touch uncomfortable with Natasha's presence. His desert abode was not really the place he would consider bringing the potential mother of a royal heir, but circumstances had left him with little choice.

'Not you.' He turned to Abdul who, unlike the maidens, had followed them through. 'I wish to speak to Natasha alone.'

'Not tonight,' Abdul said, for on this matter even

he could pull rank with the Prince. 'I have express orders from the King.'

Rakhal hissed in frustration, for it was essential that he spoke to Natasha alone. He needed to tell her he would not harm her, would not force her into something that she did not want. But he could not say such things in front of Abdul, so he turned to Natasha, who stood pale but defiant beside him.

'Normally,' Rakhal explained, 'my wife—'

'I'm *not* your wife,' Natasha cut in.

'The potential mother of my child, then.' He was finding this difficult. Her huge green eyes were hostile and scared, and that was not how she should be at this fragile time. He *must* be alone with her, for she had no idea of the royal ways of old and she had to be seen to comply. 'Here,' he said. 'I will help you with your robe.'

'I can help myself.' She lifted it off and threw it down, stood in the dress she had chosen that morning.

The coat she had left on the plane, and the dress she had put on with such excitement was now crumpled. Her gorgeous hair was knotted from the robe and from her distress before, and her lips were swollen from crying. She looked very small, very scared, and also terribly, terribly defiant as she tossed the robe to the floor, and it evoked unusual feelings in Rakhal. He wanted to soothe her, wanted to calm her, and he crossed the room. But she shrank back, as she had with the maidens.

'Sit?' he suggested. 'Perhaps eat…'

'They'll be looking for me,' Natasha said.

'Excuse me?'

'My friends,' Natasha said. 'I do have a life. You can't just whisk me off and expect no one to notice. They'll call the police...'

'Why don't you ring them, then?' Rakhal frowned.

'Ring them?'

'I will have someone bring you a phone.' He called something in his own language and in less than a moment a maid appeared. 'There is no need for histrionics, Natasha. Ring your friends and tell them.'

'And say what?'

'The truth,' Rakhal said. She took the phone and he watched the wrestle in her eyes. 'I do not want your people worrying about you. Ring them and put their minds at rest.'

She hurled the phone at him, for he had her trapped every which way. But Rakhal had reflexes like lightning, and caught the phone.

'Ring and say you have taken a holiday,' he suggested. 'Because for now you can treat it as one. For now this is your home, and you will rest and be pampered. You will come to no harm, Natasha.' He walked over and touched her cheek. She shrank back. 'My role is to ensure you are looked after.'

He had to explain things to her—had to tell of their ways.

'If I had a bride she would live at the palace,' Rakhal explained. 'For two days I would be with her, and then the maidens would take care of her. She would be hennaed and oiled and...' Much more than that he did not know, for he would not see his wife after two days of coupling—what happened after was dealt with by women. He told Natasha the little he knew. 'She would rest and be looked after, and if the oils and the flowers did not work I would return to her the next month.'

'I don't understand.'

'You do not need to,' Rakhal said. 'The maidens know what needs to be done, how you need to be looked after, the things that must be taken care of. If you do carry the future heir there are prayers to be said, traditions that must be upheld. As I said, normally you would be at the palace. I would not see you.'

He walked to a veiled area and pulled the curtain back. After a brief hesitation she followed him. 'Here is where you will rest.' It was a lavish room of purples and reds, with a large circular bed in the centre. Above it hung a thick rope. 'You pull that and a servant will come. If you need a drink or food or a massage,' Rakhal explained. 'You may join me for conversation if I am in the lounge and the music is silent.'

'I shan't be joining you,' Natasha said, but for the first time since the plane, for the first time since realisation had hit, the tightness in her chest was abating. For the first time she felt as if she could properly breathe. This was a room just for her, and she stepped into it, desperate to be alone, to gather her thoughts, to make sense of all that had happened.

'My resting area is the other side of the lounge,' Rakhal said, but she simply shrugged.

She did not care where Rakhal rested. All she wanted was to be alone—except she froze when she heard him speak on.

'It is only tonight that you will join me there.'

Natasha did not turn around; the tightness was back in her chest and sweat beaded on her forehead, yet she forced her voice calm. 'What did you say?'

'Tonight…' Rakhal kept his voice even. Aware that Abdul was listening, he could not reassure her. He wished she would turn around, so she could see the plea in his eyes, know he would not hurt her. She might somehow understand that the harshness in his voice did not match his intent. 'You are to sleep with me tonight.'

'No…' She shuddered. 'Rakhal, no.' Now she did turn around. She pleaded with the man she had just met, the first man she had made love with, who was now forcing her to join him in his bed. *'No.'*

'There can be no discussion.' He was supremely uncomfortable. Rakhal could hear the plea in her voice, but with Abdul present there was nothing he could do. 'Go now,' Rakhal said as the maidens approached. 'They will have you prepared.'

## CHAPTER NINE

RAKHAL lay on the bed, waiting for the maidens to bring Natasha to him.

Music was softly playing and he could hear the sound of water and the maidens' chatter as they bathed her. She did not return their conversation. He could see the occasional glimpse of her shadow on the white tented ceiling, could see locks of her hair and the curves of her body, and he did his best not to look at the teasing images. For though the room had been prepared, though the music and the scents had been chosen carefully to arouse, he knew he must resist.

They hadn't been alone since their time back at the hotel. There had been no chance to explain things. Natasha would never have agreed to come with him, and neither could he have left her in London to deal with her brother alone—especially if there was a chance she was carrying his child.

He had never thought she would be brought to the desert. It had not entered his head that his father would insist on this night. But at least in his bed, alone, he could finally speak with her, reassure her.

But Natasha dreaded his bed. She could see his shadow on the ceiling as the maidens bathed her, and though last night had been wonderful she could not stand the thought of sleeping with him now—could not give in without a fight.

Natasha climbed out of the bath and shivered as the maidens oiled and dressed her in the flimsiest of gowns, and then led her through the tent towards his resting area. She willed fear to subside so that she might think.

'I need my jewels,' Natasha said, for they had been taken from her. She turned to the maidens. 'If I am to be presented to him I need to wear my jewels.'

'They are in your chambers,' Amira, a maiden who spoke a little English, informed her. 'They are safe there.'

'You don't understand. They were my mother's,' Natasha said. 'And my grandmother's. It is tradition that I should be wearing them.'

Amira gave a nod and led her to her room. Tradition was the one word that seemed to reach her.

'And I need to pray,' Natasha said, 'before I put them on.'

Amira nodded and stepped outside as Natasha got down on her knees. She knew she had but a few minutes, and for the first time she was glad she had been brought to the desert—for here the walls were not made of stone, and she knew that this was her only chance.

Rakhal waited and he waited, trying to plan what he would say to her, how best he could make her understand. He knew she was out of the bath, had thought she should be with him now, but then this was unusual for him too. So he listened to the soft music, lay back on the bed. It was then that he heard the commotion, watched as a curtain parted.

But instead of Natasha, a panicked maid called out to him, 'Your Highness!' There was fear in her voice and already he was standing, whipping a sash from the bed as the maiden spoke on. 'She is not here.'

Rakhal demanded more information.

'She asked to go to her room, to collect her jewels. She insisted that she wear them for you.'

And Rakhal knew then that she had run, that the jewels had been an excuse, but that she would not have left them behind.

'She said she wanted to pray…I should not have left her alone…' The maiden sobbed for his forgiveness. 'I never thought she would run,' Amira begged, for only a mad person would run into the desert at night. Or a person who did not know how impossible it was to survive.

For the first time, Rakhal did not wait to be dressed. He pulled on his robe and sandals as the maids summoned help from the guards. When they heard Natasha had gone missing the staff, unused to such strange behaviour, ran for their horses and Jeeps, but Rakhal halted them. Somehow he kept his head, ordered them to collect lanterns and to search on foot. He did not want them racing off into the night; he did not trust that they would brake in time, and nor did he trust the horses not to trample her. That sort of search could only take place at dawn.

By then it might be too late.

No one ran into the desert night—especially dressed in a flimsy gown. Did she not understand how cold it was out there? That the winds that brought heat to the sands by day chilled them at night? That the scorpions would be out now, ready to bite at her bare feet? That even if the sand shone white beneath the moonlight and stars she would be lost before she knew it? The seemingly flat sands were dunes that shifted and changed like the ocean. The wind would carry her screams not to him but through the canyons, for the desert was especially cruel to strangers.

He did not wait for the others to gather; instead Rakhal strode into the night, shouting out her name. But then it dawned on him that Natasha was running from him. That she would rather flee into the harsh, unforgiving desert then spend a night with him. And he ceased shouting, silently asking the skies for a chance to explain, a chance to tell her that he never would have forced her, that that had not been his intent.

After fifteen minutes of running—to where she did not know—the adrenaline left Natasha, and she fell exhausted onto the cold sand. She knew that she had been crazy to run, but it had proved equally impossible to stay, simply to submit. She could hear shouts far in the distance and realised the pack was heading in a different direction, that she still had a chance to escape. Natasha looked out, to the vast space that would surely claim her, then looked back to the tent. But already it had disappeared from her vision and the voices were fading into the distance. It was either call out now and summon help, only to be returned to him, or take her chance with the night…

She chose hope.

Rakhal watched from a distance. He saw her turn, resisted the urge to call out to her, and watched as she made up her mind, as she turned from the voices that would bring her to him and faced the dark instead. It was then that he called out, his voice making her still for a second and then propelling her into a run.

'You would rather step into the night than be returned to me?'

'Yes!' Still she tried to run, but he soon caught up. He grabbed at her wrist and his grip was too strong. He spun her round.

'Even when I tell you I would never hurt you? That I will take care of you?'

'I don't need to be taken care of!' Natasha screamed, kicking and hitting and trying to bite—because, yes, she *would* rather take her chances alone in the desert than be taken care of in that way.

'But you do!' Still he gripped her wrist. He knew the hissing and sparks would fade like a firecracker and he did not argue further, just held on to her as she spun in anger, as she cursed and shouted. Finally it faded, and he let her go when spent; she sank to the sand and sat hugging her knees, and then she looked up at him and with all she had left in her she spat.

She missed.

Even defeated, Rakhal noted, she did not cry, and there was a twist in his chest, a rare need to reach out and touch. But as he tried he saw her head pull away, and then angry eyes flashed towards him.

'Do it, then!' She went to pull off her gown. 'I won't give you the satisfaction of my fighting.'

He was appalled at her thoughts, that she believed he would treat her as such. He sank to the ground and pulled at the gown, the flimsy material tearing as he fought to keep it on. 'Stop this!'

'Why? We both know what's going to happen. Just take me here and I can vomit in the sand rather than in your bed.'

'I am not going to sleep with you.' Still she fought. 'I would never force you...'

'Oh, please,' Natasha hurled. 'I was being prepared for you.'

'Because the maidens cannot know that we do not sleep together, that I have no intention...' She paused for just a moment, ceased fighting just long enough for him to go on. 'Abdul cannot know that I have only the best intentions,' he explained, 'which is why I could not speak properly with you on the plane. You were in danger back in London. I had no choice but to bring you here.'

'Danger!' She shot out a mirthless laugh. 'You think that was danger?'

'Your brother came back in the night,' Rakhal said. 'He broke windows. He was raging... Do you think I would leave you to deal with that?'

'I'd have dealt with it!'

'How?'

She didn't know—she actually didn't know. Her heart seemed to squeeze tight with fear, for had she not met Rakhal, had she not been with him that night, she would have been dealing with her brother's rages. Her hand went to her mother's necklace. She knew her brother would have ripped it from her throat, and even if she was angry with him, she was scared for him too.

'Was he arrested?'

'No.' He was sitting with her now. Her gown was torn and her breast was exposed, but he pulled up the fabric and held it as he spoke. 'He ran off, but he came back in the morning, remorseful. By then we were already on the plane. I had left instructions. My people have dealt with him.' She started to panic again, to grapple to escape him, but he held her still, kept her covered, and realised just how little she trusted him, how little she knew of their ways. 'Your family is my concern too!' Rakhal shouted above her rage. 'Your brother is on his way here.'

'Here?'

'He was made an offer,' Rakhal explained. 'His debts paid, including yours, in return for six months labour in the mines of Alzirz.'

'The *mines*!' What was this place? What were they doing to Mark? But she did not know him.

'He will leave here a wealthy man. He will work hard for six months and build muscle instead of debt. He will eat food from my land and be nourished. He is not here as a slave—he is here to rebuild his life. You can speak with him soon. And—' Rakhal revealed his deeper motivation '—if you are not pregnant, when you return to London you will have six months to sort out your life…'

His voice trailed off and Natasha sat silent, trying to take in all he had told her. And despite her fears, despite her confusion, there was a bud of calm inside her; the fear that had fluttered for months, maybe longer, was quietly stilled. Finally her brother had a chance.

'I would never hurt you. All this I was going to tell you when you were brought to me tonight.'

For the first time since the plane she could properly look at him. For the first time since then he was the man she had met—except she understood a little more of his power now, and could see, too, the foolishness of her ways. For, yes, she had been a virgin, but she shared the responsibility and so too the consequences.

'Rakhal, I accept my part in our night together.' She swallowed. 'I accept that if I am pregnant then there will be a lot of decisions that need to be made. But I simply can't try to *get* pregnant.' Her voice was urgent. 'Which is what tonight would have been about—'

'I understand that,' Rakhal interrupted. He believed in tradition, and he believed in the desert, but he was modern in other things, and in this he would defy his father, in this he would turn his back on the desert rules. 'We would not have….' Now it was he who hesitated. 'We would not have made love. I too am prepared to accept the fate we made that night.'

He looked at her and slowly she nodded, starting to believe that the man she had met was still there inside him.

'When I brought you here it was my intention that you stay at the palace. Only when I arrived my father instructed that we go to the desert, that all the rituals must take place. Here it is unthinkable that you would not want to be carrying the heir to the throne. The people could never understand that we are both hoping you're *not* pregnant. We need to let them think that we are trying to ensure that you are.'

'So we are just to share a bed?' Natasha verified. 'Nothing else will happen?'

'It is not as simple as that. They need to think...'

He was embarrassed, Natasha realised.

'They need to hear,' he explained. 'The maidens will wait outside the sleeping area.'

'We're to make *noises*?' She couldn't believe what she was hearing. 'You are going to pretend to be making love to me?'

He nodded.

'But the shadows....' She thought of his shadow, taunting her on the tent ceiling as she bathed. 'They'd see them.'

'They will see our shadows and we will look as if we are. But I give you my word, Natasha, it will be for appearances only.'

She believed him.

She looked into eyes that were the same colour as the sky above and knew he was giving her his word.

'Some people condemn our ways. That is from ignorance. If you are carrying my child, you are the most precious person in this land.'

There were shouts in the distance. Natasha could

see lights in the shadows and people nearing, and no more did she want to run and take her chances with the night.

'When this is over, if you are not carrying my child, still I will look after you. You will have a stamp in your passport that will speak volumes—a stamp that only I as Crown Prince can give. I will make sure your brother gets on well, and you will be able to visit him freely. I know I have done little to earn it, but I am asking for your trust.'

He could not have all of it, but finally there was hope for her brother when before there had been none. And she accepted, too, even if she could not fully understand, how impossible it would have been for him to leave her in London if she was carrying his child.

'I'm angry,' she warned him. For even if she trusted him a little there was a deep fury still there. 'I'm *so* angry.'

'I know that,' Rakhal said. 'But for tonight can you find a way to put that on hold? If we can placate the people—if we can appear to go along with things—then more and more we will be left alone.'

Tears glistened in her eyes as she nodded her head. Rakhal called to his people that he had found her and picked her up and carried her to his tent. The tears that threatened were not born of fear, but of the knowledge that the strong arms holding her, his need to protect her, the care he was taking, had nothing to do with her. He cared only so long as there might be a child.

# CHAPTER TEN

THE maidens gave her a drink and some fruit and then bathed her again, paying careful attention to the scratches on her legs and gently chiding her in their own language. They dabbed at her wounds before dressing her in a fresh gown and then she was led through the tent. There was music playing and the lighting was low. She could see the shadow of Rakhal through the tent wall and swore if she ever was his wife that this would be the first thing to change.

The maidens left her at the threshold of his sleeping quarters and then took their places on the floor. She was relieved rather than scared to see him this time—relieved to leave the maidens and their strange rituals behind.

Or she was relieved until she saw the man that awaited her, for he seemed even more beautiful than the last time. It was as if her brain were incapable of recording such exquisiteness in detail. He was lying on a vast bed, or rather a raised area that was draped in furs and silks. The space was all male—from the dark colour scheme to the woody fragrance that burnt.

It was clearly not an area for sharing; clearly this was *his* domain. Rakhal was on his side, naked except for a sliver of silk covering his groin. His chest and his limbs had been oiled too, and his skin gleamed in the candlelight. And now Natasha was more nervous than the virgin she had been when first she had shared his bed.

Then his promise had been to please her.

Now it was not to.

He took her hand and guided her onto the bed, moving his head in close to hers and murmuring into her ear. 'It will be okay.'

'I know.'

She could smell the pomade in his hair, as she had during their first kiss, but things were so very different this time.

'We should kiss,' Rakhal said, and he captured her face in his hands and brought her close.

But their mouths did not move, just their heads, and she trusted him a little more still. Then his hands went down her arms, and now their lips did meet—but it was just lips, and they did not press. He moved his head to her ear and she felt his breath. They stayed for a moment, his hands running along her arms, caressing her, then moving to her back as if pulling her in, and then to her front, where they rested still between them. She trusted him a little more.

'I should take off your gown now.'

She nodded her consent, lifted her arms, and he slid it over her head. They knelt facing each other. As she shook her hair she caught sight of her own shadow, could see her hard nipples, his fingers appearing to trace them—yet they did not touch her. Even when he lowered his head and seemingly kissed her breast his mouth stayed closed, and his tongue did not cool the heat. She ached for it to do so and performed for the shadows—or was it for herself?

Her neck arched back and the music quickened— their shadows, Natasha realised, were for the musician, for the tempo changed as she and Rakhal moved. The strings of the *quanoon* seemed to pluck deep inside her as his chin grazed her breast and his kiss on her skin remained elusive. Her hands moved to his head—to steady herself, she told him.

And he steadied her too—one hand around her waist and the curve of her bottom—and the music hastened and she rested a head on his shoulder. She could feel her breasts flatten on his chest and tried to slow down her breathing.

'Now,' Rakhal said, 'you must trust me.'

He laid her down and she stared at the wall, at the outline of his body and the full state of his arousal. Of course he was aroused, Natasha told herself. She was too—not that she would let him know it. It was just two bodies confined—two bodies primed with food and scents and brews for this moment—two bodies that last night had been so deliciously intimate. It would be impossible for him not to be aroused.

He lifted her knees and lowered his head between her legs—but his mouth did not touch her. She could feel only his breath when she wanted his tongue. It was a relief when he told her to make some sounds

of approval, to let it be known that the Crown Prince
Sheikh was arousing her.

She moaned not because she was told to, but because she had to. And as his hair met her thigh, as
his head danced between her legs, it was torture that
his mouth did not caress her. He pulled her hand to
his head, told her to moan louder, told her to raise her
hips. As she did so she misjudged, felt for a second
the soothing of his mouth, and then he moved back,
and she bit down on a plea for him to continue as the
music urged him. She was acting, she told herself as
his head rose.

She was acting, Natasha insisted as he lay over her.

'Soon,' Rakhal said, 'you can rest.'

His voice was hoarse. His weight was on his elbows, but their groins still met and his erection was
pressed between them. She didn't want to be resting—
she wanted him inside her.

'Say my name,' he said. 'You would call my name.'

And she did. She called his name as if he *were* inside her.

'And again,' Rakhal said as he moved over her.

She sobbed it out, saw their shadows moving in
unison, and the music hastened and urged them on to
a place she must not go.

'Trust me,' he said.

And she wished she didn't—wished he were a liar
and would take her now.

The music and the potions must have confused
her senses, must have muddled her brain, for as she
lay trapped beneath him, as she watched their im-

ages move on the tent wall, she wanted to stay there, wanted to be having his baby, wanted for ever with Rakhal. But it would not always be like this, she reminded herself. The wife of Rakhal would be kept far removed from him—if she were having his child, after the wedding she would not see him. So she tore her eyes from the wall and looked up to the sky. Only that did not dilute her arousal. Tonight, quite literally, she saw stars.

'Rakhal!' She said his name for she wanted this over. She could not play this dangerous game. 'Rakhal,' she begged, and he moved faster as the music reached a crescendo.

'Now,' he said in her ear and he lifted his body and shuddered a moan and faked his first orgasm. Without his bidding she called out, as she had last night. Should he kiss her? Rakhal wondered. If she were his bride, would he kiss her now?

Perhaps he forgot for a moment that they were acting, and for Natasha it was a relief that he did.

His tongue was a cool balm, and while their rocking was slowing, the music fading, it was contrary to the fire in their groins. It should be over—and yet his erection was still pressing, his breathing was ragged, and her fingers were on his back and digging in. Her hips rose higher against him and his tongue darted in a decadent tryst. Natasha tried to quiet the jerks of her body, tried to tell herself she was playing only the necessary game. But as he lifted his head and watched the colour rise from her chest to her cheeks, as he felt tense beneath him, there was a glimmer of triumph in his eyes as she denied her orgasm.

He rolled off her and onto his side, pulled the silk over his groin, and Natasha closed her eyes, guilty at having enjoyed it.

'Well done,' Rakhal whispered. 'Now you can rest, and tomorrow you will be taken to your own room. We don't have to be together after this night...'

His voice trailed off as a maiden entered, and she was reminded of her role as Rakhal translated the maiden's words.

'She is asking that you lift your hips.'

And she burnt with shame as she did so and a cushion was placed under her, to tilt her hips so that the supposed royal seed might get its best chance.

A vessel—that was all she was, Natasha reminded herself.

All she would ever be to him.

And she closed her eyes to the stars and tried to hold onto her tears as she waited for morning to come.

# CHAPTER ELEVEN

HER time with the master was over, Amira informed her.

Natasha had not slept; instead she had lain pretending to. When Rakhal had risen at sunlight to pray she had opened her eyes to see the maidens quietly waiting. She'd been led through the tent to eat flat bread and dates. She'd drunk infused tea and now they bathed her.

She would never relax, Natasha was sure. But the water smelt of lavender, and the fingers that massaged her scalp were firm and yet tender, and as she breathed in the fragrant steam Natasha felt the tension seep from her. She understood that she was being taken care of, that the maidens meant her no harm.

She was taken to lie on low cushions and her breath was in her throat as Amira explained that she would be decorated. Her skin was damp and warm as tiny leaves and flowers were painted around her areola and just above her pubic bone. The tiny flowers dipped above and into her intimate curls, and Amira did her best to put Natasha at ease as she explained their ways. An old lady drew a circle and then darkened one sliver. When she pointed to the sky Natasha understood it was last night's moon that had been drawn—the time recorded.

'For nine of these moons we shall paint you and pray that the flowers will grow to here.' Amira pressed into the middle of Natasha's ribcage and the old lady said something. Amira laughed. 'Sometimes ten moons,' Amira translated, and then the old lady said something else—only this time the maidens bowed their heads.

'What is she saying?'

'She speaks of Queen Layla,' Amira explained. 'The flowers only climbed to here.' She pointed to just above Natasha's umbilicus. 'There were only six moons for our Prince. It was too soon,' Amira explained, then tried to reassure her. 'But it will not happen to you. Queen Layla was not safe in Alzirz at her fertile time. She was not painted and fed the potions. She did not have us to take care of her...'

'Where was she?'

Amira looked uncomfortable and did not answer immediately; instead she carried on with her artwork. After a moment she spoke on. 'She was from the desert, and when she was in the palace she pined for it. She was so thin and so ill, and she was growing weaker... She joined the King in London—he wanted to try the doctors there.' Amira pulled a face. 'She would have been safer here. Instead she came back to us already carrying a babe. They nursed her at the palace; they did everything that could be done. But she was too weak...'

Natasha was starting to understand their terror of

breaking any traditions. When the decorating had been completed, she was oiled again till she was drowsy, then dressed in sheer organza and led to her bed. She was given a thick milk and honey drink, but it was sickly and sweet and she could not finish it.

'You must drink it all,' Amira said. 'It will help you to sleep.' She gave a smile. 'You will sleep now till tomorrow morning.'

When she was left alone Natasha put down the goblet, unsure what they were giving her, and unsure if it was okay if she were pregnant. She knew there was no way she would sleep for twenty-four hours, but the room was dark and cool and finally she did fall asleep—only to awake disorientated. The room was still dark, and she could hear music filtering through from the lounge. Without thinking she wandered out.

'What are you doing here?' Immediately Rakhal stood from the cushion he was lying on. 'You do not come out when the music plays!'

He was harsher than he'd intended, but she must not come out when there was music, for it masked other sounds. To his credit, he had just been sitting pondering—but Natasha was not to know that. More than that, the sight of her unsettled him—this side of a woman he was not supposed to see. Her hair was oiled and her skin was too; the organza robe was flimsy and clung to her. She was lush and ripe and he was wanting. But she had been bathed and painted.

'Go to your room!' he snapped, and promptly led her back. 'You do *not* come out when the music is on.'

'Then turn it off,' Natasha said, and looked at

him, this man who would send her back to her room. 'Actually, don't bother.' She shook her head. 'I don't even want to talk to you anyway.'

'Sleep,' Rakhal ordered.

'I can't sleep.'

'Pull the rope.'

He turned away, for he must rise above his feelings. She was completely forbidden now, and he was stronger than his urges, so he led her to her room. He saw the goblet still full on the tray on the floor.

'You need to drink that.' He crossed the room and picked it up.

She sat on the edge of the bed and he held it to her lips. She loathed it. It was sickly and thick like custard, and it ran down her chin, but his fingers caught it.

'All of it,' Rakhal said. 'There are herbs that help you to rest, that are good for your womb.'

He pressed the thick goo to her lips and she took it from his finger. He was hard and trying to ignore it.

He pulled back the silk and she slid into bed. Her body was on fire. It must be the herbs or the oils, for there was heat between her legs and her breasts felt taut as he stared down at her.

'Sleep,' he ordered, and left the room.

So tempted was she to call him. And it was the strangest place, the most dizzying place, for the music was louder from the lounge and it lulled her. The herbs from the drink made her dreams giddy, and then the music was quiet, and there was just the sound of laughter drifting across the desert night. A splash from the pool and then another one. She opened her eyes and a tear escaped—for it was not, as she had thought when she'd first arrived, the servants partying while the master was away.

She had only just realized. The bright colours the women had been dressed in, the dancing, the laughter that had come from the pool...

That was his harem.

# CHAPTER TWELVE

'You can continue to sulk,' Rakhal said a few days later, when she was still so furious she would hardly speak with him, 'or you can enjoy the reprieve.'

'I'll sulk, thank you.'

Natasha lay on the cushions. She was allowed out, apparently, because the music wasn't playing. She was still dressed in the flimsy organza, and would be bathed at sunset tonight. Rakhal had dismissed the maidens who usually hovered around her, and satisfied that the coupling had taken place Abdul left them alone now, but although they now had the opportunity, Natasha refused to talk.

'You wanted a holiday...'

'I wanted to lie on the beach and spend time with my friends.'

'But you weren't able to,' Rakhal reminded her, 'for your brother stole from you. Now you can rest and be pampered. I do not see what your issue is.'

*'Issues,'* Natasha corrected. She was angry at him on so many levels—so many and especially one—but she could not bring herself to speak about it, could not

swallow down her jealousy enough for it not to appear in her voice. So she spoke of other things that bothered her—and there were plenty! 'You brought me here against my will.'

'You gave me no choice,' Rakhal said. 'When you spoke of this pill that you could take.'

Natasha looked away. Really she was not sure that she would have taken the pill—wasn't sure of anything any more—but Rakhal did not leave things there.

'Did you think I would leave you to deal with your brother?'

He had a point, but she would not give in. 'You could have discussed things with me.'

'There was no time.' Rakhal had no choice but to admit it. 'I explained to you that one day I would marry. I had already been told to return to choose my bride. I was to fly out on the Monday.'

And he watched the anger grow in her, watched the fire on her cheeks, and there was rare guilt as she challenged him.

'So I was your last fling?'

'I hoped,' Rakhal said, 'to see you again…'

'Were you going to ask me to join your harem?' she spat.

'I knew that would not go well. I thought I might see you in London.' She tried to rise from the cushions but he stood over her. 'Do you understand that I could not leave you in London knowing that you might be carrying my child? That I could not marry another without first being sure you were not? If you are pregnant,' Rakhal said, 'it might be my country's only chance to continue. My father was once arrogant, assuming he would produce many heirs.'

She sat there swallowing her fury as he continued.

'If you are pregnant,' Rakhal explained, 'I know it will be a difficult transition for you—that much I do understand. However, you will never live in fear again, and you will never know anxiety—that is my duty to you...I take care of your family. I take care of your problems. You live in luxury; you raise your children.'

'Without you?'

'You would see me through your fertile times,' Rakhal explained, 'and for feasts and celebrations, and of course I would come regularly and visit the children, teach them our history—especially the eldest.'

He did not understand the tears in her eyes—had never had to try to explain this before. He snapped his fingers. He was uncomfortable with this conversation and he did not like to discuss the pointless—for these were things that could never change.

'I am going to bathe and then I will walk in the desert,' Rakhal said. 'You should rest.' And he ordered music which meant she must return to her room.

She lay there for almost an hour seething, hearing the sound of laughter that came from the bathing area. No, she would not meekly lie back and accept his ways—at least in certain things!

'What are you doing here?' Rakhal snapped as she walked into his bathing area and the laughing and chatter abruptly ceased. 'I am bathing.'

'Really?' Her eyes flashed their warning and her

voice chilled the room. 'Tell your maidens they are dismissed.'

Rakhal's eyes were just as angry, but with a few short words and a flick of his wrist they were left alone. As he had stood over her before, Natasha now stood over him.

'I'm here because you think I may be pregnant. You are considering taking me as your bride.' She spoke very slowly, her face coming close to his. 'And you have the gall to have three women wash you while I am sent to my room...'

'I was having a bath.' Rakhal was far from repentant. 'There is nothing sensual in it.'

She slipped her hand in the water and found his thick, warm tumescence. 'Oh, I beg to differ.'

He moved her hand away. She was decorated, he remembered. But he saw her pale fingers linger on the surface of the water and wanted to push her hand back down.

'You are to rest...'

'I'm bored with resting.' Her eyes were dangerous. 'And I tell you this now, Rakhal—you have your rules, well, here are mine. There are to be no other women—and that means no maidens bathing you.' She saw his jaw tighten and she glimpsed a possible future and did not like it. 'If I am pregnant that will go for our marriage too.'

'You are being ridiculous.'

'No.' She shook her head.

'You will be in the palace,' he told her. 'You will not even know...'

'I'll know,' Natasha said.

Rakhal did not like the rules being rewritten—especially this one—and simply dismissed her.

'Fine,' Natasha said. 'I'm going for a walk.'

'A walk!' He was aghast. 'You do not walk. You are to rest.'

'I have rested.' She was having great trouble keeping her voice reasonable. 'And now I would like some fresh air. I want to see the desert.'

'It is not a place for a stroll,' Rakhal said, but she would not give in.

'If you want to swim I have a private pool, and there is a garden around it...'

'I want to get out.'

'You do not just wander out to the desert alone. I thought the other night had taught you that much at least...'

'Then walk with me.'

If she stayed inside, even within the compound, for another minute she would surely go crazy. Perhaps he sensed that, for he gave a nod, and as he began to call the maidens to come and dry him and dress him he had the good sense to change his mind.

'Go and put on a robe,' Rakhal said. 'And you must have a drink before we leave.' Still she stood there. 'I'm assuming you're not here to dry me?'

Her blush chased her out of the bathroom. It was not what he had said, more the thoughts his words had triggered. She refused to think of him drying and dressing, took the small victory that he was alone, and slipped on a robe over her sheer gown. The maids came and tied on thin leather sandals, ensured she took a long drink, clearly worried that she was leaving the safety of the tent.

'I'll be fine,' she assured Amira, but she could see the dart of fear in the young girl's eyes.

As soon as she was outside she understood why, for the air was not soothing. It was hot and dry. Even the light wind cast sand in her eyes, and she realised then the haven of the compound.

'It is not a place for walking,' Rakhal said.

'I thought you said you went out in the desert a lot? That the desert is where you do your thinking...?'

'I am from the desert, though.'

'You mean your mother was from the desert.'

He looked down to where she walked beside him. 'It is not that simple—even if I never met her, her history is within me. I know how to survive here. You do not.'

'What was she like?' Natasha asked. 'You must have found out...'

Rakhal had never discussed this sort of thing—not even with his father. His childish questions had been dismissed. Yet he had found out things on his visits to the desert, and had overheard conversations with the maidens—yes, his mother had been a wise and beautiful soul, but she had been other things too, and he chose now to share them.

'She was very unusual,' Rakhal said. 'My father met her when he was walking; he found her dancing in the desert. He chose her as his bride even though he was warned against it. Normally the King's wife does not cause problems, but my mother did.'

'Tell me,' Natasha urged—not just because she had to understand this complicated man, but because the desert fascinated her so.

'My father had work to do in London. After a few months of marriage he was disappointed that my mother was not pregnant and she was too—she did not like the palace and pined for the desert. The maidens were frantic, for she stopped eating and would hardly take a drink—she spat out the custard...' He turned and gave a wry smile, for Natasha had done the same. 'She grew too thin, too pale and weak, and my father had her taken to London. He said that there the best hospitals were available, the best treatments, and once there she started to pick up and eat...'

'Maybe it was your father she missed and not the desert?'

Rakhal shook his head, but he could not completely refute it. After all, it was in London that he had been conceived.

'My father carries guilt with him—he should not have succumbed with his bride in London. None of the traditions were followed. She returned to Alzirz already pregnant. She stayed at the palace but despite their best efforts the damage was done and she grew weaker there. I was born just a few months later and she died in the process.' He looked over to Natasha. 'I do not ask you to believe in our ways, just that you understand that in going through with this I am trying to protect you too.'

And that much she did understand.

'I spoke to my brother today.'

She had at first thought herself a prisoner, and had been surprised on the second day when Amira had brought her a phone and said that her brother wished to speak with her—now they spoke most days.

'How was he?'

'He said sorry,' Natasha said. 'He's said sorry many, many times. But this time I think he means it.' She glanced up at Rakhal, to his strong profile, to the eyes she could not read. She wanted to ask him a question. 'I've been thinking...'

'The desert makes you think.'

'I know,' she admitted. 'I was so angry with my parents for making me sell the house...' her words tumbled out fast '...I think they were looking out for me—I think they knew Mark's problems. If the house had been in both our names....' She shuddered at the thought.

'They still are looking out for you,' Rakhal said.

'Do you believe that?'

'Of course.'

'Do you think your mother is looking out for you?'

Those wide shoulders shrugged and she almost had to run to keep up with him, but then he paused. 'Have you heard of dust devils?'

She shook her head.

'Tornado?'

She nodded.

'Sometimes there are small ones. Often...' He looked out to the horizon, as if looking might make one appear. 'Sometimes I think I see her there dancing,' Rakhal said. 'Sometimes I hear her laughing. It was five years ago that my father insisted I marry.' He looked at her shocked face and smiled. 'Here in Alzirz we only marry once in a lifetime.'

'So you've defied him?'

'It was not easy,' Rakhal said. 'There was much pressure. I know my people need an heir. I came out here to think and I heard her laughing, as if she was giving me her blessing to refuse. Maybe I am wrong. Maybe I should have married then...' He looked to Natasha. 'It might have saved you some trouble.'

He was uncomfortable with this discussion—had told her things he had never shared. He started to walk on.

'Anyway, she is back with the desert she loved.'

'Rakhal.' She looked out at a landscape that was fierce, brutal and staggeringly beautiful, and then she looked back to a man that was the same. She craved his mouth and his mind, but not his ways. 'It wasn't the desert she pined for—it was your father.'

'Enough!'

'Well, clearly they were happy to see each other in London.' She would not be silenced. 'I can think of nothing worse than being locked away in the palace. Especially...' Natasha swallowed. 'Especially if I loved my husband and knowing...' She could not bite down on her venom, for how she hated his ways. 'Your mother would have loathed knowing he was with his harem.'

'I said that is *enough*.' Rakhal did not need a lecture from a woman who had spent just a few nights in his land. 'You admonish our ways, yet you defend yours.

In my country women are cosseted, looked after—whereas you were in fear of your own brother. And,' he demanded, 'is there fidelity in your land?'

'Some,' Natasha said.

'Rubbish,' Rakhal said. 'In your land hearts get broken over and over because of the impossible rules. Here we accept that no one woman can suffice for a king. I will not continue with this ridiculous conversation,' Rakhal said, and strode off.

'You really don't like arguing, do you?' She ran to keep up with him. 'You only like it when I agree with you. Well, I never will.'

'You might have to.'

'No.'

She stopped and stood still in the fierce heat. She stood as he walked, and she called to his back as he walked on.

'If I am to respect your ways, then you will respect mine.'

'Natasha, we do not have time for this. The sun is fierce. It is time to return to the tent.'

'I'm not going back until you listen to me.'

'Then you will be waiting a very long time.'

But of course they both knew he was bluffing, for though he would allow Natasha to perish in the desert, she might be carrying his child and that made it a different matter indeed.

With a hiss of annoyance Rakhal turned around and strode towards her. 'I will carry you back if I have to.'

'Good,' Natasha said. 'Then my mouth will be closer to your ear.'

Reluctant was the laugh that shot from his lips. 'You have an answer for everything.'

'No, Rakhal, I don't,' Natasha admitted. 'I have no idea what is going to happen if I *am* pregnant. I don't have any answers there. But while we wait and see what is going to happen, while I'm stuck here in the middle of nowhere, while I am forced to play by your rules, then I insist on enforcing one of mine. There will be no other women.'

'Natasha.' His voice was full of reason—patient, even—as he explained the strange rules. 'I have told you: I cannot sleep with you if there is even a chance you are pregnant...'

'Then you'd better get used to being alone.' She saw the shake of his head. 'I mean it, Rakhal.'

'Suppose I play by your rules? What if you *are* pregnant? What if we are to be wed? You'd really expect me to go months, maybe a year...'

'You clearly expect *me* to.'

'But it is different for women,' Rakhal said. 'You went almost a quarter of a century without it. After all, you—'

He did not get to finish. Her hand sliced his cheek and he felt the sting of her fingers meet his flesh.

'If I am your wife, you are loyal to *me*.'

'And if I am not?' Rakhal challenged. 'What? You will lie there rigid like a plank of wood?' The triumph she had witnessed that night was back in his eyes now. 'I did not even touch you the other night, yet your body came to me...'

'You hadn't been with another,' Natasha retorted.

'You didn't sicken me...*then*.' And the wind whistled across the desert, the sun seemed to burn in the back of her skull, as she told the truth. 'I would never forgive you, Rakhal.' She made things a little more clear. 'And I don't give out second warnings.'

# CHAPTER THIRTEEN

She could not sleep, despite the custard.

Eight days here and she was growing more crazy by the day.

Her breasts felt tender and she wondered if she would soon have her period, but—more worryingly for Natasha—she wasn't so sure that she wanted it to arrive. She wanted more time with Rakhal.

She should not enjoy their conversations, she told herself.

Should not crave the evenings when they played old board games or ate and laughed or simply talked. Should not lie at night and listen to the music and remember the shadows and picture herself back in his bed.

Should not let herself fall in love with this strange land...

And when the music was silenced she wished she could sleep, wished that she did not crave his company, so she lay there, though she had been given permission. She should not condone his strange summons—except she could not sleep.

'What are these?' She had never seen anything more beautiful. There was a roll of black velvet on the floor and it was littered with jewels of all different shades of pink, from the palest blush to the darkest of wine, and Rakhal was sitting as if contemplating them. 'Are they rubies?'

'Diamonds,' Rakhal answered, and it was at that very moment she realised she was in serious trouble.

Oh, she had known it when she awoke on the plane, had known it too when she ran into the desert, but this was a different sort of trouble. When she saw the stones, and the care he was taking with his decision, she had a flutter in her stomach. Was he choosing a diamond for her? To be feeling like that was a very different sort of trouble indeed.

'There are also sapphires,' Rakhal said, and gestured for her to join him. 'It is a difficult decision. I do not want to cause offence.'

'Offence?'

'Diamonds are more valuable, especially pink ones, but here...'

He handed her two stones, both heavy and a purplish pink, and she held them up to the light, marvelling at the kaleidoscope that danced in them.

'They are beautiful, yes?'

'They're more than beautiful,' Natasha breathed, for it was as if an angel had chipped a piece out of heaven and dropped it to earth.

'The trouble is they are sapphires.'

'I thought sapphires were blue?'

She looked to him and he was smiling——a smile

she had never seen, for it was black and unkind, but it was not aimed at her. He looked to the jewels she had put down.

'That I hope will be his first thought.'

'His?'

'King Emir of Alzan,' Rakhal said. 'I am to choose a gift to send to celebrate the gift of his twin girls. I first thought of diamonds—pink diamonds—but it is too obvious a choice, so I have had my people source the best in pink sapphires. I do not want to cause offence by giving a gift that is not valuable, but these are the best.' And then his smile darkened. 'But naturally when you think of sapphires you think of blue, and blue makes you think of sons.' Rakhal had made his choice. 'As Emir must be thinking…as the entire country is thinking…'

'Perhaps Emir is simply enjoying his gorgeous new girls.'

He looked at her and lay down on his cushions, and she lay down on hers, because sometimes, when neither was sulking, they talked. She'd told him about her family, about her parents and how she missed them so. About her job as a teacher. In turn he would tell her tales of the desert and sometimes, like this time, it was the only place on earth she wanted to be. His voice was rich and painted pictures in her mind, and tonight when he asked for the music to resume he told her she could remain.

'Generations ago the Sheikha Queen was to give birth in one full moon's time.' He smiled as she closed her eyes to the sound of his voice. He had never expected her to be so keen to learn of his land, had never known another who was not from here to be so interested in the tales of old. 'But the Queen surprised everyone. The birth was early, and they were expecting only one baby, but two sons were delivered. The *doula* was taken by surprise and there was confusion. With twins, the firstborn should be branded, to avoid any mistake, only these twins were a surprise, and they could not be sure who was the firstborn. Always there had been unrest in Alzanirz. The country was divided—'

'Why?' she interrupted. She looked over to him and saw that he was watching her, knew his eyes had been roaming her, and she loved the feeling of warmth.

'This side honoured the sky, the other the land. Both thought their way the most important. The King sought counsel and it was decided to appease all people. Each twin would rule half of the land.'

'So Emir and you are related?'

'Distantly.' Rakhal shrugged.

'And now he has twins?'

'He would have preferred sons,' Rakhal said. 'His wife was ill with this pregnancy—perhaps too ill to get pregnant again...'

'Poor thing.'

'It is good for Alzirz,' Rakhal explained. 'Perhaps Alzan will return to us soon.' He gave a wry smile. 'Emir has one brother, but he is not King material—he is too wild in his ways. Emir would never step aside for Hassan...and now he has two daughters! Twins divided us and now they will reunite us.'

She did not return his smile. 'Why would you want another country to rule over?'

'Why do you seek debate when there can be none? It was written many years ago. I don't expect you to understand.'

'I don't want to,' Natasha said. 'I cannot imagine being disappointed to have a daughter.'

'You do not have to,' Rakhal said. 'For here in Alzirz the sex of a child is not a concern. All the people want is healthy offspring and plenty of them.'

And she was stupid to have hoped he might be selecting a stone for *her*—even more stupid for thinking she wanted to be a part of this strange land. She stood and headed to her chambers.

'Where are you going?' He had been enjoying their talk.

'To my room.'

'You offend easily.'

'You so easily offend.'

He was tired of her moods, tired of her speaking back to him and yet he was not tired of *her*.

Rakhal summoned Abdul and asked that the sapphires be delivered to Emir in the morning. Pleased with his gift and the bile it would induce in his rival he headed to his sleeping quarters. But the brief pleasure died as he stretched out on the pillows and asked for the music to be silenced for he remembered the night she had shared his bed.

But perhaps he should ask the musician to resume, for his body craved a woman. So many times these past nights his hand had reached for the rope that would summon the mistress of his harem to send him a woman, and now, as he lay there, his mind awake and his body too, he thought of Natasha and what she might look like beneath the organza. He had only seen her covered, but he knew she would be hennaed and oiled, and though it was forbidden how he ached to taste and to see...

He ached...

His hand reached for the rope to pull it, so that he would not think of Natasha—for even if he wanted her he could not have her. If his child grew in her womb it should rest undisturbed.

He was hard at the thought of her. He should reach for the rope, not reach for himself, for that was also forbidden. There were twenty women who could attend to his needs tonight, except his mind craved only one.

'Rakhal?'

He had not heard her footsteps. It was only her voice that told him she had entered his quarters.

'You are not permitted here,' he barked, and rolled onto his side, but he knew that she had seen the rise of the silk.

'The music isn't playing, and anyway I can't sleep.'

She could not. Natasha knew from the ache low down in her stomach what the morning would bring—knew that it was their last real chance to be alone, that it might be their last chance to talk properly. Impossible as the rules were, Rakhal was not totally unreasonable. Unlike the night she had arrived, when she had felt so terrified and alone, now—despite their differences—there was a peace that only he brought, a smile that only he summoned, and never again would she fear him.

'I'm not tired.'

'Then pull your rope and one of the maids will bring you a potion—or give you a massage if you choose…'

'I want to talk.'

'Then I will have someone who speaks English come and read to you, or hold a conversation.'

'I meant to you,' Natasha answered. '*With* you.' When he said nothing she looked up. 'The stars are amazing tonight. Can they pull back my roof?'

'Tomorrow I will ask for it to be done.'

He wanted her gone, wanted to summon a woman from the harem. He did not want a circus parading in the tent tonight and fixing the roof when he wanted— no, *needed*—her gone. He felt the indent of the cushions and was appalled by her boldness as she sat down on the Prince's bed, where only the invited were allowed. He snapped on the light to scold her—and then wished that he hadn't for she looked amazing…her hair coiled over her shoulders and her mouth his for the taking. He must not.

'Go back to bed.'

'I'm not ten years old,' Natasha said. 'You can't just send me. I'm bored.'

'I am never bored.' He said it as an insult.

'Yes, well, you've got the best view. If I could look at the stars I wouldn't be bored either.' She lay down beside him but he moved away. 'I'm not here to seduce you.'

She grinned. There was nothing more beautiful than to lie on his bed and stare at the stars. And then her smile faded, for deep in her stomach she felt again a telltale cramp and moved her hand there. He watched, and was silent for a moment.

'You should sleep,' he said finally. 'Take the custards.'

But he knew somehow they were trying to hold back a tide that had turned. He could see the swell of her breasts and recalled the flash of tears tonight when another time she might have laughed. He did not want it to be tomorrow—did not want their time in the desert to end.

'I will show you the stars.'

He did. He called for gentle music and he showed her Orion, even if she could not make it out at first. It was like the best bedtime story, his deep, low voice telling her about the magnificent hunter and the red wound on his shoulder—the red star.

And she saw it.

'It is coming to the end of its life.'

'So what will happen to Orion?' She was tired now, but she loved his stories.

'He will burn brighter for a while,' Rakhal explained. 'When he explodes and dies he will burn so bright he will be visible in the daytime.'

'In our lifetime?'

'No.' He smiled.

'How soon?

'A million years.'

'And that's soon?'

'It is to the desert.'

He wanted to turn to her, wanted the tiny years of his life to shine with a significance that was alien to him. It was not about his title, it was about a significant other, and that did not mesh with one who would be King. His mind must marry only his country. He could ponder the sky no longer, and now he was restless.

But not Natasha. His voice and his stories had soothed her and maybe now she could sleep. She was growing rather fond of the custard. Maybe a drink would help her. Maybe the cramps would fade and she would have more time here. She would ask the maidens to bring her some of that sweet brew. He had told her she could ask for anything. Her fingers reached for the rope above his head and pulled it.

'What are you doing?' His hand snatched at hers, but too late.

'I want the potion,' she explained. 'I want something to help me sleep.'

And he tried.

Rakhal tried.

He told her to leave his bed, to go to her room, that the maids would bring it there. She could not understand his urgency, for he practically ordered her from the room, looked as if he was about to carry her. Then his voice stopped, and Natasha's head turned to the woman who was stepping in from the shadows. She could hear the jangle of jewels, see the outline of her scantily clad body and the veil over her face, and even as he ordered her away in his language, even when she had gone, the musky scent of her lingered, and Natasha thought she might vomit as realisation dawned.

'She was here to sleep with you.'

'No.'

'You were going to sleep with her tonight!' Her voice was rising. 'While I slept you were planning—'

'No!' It was Rakhal who shouted. '*You* were the one who summoned her.' He pointed to the rope. 'When you pulled that...'

And she laughed—a dangerous laugh, a furious laugh, an incredulous one. 'I pull mine and I bloody well get custard!'

'I did not pull it!' Rakhal shouted his defence. 'I have not.'

'But you can!'

She looked at him and there was guilt in his eyes, for tonight perhaps he might have.

'Yes.' His voice was a touch hoarse. 'Natasha, you must see reason. No man—no husband—will wait a year...'

'A *year*?'

'You would get three months to rest after having the baby.'

She loathed him, and she loathed this land.

With a sob she left the room.

She hated this place and its strange rules—hated what she might become. Hated that she would be served on a plate to him once a year. She could not win, could only lose. And she hated that her period was near, and the music simply added to her madness. She shouted for it to be silenced, but of course she was ignored. She shouted again as Rakhal, with a sash at his hips, dashed from his room. He called for the maidens, for Natasha was raging, and they took her to her room, tried to force a drink on her and not the one she knew. But her screams grew louder. She screamed as if she was being poisoned.

Finally Rakhal intervened and took the brew from the maids.

'This is cucumber to clear your head, and chestnut to calm you, and there is wild garlic too, to calm the anger...'

'You're poisoning me!' she shouted. 'You're sedating me so you can sleep with her.'

'Are you mad?' Rakhal demanded. 'Are you mad enough to think I would give you something that would harm—?'

'Am I going mad?' she begged. She truly thought she was, because she knew then that she loved him, and all he wanted from her was a baby. And she hated the harem, and that he had shared himself with the women there. 'I can't bear to be here for another minute.'

'You must sleep.'

'I can't sleep with them watching.'

'Leave,' he said to his maidens, and when she still would not calm he took her kicking and screaming and carried her to his bed.

'I have not slept with anyone since you!' he roared, and he cursed, for it was killing him that he hadn't. But still she did not calm, so he picked up his scythe. She screamed as he raised it and then he sliced the rope. *'There!'*

And she stopped, but her breathing was heavy. The sheer organza robe had risen and he tried not to look.

'I have not slept with anyone,' he said, and his breathing was hard too. He stood over where she lay.

'And yet you won't sleep with me?'

'No,' Rakhal said.

But he watched her gold curls disappear as she covered herself with the organza and she saw his eyes linger, saw the set of his jaw as he resisted what was normal.

She had only this chance and she took it. 'You don't have to treat me like glass, Rakhal.'

Still his eyes roamed.

'What did the maidens do?' He was curious when he should not be.

'They painted me.'

He should not know of these things, but he knew a little, and his eyes flicked to her breasts. They were two tempting peaks, the nipples jutting, and he had to hold in his tongue so as not to lick one. Her body was pink beneath the sheer fabric and he knew where they would have painted her. So badly he wanted to see, to peel back the organza and explore her body, to see what a royal prince never should.

Her voice spoke on. 'I'm bored waiting for my period, I'm bored being treated like glass, and it kills me being with you and you not touching me.'

Still he did nothing. She moaned in frustration, and he sensed danger as she climbed from the bed.

'Where are you going?'

'To bed.'

'For your hands to roam your body?' He could see the lust in her eyes.

'Well, yours won't.'

'It is forbidden…'

'For you, perhaps,' Natasha said. 'What are you going to do? Tie me to the bed?'

'It could be bad for the baby.'

'Oh, please.' She could not stand it, could not bear it. She put her hands to her ears. 'La-la-la…' She would not give in to his thinking. 'You don't know what you're missing. Pregnancy is beautiful, and your wife's body would crave you, and instead you'd be with *her.*'

She jabbed at the torn rope; she was going insane in the desert, but it wasn't just sex, it was him. It was his caress that she craved, his mouth where there was heat, and she wanted his mind and his days and his nights too.

And perhaps Natasha had driven him crazy too, for he turned from the rules and to her.

He must not make love to her, but he could kiss her.

He pushed her down onto the bed. He would take the edge off her burning desire.

He hushed her with his mouth and she caved in to his tongue. But his words took the pleasure away.

'Just a kiss,' he said.

'No.'

For he'd made it worse. His touch had made it more, not less, and she climbed from his bed and went to her own.

He stared to the skies for an answer, to the shapes and the stories he knew well. There was not a jewel on the earth that matched a single star's splendour, but not even the stars could tell him what to do.

# CHAPTER FOURTEEN

NATASHA awoke to the sound of him praying and knew he would not change—perhaps she had no right to expect him to. They were from different worlds after all .

She walked out to the breakfast table, but did not sit down on the floor to wait for him to join her; instead she went to the wash area to have what she already knew confirmed.

The maidens bowed their heads as she informed them, and then she walked back to her bedroom and dressed in the clothes she had arrived in. As she pulled on her underwear she saw the fading flowers low on her stomach and ached with a strange grief that they would not blossom and grow and stretch. She mourned for something that had never been, nor could ever be.

Rakhal was seated on the floor at the breakfast table and turned when he heard her approach. His smile faded when he saw her face and registered the maidens who were quietly weeping, for they had grown fond of Natasha.

He dismissed them, and she was relieved that he did so, for she could not stand their tears. It was her period, for God's sake, Natasha reasoned, not a baby she had lost. But her own disappointment sideswiped her. Might she crave what once she had feared?

'It wasn't meant to be.' Rakhal's voice was practical, though he cursed his own restraint, berated not taking her that second night—for then they would have had the ways of old on their side. 'You must be relieved?'

'Of course,' she lied, 'and so must you...' She attempted a smile but her lips would not move.

'No.' He stood, for he did not want it to be over. 'I should be relieved.' And he did what he did not usually do—or never had till he had met her. He wrapped her in his arms and attempted to comfort her. 'But I am not.'

And she did something that no one had ever tried to do with him, for he had never needed it: the arms that coiled around his neck offered comfort to *him*.

She let the tears fall and he held her, and they mourned what had never existed, let go of what could never be.

'You can return to your life,' Rakhal said.

'You can choose your bride.'

And he felt her arms around him and offered what he'd thought he never would. But he wanted her in his life. He would somehow deal with his father's disapproval and the fear and anger from his people at such an unwise choice—more so than if she were already pregnant.

'I choose you.' Rakhal bestowed the greatest honour. 'I choose you to be my wife. I will marry you in fourteen days and you can come to my bed again.'

'Only to be removed from it two days later,' Natasha said, her eyes spilling tears as she looked up at him. 'Only to be taken away when I'm pregnant and then brought back a year later.'

'That is how it is,' Rakhal said. 'That is how it must be.'

'And the harem?'

'This is our way.'

'But it's not mine!' She tried to fathom it, tried to see herself as a part of it, but then shook her head and declined his proposal. 'No, I will not be your wife.'

'It is overwhelming, I know.' He did not linger on her refusal. In a moment she would come around. 'I will deal with my father; in time the people will accept—'

'It's not your father or the people I need to accept me.' Natasha looked at him. 'It's you, Rakhal, and you won't. So, no, I won't marry you.'

'Have you any idea of the honour I'm giving you by asking?' His arms released her.

She missed the shield of them and yet she stood firm, looked at his incredulous face and was angry for both of them. Angry that he simply did not get it—that he could not see how lonely his idea of a marriage would make her.

'Have you any idea of my shame that you did?'

'Shame?'

'Yes—shame!' Natasha was not crying now. Her eyes glittered instead with fury, and some of it was inward for she was so very tempted to say yes. But at what cost? she reminded herself as she spoke to him, as she pictured the future she simply must deny. 'To be *brought* to your bed to provide you and your country with children. To know that when the need arises you simply pull a rope… I want a partner, Rakhal—I want someone to share my life with, the good bits and the bad, someone who wants *me*, not just the babies I can give him. It's not going to happen, Rakhal. I want my passport. I want to go home.'

'Your Highness…' Abdul walked in at the most painful of moments.

'Not now!' Rakhal roared.

But Abdul did not flee. He stood and spoke to Rakhal in their own language and Natasha watched as Rakhal's face paled. He gave a brief nod and uttered a response, then turned to her.

'Abdul has just delivered some serious news.'

'Your father?'

Rakhal shook his head. 'No, but I do need to speak with him. You will wait here.'

And she waited for what was close to an hour until he returned. She'd hoped they would speak now more calmly, but Rakhal had other things on his mind.

'I have to leave,' Rakhal said. 'I need to leave on this helicopter. But my people will arrange transport for you—whatever you want—if you choose to stay in a hotel for a few days, or see your brother, or…' He hesitated. So badly he wanted to ask that she stay, but so badly it burned that she had refused him.

'Rakhal—' She was angry with him, but Natasha understood that something might have happened to his father. Yet he was dismissing her so coolly just because her period had come, just because she would not accept his ways, and that was the last straw. 'You really know how to make a woman feel used.'

'I asked you to be my bride less than an hour ago,' Rakhal said, 'and yet you accuse me of making you feel used.' He did not have time for another row, and neither did he have time to explain properly, but he tried. 'Emir...' Rakhal's words were sparse. 'His wife died at dawn.'

'The twins' mother...?'

He gave a brief nod. 'I must attend the burial, offer him condolences.'

'Of course.'

And then Abdul came, and he must have informed Rakhal that his transport was ready for he nodded and said to Natasha that he must now leave. Abdul said something else, more words that she did not understand, but they were said with a smile that had Natasha's stomach churning.

'What did Abdul just say?' she challenged when he had gone.

'Nothing.'

'Is this good news for Alzirz?' She would not relent. 'Has it bought you some time?'

'They were his words, not mine,' Rakhal pointed out. 'Yes, it gives us some time. But for now...' He felt as if a mirror was cracking in his mind. 'Now Emir will be deeply grieving. In Alzan...' how he wished she could understand '...because the King can take another wife they live as you would choose.'

And it was as if he was back in London, staring

out of the window. The blackness in his soul had returned—only he recognised it this time. Recognised the jealousy that had burnt there. For in Alzan, where there could be more than one partner in a lifetime, all hope for the country's future was not pinned on one bride. There the royals could live and love together and watch their family grow.

'So could you,' Natasha said, when he'd tried to explain to her.

Rakhal shook his head, for it could not be. 'The people would never accept it. The King can be married only to his country. The wife of the King is to be—'

'Locked away!' Natasha shouted. 'Kept on a luxurious shelf and taken down when needed!' She hated Alzirz, hated this land and its strange ways, except she loved *him*. 'Please, can you just think about it? Even if not for me. If you do marry a more suitable woman, can you at least think about it for *her*?'

'I have to leave.' There was no time to argue and Rakhal knew there was no point either. Had Natasha been pregnant there would have been no discussion— she would have had to conform to their ways—but she was not, so why didn't he feel relief?

He should just go, and he moved to do so—did not give her a kiss. She had refused his offer and so it was not his place. But still he could not end it.

'Stay.' He swallowed his pride and forced the word. 'We can speak on my return…'

'And you'll think about it?'

He gave a nod, for how could he not think about it? And yet it was an impossible ask. The King's mind must be only on his country, not on his children or his wife.

As he boarded the helicopter and it lurched into the sky, so too did his stomach lurch as Abdul made another comment about Emir that a few weeks ago might have brought a wry smile to Rakhal's lips.

Today it did not.

'You will show respect.' He stared at his aide.

'I would not say it to *him*.'

'And neither should you say it to me.'

He saw the set of his aide's chin, saw the pursing of his lips, for the Prince was more than chastising him. He was turning his back on a rivalry of old and it would no doubt be reported to the King. But his time with Natasha had changed things. This morning he had woken with a woman in his bed and hope for the future—he had glimpsed how Emir had lived.

And he wanted it.

Even the grief...

*Such* grief on Emir's features as Rakhal entered the Palace of Alzan and he kissed him on both cheeks, as was their way. He offered him his sympathy, as was their way too; only for Rakhal it felt different. This time Rakhal spoke from a place he never had before. His words came from his heart.

Not that Emir noticed.

An English nanny held the tiny twins and she was weeping whcn Rakhal went over. He kissed each twin's tiny cheek and offered them too his condolences. The babies were teary and fretful, and a veiled woman apologised to Rakhal.

'They miss their mother's milk.'

He did not nod and return to the men; instead he lifted one tiny child, whose name, he was informed, was Clemira, and told the veiled woman that it was her mother she missed. In that moment he missed his own.

Pink sapphires did not seem such a suitable gift now.

And the Sheikha Queen, Rakhal realised, was in fact indispensable. For he looked at Emir and realised he had loved his wife. Now Emir would have the agony of finding another bride while still grieving his loss.

As might he.

# CHAPTER FIFTEEN

'You have been granted full privileges.'

She wanted Rakhal, but instead it was Abdul who returned that night and told her of her *reward*—that she could travel freely to visit her brother, go to the desert or to the harem and perhaps surprise Rakhal. Rakhal would see her at times in London too.

The meaning and intent were clear, and Natasha glimpsed her future—a life that was a little more taken care of, for he had paid funds for her time here that were generous, and her brother's debts were sorted out. She could return to Alzirz when she chose—except it would kill her.

To have the man she loved as an occasional treat, a reward for them both now and then with no strings, an exotic fantasy she could return to at times...

For how long? Natasha thought with tears in her eyes.

Till the time when her body was no longer the one he wanted? When she did not amuse him any more?

'Rakhal knows that I would never agree to this.' She shook her head. 'I want to speak to him.'

'Prince Rakhal wants to concentrate now on duty,' Abdul explained. 'I have arranged transport to take you back to London.'

'No.' He had asked her to stay till he returned and she did not believe Abdul. 'I want to see him.'

'It is not about *your* wants,' Abdul said. 'And Prince Rakhal knows that, which is why he has placed this stamp.'

She looked at the passport he handed to her. On it was the gold stamp that Abdul could not fake, for it could only come from Rakhal. What hurt her the most was not his coarse offer, but the fact that she considered it in the knowledge that somehow her body was now forever his. Somehow so too was her heart, even if she must leave. After Rakhal no one else would ever suffice.

'I must return to the Prince now. A helicopter will take you to the airport.'

She lay alone on his bed and waited for the transport that would prise her away from the desert she loved and the rules that she loathed. She wanted to speak with him just one more time—wanted Rakhal to look her in the eye and tell her it was over.

She could hear the laughter and noises of the harem, the splashes in the pool and the music that seduced. She begged the stars for an answer, but all they did was shine silver—except one that was maybe a planet. That one shone a little gold, as she had on the night she had met him, and as her heart shone now with hope.

'You should not be here.' The madam scolded her as she parted the curtain. 'You should not wander.'

But she showed the madam the gold stamp and with that she could not argue.

'It will be at a time of my choosing, though,' the madam warned her. 'You will not be called on for now. When he returns from the funeral the Prince will be in deep *tahir*, but that will change before the wedding.'

And the gold stamp gave her rare status, for when a furious Abdul came to the tent late in the night, to insist that she take her flight to London, the madam shooed him away—for here the madam ruled.

She learnt so much in those days—the harem was nothing like she'd imagined. The women there were spoiled and pampered too. They were massaged and oiled and kept beautiful, and they spent their time chatting and laughing, reading and swimming, as any group of girlfriends on a luxury holiday together would.

'We are spoiled by the Prince,' said Nadia, who had a throaty French accent.

Natasha had been surprised to find out that not all the women were from Alzirz. The Prince, it would seem, liked variety.

'Before I came here,' explained Calah, who was from Alzirz, 'my family was poor and I was to be married to an old man—to keep his home and share his filthy bed. I ran away, and I would have been working the streets, but I was lucky and I was chosen. Now I live in luxury and my family is being taken care of. I am studying for a degree—' she smiled at Natasha '—and sometimes I get to be with the Prince.' Her eyes challenged the doubt in Natasha's. 'Which is always a pleasure.'

Natasha's cheeks burnt as she heard the other women discuss him, and she dreaded the ring of the bell that, for Natasha, would sound the end if the madam did not first choose her.

But days passed and the bell did not ring—and then Natasha found out why. 'He is meeting with the King,' the madam explained. 'Soon his bride will be announced. Tomorrow, they say.' She smiled to her girls and all but Natasha returned it. 'Our Prince will announce his bride.'

# CHAPTER SIXTEEN

RAKHAL stared out of the palace windows to the celebrations that were starting in the street.

'It is good to see the people so happy,' the King said. 'They fear my passing, they know now that it will be soon, and the wedding will please them.'

'The people have nothing to fear,' Rakhal said. 'I will be a good leader.'

He would be. He had visions for his country and he knew that the people were ready. The wealth from the mines needed to be better returned to the people; infrastructure was needed—hospitals, schools and universities. But at a pace that would do no harm. His heart told him to protect the desert, not to inflict upon it modern ways—and he needed a clear head for that. He needed time alone and deep reflection for every decision he would make—not a wife who would demand he speak to her, who would pout when she was bored. Yet at that moment his heart ached for the same.

'I have just days,' the King said. 'Soon the people will be in mourning. You must change that. You must give them an heir, give them hope...'

PROPERTY OF MERTHYR TYDFIL PUBLIC LIBRARY

Rakhal looked out to the sea of people and thought of the grief that would soon seep into them. He knew his plans for the future would scare them rather than please. Theirs would be a grief that only a bride and a baby would appease.

But the bride he wanted could not be found—his people were still searching for her. She was back in London, Abdul had informed him, and yet she would not take his calls.

Rakhal had not thought it possible to mourn a living person, yet it felt as if he did, and he mourned too a baby that had never existed. He did not understand how Natasha could leave without speaking with him.

'If I fly to London—'

'Enough!' The King was furious with his son—furious that still Rakhal insisted on bringing up this Natasha—and he let his displeasure show. 'Still—even as death creeps in—you try to postpone your duty.'

'I do not want to postpone it—I accept that I must marry. But if I could just speak to her…'

'And say what?' the King demanded. 'That you bend to her whims instead of serving your people? *Never.*' The King had had enough. 'Now we will feast, but tomorrow you will step onto the balcony wearing the gold braid and let the people know you have chosen your wife.'

Rakhal frowned, for this was straying from tradition .

'Tomorrow I will step onto the balcony wearing the gold braid, but now I return to the desert,' Rakhal said.

'And I will feast and celebrate there, and tomorrow I will return and choose from your selection.'

'Better you are here,' the King snapped. 'Save your seed for your bride.'

'I'm sure,' Rakhal snapped back, 'that there is plenty.'

And he did not bend to his father—not even now; instead he returned to the desert, and then to the land his mother had once roamed. He roamed it now with his eagle.

Since Natasha had left he had not shaved nor bathed.

He prayed and he sat and he tried to meditate.

A dust devil formed and he heard his mother laugh at his problems. She did not understand that tomorrow he must announce a wife, that the people would panic if it did not happen. She laughed and she danced and he did not understand.

He felt the sun on his skull and tried to clear his thoughts, to let them slip out of his mind as fast as they came in, to clear his head so he might be centred.

He did this often.

Rakhal would clear his head and let the silent desert fill it, let the voice of the wind and the stories in the sand infuse him. He trusted in the answers. But no matter how long he sat, no matter how he tried to empty his mind, to focus on his country and the leadership that would soon be his, all too soon Natasha would fill his thoughts.

He could not speak to his aides, nor his family—for they would not give unbiased counsel. They would not contemplate let alone discuss changes to the monarchy, to the rules and their ways; they would never permit his thinking. His grandfather had taught a young Rakhal the desert ways, though, and even if his son had rejected them his grandson had not.

He loved the desert as he loved the stars, sought wisdom from the dunes, and he knew then what he must do.

He took his eagle and let it circle.

And then he sent his eagle to the skies again.

If he did it a third time the Bedouins would be alerted.

If he did it a fourth they would continue with their day.

But if the bird ceased flying after three times the wizened old man would be summoned.

Rakhal sought his counsel rarely, though it was rumoured that Emir, at times, met with the old man too.

Within the hour Rakhal sat with a man who had seen one hundred and twenty yellow moons and heard again about two tests. And Rakhal silently questioned why he would ask someone so old about ways that should be new.

'I need to think of my country,' Rakhal said, 'except I think of her. I need my mind to be clear of her.'

'I will guide you in meditation,' the old man said.

Rakhal sat and let his mind empty, but still it was Natasha's face that he saw.

'Take your mind to the stars and beyond them.'

Rakhal did. But still she was there.

The old man took him further, past Orion, beyond the planets, and still there she was.

'To the edge of the universe,' the old man said.

But still she was there.

'To the end of the universe.'

She was there waiting.

'And beyond the end,' the old man instructed.

But there she was.

'And beyond the end again.'

Her image was not fading.

'It does not end.' Rakhal opened his eyes to the old man and hissed his frustration.

'It cannot end,' the old man said, and stood. 'Trust the desert. Trust in the traditions and the ways of old.'

'She doesn't want the ways of old.'

'Tonight you should trust in them.'

But the ways of old were not being adhered to.

Rakhal returned to his tent and declined a feast of fruit and music to please him. He watched as the arak turned white when Abdul added ice, and he turned down the hookah—all the traditional ways for a prince to behave before he made his choice.

'I wish to bathe.'

He summoned the maidens and asked that Abdul leave, for tonight he would be busy and the arak and the hookah would not help with that.

He laughed and chatted with the maidens who bathed him, and lay back as he was shaved, and then he rose from the bath, dressed in as little as was expected. And still Abdul remained.

'You will leave,' Rakhal said, and instructed the musician to play a more suitable choice for his mood.

'Drink.' Again Abdul pushed a glass towards him. 'Celebrate these last hours of freedom.'

And Rakhal was certain now that she was near.

# CHAPTER SEVENTEEN

'He has bathed!' The madam clapped her hands and got her girls' attention. 'And he has shaved, and he has summoned music and the most potent of foods....'

Her voice trailed off as Abdul appeared, and Natasha watched the madam's eyes narrow as he whispered some words.

They all waited but the bell did not ring, and she held her breath in hope, for maybe Rakhal could change even if not for her. But then came the kick in the guts of disappointment when finally it rang, and she could picture his hand reaching out to the rope on the bed where they had lain. There was a flurry of activity, the girls rubbing in oils and teasing their hair, doing their make-up and chattering excitedly as they tried to guess who might be chosen. Natasha held her breath and prayed it would be her.

'Nadia.'

The madam slipped a *yashmak* over the scantily dressed woman and sprayed her with a musky scent. It filled Natasha's nostrils and she felt like retching, for it was the same scent that had entered their room that night.

'It has been a while. His need will be great.'

The madam gave Nadia instructions and as she disappeared into the night Natasha lay on the cushions, closing her eyes against tears, trying and failing not to imagine what they were doing. She felt pure loss as their time together was terminated by a single ring of the bell, as her prince returned to the ways he knew best.

And her last tiny glimmer of hope died—a foolish hope, a stupid hope, she thought—when Nadia returned just fifteen minutes later.

'Leave Nadia,' the madam scolded as all the women except Natasha gathered around Nadia to ask how the Prince was. 'She will bathe and get some rest.'

But the madam frowned as Nadia went to her cushions and lay silent. The other girls frowned too, for usually there was a more excited return.

Over and over he shamed her.

The bell rang through the night, and Natasha screwed her eyes closed as one by one the women returned and he made a mockery of all they had been, all she had asked him to consider. Finally, when the bell was quiet, when the women all dozed and slept, she prayed for sunlight. Dawn would be here soon. He would go to prayer and she would leave, Natasha decided. At first light she would leave.

And then the bell rang.

The madam stood and parted the curtain, looked

outside and then over to Natasha. She put her fingers to her lips and summoned her.

Natasha was draped in a small skirt with a tiny coined fringe and beneath it she was naked. Her breasts were dressed with the same noisy fabric too, and a veil was placed to just reveal her eyes. She was told what it would mean should he gesture that she remove the veil. If he did that she would slap his face instead, Natasha decided. As the madam came to her with the musk Natasha shook her head, again remembering that night one of the women had come to the room. The scent still made her ill, but the madam insisted.

'He will be sleepy,' the mistress explained, 'so you may not get to surprise him.'

Surprise him? Natasha thought darkly. She'd more likely spit at him—not that she would tell the madam that; instead she stood as she was delivered more instructions.

'He might not want any conversation. Do your duty silently with him, so that the Prince's mind can wander where it chooses. Let his hand guide you and if he talks just say you speak English,' the madam said. 'But rarely does he speak. Prince Rakhal does not waste time with conversation.'

She put a gold bangle on Natasha's wrist, and large earrings in her ears that fell in gold rows—because, the madam said, he liked the noise. Natasha hated finding that out from another woman.

And then it was on with a *yashmak*.

As she left the tent the madam again put a finger to

her lips, for outside lay a sleeping Abdul. There was a flutter of hope in Natasha's stomach, a hope she dared not examine, for she understood Abdul's instructions were that she be kept from him.

The madam hurried Natasha through to his tent, and as they got there the madam paused. 'He deserves happiness,' she said, and there were tears in her eyes as she kissed Natasha on the cheek.

She was left alone to enter—there were no maidens guarding his shadow tonight—and she could see his profile on the bed. In a moment she would face him.

Or rather, Natasha thought, holding her head high, Rakhal would face *her*.

# CHAPTER EIGHTEEN

STILL her phone was not answered, and Rakhal lay back on the bed and knew he was foolish even to hope.

All night he had hoped she would come to him—had done as he'd been told and trusted in the ways of old—had stupidly almost convinced himself that his father and Abdul were keeping the harem from him for a reason.

Soon the morning would be here. He would pray and then head to the palace, and there could be no more putting it off. Today he would announce his bride, and from there there could be no turning back.

He heard soft footsteps and then the jangle of jewellery, and as the woman entered and the heavy scent of musk reached Rakhal the last vestige of hope died. For he knew she did not like jewellery or scent. He also knew in his heart that Natasha would never join the harem—it had been but a pipe dream.

The room was dark and the music played louder as Natasha stepped into his abode. Nervously she stood for a moment, looked to where he lay on the bed naked,

a silk drape over his groin. He did not look up as she
walked towards him. He did not look over, but spoke
in Arabic to her.

She did not answer. Her throat was dry, and she was
terrified that he would recognise her, that he would be
furious. She walked slowly to the bed, reaching out her
hand to him, to speak with him, to explain that she was
here finally to talk. But what was the point? Natasha
thought bitterly. She felt cheated on after the past night.

'Did you not understand what I said?' His hand
grabbed hers as she reached out to touch him. 'I said
that you are to take the jewel that is on the table.'

She did *not* understand—although he had spoken
in English this time. The madam had said nothing of
this. Perhaps he meant afterwards, Natasha thought,
and when his grip released her hand she hovered over
his stomach. She saw the snake of hair that had teased
her the day they had met. Rather than a row or a confrontation, she wanted one last time with him before
the magic must end, and her finger moved to lightly
trace the hair. She watched as his stomach tightened.

'Take the jewel,' he said, 'and never speak of this
to anyone. Go now and sit on that chair for a suitable
time.' The musky scent filled his nostrils, the sound
of her bangles jangled, and all he wanted was Natasha.
'If you talk, even amongst the others, I will know. You
are to take the jewel as payment for your silence. My
mind is with another. I need to think.'

Except his body betrayed him, for still those fingers traced the hair on his lower stomach. He grew
hard even as he resisted, and the silk slithered away.

Still the finger explored the flat plane of his stomach, and it was as if his skin recognised her. So light was her touch that it could have been Natasha's—but he halted her there, his fingers lingering with regret on the bangles that had tainted his fantasy that it was her. She released him—but only to take the bangles off.

'Take the jewel and leave.' He was close to begging as her hand returned, yet he did not halt it, for the hand that now held him was silent, and it allowed him to remember. 'Take the jewel,' he said, as he had to the other girls throughout the night. He had hoped so badly to find Natasha, but now his body gave in.

She watched, fascinated, watched him rise and grow at such a slight touch. It was as if his body welcomed her back even as he tried to douse it.

'My mind is with another.'

'I can be her,' she whispered, for she knew it was *her* that he was thinking of, and she smiled at what he had done.

She understood now Nadia and the other girls' silence when they had returned. He had kept himself unto her, and though his hand was tight over her wrist she moved her other hand over the magnificence that was waiting, stroked a finger lightly along it.

'You can think of her…' She took the hand that gripped her to her breast, felt his hand flat and resisting against it, then a reluctant exploration as still she stroked him.

'Take the jewel.' His teeth were gritted, for his mind was playing tricks. Beneath the musk he could smell her delicious fresh scent, and he did not want to open his eyes and be disappointed all over again—did not want to taint the fantasy that it was her. Was this what he was destined to do for the rest of his life? To close his eyes and imagine it was her?

Yes, Rakhal realised, for she could not be found.

'Please...' he begged this wanton woman who should follow orders.

But without order she had removed her veil. Her lips were at his tip now, and he could feel her hair on his stomach. He curled his fingers into her hair to lift her head, to tell her to stop, but there was a devil that begged him let her work on, for her mouth was a soothing balm and her tongue knew just what to do in a way others did not.

'Let me be her.' Natasha smiled and licked him, licked his delicious length, and then took in the moist tip and slowly caressed it. She berated the sound of her earrings, for they had distracted him, and could only admire his roar of restraint as he yanked at her hair and pulled her head back, almost weeping to the dark.

'I love another!'

How angrily he said it, but how delicious it was to hear it.

'Then let me love *you*,' she said, taking her earrings out as she returned her mouth to him.

'I am to share my bed only with her. My people are searching for her now,' Rakhal said. But her mouth was back and he was weak.

He must get rid of this woman who had crept into his head, who knew what he liked, who made him weak, made a strong man give in. He reached for the lamp, for he must end this fantasy, yet as he turned on the light there were red curls cascading over him and it killed him not to come. There was white pale skin and it was a cruel torture to be tested like this.

He lifted her head and saw her eyes and it was Natasha—or was his mind playing tricks? Could he convince himself so fully as he made love with another that it was her?

'Natasha...' And there beneath the make up and musk it was surely her. 'I have been searching...'

'I've been here.' There was hurt in her eyes. 'Your gold seal assured me access to all areas.'

Ardour was replaced by anger as realisation dawned. 'I did not grant that...'

'Only you can.'

'Or the King.' He knew the lengths his people would go to, to keep traditions safe, but that his father would take such an active part in it—would do anything to keep the ways of old—etched a new river of pain. 'They were not even looking for you.'

'Abdul knew where I was,' Natasha explained. 'He's outside guarding the harem now—or supposed to be.'

Anger propelled him from the bed. He pulled on a sash, scanned the room for his robe. He would go to Abdul first, kill him with his bare hands so blind was he with fury.

'He fell asleep. I think he thought you were done for the night.'

He heard the tremble of rage in her voice and knew he would deal with Abdul later. There was something more important to address than his aide.

'I paid them a jewel for their silence,' Rakhal said. 'I could not think of being with another since I have been with you.'

'But one day you might. When I am away being *pampered*, or when we've had a row and I haven't agreed with something you said, or when I'm old or sick...'

She looked to the rope and she loathed it, but his eyes did not wander there; instead he looked at the woman he had missed every night they had been apart. He never wanted to sleep alone again—which sounded a lot like the love she insisted upon.

'No.' He shook his head. 'Those ways are over.'

'You say that now.'

He meant it. For here was the one living person who did not care about his title, who did not care for his luxuries, did not care about the prestige that marrying him would bring. All she wanted was *him*, and it was humbling indeed to look love in the eye and recognise it.

So he *asked* her for the first time, when before he had bestowed an honour. 'Will you be my wife?'

And Natasha stood there silent—because if she opened her mouth she'd say yes, would settle for two nights a month knowing that he loved her.

But her silence forced him to continue.

'Will you share in my life?' Rakhal asked. 'All of it?'

'The people...' She could not take it in. 'The traditions...'

'The people want a strong ruler,' Rakhal said. 'And

I will be stronger with you by my side. In time they will come to understand.'

He pulled her towards him. He saw her as if for the first time. He traced her lips with his fingers to be sure, and then he tasted them again to prove it to himself. And he dipped his sash in the water by his bed and washed off the musk, took off the clothes she had worn for him. He wanted only her now, and he kissed her till she was writhing, till their bodies were locked deep in their own rhythm and her neck arched back and her mouth moaned. The music heightened and their bodies moved in the shadows above.

There would be changes, she thought faintly, but for tonight she would celebrate the ways of the desert and the music that was made for them.

'I can spend the rest of my life making love to you.' How could he have thought it was a concession? This was heaven he had found. She was a part of him and he could love her for ever.

He imagined her heavy with his child, those breasts full and milky. He would love every change in her. He would witness each one.

She was over and on top of him; she made love to him as he had once made love to her; she gave in to him completely, taken to a new place, to a future that would be different. And she did not fear it, for Rakhal would be walking with her.

She felt the tremble of her orgasm and there was no halting it. The music urged them on and, unsheathed, he spilled inside her, for they never needed to hold back from each other again.

'We marry soon.'

He held her as he told her, and she did not resist, for she wanted that too.

'The people will hear today that my bride has been chosen.' He wanted more than that for Natasha, though—wanted the changes to start this very day. 'Today they will *see* who I have chosen. I will return to the palace with you by my side. You will step out on the balcony with me.'

And later she was taken and bathed. The maidens knew the secret, for perhaps she might be with child, and this time when she was oiled and hennaed she knew she would be returned to him. She even had a little joke with Amira, for she was not wearing her mother's jewels.

'I will fetch them for you,' Amira said, and it felt nice to wear them on this day as pretty flowers were painted over her womb. So badly she wanted to see them grow.

Rakhal too was bathed, and dressed in a robe of black. His *kafiya* should be tied with a silver braid till his selection, but it was already decorated with a braid of gold, for the choice had already been made— by both of them.

Natasha was nervous as she sat for the second time in a helicopter—though not so terrified as she had been the first time. Rakhal sat beside her and she looked down at her hand in his, saw the long fingers and manicured nails and felt the warmth of his skin around hers. She glanced over to Abdul, who sat sweating and pale opposite them—for Rakhal had not yet said a word to his aide.

And Natasha said nothing either, as she sat in a lounge with the maidens and Abdul went in with Rakhal to address his father.

She waited for shouts, for protests, for rage. But the walls must be thick, for all she heard was the low murmur of Rakhal's deep voice, and then the door opened and as always he made her heart hammer. As on the first day, a blush rose in her cheeks and she fought the urge to run to him.

'What did he say?'

'That he does not consent. That the wedding cannot go ahead without his blessing,' Rakhal said.

She felt her stomach tighten in dread, felt the weight of tradition force them apart, but Rakhal gave a dismissive shrug to his father's threats.

'I told him that I did not need his blessing. That I will show my bride to the people today and we will marry when I rule, if that is how my father chooses to be.'

She had not met the King, had only heard of his power and might, but today no might could match Rakhal's, for his eyes were as dark as the night sky, his stance resolute, and it was clear he would not be deterred.

'I told him I have learnt not just from our teachings but from our mistakes—from *his* mistakes, from his regret at not having my mother by his side.'

She could hear Abdul weeping beside her.

'For years he has mourned her. He could have been with her. She pined not for the desert but for him.'

Rakhal closed his eyes for a brief moment, dragged in air, and she could only imagine how hard it must have been to say it, let alone for the King to hear it.

'I have learnt from his mistakes and I choose to do things differently. Or else...' He looked at his soon-to-be bride but did not continue.

Natasha now spoke for him. 'You would never walk away from your people.'

'Of course not,' Rakhal said. 'My people trust me to make the right decision and they will not turn away from me.'

But a muscle flickered in his cheek as he said that, and Natasha was not so sure.

'We must greet the people now,' he said.

They walked up a vast staircase. She could hear shouts and cheers from the people outside, waiting for their Prince to come out, and she was terribly, terribly nervous—especially when the maidens took off her robe and arranged her hair. She looked to Rakhal, who was also being readied, a sash placed around his shoulders, his *kafiya* already roped in gold. He stood tall and strong, ready to face the judgement of his people.

'Whatever their response,' Rakhal said, 'know that I am proud.'

She could not do this to him—to the people, to the King. But Rakhal silenced her protests and ordered the balcony doors open. He took her hand and stepped out to face the crowd.

The noise was deafening, and the silence, as the

shouts faded, was deafening too. They saw their Prince with his chosen bride and there were gasps of bewilderment as they realised she stood by his side. Her hair was blowing in the breeze and his hand gripped hers tighter.

And then she heard a cough behind her, turned. For the first time Natasha met the King—a thinner, older version of Rakhal, his face etched with the pain of half a lifetime buried in regret. Her heart could not fail to love him—especially when he stepped forward and took her other hand and then raised it to the crowd. The cheering resumed, with claps and the shouts from the people, as the King blessed his son's choice.

A few days later she was draped in gold, as she had been the night he found her, and led to him. She curtsied to the King and smiled at her proud brother.

They were married in the gardens of the palace, then driven through the streets—and the people cheered for them, for there had always been a sadness in the Sheikh Crown Prince's eyes and it was gone now. They had mourned the passing of his mother and seen the happiness die in their King's eyes, but now love had returned to Alzirz and now they cheered for it.

For the love their Prince had found with his bride.

# EPILOGUE

THE King was returned to the desert just before sunset. He had lasted another three months but death, when it came, was swift, and that morning they had been urgently summoned to farewell him.

One by one they went to him, even King Emir of Alzan and the tiny princesses. For though there was rivalry, there were deep traditions too. And after Natasha had been in to see him she sat with Amy, the nanny, because she was English too.

'How are they?' The girls were gorgeous, with big black eyes that were as solemn as the day.

'They're doing well.' Amy gave a tight smile.

'And King Emir?'

'I don't know,' Amy said. 'We don't really see him.' She looked down at the babies, and there was a wry note to her voice and a flash of tears in her eyes as she addressed them. 'Do we, girls?'

'But…' It was not her place to question, but Rakhal had told her that it was different in Alzan, that the royals raised their own children. Clearly this wasn't the case. Natasha looked over as Emir came out from his time with the King, but he did not glance over to his girls; instead he sat in quiet prayer.

And then it was Rakhal's time to go in, and there he remained with his father till the end.

Today they stood where the palace gave way to the desert, and there was wailing and tears, but Rakhal stood stoic and strong as he had all day.

'We will stay in the desert.' Rakhal explained the ways of his country. 'The rest of the party will return now to the palace, but it is a time for deep *tahir* for me, so you need to farewell our guests.'

'Thank you for coming.' She smiled and embraced her brother Mark. He hugged her and checked she was okay, as a brother should when his sister was grieving. He was doing so well now. He loved the land as much as Natasha did, and still worked the mines even though he was a royal now too. She was proud of him. It was so wonderful to see him strong and healthy.

Natasha then went back to her husband, who was saying goodbye to Emir and thanking him for his attendance. A dark, brooding man, Emir greeted her formally as she approached.

'How are the twins?' Natasha attempted conversation, but he hardly returned it.

'They are with the nanny.'

He kissed Rakhal on both cheeks, as was their way, and then went to his car. Natasha could see the nanny and the babies in the car behind him.

She knew what Amy had said earlier was true. They were present for duty, for appearances' sake. Not once had he looked at them.

But she could not think of Emir's pain tonight. They were driving in silence to the tent they both loved—though it would not be joyous this time. In the last three months she had grown fond of the King, and Rakhal's relationship with his father had warmed.

She took off her shoes. She was drained and exhausted, but for the first time since they had been summoned to the King's bedside they could speak properly.

'He did not suffer,' Natasha said.

'He was happy to leave.'

Rakhal surprised her, for his voice was not morose—in fact there was a pale smile.

'When everyone had said their goodbyes and I sat with him, he said he could see my mother dancing sometimes in the dust devils, and that he could see her more clearly today. It wasn't just me who saw her out in the desert.'

Natasha felt like crying, but she joined him at the low table and sat down on the floor as a maid poured water into a goblet. She drank and waited for their meal to be served.

'Now I will pray.' Rakhal rose. 'Rest if you are tired.'

'I'm actually really hungry.' She felt just a little guilty admitting it—especially when Rakhal grimaced.

'I have not explained. For two days the country will be in the deepest of mourning. For two days we will fast and pray. When I return to the palace there will be a meal at which I will preside. That is when I will assume the role of King. For now I am to prepare for that duty. For now we pray for my father who is still the King.'

'I don't know if I can…' She saw him frown, saw his features darken.

'Natasha, in so many things I do my best to listen and to make changes where I can, but do not disrespect me in this—for you are disrespecting my father too, and he is not even cold.' And he strode off to his abode.

She followed him. 'Rakhal, please.' There were tears in her eyes that he thought she might be so callous, so precious, that she would not miss a meal and keep his ways. 'I didn't want to tell you today—not when you are grieving—but I found out just before we were summoned to your father.' She saw his mouth open, saw some light in those dark eyes. 'I couldn't wait for the moon. I saw the palace doctor this morning—just before your father did.' She watched as his face paled, as on this darkest of days somehow hope shone in. 'He confirmed that I am pregnant. I honestly don't know if I am allowed to fast. Of course if I am, I will do it…'

*'No!'* He couldn't take it in. He should be on his knees in prayer, but instead he held her. 'It feels wrong to be happy in grief,' he admitted, 'but it feels so good to have this hope.'

He looked to her and she knew what he was thinking.

'He would rejoice.'

'He did,' Natasha whispered. 'When I farewelled him I told him.' And she was so glad that she had—just so she could have this moment. 'Of course I should have told you first, but I had only just found out my-self. But he knew.' She repeated as best she could what his father's response had been.

'"My life is complete."' Rakhal translated the words his father had said to her. He knew his father was with his mother now, back with Layla and danc-ing in the desert. 'He kept saying that soon Alzirz would celebrate—I did not understand that he knew something I did not.'

But there would be time for smiles and celebrations later. For now he must pray, and she must eat a light supper. For two days he would not make love to her, for two days he would pray for his father and for his country, but when he climbed into bed that night it was sweet relief to hold her—a relief he might never have known, for with the old ways this night would have been a long and lonely one.

'Are you scared to be King?' she asked as they lay together.

'I am never scared.' He answered the same way he had the first time she had asked.

'I would be.'

'I would be too,' he admitted, 'had I not found you.'

'You're going to be a wonderful ruler.'

'I know.' He was not vain. He was right. 'I am good for the people.'

'So too is Emir—as would be his girls.'

He did not respond, and tonight she chose not to push it, but one day she knew that she would.

'We will die in this bed together.' He held her. 'Or

lie alone and grow old thinking of the other...' She had his heart for ever.

Deep in the night she awoke, her light supper not quite enough, but because they were in mourning she checked with him just to be sure.

'Have some of the custard.' His voice was sleepy, his arms around her. 'It is good for you.'

As was Rakhal for her.

As was Natasha for him.

And she smiled as he reached for the rope.

\* \* \* \* \*

# The Tarnished Jewel of Jazaar

## SUSANNA CARR

**Susanna Carr** has been an avid romance reader since she read her first at the age of ten. Although romance novels were not allowed in her home, she had always managed to sneak one in from the local library or from her twin sister's secret stash.

After attending college and receiving a degree in English Literature, Susanna pursued a romance writing career. She has written sexy contemporary romances for several publishers and her work has been honoured with awards for contemporary and sensual romance.

Susanna Carr lives in the Pacific Northwest with her family. When she isn't writing, Susanna enjoys reading romance and connecting with readers online. Visit her website at susannacarr.com.

To Lucy Gilmour,
for her insights and encouragement.
Thanks for making my dream come true!

# CHAPTER ONE

DARKNESS descended on the desert as the black SUV came to a halt in front of the village's inn, a large but plain building. The arches and columns that guarded the courtyard were decorated with flower garlands. Strands of lights were wrapped around thick palm trees. Sheikh Nadir ibn Shihab heard the native music beyond the columns. In the distance, fireworks shot off and sprayed into the night sky, announcing his arrival.

It was time to meet his bride.

Nadir felt no excitement. There was no curiosity and no dread. Having a wife was a means to an end. It was not an emotional choice but a civilized arrangement. An arrangement he was making because of one rash, emotional reaction two years ago.

He pushed his thoughts aside. He wasn't going to think about the injustice now. With this marriage he would repair his reputation and no one would question his commitment to the traditional way of life in the kingdom of Jazaar.

Nadir stepped out of the car and his *dishdasha* was plastered against his muscular body as his black cloak whipped in the strong wind. The white headdress billowed behind him. Nadir found the traditional clothes confining, but today he wore them out of respect to custom.

He saw his younger brother approach. Nadir smiled at

the unusual sight of Rashid wearing traditional garb. They greeted each other with an embrace.

"You are very late for your wedding," Rashid said in a low and confidential tone.

"It doesn't start until I arrive," Nadir replied as he pulled back.

Rashid shook his head at his brother's arrogance. "I mean it, Nadir. This is not the way to make amends with the tribe."

"I'm aware of it. I got here as quickly as I could." He had spent most of his wedding day negotiating with two warring tribes over a sacred spot of land. It was more important than a wedding feast. Even if it was his own wedding.

"That's not good enough for the elders," Rashid said as they walked toward the hotel. "In their eyes you showed them the ultimate disrespect two years ago. They won't forgive your tardiness."

Nadir was not in the mood to be lectured by his younger brother. "I'm marrying the woman of their choice, aren't I?"

The marriage was a political alliance with an influential tribe who both respected and feared him. Nadir had heard that his nickname in this part of the desert was The Beast. And, like mere mortals who knew they had angered a demon god, the elders were willing to sacrifice a young virgin as his bride.

Nadir approached the row of elders, who were dressed in their finest. Glimpsing the solemn faces of the older men, Nadir knew Rashid was right. They were not happy with him. If this tribe wasn't so important for his plans to modernize the country, Nadir would ignore their existence.

"My humblest apologies." Nadir greeted the elders, bowing low and offering his deepest regrets for his tardiness. He didn't care if these men felt slighted by his delay, but he went through the motions.

He had no use for the prolonged greeting ritual, but he had to be diplomatic. He was already battling political retribution from the elders, and had countered it by showing a willingness to marry a woman from their tribe. That maneuver should have improved relations with the tribal leaders, but Nadir sensed they were anything but honored.

The elders politely ushered him into the courtyard as the ancient chant accompanied by drums pulsed in the air. It tugged at something deep in Nadir, but he wasn't going to join in. While the guests were happy that the Sheikh was marrying one of their own, he wasn't pleased about the turn of events.

"Do you know anything about the bride?" Rashid whispered into Nadir's ear. "What if she's unsuitable?"

"It's not important," Nadir quietly informed his brother. "I have no plans to live as husband and wife. I will marry her and take her to bed, but once the wedding ceremonies are over she will live in the harem at the Sultan's palace. She will have everything she needs and I'll have my freedom. If all goes well we will never set eyes on each other again."

Nadir surveyed the crowd. Men were on one side of the aisle, dressed in white, chanting and clapping as they provoked the women on the other side to dance faster. The women's side was a riot of color liberally streaked with gold. The women silently taunted the men, their hips undulating to the edge of propriety. Their loose-fitting garments stretched and strained over voluptuous curves.

His presence was suddenly felt. He felt the ripple of awareness through the crowd. The music ended abruptly as everyone froze, staring at him. He felt like an unwelcome guest at his own wedding.

Nadir was used to seeing wariness in the eyes of everyone from statesmen to servants. International businesses accused him of being as devious as a jackal when he thwarted their attempts to steal Jazaar's resources. Journalists declared that he enforced the Sultan's law with the ruthless sting of a scorpion's tail. He had even been compared to a viper when he'd protected Jazaar with unwavering aggression from bloodthirsty rebels. His countrymen might be afraid to look him in the eye, but they knew he would take care of them by any means necessary.

Nadir strode down the aisle with Rashid one step behind him. The guests slowly regained their festive spirits, singing loudly as they showered him with rose petals. They seemed indecently relieved that his three-day marriage ceremony had commenced. He frowned at the men's wide smiles and the women's high-pitched trills. It was as if they believed they had appeased The Beast's hunger.

He kept his gaze straight ahead on the end of the courtyard. A dais sat in the center. A couple of divans flanked two golden throne-like chairs. His bride sat in one, waiting for him with her head tucked low and her hands in her lap.

Nadir slowed down when he saw that his bride wore an ethnic wedding dress in deep crimson. A heavy veil concealed her hair and framed her face before cascading down her shoulders and arms. Her fitted bodice was encrusted with gold beads, hinting at the small breasts and slender waist underneath. Her delicate hands, decorated with an ornate henna design, lay against the voluminous brocade skirt.

He frowned as he studied the woman. There was something different, something *wrong* about the bride. He halted in the middle of the aisle as the realization hit him like a clap of thunder.

"Nadir!" Rashid whispered harshly.

"I see." His tone was low and fierce as the shock reverberated inside him.

The woman before him was no Jazaari bride, fit for a sheikh.

She was an outcast. A woman no man would marry.

The tribal leaders had tricked him. Nadir stood very still as his anger flared. He had agreed to marry a woman of the tribe's choosing in a gesture of good faith. In return they had given him the American orphaned niece of one of their families.

It was an insult, he thought grimly as he ruthlessly reined in his emotions. It was also a message. The tribe thought that Nadir was too Western and modern to appreciate a traditional Jazaari bride.

"How dare they?" Rashid said in growl. "We're leaving now. Once the Sultan hears about this we will formally shun this tribe and—"

"No." Nadir's decision was swift and certain. He didn't like it, but all his instincts told him it was for the greater good. "I accepted their choice."

"Nadir, you don't have to."

"Yes, I do."

The tribe expected him to refuse this woman as his bride. They wanted him to defy tradition and prove that he didn't appreciate the Jazaari way of life.

He couldn't do that. Not again.

And the elders knew it.

Nadir's eyes narrowed into slits. He would accept this unworthy woman as his bride. And once the wedding was over he would destroy the elders in this tribe one by one.

"I must protest," Rashid said. "A sheikh does not marry an outcast."

"I agree, but I need a bride, and any woman from this

tribe will do. One woman is just as much trouble as the next."

"But…"

"Don't worry, Rashid. I am changing my plans. I won't let her live in the Sultan's palace. I will send her into seclusion at the palace in the mountains." He would hide this woman—and any evidence that he had been shamed by this tribe. No one would ever know how he had paid a huge dowry for such an inferior bride.

Nadir forced his feet to move, his white-hot anger turning to ice as he approached his bride. He noticed that the woman's face was pale against her dark red lips and kohled eyes. A thick rope of rubies and diamonds edged along her hairline. She had a tangle of necklaces around her throat and a long column of gold bangles on both arms.

She was dressed like a Jazaari bride, but it was obvious that she wasn't the real thing. Her downcast eyes and prim posture couldn't hide her bold nature. There was a defiant tilt to her head and a brash energy about her.

The woman also had an earthy sexiness, he decided. A proper bride would be shy and modest. She looked like a mysterious and exotic maiden who should be dancing barefoot by a bonfire on a dark desert night.

His bride cautiously glanced from beneath her lashes and he captured her startled gaze. Nadir felt the impact as their eyes clashed and held.

Zoe Martin's blood raced painfully through her veins as she stared into dark, hypnotic eyes. As much as she wanted to, she couldn't look away. The eyes darkened. She felt as if she was caught in a swirling storm.

*Please don't let this be the man I am marrying!* She needed to trick and manipulate her husband throughout their honeymoon, but she could tell immediately this man was too dangerous for her plans.

Sheikh Nadir ibn Shihab wasn't handsome. His features were too hard, too primitive. His face was all lines and angles, from his Bedouin nose to the forceful thrust of his jaw. His cheekbones slashed down his face and a cleft scored his chin. There was a hint of softness in his full lips, but the cynical curl at the edge of his mouth warned of his impatience. She had no doubt that everyone kept a distance from him or suffered the brunt of his venomous barbs.

The pearl-white of the Sheikh's *dishdasha* contrasted with his golden-brown skin and it couldn't conceal his long, tapered body. Every move he made drew her attention to his lean and compact muscles. Zoe decided that his elegant appearance was deceiving. She had no doubt that he had been brought up in a world of wealth and privilege, but this man belonged to the harsh and unforgiving desert. He had the desert's stark beauty and its cruelty.

The Sheikh showed no expression, no emotion, but she felt a biting hot energy slamming against her. Zoe flinched, her skin stinging from his bold gaze. She wanted to rub her arms and wrap them protectively around her. She felt the inexplicable need to slough off his claim.

*Claim?* A flash of fear gripped Zoe as her chest tightened. Why did it feel like that? The Sheikh hadn't touched her yet.

She had the sudden overwhelming need to turn and run as fast as she could to escape. Her heart pounded in her ears, her breath rasped in her constricted throat, and although every self-preservation instinct told her to flee, she couldn't move.

*"As-Salamu Alaykum,"* Nadir greeted as he sat down next to her.

Zoe shivered at the rough, masculine sound. His voice was soft, but the commanding tone coiled around her body, tugging at something dark and unknown inside her. The muscles low in her abdomen tingled with awareness.

"It's a pleasure to meet you," he said with cool politeness.

Zoe gave a start, her excess of gold jewelry chiming from her sudden move. He'd spoken to her in English. It had been so long since she'd heard her mother tongue. Unshed tears suddenly stung her eyes and she struggled to regain her composure.

She shouldn't have been surprised that the Sheikh spoke English. He'd been educated in the United States, traveled frequently, and knew several languages as well as all the dialects spoken in Jazaar. His need to travel internationally was one of the reasons why she had agreed to marry him.

But curiosity got the better of her. She couldn't imagine this man doing something thoughtful without getting something in return. Her voice wavered as she asked, "Why are you speaking to me in English?"

"You are American. It's your language."

She gave a curt nod and kept her head down, her gaze focused on her clenched hands. It had been her language once. Until her uncle had forbidden it. "It isn't spoken here," she whispered.

"That's why I'm using it," Nadir said in an uninterested tone as he surveyed the courtyard. "English will be just our language and no one will know what we're saying."

Ah, now she understood. He wanted to create an immediate bond between them. Or at least the illusion of one. It was a clever strategy, but she wasn't going to fall for it.

"I'm not supposed to talk during the ceremony," she reminded him.

She sensed his attention back on her. The energy crackling between them grew sharper. "But I want you to talk."

*Right.* Was this some sort of test to see if she was a good

Jazaari bride? "My aunts gave me strict orders to keep my head down and my mouth shut."

"Whose opinions are more important to you?" She heard the arrogance in his voice. "Your aunts' or your husband's?"

*Neither,* she wanted to say. It was tempting, but she knew she had to play the game. "I will do as you wish." She nearly choked on the words.

His chuckle was rough and masculine. "Keep saying that and we'll get along just fine."

Zoe clenched her teeth, preventing herself from giving a sharp reply. She swallowed her retort just in time as the first elder came onto the dais. As she'd expected, the older man ignored her and spoke only to the Sheikh.

She stared at her hands in her lap and slowly squeezed her fingers together. The bite of pain didn't distract her from her troubled thoughts. She was never going to pull off the demure look. It was just a matter of time before she messed up. Her family knew it, too. The disapproving glares from her aunts were hot enough to burn a sizzling hole in her veil.

Zoe knew her appearance and manners didn't meet family expectations. They never had. Her face was much too pale and she lacked refinement and feminine charm. It didn't matter if the veil concealed her features, or if her bent head hid her big, bold eyes. They knew she wasn't a proper young woman. She talked louder than a whisper, walked faster than she should, and no matter how often she was told she never knew her place.

She was too American. Too much trouble. Simply too much.

Her relatives thought she should be timid and subservient, and they had tried to transform her using every barbaric punishment they knew. Starvation. Sleep deprivation.

Beatings. Nothing had worked. It had only made Zoe more rebellious and determined to get out of this hell. If only she had a better escape plan. If only her freedom didn't rely on pretending to be the perfect woman.

As the last elder left the dais, Zoe felt the Sheikh's intent gaze on her. She tensed but kept her focus on her hands. Did he find her lacking or did she pass inspection?

"What is your name?" the Sheikh asked her.

Zoe's eyes widened. *Seriously?* This was not something a woman wanted to hear from her husband on her wedding day. Zoe held back the urge to give him a false name. A stripper name, she thought with a sly smile. If only she could. But it wouldn't be worth the punishment.

"Zoe Martin," she answered.

"And how old are you?"

*Old enough.* She bit the tip of her tongue before she blurted out that reply. "I'm twenty-one years old."

How was it possible the Sheikh didn't know anything about her? Wasn't he curious about the woman he married? Didn't he care?

"Do I detect a Texan accent?" he asked.

Zoe bit her bottom lip as a memory of her home in Texas bloomed. The last time she had felt as if she belonged to a family. Once she had been loved and protected; now she was chattel for her uncle.

"You have a very good ear," she answered huskily. "I thought I had lost the twang." *Along with everything else.*

"Texas is a long way from here."

*No kidding.* But she knew what he was really asking. How the hell had she wound up in Jazaar? She'd wondered that many times herself. "My father was a doctor for a humanitarian medical organization and he met my mother when he visited Jazaar. Didn't anyone tell you about me?"

"I was told everything I needed to know."

That made her curious. What had been said about her? She wasn't sure if she wanted to know. "Such as?" she asked as she watched the servants bringing plates of food to the dais.

He shrugged. "You are part of this tribe and you are of marriageable age."

She waited a beat. "Anything else?"

"What else do I need to know?"

Her eyes widened. His indifference took her breath away, but she knew she should be grateful for it. It was better that he had not asked any questions or dug for information. He would have discovered what kind of woman he was marrying.

Zoe barely ate anything from the wedding feast. She usually had a healthy appetite—some felt too robust—but tonight the aromas and spices were overwhelming. Immediately after the meal a procession of guests approached the dais to congratulate the happy couple. She was glad that no one expected her to speak. She barely listened to what was said, too aware of the man sitting next to her.

"You will have your hands full with this one, Your Highness. She's nothing but trouble."

Zoe glanced up when she heard those words. She knew she should keep her head down, but she was surprised that someone would warn the Sheikh. Weren't they trying to get rid of her by marrying her off?

Yet she had never got along with the wife of the wealthy storekeeper. The older woman had forbidden Zoe from entering the store. But Zoe was used to being excluded and had frequently managed to make her purchases through strategy and stealth.

"She's an incredibly slow learner," the older woman continued. "It doesn't matter how hard her uncle slaps her, Zoe keeps talking back."

"Is that so?" the Sheikh drawled. "Perhaps her uncle is the slow learner and should try a new approach?"

Zoe jerked in surprise and immediately ducked her head so no one could see her expression. Was he questioning Uncle Tareef's methods? She thought men sided with one another.

"Nothing works with Zoe," the storekeeper's wife informed the Sheikh. "Once she burned the dinner. Of course she was punished. You'd think she'd learn her lesson, but the next day she poured an entire pot of hot pepper in the dinner. Her uncle had blisters inside his mouth for weeks."

"It wasn't my fault he kept trying to eat it," Zoe said as she glared at the woman. "And at least it wasn't burnt."

Zoe cringed inwardly when she recognized her mistake and immediately bent her head as if nothing happened. There was a long, silent pause and Zoe felt the Sheikh's gaze on her. She instinctively hunched her shoulders, as if that would make her smaller. Invisible.

"I hope your cooking has improved," he said.

Zoe nodded cautiously. It was a lie, but he would never find out. She was grateful that he'd ignored her outburst, surprised that he didn't comment on it.

He was probably saving it all up for later, she decided, as the tension vibrated inside her. She was going to face one monstrous lecture after the ceremony.

"When all else failed," the older woman valiantly continued, "Zoe was forced to treat the sick until she learned how to behave. She has taken care of the poor women for *years*."

Zoe knew that the task of treating the ill was reserved for servants in the tribe, but she didn't care. It was what she wanted to do. The science of nursing and the art of folk remedies fascinated her.

"Zoe," Nadir said, "you no longer have to treat the sick."

Zoe frowned, not sure how to answer. "That's not necessary. I'm not afraid of hard work and I'm very good at it."

"Zoe!" the storekeeper's wife said in a scandalized tone, her eyes dancing with delight. "A Jazaari woman must be humble."

Nadir rose from his seat and Zoe couldn't help noticing how tall and commanding he was. He motioned for the most exalted elder to approach the dais. Zoe's stomach twisted sharply and she tasted hot, bitter fear in her mouth. What was the Sheikh doing? She had displeased him. Somehow she would be punished for it.

The older woman smiled victoriously and walked away with a spring in her step as the elder approached. Zoe was angry at herself for letting the old bat rile her.

The Sheikh placed his palm against his heart and told the chief elder, "You have honored me with Zoe as my bride."

The elder couldn't hide his surprise and the nearby guests started to whisper excitedly behind their hands and veils. Zoe didn't feel any relief. Instead, she battled the trickle of suspicion. Honored? He didn't know the first thing about her.

"I gladly accept the duty to protect her and provide for her," the Sheikh continued, his voice strong and clear. "She will want for nothing."

Her suspicions deepened as the buzz of conversation swelled. What was this man up to? She had learned firsthand that when a man made those kinds of promises it was very likely he would do the opposite. Like when Uncle Tareef had promised to take her in and look after her. Instead he'd stolen her inheritance and she'd become an unpaid servant in his household.

"And as your Sheikha," Nadir announced, "she will spend her days and nights tending to me."

Zoe lowered her head as the guests cheered. Anger swirled inside her chest. The tribe was thrilled that she pleased the Sheikh. He wasn't going to let her leave his side and she wouldn't have time to nurse the sick because she had the honor of being at his beck and call.

The man had no idea how important it was for her to work. Before her parents died Zoe had volunteered at the local hospital with her mother. It had been exciting and she'd known then she wanted to have a medical career like her father's.

Her dreams of practicing medicine with her father had been shattered when her parents died in a car accident and suddenly she had found herself living in a foreign place with people she didn't know. She had suffered through the language barrier, strange food and an unwelcoming tribe. But when she'd watched the healer treat the sick, Zoe had felt she was back in familiar territory.

In a matter of months she had become the healer's assistant. It was supposed to be a punishment, but she had wanted to learn. When Zoe noticed that the poor women were reluctant to seek medical help from a male healer, she gradually took on the female patients. It was her way of continuing her family's legacy, and practicing medicine had become her lifeline.

She had finally found a way to stay away from Uncle Tareef's house and focus on something other than her difficult situation. And when she handled a medical emergency she felt the same excitement she had when she'd been back home in the local hospital. Taking care of women in need had let her find a sense of purpose. It was the one thing that kept her going.

And now the Sheikh wanted to take that away from her? Zoe closed her eyes and tried desperately to control her temper. She had to give up the one thing that interested her, the one thing she was good at, because Nadir didn't like it? It wasn't fair. She wanted to argue right here and now.

What was she upset about? Zoe slowly opened her eyes. What Nadir wanted didn't affect her life. She wasn't going to stay married long enough for him to take her interests away from her.

"I must say you surprised me."

Zoe looked at the tall and slender woman who was now sitting next to her—her cousin Fatimah. Zoe clenched her teeth as she braced herself for what she was sure would be a few unpleasant moments.

Fatimah wore a shimmering green gown. Heavy gold jewelry dripped from her ears, throat and wrists. She always made a glamorous and dramatic impact wherever she went.

"I didn't think you would do it," Fatimah told Zoe in a breezy, chatty tone. "I know how you Americans believe in love matches."

Zoe didn't respond. She had never liked her cousin, and they weren't friends. Fatimah would not form an alliance with an outcast like Zoe. Instead, she preferred to feel powerful by preying on the defenseless, and Zoe had seen her in all her destructive glory. Now she noted the dark look in her cousin's eyes. Fatimah was on the prowl for trouble and had found her target.

Her cousin bestowed a tight smile upon her. "I can't wait to tell Musad."

Zoe did her best not to flinch. "Please do."

She hoped she was getting better at not reacting to his name. Musad had once represented a fragile yet blossoming love in a world of quicksand filled with hate and indifference. Now his name reminded her that no man could be trusted.

"What should I tell our old friend?" Fatimah asked

as she studied Zoe's face closely. "Shall I send him your love?"

Zoe shrugged, refusing to let the word "love" pierce her wrung-out heart. Musad had ceased to matter a year ago, when he'd moved to America without a backward glance. She had filed him under "lesson learned."

Zoe leaned back in her chair as if she didn't have a care in the world. "Tell him what you want."

Fatimah rested her hand on Zoe's arm and leaned forward to whisper, "How can you say that, considering how *close* you were?"

Zoe felt the blood leaving her face as icy fear seeped in her veins. Fatimah knew. She saw it in the malicious glow of the woman's eyes. Somehow Fatimah knew about her forbidden liaison with Musad. She was the one who'd started the rumors that were beginning to percolate in village gossip.

Zoe had to get away. She had to silence Fatimah. If she breathed a word of this to her family…to the Sheikh…

"Zoe?"

Zoe looked up to see her aunts and other female cousins. They were smiling. Real smiles. It was unlikely that they had heard Fatimah's accusation. Zoe wanted to sag with relief.

"Come, Zoe." One of her cousins unceremoniously pulled her from her chair and her female relatives surrounded her. "It's time to prepare you for your wedding night."

Her wedding night. Her stomach twisted sharply and she battled back nausea. Her aunts smiled and giggled as they swept her out of the courtyard and up to the honeymoon suite. She hunched her shoulders as corroding fear, thick and searing hot, bled through her body. It pooled under her skin, pressing harder and harder, threatening to burst through.

It suddenly sank into her. She belonged to the Sheikh. A man they called The Beast. She was married to him. *Married.*

Her married cousins were offering words of advice, telling her how to please her husband, but Zoe didn't hear a word of it. There was a desperate energy among the women. Their laughter was a little shrill, their advice raw and uncoated.

Zoe didn't resist as the women settled her in the center of the bed. She knelt on the mattress, her hands folded in front of her, her head bent down. She wanted to jump out of bed and run, but she knew these women would bring her back and guard the bedroom.

She closed her eyes and took a deep, jagged breath. She heard the women leaving the room, their laughter harsh as they tossed her more marital advice. She had always thought her wedding day would be different. In her daydreams it had been full of laughter and joy, not to mention love.

The reality was much bleaker. Zoe slowly opened her eyes. She was marrying because she was out of options and running out of luck. She was taking a leap of faith, believing she could use this marriage to her advantage. But she might have given up more than her freedom to a man who was a dangerous stranger.

What had she done?

Pure terror clamped her chest. She felt the room closing in on her as she tried to gulp in the hot air. Dark spots danced before her eyes.

"I can't do this. I can't sleep with him," Zoe said aloud. She thought she was alone until Fatimah answered.

"He's required to consummate the marriage," her cousin

said as she straightened Zoe's skirt, making it a smooth circle on the bed. "Otherwise it's not acknowledged."

"Required?" Zoe's stomach gave a sickening twist. That sounded so clinical. So unromantic.

Fatimah cast an annoyed look in her direction. "That's why you have the last ceremony on the third day. It's based on an ancient law to celebrate the consummation of the marriage."

Zoe's jaw dropped. "Are you kidding me?"

"And if you aren't to his liking," Fatimah said, giving her a sidelong look, "he can throw you back."

Zoe frowned. "Throw me back? You mean back to your family? No, he can't. Nice try, Fatimah, but I'm not falling for another one of your lies."

"I'm not lying," Fatimah swore, flattening her hand against her chest. "The Sheikh did that to his first wife."

*First wife?* Zoe drew back her head and stared at her cousin as surprise tingled down her spine. What first wife? "What are you talking about?"

"Didn't anyone tell you?" Fatimah's face brightened when she realized she would get to reveal all. "Two years ago the Sheikh was married to the daughter of one of the finest families in the tribe. Yusra. You remember her?"

"Barely." Yusra had been drop-dead gorgeous, ultra feminine and the perfect Jazaari girl. Zoe had privately thought Yusra was a spoiled brat and a bit of snob. She had been glad when her family left the village.

"It was a fabulous ceremony. Unlike any I've ever seen. Don't you remember it? It was better than yours."

"I probably wasn't invited." She was an outcast. She was either ignored or bullied. Any member of the tribe could publicly humiliate her without consequence. They all knew her uncle wouldn't protect her. They had all witnessed the treatment she'd received under his cruel hand and followed his lead.

"Well, the third day of the ceremony had barely started when he tossed Yusra back to her parents." Fatimah gave a flick of her wrist, the jangle of gold bracelets loud to Zoe's ears. "In front of the entire tribe. He said she was not to his liking."

If he'd had a problem with his first choice of a wife, he was definitely not going to be pleased with her. "He had sex with her and then dumped her? Can he do that?"

"It caused a huge scandal. How is it you don't know any of this? You were living here when it happened."

Zoe probably had heard about it but thought it one of those "bonfire stories." She had heard plenty of folk tales that were designed to scare boys and girls into behaving properly.

She was in so much trouble. Her knees wobbled as a wave of fear crashed over her. If she didn't have sex with the Sheikh he would send her back to her family. If she did have sex with him she might well have had the same problem. "So basically this ancient law is a return policy?"

"It's rarely used. A man has to have a very good reason to invoke it. Unless you're a sheikh, of course. Then no one will question your actions."

"But—"

One of Zoe's aunts peeked inside the room. "Fatimah, what are you still doing here?" the woman said in a fierce whisper. "The Sheikh is coming."

"Good luck, Zoe," Fatimah said with a sly smile as she slipped out of the room. "I hope you can satisfy the Sheikh better than his last bride."

# CHAPTER TWO

WHAT was she going to do? Zoe glanced wildly at the open windows and the colorful gauzy curtains fluttering in the breeze. No, she couldn't escape that way.

Even if she got out safely she had no place to hide. She had learned that over the years, after her failed attempts to run away. No one would provide her with sanctuary and the desert was a deathtrap. She had barely survived the last time.

She was trapped and she needed to come up with a plan. Zoe squeezed her eyes shut as the panic swelled in her chest. *Think, think, think!*

Her mind was locked on only one thing: chastity was highly prized in a woman, and she wasn't a virgin.

The tribe had very strict rules about sex outside marriage. The men were punished, but not as harshly as the women. Zoe tried to block out the memory of the scars her female patients had from being caned and whipped.

A man like the Sheikh would demand an untouched bride. Zoe's stomach cramped with panic. She had known that before she accepted the arrangement, but had thought she would be safe once the marriage contract was signed. It had been a risk, and it had backfired.

The door opened and Zoe went still, her breath lodging in her throat. She heard the guests offering their best wishes over the jubilant music. The jumble of noise scraped against her taut nerves. She wanted to scream, to bolt, to break down and cry, but she carefully lowered her head and clasped her hands tightly.

She flinched violently when the door closed and Zoe winced at her response. She needed to please the Sheikh, not offend him.

"Would you like a drink, Zoe?" he asked softly as he slipped off his shoes next to the door.

She wordlessly shook her head. Her mouth was dry, her throat ached, and she wished there was alcohol to numb her senses. But she didn't think she could accept a drop without choking.

How was she going to get through the night? Maybe he wouldn't notice that she wasn't a virgin? Her head ached as she tried to plan. Perhaps she could fake her virginity? She wasn't sure if she could get away with that strategy. From what she had heard about her husband he was very experienced, with an insatiable sex-drive.

She heard his cloak fall to the ground. Something soft followed. Zoe couldn't help but look, and discovered the Sheikh had removed his headdress. His hair was short, thick and black.

He didn't seem any less intimating. If anything, her husband appeared even harder, more ruthless. His profile was strong and aggressive. Power came off him in waves. She was aware that this was a man in his prime.

Zoe pulled her gaze away and stared at her hands. What was wrong with her? She was not interested in the Sheikh. He could become an obstacle to her dreams of returning home.

"It was a good ceremony," the Sheikh said, his voice closer. "Short. My favorite kind."

Zoe nodded again, although *she* thought the ceremony

had been miserably long. However, she hadn't shown up late. Not that she would point it out.

But this night was going to be endless. How was she going to prevent the fallout that was sure to come? Maybe she should fake modesty so he could never get close enough to finding out if she was a virgin or not. After all, what man would admit he'd failed to bed his wife on their wedding night?

Or she could pretend to faint dead away at the sight of him without a shirt. Zoe bit her bottom lip as she considered the merit of the idea. Or she could cry. A lot. For two solid days and nights. Men couldn't stand being around a woman in tears.

Although the Sheikh might be different. He was probably used to women trembling and crying in his presence.

She heard his footsteps approaching the bed. Zoe took a gulp of air but it fizzled in her throat. She heard the faint chime of metal and discovered her bracelets clinking against each other as her arms and hands shook.

"Zoe?"

She stilled when she heard his voice. The chiming ceased. The Sheikh was right next to her. She felt vulnerable with her head down, but she was trying to be a good Jazaari bride. It was difficult pretending to be meek when she preferred to face trouble head-on.

She decided to follow her original plan. She wouldn't run away but she wouldn't sleep with the Sheikh. Fatimah was trying to play mind games again. She wouldn't fall for it. All she needed to do tonight was keep her husband at a distance. Play the reluctant and timid bride until they left for their honeymoon. Once they were out of Jazaar she could make her escape.

"Are you giving me the silent treatment already?" He

sounded amused. "We haven't been married for more than a day."

Silent treatment? She had never been accused of that before. Her problem had always been speaking her mind. "I'm nervous, Your Highness," she replied, hating how her voice cracked.

"You may call me Nadir. And you don't have to be nervous with me."

Of course she did. He had the power to destroy her life or, unwittingly, help her to create a new one. She gave a tilt of her head to show that she understood him, and immediately tensed when he knelt on the mattress in front of her.

The bed suddenly felt smaller. *She* felt smaller as Nadir towered over her. Zoe kept her eyes firmly on her fists that rested on her lap. She watched cautiously as he reached for her hand. She jerked when she felt a hot spark between them as his skin touched hers.

Nadir's hand was dark and large against hers. Zoe felt his latent strength as he gently uncurled her fingers. She watched as he quietly slid the stack of bangles from her wrists and over her hand. She noticed how much lighter her arms felt as the bracelets fell onto the floor.

Once he'd removed her bracelets Nadir lazily traced the henna pattern on her hand with a fingertip. Her skin tingled as the pulse skittered in her wrist. Zoe was tempted to pull away.

"Your veil looks heavy," Nadir said softly.

*He had no idea.* "Yes."

Nadir skimmed the top of her head with his hands. Zoe's muscles tightened as she fought the urge to bolt. His gentle touch felt like a silent claim that she didn't want to accept or obey. She wanted to retreat. Brush his hands aside. Get away from the bed. Her skin prickled, heat sizzling through her blood as she struggled to remain still.

She heard the beat of her heart mingled with her short, choppy breaths. She felt Nadir guide his hands along the jeweled edge of her veil. He located the hairpins anchoring the veil and slid them free. Tossing the pins onto the floor, he glided the veil off her head and let it fall behind her.

She immediately felt its loss. While Zoe was grateful to shed the weight, the veil had allowed her to hide. She no longer had that luxury.

She kept her head down as Nadir threaded his fingers through her long brown hair. She couldn't tell if he was fascinated or disappointed by the unusual shade.

"Look at me, Zoe."

Her pulse gave a hard skip. She wasn't ready to look at him. With more courage than she'd thought she possessed, she slowly, jerkily, raised her head to meet Nadir's gaze.

Heat bloomed inside her when she saw the desire in his eyes. He lowered his head and her eyelashes fluttered. Zoe knew she should turn away but she remained motionless. She didn't know if she was relieved or disappointed when she felt his lips brush along her forehead.

Her lips stung with anticipation as Nadir skimmed his mouth along her cheek. His warm breath wafted over her skin before he placed a trail of soft kisses on her jawline. His hands were tangled in the mass of her hair, and she felt his fingers tighten when she gave a small sigh of pleasure.

Zoe leaned in closer and immediately stopped. She'd almost given herself away. She was supposed to be a bashful virginal bride. She needed to shy away, not participate!

Why was she responding so eagerly? She shouldn't soften from a few tender caresses. Was her body greedy for a man's touch because it had been so long? Or did Nadir know how to touch a woman and make her forget her best intentions?

She wasn't going to fall for this. Obviously he wanted

her to become used to his touch. He wanted her to welcome his advances and not see him as a threat.

It was too late. Nadir had been a threat from the moment he touched her. She didn't think she had ever longed for a man's touch, hungered for a kiss, as much as she did at this moment.

Her defenses couldn't crumble. She would not let him get too close. Her future depended on it.

Nadir cradled her face with his hands and covered her mouth with his.

Wild desire exploded inside her. It rushed through her veins and she melted against him. She had never been kissed like this before. Nadir's kiss claimed. Dominated.

She couldn't surrender to him. She couldn't let him find out the truth about her. Zoe knew she shouldn't let this seduction continue, but somehow she parted her lips and allowed him to thrust his tongue deep into her mouth. She returned the kiss and was instantly swept away.

Sensations overwhelmed her and she clung to Nadir's shoulders. Her hands crushed the luxurious fabric of his *dishdasha* and she drew him closer. She wanted more, so much more.

Zoe ignored her growing sense of alarm until she heard Nadir's groan. She couldn't tame the instant attraction that had flared between them. Nadir was too sensual, too dangerous. She broke the kiss and turned her head away swiftly.

She felt Nadir shudder as he tried to harness his emotions and knew she was pressing her luck. The last thing she wanted to do was frustrate him. "I'm sorry," she whispered as she looked away.

Zoe pressed her fingertips against her swollen lips. Her breasts felt heavy and there was a delicious ache low in her belly. She had to get out of this bed. Now.

As she battled back the hunger Zoe realized she had not anticipated this fatal flaw in her plan. She'd never thought she would desire the Sheikh. That he would tempt her to throw caution to the wind.

She had to be careful. This was becoming a very dangerous game. She had to hide her shameful attraction and she could not act on it. Under no circumstances could she allow him to get any closer. No more kissing!

"It's all right," he murmured. He slowly kissed down the length of her throat. "I want you to kiss me back."

That was the problem: she wanted to do more than kiss. Only she had to appear untutored and modest, Zoe reminded herself as Nadir removed her necklaces one by one. And when she kissed him she felt untamed. How did he have that much power over her responses?

She felt his hands travel down her spine and her top sagged open. Zoe's heart lurched. He had found the fasteners hidden under the beading in the back. This wedding night had gone further than she wanted and she wasn't sure how to stop it. Nadir pushed her top down her shoulders, revealing a thin white chemise.

She felt his heated gaze on her. She shivered as a dangerous excitement swept along her body, but she knew she should be feeling exposed and uncertain. What would a virgin do? Zoe belatedly crossed her arms to hide herself, but Nadir grasped her wrists.

"Don't," he ordered in a gruff voice. He lowered her arms. "Never hide yourself for me. You are beautiful."

Zoe wanted to believe that the compliment fell automatically from Nadir's lips, that he said it to all his lovers, but she felt beautiful. Desirable. Wanted. She hadn't felt like that for a long time. She had to be very careful and *not* follow her instincts, but the blood was roaring in her veins.

Nadir dipped his head and captured her mouth with his.

This time he wasn't as gentle. She fed off his aggression. His kiss was hard and hungry. He couldn't hide how much he wanted and needed her.

Heat swirled inside her. She was caught up in the kiss as he slowly lowered her. She speared her hands into his thick hair as he laid her on the bed. She'd accept one more kiss and then she'll pull away. One more...

She didn't protest when Nadir stripped her heavy skirt from her hips. He tore his mouth from hers and knelt back. She watched dazedly as he yanked off his *dishdasha* and tossed it on the floor.

Zoe gasped when she saw his golden brown skin and muscular physique. Okay, new rule, she decided frantically. No more taking off clothes. This was as far as they could go.

Without thinking she reached out and stroked his chest. She rubbed her fingertips in the sprinkle of coarse hair. She enjoyed the rasp of friction and imagined his chest, hot and sweaty, pressed against her soft breast.

She bucked her hips as the ache in her pelvis intensified. *Uh-oh.* She shouldn't have done that. Had Nadir read anything from that shameless move?

Zoe hesitated, her chest rising and falling. She needed to hide her bold responses—a virgin would be shy and uncertain. She couldn't let Nadir know how much she enjoyed exploring his body.

"Touch me again," Nadir said in a hoarse whisper. "Touch me as much as you want."

He shouldn't give her that kind of encouragement. If she touched him as much as she wanted she would not stop touching him. She would touch this legendary playboy in ways that would shock him.

But she shouldn't refuse him. Okay, revised new rule. She wouldn't go past his chest. That was safe. Zoe splayed her fingers and caressed his arms and shoulders. She smoothed her hands along his back before trailing her fingers back to his chest.

Nadir's muscles bunched as she scored his nipple with her fingernail. She hid her smile as a sense of power poured over her. She drew her hands down to his rock-hard abdomen before she reached the waistband of his white boxer shorts.

There must be something in her eyes. Something that gave away how she felt. She saw Nadir's expression tighten and the fire glow in his eyes before he swooped down and claimed her mouth again. The long, wet kiss took her breath away.

She didn't mean to part her thighs when he nestled his hips between her legs. Zoe knew he was trying to go slow and she didn't think she could slow him down further. His muscles shook with restraint as he caressed the length of her leg.

Nadir deepened their kiss and cupped her breast. Zoe was surprised by his possessive touch. It felt good. It felt right. It was all she could do not to arch into his hand. Her nipple tightened under his attention, her breasts full and heavy.

She shouldn't allow this, Zoe thought dazedly. But she was still partly clothed. She wasn't too close to the point of no return, but she was far away from her original plan. She should stop this now, no matter how much she wanted it.

Zoe gasped, the sound ringing out into the room, as he pinched her nipple between his fingers. Intense pleasure spread under her skin like wildfire. She wiggled under his body and demanded more from his kiss.

Nadir didn't follow her insistent silent command. He pulled away and she whimpered. His gaze focused on her shoulder as he pushed down the chemise strap. She felt the tremor in his hand as he peeled the fabric from her small breast. She thought she heard a purr of satisfaction before he lowered his head and took her breast into his mouth.

Zoe's moan staggered from her throat. It didn't sound virginal at all. She tilted her head back as hot pleasure poured through her. She closed her eyes, unwilling to reveal how weak and needy she felt. Nadir seemed to know exactly what she wanted. She felt the strong pull all the way to her core.

She instinctively wrapped her legs around his lean waist and drew him closer. When she felt his rock-hard erection against her flesh she realized she was in the danger zone. She wanted him inside her so much, but he would find out the truth about her.

She quickly dropped her legs as panic swelled in her chest. She grabbed his wide shoulders and tried to push him away, but he was too strong. "We've gone far enough," she blurted out. "I am *not* sleeping with you!"

She clapped her hand over her mouth. Taut silence pulsated in the room. Nadir didn't move, but she felt the ripple of tension in his body.

Now she'd done it. Zoe hunched her shoulders and waited for the explosion that was sure to follow. There was virginal reluctance and then there was outright refusal. The Sheikh was going to cast her back to her family before the night was over.

Nadir shuddered as he tried to hold back. He wanted Zoe badly. He was willing to change her mind. Lie. Cajole. Beg. He needed to taste her, sink into her wet heat and make her his in the most basic, primitive way.

He didn't understand this white-hot instant attraction, but he wasn't going to question it. It was an unexpected bonus to be attracted to his arranged bride, and he was willing to make the most of his good fortune for a few nights before he sent her away.

But Zoe didn't see it that way. Was she frightened by the unfamiliar sexual feelings or was it something else? He wondered if she had heard the rumors about him. They would send any bride into a panic.

"Zoe." He reached out for her but stopped when she flinched. Did she think he was going to hit her?

"I'm sorry," she said behind her splayed hand. "I didn't mean to say that."

"Yes, you did." He watched her expression closely. She was thinking fast, as if considering her best option.

"Okay, I did," she admitted as she dropped her hand. "But… But…you have to understand. I don't know you."

He braced his arms on the mattress and met her gaze. He sensed that wasn't her main concern. There was something false about her behavior. "I'm your husband. That's all you need to know."

Her mouth drew into a firm line and he knew she was choosing her next words carefully. "I don't know anything about you," she clarified.

That wasn't what she really wanted to say. Her eyes were very expressive. She had already made up her mind about him and it wasn't favorable. "I don't know anything about you, either," he said, "but I'm okay with that."

Zoe's eyes narrowed. "Women are different that way."

Nadir exhaled sharply. It was true. Sex wasn't just sex with women. It was a connection. It was about intimacy. And with a virgin it was supposed to be a magical experience. A sacred rite of passage.

Damn these virgins. They had to make a simple pleasure so complicated.

"In all honesty," she continued softly as she looked

away, "I don't know anything about you other than your name."

Which she hadn't used yet, he noted. He'd had visions of her crying out his name over and over, but that wasn't going to happen tonight. Nadir reluctantly slid the delicate strap of her chemise up her arm and settled it securely on her shoulder.

"I don't know your favorite color or your favorite drink."

The words rushed past her reddened lips as she tried desperately to explain herself. But he didn't believe a word of it. Zoe was trying to build barriers.

"I don't know your pet peeves or your goals. It's kind of hard to sleep with a stranger even if you are married to him."

"Women have been in arranged marriages for centuries," he argued as lust continued to scorch through his veins. "It's normal. It's natural."

"Not for me!"

Nadir gritted his teeth. An American virgin was probably the worst of the lot.

In fact his bride was very American. How long would it take for her to see the same Western sensibilities and spirit in him? If she suspected that he wasn't as conservative as he pretended she could use that against him. He needed to stay on guard around Zoe.

"Now I've made you angry," she said as her bottom lip wobbled.

Was she going to cry? Nadir rubbed his face with his hand. He hadn't even raised his voice. How would she react when he wasn't on his best behavior?

He knew she wasn't just a virgin whose expectations were different. He understood this was an emotional day for her. She was obviously coming to terms with the fact that she was married and in bed with The Beast.

That wasn't good. She was too nervous to be seduced into a sensual honeymoon, and despite what she thought he wasn't going to force her.

The last thing he needed was a bride who was scared of him. That would encourage more questions and rumors. He needed to show the tribe that he could tame this American wildcat into a traditional Jazaari woman. Once they left the village he would send her away. But for now it meant he had to be more attentive. Patient.

But he was not a patient man. He had got where he was today by being merciless, intimidating and unyielding. That strategy wouldn't work on his trembling wife. He needed to romance her. Show his tender side.

If only he had a tender side.

"Zoe, I'm not angry. Just stop cowering."

She inhaled sharply. "I don't cower," she shot back.

Ah, those tears were fake. She wasn't above using that age-old feminine technique, Nadir realized as he rose to his knees. That was good to know.

"You make a valid point about how we are strangers. We need to learn about each other more."

She nodded fiercely and relief shone brightly in her eyes. "Exactly."

"But you're still sharing a bed with me," he announced. He saw the hunted look on her face as he settled onto the other side of the bed. "How else will we know each other more?"

"I—I—"

Her gaze shifted from one point of the room to another. He knew she was trying to come up with an argument.

They had to sleep in the same bed. All it would take was one servant to notice their separate sleeping arrangements for gossip to spread like wildfire. That was the last thing he needed the tribe elders to discover.

"I won't touch you until you're ready," Nadir said.

Zoe's jaw shut with a snap. She narrowed her eyes as if she was trying to find some hidden loophole in his words. That offended him. Why should she question his word? He was a sheikh. He was her husband.

"I don't need to force myself on a woman," he said with lethal softness.

Her face paled. "I n-never said…"

"I know." She didn't have to. The look in her eyes indicated that she thought he was the fabled beast who would devour her in her sleep. Nadir swallowed back another deep sigh and turned off the lamp. "Go to sleep, Zoe."

She gave a huff, as if to say that it would be impossible. Nadir watched as she scooted off to the far edge of the bed. She lay on her side, facing him, as if she had to keep an eye on him.

"You flatter yourself," he muttered, and reached for her. She protested with a squawk, her muscles locking as he curled her against his side. He tried to ignore how well she fit against him.

"You said you wouldn't touch me until I was ready," she said stiffly.

"I won't have sex with you until you're ready," he amended. And they would have sex very soon. He would make certain. "But you're not going to get to know me, be comfortable with me, if you're hanging on the edge of the mattress."

She didn't fight out of his loose embrace, but he could tell she wanted to. Zoe would probably leave the bed the moment he fell asleep. He had to build a quicker rapport between them, but how could he do that without sex?

He looked up at the ceiling as he considered possible alternatives. He remembered what Zoe had said and he rolled his eyes. It was ridiculous, but he might as well give it a shot. "And it's blue."

"What is?" she asked.

"My favorite color," he answered gruffly. "A deep sapphire-blue. The color of the desert sky right before night falls."

The silence stretched between them. "Blue is my favorite color, too," she reluctantly admitted.

"Imagine that." Nadir didn't know if she was saying it to please him or if it was the truth. It didn't matter as long as she'd learned a little bit more about him. Tomorrow she would accept—no, *welcome* him in her bed. And then he would tame his wife with one night of exquisite pleasure before sending her away.

He closed his eyes, his body still hard, his blood racing as he inhaled Zoe's scent. Her long hair spilled over his shoulder and her soft body pressed against his. They were skin to skin.

And he couldn't do anything about it.

He hadn't expected to suffer like this, but it was a hell of a lot better than his last wedding night.

# CHAPTER THREE

ZOE woke up with a violent start. Her heart banged against her chest as her muscles locked so hard they ached. She tilted her head up like a small animal scenting danger. Sunlight streamed in the windows and she heard the muted chatter of people in the courtyard. She cautiously looked to her side, praying that Nadir hadn't been watching her sleep, and found the bed blessedly empty.

She brushed her tangled hair from her eyes, finding it difficult to believe she had fallen asleep. She wanted to blame it on exhaustion and stress. It wasn't because she'd started to take Nadir at his word! All night she had lain uncomfortably in Nadir's arms. Not only had it felt strange to share her bed, but it had been a challenge to keep her hands to herself. She had been inexplicably tempted to explore Nadir's muscular body.

Zoe bolted out of bed and went straight to the bathroom. She saw some of her clothes hanging in the closet and grabbed a mustard-yellow caftan. Passing by a mirror above the sink, she caught a glimpse of her reflection and stopped.

*Oh, my goodness.* She shoved her hands in her tousled and wild hair and stared at her smeared make-up. She saw the outline of her body through the thin chemise. She looked bold and sexy, as though she just returned from a

night of debauchery. Considering Nadir's legendary sex-
drive, it was something of a surprise that he hadn't bedded her last night.

Why hadn't he? Nadir had to be up to something. Men
were like that, she decided as she started the shower. They
promised to love and take care of you, but really they were
using you.

But this time she was using a man, she thought with
dark satisfaction as she stepped into the shower stall. She
was taking advantage of her husband.

As the hot water pounded against her tired body Zoe
reviewed her plan. She wasn't allowed to travel at all unless she was accompanied by a male relative. It didn't matter that she was over eighteen, and it didn't matter that she
was an American citizen. The law here was the law. But
once she got through the third day of wedding ceremonies
she would go on her honeymoon with Nadir. The moment
she passed the borders of Jazaar she could escape to Texas.

She needed to find out where they were going on their
honeymoon, Zoe decided as she grabbed for a washcloth.
She hoped it was somewhere close to America. Once she
got home—her real home—she could complete her education and live her life on her terms.

Zoe looked at her hands, which were still decorated with
henna. Of course she would still be married to the Sheikh
when she arrived in America, but she could get that annulled if Nadir didn't do it first. He wouldn't come after
her once she reached Texas. He had his choice of women.
She was interchangeable to a man like Nadir.

After Zoe got dressed, she glanced in the mirror before
stepping into the living area of the hotel suite. She had
done everything she could to look plain and dowdy. Her
brown hair was still damp and pulled back severely in a
tight braid. Her face was free of make-up and she wore no

jewelry. Her faded caftan did nothing for her figure, and the shade of yellow made her skin look sallow.

Nadir was going to be horrified—but that was a good thing, she reminded herself as she quietly entered the room. If he didn't find her attractive he wouldn't rush her into bed.

She saw two servants carrying trays of food and found Nadir sitting on the silk floor pillows near the low table. Her heart gave a flip when she saw he wore a gray short-sleeve shirt and dark trousers. He rose fluidly when he saw her. She didn't realize he was speaking on a sleek cell phone until he swiftly disconnected the call.

Nadir frowned as he studied her appearance. She knew that look. Displeasure. Disapproval. Disappointment. Zoe wondered if he already had buyer's remorse.

"I hope you slept well," he finally said.

"I did," she lied. "Thank you."

His dark eyes gleamed and she assumed he knew the truth. He knew she had been on alert all night. Every time she had thought it safe to move away his hold had tightened.

"Please, have some breakfast." He gestured at the low table that was laden with food. She inhaled the aroma of strong coffee and savory breakfast dishes.

But she wasn't used to the luxury of eating first thing in the morning, and the idea of sharing a meal with Nadir felt too intimate. "No, thank you. I don't eat breakfast."

"You didn't eat much last night," he said, and he placed his hand on the small of her back. The unexpected touch startled her and she flinched. Nadir frowned as she automatically stepped away. "I insist you have breakfast."

She was surprised that he had noticed her lack of appetite. What else did this man see? She needed to stay on guard, Zoe decided as she reluctantly moved to the opposite side of the table.

"No, Zoe, sit next to me." He pointed at the large silk pillow they would share.

Zoe's gaze flew to his face. She saw a flicker in his eyes before he banked it. His expression was polite and innocent. She knew better. He was playing the role of besotted husband.

She glanced at the servants, who now stood several feet away from the table, ready to assist when needed. Zoe wondered if this display was for them. Did Nadir think the servants would gossip about their behavior? That the tribe would analyze everything including how close they sat during meals?

Or was this act simply for her? He had a reluctant bride on his hands. What better way to woo her into his bed than by playing the tender and thoughtful husband? She didn't think the act would last long, but he was going to be on his best behavior and she needed to use it her advantage.

Zoe gritted her teeth. She should never have complained about how little they knew each other. Would she be expected to stay at his side for the next couple of days?

She knew this was not a battle she wanted to fight and quietly sat down. Nadir sat next to her, his arms and legs brushing hers. She didn't like sitting this close to someone, especially a man. After years of dealing with her uncle's temper she preferred to be more than an arm's length away from any male.

She reached for the coffeepot like a drowning man would grab for a life preserver as Nadir tore off a piece of flatbread. He scooped up some mutton with the flatbread and held it out to her. Zoe gave him a questioning glance.

"Eat this," he said.

"There's plenty of food." She motioned at the bowls

and plates that covered every inch of the table. "I don't need to eat yours."

"I want to share this with you," he explained softly as he grazed her lips with the bread. "Eat."

It was not easy for her to comply. Eating from Nadir's hand required a level of trust and acceptance from her. She opened her mouth slightly and he popped the morsel in.

Zoe closed her mouth too quickly and caught the edge of his thumb. Nadir took the opportunity to stroke her bottom lip with the side of his thumb as she struggled to swallow the food.

Was he doing all this as an excuse to touch her? Why would he when she looked jaundiced? She was suddenly glad there were servants in the room, knowing that any intimacy Nadir planned would be curtailed.

Or was he trying to get her to depend on him? Did he think that if he fed her she would develop the belief that he provided for her? She couldn't figure it out, but she knew not to trust this attentive side of Nadir.

"It was a pleasure meeting your brother at the ceremony," she lied with a smile. The man had made it clear she was unworthy to sit in the same room with him. "Will he visit us today?"

"No, Rashid has already returned to the palace. He sends his regrets."

Sure he did. It was more likely that Rashid couldn't stand the idea of her marrying into the family. "Do you have any more brothers and sisters?"

"No, my mother died while giving birth to Rashid. It's just me, my brother and my father."

"Will your father attend the last ceremony?"

Nadir shook his head. "My father is unable to make the journey."

"I'm sorry to hear that. When will I meet him?" Zoe frowned when she saw Nadir hesitate.

"That's hard to say," Nadir didn't meet her gaze. "The Sultan is unwell and is not receiving visitors at this time."

Zoe's eyes narrowed. She got the feeling that Nadir didn't want her to meet his father. Was he ashamed of the match? The possibility stung.

"I forgot to ask you," she said hurriedly, changing the subject as she grabbed her coffee cup. "Where are we going on our honeymoon?"

He paused and returned his attention to his plate. "To my home in the mountains."

Her fingers clenched on the coffee cup. She was surprised it didn't shatter in her hands. "Oh," she said on strangled breath.

*They weren't leaving Jazaar? No, no, no! That wasn't part of the plan.*

He scooped up another chunk of mutton with a piece of flatbread. When he held it out to her his eyes narrowed on her face. "You're disappointed?"

"I'm sure it's a lovely home," she said in a rush. She couldn't afford to offend him. "I just assumed we would go overseas because you travel so much."

"The traveling is part of my work, not my private life." He held the bite of food against her lips. "I would never take my wife with me on business trips."

"Oh." She cautiously accepted the food as her mind went into overdrive. His decision ruined everything!

Nadir tilted his head as he studied her face. "You want to go somewhere?"

She hurriedly chewed and swallowed the mutton. This was her chance. She couldn't blow it. "Well, I haven't been anywhere for a while. I'd like to do some traveling."

"Do you have a place in mind?"

She shrugged. She needed to appear casual even as nervousness bit into her chest. "Europe. Australia. Maybe America."

He frowned. "But you're from America. That couldn't be of much interest to you."

"America is a big place," she replied as she took a sip of the hot, bitter coffee. "There so much of it I haven't seen."

"Why would you want to travel?" he asked as he took a bite of his breakfast. "What would you do?"

Escape. Study medicine. Reclaim the life that should have been hers.

"I'm sure there would be lots of things that would interest me."

"You're not ready to represent Jazaar," he declared as he took a pitted date from the fruit platter. "The future Sultana must be the ideal Jazaari woman and demonstrate those values."

*Beauty, refinement and obedience.* Zoe closed her eyes in defeat. Of all the days to dress down. Damn it.

Nadir chuckled as he held the date to her mouth. "Like I said, the outside world is not ready for a sheikha like you."

Zoe's eyes widened in horror. Had she cursed aloud? It was getting worse and worse. She automatically parted her lips to accept the date. "Didn't I look like the perfect Jazaari bride at our wedding?"

He shook his head. "I knew the truth the moment I saw you."

She hoped not. But if she couldn't convince Nadir that she was a beautiful and obedient wife, she wasn't going to get out of this country. "I can meet your expectations. All I need is a new caftan and a better pair of sandals."

He gave her a disbelieving look before he studied her yellow caftan. "Is that all you have to wear?"

"I have my wedding gowns. Why?"

"You'll need some more clothes," he said as he offered her another date.

She accepted the fruit and chewed furiously. "Are you considering a trip?"

"No, but you need to wear something befitting of a sheikha." He looked at her caftan with distaste.

It was hard to remember she was a sheikha when just a couple of days ago she'd been scrubbing floors. "There aren't that many shops in the village."

"We'll take my helicopter to Omaira."

Her eyes widened and her pulse skipped a beat. Omaira was the biggest city in Jazaar. It was a metropolitan center that she had heard rivaled Marrakesh and Dubai. Chances were there was an American embassy. She could escape Jazaar and request sanctuary the moment she stepped into the government building.

"Let me know when you want to go."

She set down her coffee cup with a clatter. "I'm ready now."

This was not one of his better ideas.

Nadir had learned quickly that he needed to watch Zoe like a hawk as they explored Omaira. His wife was endlessly fascinated with the city. She had immediately requested a map even though he could reveal any secret of the place. She insisted on asserting her independence, constantly getting lost in the dark alleys and winding streets the moment he turned his head.

Zoe was facing the excursion with startling intensity. She had craned her neck to study the architecture and stared at the red clay that edged up to the deep blue ocean. She was thrilled by the activity in the ancient marketplace, enjoying the spices and food. She was enthralled with the stores and the people.

She was interested in everything and everyone but him. In fact she seemed frustrated that he was protectively at her side and didn't allow her to venture far.

Didn't Zoe know that a good Jazaari bride focused all of her attention on her husband? Perhaps it was time to go back to the village where there weren't as many distractions? Or was she so shy with her arranged husband that she was using the city as an excuse to keep busy?

No, that wasn't it. Zoe was stubborn and disobedient, but never shy. If she grew quiet she was up to something. He already knew that much.

She tilted her head and took a few steps back to peek at a dark alley. Nadir slid her arm through his and held her firmly. "This way, Zoe."

"I can walk on my own," she replied as her fingers curled in a fist. "You act is if I need to be on a leash."

"Don't tempt me." At first he had thought she was overwhelmed with the noise and the crowds. He had thought her rebellious streak was overcompensating for her lack of sophistication.

But he'd discarded that possibility when she'd got lost for the fifth time. Her sense of direction couldn't be that poor. Nadir couldn't shake the feeling that she was *trying* to get lost. Trying to run away.

"Ah, here we are." He stopped at the entrance of a modern steel and glass building.

Zoe tried to act nonchalant as she removed her hand from his hold. She glanced at the window displays. "A jewelry store?"

Nadir fought back a smile. No woman in Jazaar would describe it as such. Paradise, maybe heaven, but never just "a jewelry store." "Fayruz has been the royal jewelers for decades."

Zoe wasn't impressed. "Why are we here?"

"You need a few things." He had noticed in the morning light that the necklaces and earrings she'd worn for her wedding were paste. Her bangles were cheap metal and the rubies and diamonds were fake. It surprised him that her family would send her off with no real jewelry. Her jewelry collection was supposed to be her financial nest egg.

She dismissed the store with a wave of her hand. "I'm fine with what I have."

She obviously didn't know about her jewelry, and he wasn't going to reveal the truth to her. "Zoe, it reflects poorly on me if you don't wear jewelry. I am buying you a necklace, some earrings, and maybe a few bracelets."

She needed the basics for her new role. Normally a sheikha would wear the royal jewels, but this was a paper marriage. She would not be at his side or living with him. If he gave her a few important pieces of jewelry people would know that she was still under his protection and care.

"No, you shouldn't. You have already bought too much." She flattened her hands on her cheeks and groaned. "All those clothes."

Most women loved to get new clothes, yet Zoe had tried on each designer outfit with reluctance. She'd tried to talk him out of his purchases, but he wouldn't listen.

"You need the clothes for your new role," he reminded her.

"But they are so expensive. I could have bought medical equipment to serve all the pregnant women in the village."

"The women don't need that."

Zoe's jaw dropped. "Are you kidding me? The women in the village don't have access to basic medicine."

"Impossible. Jazaar is a wealthy kingdom. The Ministry of Health has allocated millions to the most remote villages."

"That goes to the men," she muttered. "Because the elders decide where the money is spent."

"Enough. I'm not going to discuss this anymore," he declared as guided her to the famous turquoise doors. Jewelry was the way to gain a woman's deference. He knew from experience that even the most temperamental girlfriend could be soothed by an expensive bauble.

Zoe held back. "I appreciate the new clothes…"

"Apparently."

"…but if you need to demonstrate how wealthy Jazaar is I'd rather you use the money on building a women's medical clinic for the village."

He looked intently at her earnest face. "Your village doesn't need one."

"It does. I, however, don't need a necklace."

His cell phone rang and he bit back an oath. He was in delicate negotiations with his stubborn wife and didn't need the interruption. "Excuse me. I have to take this call."

He accepted the call and tried to listen to one of his executive assistants as he watched Zoe's expression. She looked as if she wanted to chuck his phone into the traffic and continue to argue her point. Nadir knew he had caught a glimpse of the real Zoe. Finally.

Something his assistant said caught his attention. "Would you repeat that?" he asked into the phone. He motioned his apology to Zoe as he turned away from the traffic and listened to the assistant. After giving a few orders, he ended the call.

If only getting Zoe to accept his gifts could be so easy and straightforward. "As I was saying…"

He turned around and discovered Zoe wasn't standing next to him. He glanced around the sidewalk and didn't see her anywhere.

* * *

Zoe walked briskly as her heart thudded against her chest. She wanted to run as fast as she could, but that would create a scene. She needed to do more than escape. She needed to disappear.

She glanced at the streets, recognizing the storefronts and landmarks. Having spent most of the day memorizing the layout of Omaira, she had a good idea where she was. Unfortunately the American embassy was on the opposite side of town.

Nadir might have completed his call by now. He would start to look for her. As much as it went against her instincts, Zoe ducked into a store. She wanted to put as much distance between herself and her new husband as possible, but he would easily spot her on the street. It was best to hide for a while.

She looked around and realized she had walked into a bookstore. Zoe froze, but it was too late. She had already inhaled the familiar scent of books.

Zoe picked up a book from the metal rack. It had a blinding red cover, but she didn't know the author or the title. She thumbed through the pages, enjoying the sound of the paper.

"Zoe! There you are."

*Damn.* Zoe tensed at the sound of Nadir's voice. He'd found her already. She had squandered her best chance of escaping.

She sensed Nadir surging forward and he was suddenly at her side. As he towered over her head she felt his frustration and chafing temper.

If she'd been facing her uncle she would have known to hunch her shoulders to protect her ears and wait for the stinging slap. Being in public and having witnesses meant nothing. Experience had also taught her that ducking out of reach only made Uncle Tareef angrier.

But she couldn't predict Nadir's response. She was jumpy, desperate to get out range, but she forced herself to remain still as she waited for his next move.

He didn't touch her, but it felt as though he surrounded her. "I've been looking for you." He was annoyed, but he didn't raise his voice. "You need to tell me where you're going."

Zoe felt impatience billowing off him, and she had to do her best to play innocent. She had to act as though she hadn't intentionally run away from him, as though she had not tried to escape.

She kept her focus on the book and continued to stroke the shiny red cover with her fingers. The book felt sleek in her hands and the weight was familiar. She remembered how good it used to feel, having a book in her hand.

"Zoe." His voice was low and rough. "I will not be ignored."

"I'm sorry." She slowly turned to face Nadir. "It's been a while since I've been in a bookstore."

He cast a glance at the small shop, shaking his head at the glossy magazines and colorful books. "You saw this bookstore from where we were standing?"

"Yes," she lied through clenched teeth.

Nadir slowly exhaled, and she suspected he was drawing on the last of his patience. "You could have gotten lost. Again," he said with calm control. "Stay with me and I won't let anything happen to you."

She pressed her lips together, not trusting herself to speak. The idea that a man would be there when you needed him the most was a fantasy. She'd learned long ago not to rely on anyone.

"Is that what you want?" He nodded at the book in her hands.

Her grip tightened on the book. Zoe sighed with regret and reluctantly replaced the book. "No."

"Pick a book. Pick a hundred of them," Nadir suggested as he gestured at the bookshelves.

From the corner of her eye Zoe saw the bookseller approaching. She dipped her head. "That's very generous of you, but it's not necessary."

He inhaled sharply and rubbed the back of his neck with his hand. "Why are you refusing every gift I offer?"

Was that what he thought? She had to tell him the truth, no matter how much it embarrassed her. "I can't read these books," Zoe whispered as her face burned red.

Nadir stilled. "You can't read?"

She jerked her head up and tilted her chin. "I can read! I love to read. But I can only read English."

His gaze held hers for one charged moment. He dragged his attention away to greet the bookseller smoothly and assure him that they were only browsing. He waited until they were alone until he said quietly, "Didn't your uncle send you to school?"

"No." She could recite all the made-up reasons she normally used when anyone asked her that question, but today she didn't feel like playing that game. "I don't want to talk about it."

"I'm sure he had a very good reason," he said.

"I'm sure." She crossed her arms tightly. Uncle Tareef had thought he had a very good reason. He'd enjoyed using her thirst for knowledge as a bargaining chip. He also hadn't liked how her intelligence challenged his.

Nadir looked at the shelf full of books and then looked back at her. "How did you read our marriage contract?"

Zoe winced. She might have just gotten tangled in a deeper problem. The only thing she could do was answer truthfully and hope for the best. "I didn't."

"Do you know what was included?" he asked. "Did anyone explain it to you?"

"No." She stared at her feet, not sure what would happen next. Did that make the marriage invalid? Was he going to call the whole thing off? Toss her back to her relatives?

"This will not do. You are a sheikha. You should be able to read and write in our language. I will remedy this immediately."

She watched him pull out his cell phone. "What are you planning?"

"I'm going to have my executive assistant schedule a tutor for you," he said as he tapped out a message. "By our first wedding anniversary you will read and write Arabic."

She didn't know if she should believe him. She had heard too many broken promises. How many times had Musad made promises, until "tomorrow" became "next time" and "soon" became "someday"? How many times had her uncle promised that if she was a good girl he would enroll her in school? The problem was that she was never good enough and eventually had stopped trying.

"That's very kind of you," Zoe said politely. She knew she should sound more grateful. More excited. But she wasn't going to get her hopes up. It would be easier this way if Nadir failed to deliver on his promise.

"It has nothing to do with kindness. You need these skills."

Not if her plans succeeded. With any luck she would be out of the country if and when the tutor showed up. "Thank you."

"You're welcome," Nadir said, and tapped another text in his cell phone. "Now it's time for tea."

"Of course." Zoe followed Nadir, but when she passed the threshold she couldn't resist taking a final look at the bookstore.

By this time next year she would be surrounded by books that she could read. By this time next *month,* she decided. The minute she returned home she would go into a public library and read her heart out.

She was silent as Nadir took her across the street to an elegant restaurant. Upon entering, Zoe realized that her attire was cheap and faded next to that of the other patrons. She wanted to disappear, but they were seated at the best table in the center of the room.

She knew she lacked the refinement and sophistication Nadir expected in a wife, but he didn't complain or make any snide comment. He didn't need to. She could tell from the faces of the other customers that her appearance reflected poorly on him.

She gradually forgot about her outfit as Nadir asked her about favorite books. She wasn't sure about his ulterior motive. Was he just making conversation, or was he figuring out how her mind ticked? She played along and discovered that having his attention was like a rollercoaster ride—enthralling and a little bit scary.

Zoe silently enjoyed the taste of freedom. The moment she had left the village she had felt as if she could breathe a little easier and spread her wings. Everything seemed brighter. Bolder. Zoe appreciated the audacious spirit in Omaira. She saw it in the daring architecture and in the enterprising people around her. It made her believe anything was possible, and that her dreams weren't out of reach.

She was grateful that her new husband didn't try to squash her growing enthusiasm. Usually when she was with her uncle she had to hide her interest. Protect it. Instead, Nadir nurtured her curiosity, pointing out what he knew she would like and encouraging her to ask questions. When she was with Nadir she felt as if her world expanded.

When they stepped out of the restaurant and walked

through the breathtakingly modern lobby Zoe saw Nadir turn on his phone. His frown seemed to deepen as he checked his messages.

"Is something wrong?" she asked.

He shrugged. "A business problem in Singapore."

Singapore. Her mind grabbed onto the word and wouldn't shake free. Singapore wasn't close to America, but it was far away from Jazaar. "I've never been there. I hear Singapore is quite beautiful."

"It is," he muttered absently as he tapped a key on his cell phone.

"I bet it's a perfect place for a honeymoon."

Nadir cast a quizzical look in her direction just as their luxury sedan rolled up to the curb. He escorted her to the car, and when they were both inside she saw a gift-wrapped package by her seat.

"That's for you," Nadir said as he continued scrolling through his messages.

"Thank you." She didn't want to accept another gift from him. He was trying hard to win her over, but all she felt was guilt.

She carefully tore off the ribbon. Once she had ripped off the paper she reluctantly opened the box. Zoe had been expecting jewelry. Something obscenely extravagant like a tiara. Instead she stared at a small gray electronic device with a screen. It was too big for a phone, but smaller than most computers she had seen. "What is it?"

"It's an e-book reader."

She picked up the light device as excitement bubbled in her chest. "E-book?"

"My assistant has programmed the reader and you can download books instantly. Now you may read whatever you want, whenever you want."

Whatever she wanted, whenever she wanted... Her head spun at the thought. "You gave me a library?"

He set his phone down and smiled at her. "That's one way of looking at it."

It was almost too good to be true. There had to be a catch. But she didn't want to think about it right now. After all these years of not having the opportunity to read, she now had all the books she wanted at her fingertips. She clasped the e-book reader to her chest. "Thank you, Nadir," she whispered.

His eyes flared bright when she said his name. "You're welcome, Zoe." He gently caressed her cheek with his fingertips. "Now we must go. The helicopter is waiting for us."

They were going back to the village? The idea suffocated Zoe. She had had a taste of freedom and she wanted more. "Are you sure you don't want to stay in Omaira?" she asked wistfully. "Didn't you say you had a place here?"

"I would like to show you our home here," he said, "but tradition requires us to return before sundown. The servants have already started preparations."

"Preparations for what?" As far as she knew they had no ceremonies to suffer through tonight.

"Our first full night together alone." Nadir's mouth tilted into a sexy smile of anticipation. "Tonight it will be the two of us. No distractions and no interruptions."

Zoe's breath hitched in her throat as her heart clanged against her ribs. She had wanted to hold him off for one more night, but Nadir was planning a full-out seduction.

And she was no match for a man like him.

# CHAPTER FOUR

ZOE stared at the mirror with growing alarm. She sat quietly in front of her dressing table, panic clawing her chest as the two maids added the finishing touches to her transformation. She no longer looked like an innocent girl or a shy bride. She looked like a seductress.

This was terrible. How could she maintain the virgin act when she looked like this? Zoe took in a shallow, choppy breath and inhaled the spicy perfume she wore. The jasmine and incense were an invitation for exotic, forbidden sex. They were designed to tantalize, and the last thing Zoe needed to do was entice Nadir even closer.

She bit the inside of her lip and tightly squeezed her hands together as the maids' voices ebbed and flowed around her. The older women were experts in the traditional ritual of preparing the bride for her groom and they dismissed her concerns with a wave of their weathered hands. They didn't need a prudish bride to tell them how to prepare her for a man.

Zoe peeked from under her thick lashes and gave another glance at her reflection. She froze, and swore she wouldn't make any slanted looks in front of Nadir. It was too sexy, too suggestive.

Everything about her said she was ready for an endless night of sensual pleasure. She had been bathed, oiled, perfumed and made up for Nadir's desire. Zoe frowned at her reflection and shifted uncomfortably in her seat. She might as well place a shiny red bow around her neck along with a gift tag that said "Take me."

A fine tremor swept through her as she imagined what his response would be to such a blatant offer. She was sure that Nadir could give her mind-blowing pleasure, but she couldn't let that happen. Not tonight, when he might discover she wasn't a virgin bride. Probably not ever. She couldn't afford to lower her guard with any man, especially one as powerful and ruthless as the Sheikh.

If only she could acquire some kind of armor for the upcoming battle. The buttoned-up yellow gown that hid her figure was gone. She had heard Amina, one the maids, muttering under her breath about burning it. In its place was a long sapphire-blue negligee with a high slit at the side, offering a glimpse of her bare legs. But who would be looking at her legs when the clinging silk emphasized the thrust of her breasts and the gentle swell of her hips?

"The Sheikh is very pleased with you," Amina said as she brushed Zoe's long, thick brown hair.

"Mmm." Zoe didn't know how to respond to that opinion. Pleased? She wasn't so sure about that. He was patient because he wanted something from her.

"You survived the wedding night," said the other maid, Halima, as she tidied up the dressing table. "Not a drop of blood."

Zoe's eyes widened and her heart stopped. Her stomach gave a sickening twist. What were they referring to? Had they been looking for a bloodstain on the bedsheets that proved she had been a virgin? She hadn't considered that possibility.

"The Sheikh's last wedding night…" Halima clicked her

tongue and shook her head. "There was so much blood on the bed his bride had to be taken to the hospital in Omaira."

Zoe stared at the older woman, her heart pounding erratically. They were talking about a different wedding night. A different bride.

Nadir's first wife had had to be hospitalized after her wedding night? Fatimah hadn't mentioned that, and her cousin would have been eager to add that to her tall tale. There had to be something more to the story. "What are you talking about?"

Amina stopped brushing her hair and leaned forward, their eyes meeting in the mirror. "Didn't you ever wonder why he's called The Beast?" she asked in a low, confidential tone.

These women automatically assumed the worst of Nadir. Or were they trying to gather gossip? They wanted scandalous tidbits about her wedding night. Zoe narrowed her eyes. She wouldn't give them the satisfaction.

"Don't believe a word of it," Zoe warned the maids. "The Sheikh is a man of honor. A gentleman."

Halima raised her hands in mock surrender. "We didn't mean to offend."

"We thought we should warn you," Amina said as she resumed brushing Zoe's hair.

Frighten her was more like it. Zoe knew she shouldn't care. She should find it amusing or inconsequential. But she didn't. Maybe it was because she knew how gossip could harm a person. How it could destroy a future or ruin a life.

Zoe didn't know why she felt the need to set the women straight. She might be married to Nadir, but she hadn't sworn her allegiance to the man. "My husband would never harm a woman," she said with quiet certainty.

"You weren't there that night," Amina pointed out.

"No, but I was with him last night. I know what I'm talking about." But did she? Right now Nadir was on his best behavior, determined to create a bond with his bride.

As a healer for the women in her tribe, Zoe had taken care of domestic abuse victims. She'd listened to the women's stories as she tended to their wounds, but her concerns about them had fallen on deaf ears with the tribal leaders. She had also seen what went on in her uncle's house, and learned the pattern of his moods for her own safety.

Zoe didn't trust men in general, but she didn't think Nadir was violent. His actions last night alone told her that. He hadn't forced her into bed, but instead had allowed her to set the pace. A beast would take and take without consideration.

A man like Nadir would never have to raise his hand or his voice to get what he wanted.

"Don't underestimate the Sheikh," Amina whispered, her voice filled with foreboding. "You should have heard what Yusra's mother said. It would curl your hair."

Zoe rolled her eyes. "This is your source? Yusra's mother? Everyone knows that woman is a malicious gossip. I would never believe a word she said."

"But how do you explain—?"

"I don't have to," Zoe interrupted Halima. "I won't have anyone gossip about my husband, especially in my presence."

"Zoe, are you defending my honor?" Nadir drawled in English.

Zoe whirled around, her pulse skittering wildly when she saw Nadir at the door. His dark eyes glittered and an unpredictable energy pulsed in the room. Although he was resting his shoulder against the doorframe, she knew he was not feeling casual. He was tired of waiting and was ready to claim his bride.

Nadir tried to hide the satisfaction that spread through his chest as he held Zoe's gaze. He had not expected his new bride to defend his honor. It was more than he had hoped for.

But it didn't mean that she was loyal or committed to him, Nadir reminded himself as he watched Zoe hurriedly dismiss the shamefaced maids. She might be one of those rare women who didn't like gossip. Still, her response was a good start.

Or was it? She was already getting an idea of what kind of man he was. It wouldn't be long before she discovered that he was trying to balance tradition and innovation. That he was not like the men he would one day rule.

"Don't you know never to enter a woman's dressing room?" Zoe asked sharply as she crossed her arms.

"I can see why. One never knows what one might learn."

"Those maids have a tendency to repeat gossip without questioning the source. Don't worry about them."

"I wasn't." His only concern was what Zoe thought of him. She didn't believe the rumors about his first wedding night. There had been no hesitation when she defended him.

"Why are you here?" Zoe asked after a prolonged pause.

"I was beginning to wonder where my bride was," he said with a slow smile. "Night has fallen and the suite is empty. I was checking that you hadn't succumbed to bridal jitters and escaped out the window."

She gave a start. "Nonsense."

He caught the guilty flash in her eyes. She wanted to hide. Make a run for it. She'd declared that he wasn't a beast, but did she really believe that?

Nadir knew he had to tread lightly tonight. He needed to bind her to him, but not scare her. It required him to be romantic and charming while holding back the raw lust that whipped through him. He was determined to give Zoe the night of her life and not scare her with the intensity he felt. The very last thing he needed was a runaway bride.

"I'm sorry for the delay," Zoe said as she reluctantly stood up. "The preparations took longer than expected."

Nadir remained very still as he watched her slowly walk toward him. The way she looked, the way she moved, promised to fulfill his every fantasy. "The results are worth the wait," he said softly. "You are exquisite."

He watched Zoe blush from the compliment and sensed she wasn't comfortable with praise. He needed to be very careful as he sweet-talked her into his bed.

"Come," he said as he took her hand. He ignored the heat coursing through his veins from the simple touch. "Night has fallen and dinner is ready."

Zoe didn't think she was going to make it through the dinner without dissolving into a full panic attack. They were alone once Nadir dismissed the servants. They sat together at the low table, side by side. Her posture was rigid, her arms and legs close to her body, but somehow she kept brushing up against Nadir.

She needed something to interrupt them. Something to shatter this spell he was weaving around her.

"I haven't heard your phone ring," she commented. "Has everything been resolved?"

"Unfortunately, no. But I turned off the phone for the night. I will deal with business tomorrow."

Zoe's eyes widened. "You—you turned off your phone? Why?" *Why tonight of all nights?*

He gave a shrug. "I didn't want anything to intrude on our first full night together."

Zoe's smile froze on her face. "Good planning." Why did he have to be so attentive? She knew most brides would be thrilled by the gesture, but she needed something—anything—to disrupt his plans of seduction.

Her husband was incredibly charming and attentive, which made Zoe even more nervous. She barely ate, was almost afraid to move in case one of the delicate straps of her negligee fell, and she was very aware of Nadir's gaze upon her.

She wasn't used to this kind of attention. Most of the time she had been in the background, excluded and ignored. She preferred it that way. It was safer.

But now a part of her wanted to drink in the attention. How often had she met an incredibly sophisticated and sensual man? If she had met him under different circumstances, like at a nightclub or at a coffeehouse, she would have flirted back.

But this was Jazaar, and if Nadir found out she wasn't a virgin he could end this marriage with incredible ease. She knew she had to keep her distance, but her wall of icy politeness began to crack as he regaled her with stories of his travels. The man knew exactly how to lower her guard.

She understood he was a man of the world, but he was constantly surprising her with his insights. Educated in the best schools in America, Nadir was well-read and informed. Zoe discovered he had an adventurous spirit and some very modern ideas for Jazaar. She didn't always agree with his opinions, and was tempted to voice her ideas, but she still bore the scars from the last time she'd questioned a Jazaari male.

As she watched him drink from his glass goblet, Zoe wondered not for the first time why he had accepted marrying someone like her. He could have had any woman in the tribe. Why had Nadir agreed to her?

She was not in his league. It had to do with more than just social status. This man knew how to seduce a woman.

One kiss and she forgot everything. He knew it, too, so what was holding him back now?

When they were shopping in Omaira Nadir had gotten his way every time—and that was when he was on his best behavior. Zoe wondered how he would act if he faced a real obstacle. She always felt she would know a man's true character when he faced pressure. Her uncle had lashed out. Musad had placed her in the line of fire and ran. What would Nadir do?

She watched him pluck a grape from the fruit platter. Zoe was sure this man never had a clumsy moment. Her skin heated as she remembered how those big, masculine hands felt when he caressed her body.

"Taste this," he said as he offered her the grape.

Zoe pressed her mouth closed for a moment, but she knew declining would be useless. She shyly parted her lips as Nadir slid the dark purple fruit in her mouth. She closed her mouth as he stroked her lips with his thumb. The juicy grape burst in her mouth just as she saw the lust in his dark eyes.

She swallowed hard as hot desire sparked and showered inside her. Her eyelashes fluttered as she tried to hide her feelings, but it was no use. Nadir lowered his head and brushed his mouth against her lips.

The kiss was soft. Gentle. It was like the flutter of a butterfly's wing grazing her mouth. Nadir pulled away slightly and her lips clung to his for a moment. The unexpected sweetness pierced her, and she almost didn't want to move in fear of ruining the moment. Nadir waited silently for her to return the kiss.

Zoe turned her head abruptly. What was wrong with her? She'd expected an aggressive sensual assault, but Nadir had caught her off guard. She didn't know how to confront tenderness. The man wasn't a beast, but he was as sly as a fox.

She had to take control immediately. Set the pace for the night. She needed to act like a scared virgin for one more night. It would require a balancing act: she could not let things go too far and she must keep him from getting too frustrated.

Zoe stared at the dinner table, her eyes wide as her mind whirled with strategies. Her gaze focused on the fruit platter. "You should try one," she said hoarsely as she plucked a grape. She held it up to him and stalled, belatedly realizing that she would have to feed him.

It was a simple act, but the gesture of feeding him was too intimate. It held too much symbolism if the look in Nadir's eyes were anything to go by.

Nadir wrapped his fingers around her wrist and guided her hand to his mouth. His hold was gentle but firm. Zoe didn't like the way he took control, but she couldn't do anything but watch.

She frowned as he ignored the grape in her hand and lightly kissed her knuckles. If he felt the gradual tension in her fingers he didn't comment. Instead he grazed the edge of his teeth against the tip of her little finger.

Zoe didn't know if the sharp nip was a warning not to play games. He caught her next finger between his lips and suckled the tip. She struggled for her next breath as she felt the erotic pull deep within her.

Startled, she dropped the grape and let it roll onto the floor. She didn't yank her hand away; she didn't even try as she fought off the sting in her nipples and the heavy ache low in her hips.

She saw the gleam in his eyes. He knew how she was responding despite her attempts to hide it. He knew her body better than she did.

That scared her. She had to stop this. Stop him before he took over completely.

"Nadir?" she said, her voice rough as she tugged her hand. To her surprise, she easily broke from his hold.

Nadir leaned closer, his hands on either side of her, his muscular arms trapping her where she sat. He nestled his face in the crook of her neck. She curled her shoulder to fend him off, but she was too late.

She closed her eyes and swallowed roughly as he placed a trail of kisses along the length of her neck. She understood he was changing tactics, that tonight he was going slowly to lull her into submission. She should feel relieved that she wouldn't face the full brunt of his power, but this brand of seduction played havoc with her senses.

"Nadir…" She stifled a gasp as he placed a soft, gentle kiss against the sensitive spot under her ear. "We…we should—"

"Yes," he whispered against her ear, his warm breath tickling her skin. "We should."

He captured her mouth with his. His touch was a tender exploration. He leisurely bestowed small kisses from one corner of her lips to the other. By the time he darted his tongue along the seam of her mouth she automatically parted her lips and let him in.

Nadir cradled her head in his hands and deepened the kiss. The care in which he held her, the reverence in the kiss…it sparked something inside Zoe. She glided her hands up his chest and rested her fingertips against the broad column of his throat. She felt the beat of his pulse quicken as she hesitantly returned his kiss.

Her world slowly centered on his mouth. Their breaths mingled as he drew her tongue past his lips. There was something revealing about his kisses. He desired her, but he longed for her trust. He wanted her to surrender, cling to him, but that could never happen.

Nadir slid his hand down her shoulder and against her back. She didn't notice that he'd lowered her onto the pillows until her spine rested against cool silk. She tensed and Nadir tried to soothe her with the stroke of his hands.

Zoe was tempted to pull back and slow down, but they were only kissing. Their clothes were still on and they were nowhere near the bed. But she felt close to the danger zone, the point of no return.

She wouldn't let this slow seduction get too far, Zoe decided, as she speared her hands through Nadir's thick hair and drew him closer. The sound of his muffled groan thrilled her and a heady mix of power and pleasure swirled inside her.

This was how a kiss should be. Two people yielding to each other. Trusting and accepting. Zoe felt as if Nadir shared a little of his soul with each kiss, while stealing a little of hers.

She felt his fingers tremble as he curled them underneath her negligee strap. Her heart skipped a beat. Did he feel the same addictive excitement? Was he also struggling between accepting and resisting? Or was his restraint slipping?

Nadir pushed one strap down her shoulder and splayed his hand over her bare breast. His touch was undeniably possessive. Her tight nipple rasped against his palm. She arched against his hand, biting back a cry of pleasure.

Zoe saw the feral glow of passion in Nadir's eyes before he banked it. Trepidation trickled down her spine but it immediately disappeared as he laved his tongue against the tip of her breast.

A long moan was torn from her throat. Zoe clenched the back of Nadir's skull as a streak of white heat suffused her body. He teased her with his mouth and fingers and the slow fire inside her burned brighter.

Her breasts felt tight and heavy and a fierce ache radiated in her pelvis. The sound of her panting filled the air. Nadir slowly hitched up her negligee and skimmed his hand along her leg. When he boldly cupped her sex she bucked eagerly against his hand.

Zoe's mind shut down the moment Nadir pressed his finger against her slick clitoris. Tingling heat coiled inside her, winding tighter and tighter with each stroke of Nadir's finger. When he dipped his finger into her wet heat, she writhed under his masterful touch.

"That's it, Zoe," Nadir said roughly as he watched her chase the pleasure.

Satisfaction, warm and delicious, rippled from her core through her body. She tried to hold on to the beautiful moment and savor the pure sensation for as long as possible.

She went limp and sagged against the pillows. Her pulse pounded in her ears as she tried to catch her breath. She didn't hear the rustle of clothing. Her heart jolted, her muscles tightened when Nadir nudged his knee between her legs and settled in the cradle of her thighs.

Zoe shook her head as she tried to form words. "I'm not... I can't..." She felt the tip of Nadir's arousal press against the folds of her sex. Her traitorous body still pulsed with aftershocks and eagerly accepted him.

Nadir surged into her and stilled. Zoe saw him squeezing his eyes shut and the clench of his jaw. The muscles bunched in his cheek as his arms shook.

Zoe didn't think she could handle any more of this slow and gentle lovemaking. She instinctively tilted her hips, drawing him in deeper. Nadir tossed back his head and it was as if his restraint snapped. She felt the rumble of his moan deep in his chest before he sank into her.

She had never felt like this before. Wild sensation built inside her with each forceful thrust. It burned hotter and brighter, searing through her, scorching her mind and pressing against her skin, threatening to burst. The satisfaction Nadir gave her was ferocious.

She wrapped her arms around him and held on to him tightly, her breasts flattening against his chest, her legs winding against his hips. She clung to him, knowing that if she shattered into a million pieces Nadir would hold her together.

The red-hot climax ripped through her as Nadir drove into her with abandon. He growled low in her ear. Zoe tipped her head back, her mouth sagged open, but no sound came as she rode out the intense pleasure.

She couldn't get enough of each savage thrust and mindlessly followed his untamed rhythm. She gulped for air, inhaling the scent of hot, primitive male. Her core pulsed and clenched around him. Nadir's muscles rippled and tightened beneath her hands. With one powerful thrust he gave a gruff cry and found his release. She felt the tautness of his body before his arms collapsed and he toppled onto her.

Silence immediately descended in the room. All she heard was hoarse, jagged breathing. She gradually became aware of the heavy tension surrounding them. The moment of pure bliss evaporated as Zoe reluctantly opened her eyes.

Her seductive lover had transformed into a dangerous man. She saw the anger and menace in his glare. He pinned her to the floor, his body still joined with hers.

Fear twisted inside her. Zoe had never felt so vulnerable. So exposed. He knew the truth about her. She could tell before he said the words through his clenched teeth.

"You were no virgin."

# CHAPTER FIVE

ZOE couldn't escape. She was defenseless on her back and Nadir hovered above her. His hands were flattened on the floor, trapping her.

Her heart pounded so fiercely that it hurt. She had bared herself to him and was now unprotected. Her body still pulsed from his touch. She cautiously met his glare.

Nadir's dark mood was almost tangible. Zoe couldn't believe that only moments ago he had caressed her so gently, so lovingly.

She wanted to hide. Just disappear. She wished she could close her eyes, but that wouldn't save her.

She knew she shouldn't have allowed him to get this close to her. His tenderness was all pretend, and even though she had recognized his strategy she had still fallen for it. Why? Was it because for one moment she hadn't felt so alone? So unlovable?

Tears stung the back of her eyes. She was pathetic. Stupid. When would she ever learn? Men were only nice to her when they wanted something.

Nadir must have sensed her loneliness and used it to his advantage. And, like a fool, she'd let him. Her self-disgust pricked at her like a thousand needles. Now she had to suffer the consequences.

"Answer me, Zoe," he said in a low growl.

She pushed at his arms but he was too strong. "Get off," she said through clenched teeth.

Nadir scoffed at her demand. "Not a chance."

"How dare you make that kind of accusation?" she asked. Denial was the only strategy she could think of, even though Nadir knew the truth.

"That's not going to work," he said. "I know you weren't a virgin. There was no barrier or resistance. You felt no pain, and I'm sure there will be no blood to prove your innocence."

"That doesn't mean anything."

"You don't want to push your luck with me. Start talking. What made you think you could get away with this?"

Her heart was beating so hard she thought it was going to burst out of her chest. "I don't know why you would say such a thing."

Nadir's eyes narrowed. "Did you think that I wouldn't notice?" he asked as he tilted his hips against her. Zoe gasped as her body responded. "That you could hide your reactions?"

She was appalled at the way her flesh clung to him. She hated the way she felt vibrantly alive when Nadir touched her. All her senses should be on the defense, ready to fight or flee. Didn't her survival instinct tell her that Nadir could destroy her without breaking a sweat?

"Fine!" she bit out as the dread and fear threatened to smother her. Keeping up the pretense would only make things worse. Zoe sagged against the pillow underneath her. She looked away as she confessed. "I wasn't a virgin."

The silence was thick and heavy. Zoe bit her lip as coldness seeped into her bones. What was going to happen to her? What was Nadir going to do? She wasn't sure if she was strong enough to face her future.

Zoe blinked frantically as the tears threatened to fall.

"Would you get off me…please?" she asked, her voice wavering.

She felt Nadir hesitate. He wasn't going to listen, she decided. He had her cornered and it was against his nature to give her any relief. To her surprise, Nadir reluctantly pulled away and stood up.

But then, why would he want to touch her? She wasn't the perfect Jazaari bride, and she was hardly a worthy opponent. Why put any effort into intimidating her when she'd already given him the answer he was seeking?

"Do you have a boyfriend? A lover?" Nadir asked, his movements sharp and aggressive as he adjusted his clothes. "Is he still in the picture?"

She hadn't expected him to ask. Why would he care? "No," she said as she slowly sat up. But she wasn't sure if that was the truth. Musad was the past yet he still threatened her future.

"I want the truth, Zoe. I don't want any ex-lovers hanging around. You now belong to me."

Oh, she should have known. Men were all the same. Let's not consider how the secret had serious repercussions for *her*. All Nadir was worried about was his territory. Some guy had stolen what Nadir thought was his. Some guy had got to his woman first.

Zoe felt jittery as dark emotions tore at her. Destructive emotions. She needed to play it safe, beg for mercy and promise him anything. But it was as if her body rejected the idea and she was on automatic pilot to crash and burn.

"Belong? Are you serious?" she asked bitingly. She didn't belong to anyone or anyplace. No one wanted her; they only wanted to use her temporarily.

Zoe quickly pulled up the strap of her negligee to cover herself. "Why don't you give me a list of all the women you have slept with? Just so I know in case I bump into them."

Nadir slowly placed his hands on his hips in classic battle stance. "How many men have you had sex with?"

Oh, this was getting worse and worse. Zoe knew she should have bitten her tongue and listened to his ranting until he'd exhausted his anger. She just couldn't stop herself.

"How many, Zoe?" His low, raspy voice made her shiver.

"One. Just one," she said unwillingly as she rose to her feet. It had only taken one man to ruin her life. She really knew how to choose them.

"I don't believe you."

Of course. She couldn't possibly be telling the truth. Zoe clenched her teeth and righteous anger bubbled inside her. It stood to reason that since she wasn't a virgin she must be promiscuous. "Don't judge me by your standards."

A dull red flushed Nadir's high cheekbones. She could tell that he was reining in his temper. "I didn't pretend to be an innocent," he pointed out.

"You didn't have to, did you?" He was a sheikh and followed different rules. She, on the other hand, had to be as pure as snow. "But I never said I was a virgin. You assumed."

"You played the part perfectly," Nadir said and bowed his head in deference to her acting abilities. One look into her brown eyes and he had been willing to believe anything.

He had been so patient, Nadir thought with disgust as he started to pace around the room. All this time he'd thought Zoe was shy about this rite of passage. She'd seemed uncertain about how he made her feel. Almost frightened by the intense power of those sensations. He was a fool.

No, he was worse. Nadir bowed his head as he struggled with an ugly truth about himself. From the time he was in his teens he'd truly believed he was a modern man. While he was bound to his homeland, he didn't blindly follow its customs. He questioned everything, participated only in the traditions that made sense to him, and was determined to make changes in the name of progress.

Yet the moment he'd realized Zoe wasn't a virgin he hadn't felt very civilized. His primal instincts roared to erase any other claim on her. Wipe out her memories of her first lover. Obliterate the other man's existence.

Nadir inhaled deeply and rubbed his hands over his face. He was not like his barbaric ancestors. He was not going to be ruled by primitive customs or his emotions.

But his greatest challenge would be the fierce attraction he felt for Zoe. He should have stopped the moment he discovered she wasn't a virgin, but he had been driven by an uncontrollable need. He'd had to make Zoe his.

She had a past. A love-life. That changed everything. Zoe wasn't a naïve virgin he could seduce into obedience. She wouldn't blindly follow his command after a few caresses and sweet words. She would not go quietly to his mountain palace. And he didn't think he could stay away from her.

Even now he was tempted to bed her again. This time he wanted to strip her bare and have her chant his name. Possess her body and soul. She didn't need to touch him and still he wanted to press her against his chest, kiss her senseless and fall into bed.

Nadir had never thought any woman would hold this kind of power over him—especially his arranged bride. Zoe had no idea of her sexual magnetism, for which he was thankful. If she discovered the power she wielded he would be lost. He needed to master this potentially dangerous need quickly.

He stepped in front of the window and looked out into

the star-studded night. It was better if he wasn't looking at Zoe, wasn't inhaling her scent or remembering the softness of her skin while he tried to decide his next move.

Zoe wasn't a virgin. He was disappointed that he wasn't her first, but her lack of virginity wasn't a crime. Was this the reason why she kept trying to run away? Did she think he would annul the marriage and have her caned?

Of course she did. He was The Beast, after all. She probably thought he would wield the cane himself.

Maybe he could use that to his advantage? Would she behave like a proper Jazaari woman to appease him? Just until the last wedding ceremony?

He turned and leaned against the window to study her. Her hair was mussed from his fingers, her lips red and swollen from his mouth. She had one hand on her shoulder and the other one wrapped around her waist. The self-protective gesture was no use; he still remembered her sensual beauty and how her skin tasted.

He dragged his gaze to her eyes. He saw hurt and anger. And something else. Zoe held a few more secrets. The possibility burned through him like acid. Those secrets could blow up in his face. He needed to go on the offense.

"Who knows the truth about you?" The tribe might have set him up with an impure bride just to test how he would react. "The elders?"

She looked at him as if he was crazy. "Hell, no."

"Are you sure?" He wouldn't expose Zoe's secret, but it could cost him if someone else knew it.

Her eyes flashed with anger. "If they did I would have been caned and I'd bear the scars."

That was true. His chest had clenched with anguish when he'd first seen her scars and burn marks. He had wanted to hunt down those who had made her suffer and punish them without mercy. The marks on her skin were from years of brutal hardship and abuse, but they didn't come from a cane or whip.

"You realize this is a reason to annul the marriage?" he said. He fought to keep his tone impersonal. If she thought she was safe because he couldn't afford to offend the tribe, he needed to scare her.

Zoe flinched as if she had been punched. "An annulment?" she whispered as the color leeched from her face. She looked wounded. "You would do that to me?"

He wasn't going to feel guilty. "It's in the marriage contract."

Zoe's features tightened as she glared at him. "I don't believe you." She took a step forward and pointed an accusing finger at him. "You're just trying to scare me because you know I can't read it. I should have known you'd use that information against me."

He folded his arms across his chest. He had to be ruthless and he wasn't going to apologize for it. "I'm telling the truth," he said. "According to the contract, you entered the marriage on fraudulent grounds."

"What man in this century would end a marriage because his wife isn't a virgin?"

He wouldn't end a marriage because of that. The political repercussions from another annulment would be catastrophic. He felt as if he had more to lose than Zoe, but he couldn't show it. He didn't want to give her any ammunition.

"You entered this marriage with a lie." Nadir gestured at the door. "No Jazaari man would stay with a woman he couldn't trust."

"You're right." She tossed her hands up in the air with anger. "Most of the men I know don't understand the meaning of commitment."

Nadir threaded his hands through his hair and laced

them behind his head. He found it hard to breathe as heaviness lay on his chest. He knew he had to see this marriage through, but he had to wonder if that was what Zoe was betting on. Was this why she had accepted marrying The Beast? Because he couldn't risk another annulment?

Nadir studied her intently. No, if she knew why he needed this marriage to work she would have used that already in her argument. But from the look in her eyes, Zoe seemed more interested in hiding *her* reasons for marrying *him*.

"What?" Zoe asked as she broke eye contact. "What is it?"

He tilted his head as he studied her demeanor. She was holding something back. "What else are you hiding?"

She jutted out her chin. "I don't know what you're talking about. I'm not hiding anything."

Yes, she was. "Are you sure?" he asked as dread knotted in his chest and pressed against his ribs. "Nothing like a baby?"

"A baby?" She was visibly shocked. "You think I'm pregnant?"

Nadir shrugged and breathed a little easier. His accusation had shocked her. She couldn't have faked that reaction. If it wasn't a baby, what *was* she hiding?

Zoe's eyes widened with horror. "Do I look pregnant?"

"You look guilty."

"So let me see if I've got this straight," Zoe said with exaggerated care. "Because I'm not a virgin I must be a slut. And you think that because I had sex in the past I must be pregnant now?"

He raised one eyebrow as he watched her bristle with indignation. "Sex *is* the way to get pregnant."

"I'm not pregnant," she said through clenched teeth.

"And I should take your word for it?" He gestured at her. "Based on your record of honesty?"

She tossed her head back, her long brown hair cascading down her shoulders. "I'll gladly take a pregnancy test. Right now if I have to."

"Excuse me if I don't call the front desk and request a pregnancy test on the second day of my honeymoon."

"I'm not hiding a pregnancy." She flattened her hand against her chest as if she was making a pledge. "I would never do that. Not to a man or to a child."

That was one point in her favor, but it didn't mean he was going to instantly trust her. "That's very admirable of you," he said with deep sarcasm, "but you haven't been totally honest with me."

"I'm sorry that I'm not a perfect Jazaari bride fit for a sheikh," she said bitterly. "But you are no prize either."

He took a step toward her. "Pardon?"

"Why did I think you would keep your promise?"

"What are saying? I always keep my promises." Nadir cupped his hand on Zoe's shoulder. "My word is my bond."

She shrugged off his hand. "You promised we wouldn't have sex until I was ready. You seduced me tonight and you broke your promise."

He wasn't going to be blamed for that. "You could have stopped me at any time."

Zoe arched an eyebrow and pursed her lips. "We both know that isn't true."

Nadir clenched his jaw. Perhaps she was aware that he couldn't keep his hands off her. He needed to keep his distance. He didn't trust her, but more importantly he didn't trust himself.

He needed to focus on the fact that Zoe was still hiding something from him. "The only reason you extracted the promise from me was so that I wouldn't find out you weren't a virgin."

She nodded slowly in agreement. "That's true."

Her confession surprised him. Why was she suddenly so free with the truth? It made him more suspicious than when she boldly lied to him.

"You knew there was a risk that I would discover the truth," he added. "You had to have known that an annulment was a possible outcome."

"I had hoped you wouldn't discover it until after the last wedding ceremony."

That made sense. After the last ceremony it would have been almost impossible to divorce. "When I was stuck with you?"

"When we were stuck with each other," she corrected him. She bit her lip and took a deep breath. "Just give it to me straight, Nadir. What are you going to do?"

He didn't know. He needed this marriage, but he didn't trust Zoe. Even though he planned to stow her away in a remote palace, he would still be married to her.

She looked up at him, her eyes glistening with unshed tears. "Are you going to punish me for an action I made before I met you?"

She thought he was upset that she wasn't a virgin. He'd let her think that while he tried to uncover her other secrets. "It's not your right to ask me."

"It *is* my right!" Anger flashed in her eyes as she stomped her foot on the floor. "Your decision will cast my future."

"You should have thought about that before you slept with me or the man before me!"

"Really?" She planted her hands on her hips. "What would you have done in my position? How would you have brought up the subject?"

"It's a waste of time to think about," he said as he walked past the low table. "What is done is done."

The pillows by the table snagged his attention. Hell, what had he been thinking, taking his bride on the floor? It wasn't how he had planned the night.

He halted abruptly when it occurred to him. The seduction hadn't gone as planned. He hadn't used any protection.

Nadir closed his eyes and bunched his hands into fists as he fought the alarm zigzagging through his veins. There was a chance that Zoe might be pregnant with his child.

That changed everything. Even if he was ready to face the wrath of an influential tribe for annulling yet another marriage, he couldn't do that to his child.

He had to see this through and bind himself to a woman he didn't trust. His mind was numb from the injustice of it all. Deep down he knew the Fates were punishing him for the way he'd handled his first wedding night.

"Nadir, what is it?" Zoe asked right behind him.

"I'm leaving." He needed to think this through and consider his options. He already knew he would remain married to Zoe. He just wasn't ready to voice it.

"Where are you going?" she asked anxiously.

"I'll find another place to stay for the night," he said as he made his way to the door. He needed to think before he made his next move.

Zoe yanked at his arm. "You can't do that!"

He looked down at her hands covered in henna designs clenching his shirtsleeve. "Why not?" he asked dully as heavy emotions battered inside him. "Are you worried about your reputation?"

"Yes, as a matter of fact I am!" She pulled at his sleeve with urgency. "The groom stays in the honeymoon suite. If word gets out that I displeased you I'm in big trouble."

"No one would think that." The moment he said it he

wasn't sure if it was true. Zoe was part of a tight-knit tribe. By sunrise everyone would know that she was not to his liking. She was already an outcast and this development would make life incredibly hard on her.

"Nadir, listen to me." Her bright red nails sank into the soft cloth of his shirt. "You can't give me back to my uncle."

He knew sending her back to her family would be cruel.

"I won't be spared. This will bring dishonor to my uncle and he will kill me." Her voice shook. "No one will intervene. My aunts will support his decision. The tribe will encourage it."

"Honor killing is forbidden in Jazaar," Nadir said. He suspected she had been mistreated in her uncle's house. She was very young to be this cynical. Hadn't her uncle protected her? Had her relatives given her the scars and burns? He needed to know more about her past and her family life.

"That won't stop him," Zoe said. "Please, Nadir. You can't throw me to the wolves."

"Don't tell me what to do," Nadir said as he opened the door.

"You're still leaving? After everything I told you?" Zoe dropped her hands from his arm. She took a deep breath and looked away. "Are you going to annul this marriage?"

"Don't rush me," he warned her as he walked out the door. "You will find out along with everyone else at the ceremony."

# CHAPTER SIX

NADIR strode to the honeymoon suite late the next evening. He had made his decision and he wasn't happy about it. His plan of action had never really changed from the moment he realized Zoe might already be carrying his baby.

He had done his best to stay away from her until now. Just as he had expected, no one had dared question his need for another room. It helped that his cell phone kept ringing. A brief mention that he didn't want to disturb his new wife with business calls and he was given another suite.

His upper lip curled into a sneer. He was almost as good of a liar as his wife.

*His wife.* The words sliced through him like a dagger. His deceitful, untrustworthy wife. The thought of her had kept him up all night.

Worse, he'd had trouble focusing on urgent business negotiations during the day. His mind had kept veering to the memory of her soft, fragrant skin or the way her legs had gripped him in the heat of passion. He wanted to be with her as much as he wanted to stay away.

Nadir paused as his body hardened from the sensual memory. He had to master this raw, powerful lust. The absence of his legendary willpower was not improving his dark mood. He clenched his jaw and slid the key card into the door with more force than necessary.

He needed to be in command by the time he saw Zoe. Show her that he would not be swayed by her feminine charm or tears. The night was going to be torture, knowing he had to play the happy groom but trying to keep all physical contact to an absolute minimum.

He entered the honeymoon suite and his frown deepened when he realized that his troublesome bride wasn't in the sitting room waiting for him. That was a bad move on her part, he decided. If Zoe wanted to remain married she should be ready for him, preferably meek, obedient and silent.

He grimaced as the last thought lingered in his head. Now he was sounding like his father, with his archaic ideas and outdated values. Zoe had the remarkable ability to test his ideals and drive him crazy.

Nadir turned toward the bedroom and saw Zoe's two maids. They were dressed in colorful *abayas* and head-scarves. He noticed they were knocking timidly on the closed door with their bejeweled hands.

"Why are you not preparing the Sheikha?" Nadir asked as he approached them.

Amina twirled around and gasped, clutching her thick necklace with a tense hand. Halima slowly faced him, flattened her hands on the door and bent her head in defeat.

"We were adding the finishing touches," Amina said as she motioned at the door. "Then she l-led us to the door and l-locked herself in the bedroom."

Nadir didn't say anything and showed no outward appearance of concern. But he knew that Zoe wasn't coming out of the bedroom without a fight.

"She says she's not going to the ceremony," Halima added as she continued to hang her head low.

Zoe was very wrong to give such a challenge. She would

soon learn not to test him so brazenly. "You may leave," he told the maids. "I will get my wife ready for the ceremony."

Amina and Halima exchanged glances. The older women were not convinced by his display of husbandly patience.

"No need to be alarmed," he said, with a smile he didn't feel. "My wife hates ceremonies and she's not used to being the center of attention. I will take care of this."

They still hesitated.

"Please join the party." Nadir wrapped the order in the form of an invitation and gestured for them to leave. "The Sheikha and I will be there momentarily."

The maids knew a command when they heard one and scurried away. As Nadir waited impatiently for them to leave he considered the methods his father and grandfather would have used to tame a disobedient bride.

No, Nadir thought as he closed his eyes and harnessed the last of his patience. He wouldn't act like his ancestors. Zoe was a modern woman and he would behave like a civilized man.

Once the women had vacated the hotel suite, Nadir gave an imperious knock on the locked door. "Zoe? It's time to leave for the ceremony."

"I'm not going."

She wasn't near to the door. In fact, she sounded as if she was on the opposite side of the room. Yet the defiance rang clear in her voice.

Nadir suspected that he was getting a glimpse of the real Zoe. Stubborn. Unmanageable. Intriguing. "Open this door," he said with a hint of warning.

"So you can present me to the tribe, tell them I'm not worthy of you, and toss me back to my uncle? Forget it."

He didn't have time for this. There was no way he would

discuss this matter through a locked door. "This is your last warning."

"You can make the announcement without me," Zoe said. "Tell me how the party went."

Nadir took a step back and gave the door a fierce kick. He barely heard Zoe's startled yelp over the sound of splintering wood. The door flew open and crashed against the wall.

Zoe whirled, her gold ceremonial gown swishing around her. She was stunning. Nadir gripped the doorframe for support as his knees threatened to buckle.

He took a long, silent look. His heart thudded in his ears as his gaze drifted to her dark hair. It was swept up in soft waves, and instead of a veil she wore a small sparkling tiara. Zoe had been transformed into a regal beauty.

The gold caftan gleamed in the light. He couldn't help notice that the silk skimmed her body and hinted at the curves underneath. He swallowed hard and tightened his hold on the doorframe. She was magnificent. He had thought Zoe was sexy when he first saw her, but nothing had prepared him for the impact of her beauty now.

She stood defiantly before him. Her hands were curled into fists at her sides and her eyes flashed with rebellion and fear. "If you try to drag me down to the ceremony," she said in a low, fierce voice, "I will kick, scream and claw at you every step of the way."

"I have no doubt," Nadir said as if he was hypnotized. The beat of his heart slowed. He blinked hard to break the trance.

Her eyes narrowed as she watched him enter the room. "I am not going to stand beside you in front of everyone only to have you publicly humiliate me."

Nadir approached her with caution. She was irresistible

and he didn't trust his self-control. "Behave and I won't ask for an annulment."

Zoe didn't look relieved. She looked suspicious. "I don't believe you. Your mind-games won't work on me."

"I don't care that you weren't a virgin on our wedding night."

Zoe cast a quick look at the doorway. "Keep your voice down."

"I care that you are keeping secrets from me. I don't need any unpleasant surprises. For all I know, you're going to sabotage me at the ceremony."

"Right. Like I have that kind of power. Don't try to sweet-talk me. You'll say anything to get me down to the ceremony so you can have the pleasure of discarding me like garbage."

"If I really wanted to end this marriage, all I'd have to do is bring the elders up to this room and complete the necessary rituals."

She held out her hand. "Don't step any closer."

He ignored her and kept approaching until his chest reached her outstretched hand. He felt her fingers trembling. "Zoe, you will attend this ceremony and you will stand at my side looking happy and satisfied."

Zoe gave a mirthless chuckle. "That's never going to happen."

Nadir took a deep breath. "You need to understand that my last wedding caused irreparable damage to the relationship I have with your tribe."

She slowly lowered her hand. "So?"

He took the opportunity to step closer. "The elders believe that I am too Western to one day rule Jazaar. That's why they gave me you. An American bride. Many have used how I handled my last wedding as an example of my disrespect for tradition."

"So you'll be a modern leader. They'll learn to accept it. What's the big deal?"

He hesitated. Did he really want Zoe to know that he had to rely on her? She could use the information against him, but he had to get through to her.

"Zoe, they will try to destroy me in order to protect their way of life."

She stilled and cautiously stole a look at him, searching his eyes to determine if this was an elaborate lie. She didn't say anything.

"If I seek another annulment there will be serious political repercussions," he admitted.

She looked away. He could tell that she was deep in thought. Was she considering what he was saying, or was she plotting his downfall?

"Don't think of me," he said quietly. "Think about the ones you healed. The families you've taken care of and the children you have helped bring into this world. They will lose everything if they try to fight me."

He saw the struggle in her eyes. Zoe might be an outcast in her tribe, but she wasn't vindictive. She truly cared about those she helped in her community.

"You must trust me," he said roughly as emotions squeezed his chest.

She shook her head as if she was trying to clear her mind. "You've broken your promise to me before. You tossed your first wife back to the tribe, and I'm supposed to believe you won't do it again?"

He had to admit he was asking a great deal from her, but he expected nothing less from the wife.

"And now you're telling me you're going to win any conflict with the tribe." She folded her arm tightly. "You might suffer a setback, but I'm the one who will be destroyed. Nothing is really stopping you."

"And nothing is stopping me from throwing you over my shoulder and carrying you out of this room," he replied, his voice shaking with the last of his restraint.

Their gazes clashed as heightened tension shimmered between them. Nadir hid nothing from her, determined to show that he wasn't lying. He hated this feeling. He couldn't remember a time when he'd felt so exposed.

Zoe suddenly moved past him. "So help me, Nadir," she said through clenched teeth, "if you're lying to me I will kill you with my bare hands."

Relief poured through him. He grabbed her wrist as she walked past him. She jerked to a standstill. He felt her racing pulse under his fingertips. "Stay at my side and take my arm."

She muttered something under her breath. He didn't catch it under the roar of his blood. She clamped her hand on the crook of his arm and an unpredictable energy vibrated from her.

Did she really believe him, or was she setting him up for a catastrophic night? Nadir couldn't tell and he didn't like walking into a battlefield without knowing his allies and enemies.

He gently covered her hand with his. "Now follow my lead."

She refused to look at him and kept her gaze straight ahead. "Don't make me regret it."

Zoe didn't want to hold on to Nadir's arm, but she didn't think she could stay upright by herself. Her legs were shaking violently. Her body was numb as fear congealed in her stomach. She couldn't obey the instincts screaming for her to run and hide.

When a servant held the elevator for them, Zoe's body protested against moving forward. She gulped for fresh air and her muscles locked. She almost stumbled as Nadir gently nudged her.

She dipped her head, the world slowing down as she stepped into the elevator. Her heart raced and her skin flushed. When she heard the elevator doors clang shut, she jumped.

"Relax," Nadir whispered as he stared straight ahead.

Right. Relax. Did the executioner say that to the prisoner right before he wielded the ax?

Zoe closed her eyes and took in a shaky breath. She didn't trust Nadir, but she wanted to. She didn't have much practice trusting men. The idea of even trying scared her. Sooner or later they had always disappointed her. Betrayed her. Used her. Why should Nadir be any different?

Zoe nervously glanced at him, but he wasn't looking at her. She didn't know if that was a good or bad thing. She needed to see his eyes. If there was a glimmer of kindness she knew she would be all right.

"Nadir?" She hated how her voice cracked.

He glanced up at the lights that told him which floor they were on. "It's time to give your best performance."

She heard the chime and took a step back. *She wasn't ready!*

Zoe didn't think she had the strength to leave the elevator. Nadir's grip tightened on her hand. There was no backing out.

She took a deep, shuddering breath. She dipped her head and silently prayed for a miracle. As the elevator door swung open she lifted her head, pasted on a polite smile and stepped across the threshold.

The small lobby was quiet and almost empty, since many of the guests were waiting for them in the courtyard. Zoe heard light music and conversation drifting from outside.

"Zoe!" Her cousin Fatimah was standing by the bank of elevators. She was dressed in a vibrant red caftan that was designed to turn heads.

*No, no, no.* Zoe's smile froze on her face. She didn't need to deal with her poisonous cousin. Not now. The last thing she needed was for Fatimah to give Nadir any additional reason to abandon her.

"Many felicitations on your wedding."

"Thank you, Fatimah," Zoe said stiffly. Her cousin was *never* this happy for her.

Fatimah gave a sly look to Nadir. "And to you, Your Highness. I'm so glad that Zoe has pleased you."

Zoe tilted her head with suspicion. There was something about Fatimah's tone. She had heard it many times before. Her cousin was about to make the first strike.

"But it doesn't surprise me," Fatimah said conversationally as her eyes glittered with menace, "considering her wealth of experience with men."

Zoe froze as her cousin's condemning words flayed her like a whip. The pain consumed her like fire. She couldn't believe the depth of Fatimah's hatred. How could one woman cause so much damage with one breath?

"Fatimah, be very, very careful," Nadir said in a low voice that hinted at dangerous undercurrents. "Anything you say against Zoe, you say against me."

Fatimah faced Nadir as she would an unfamiliar opponent. "I'm not sure I understand what you mean," she said sweetly as she studied Nadir through her batting lashes.

"Then let me be clear." He didn't raise his voice, but it held a frightening quality that made Zoe shiver. "If there are any malicious rumors about Zoe, I will hold *you* responsible."

Fatimah jerked as her jaw sagged. "But that's not fair."

Nadir shrugged. He didn't care. "You've been warned.

I'm a reasonable man, but when I'm crossed I will show no mercy."

Zoe clung onto Nadir's arm as he guided her away from Fatimah and toward the courtyard.

"Fatimah will try to take another swipe at you," he murmured to Zoe, "but I have declawed her. She shouldn't be a real threat anymore."

"Thank you," she said weakly. She wasn't sure what to say or do. It had been a long time since someone had come to her defense.

His hand tightened on hers, causing her to look up at his face. There was coldness in his expression, not one hint of softness. "I thought no one knew."

Zoe tensed. She would not be blamed. "I never said a word to anyone. That would have been suicide."

"Then your lover didn't care enough to protect you," he said with brutal honesty. "And you were extremely reckless."

"Can we not discuss this right now?" she asked as the sounds of the party grew louder.

"With pleasure."

The wedding guests were waiting impatiently and greeted them with applause as Zoe and Nadir stepped onto the courtyard. Zoe desperately wanted to close her eyes and hang back. Disappear altogether.

As they walked to the dais covered with faded Persian rugs, Zoe noticed that the greeting was cautious. Were the tribe trying to determine if history would repeat itself? Panic fluttered in her chest and the sweet fragrance of the flowers choked her.

She fought to maintain her smile as she watched her tribesmen study Nadir's expression. She didn't know what they were concerned about other than money lost. They had probably placed bets on the outcome of this wedding.

She was the one who would lose her dreams, her future and her freedom.

Zoe cast a glance at Nadir. He gave nothing away. There was no smile, and yet no anger, either. His expression was somber.

*He's not going to cast you back to your uncle,* Zoe told herself fiercely as she got closer and closer to the dais where her fate would be decided. *He stood up for you against Fatimah.*

But that could have been a gesture of protection before she was discarded. Not that his protection would do her any good if Nadir wasn't there to enforce it.

He was going to annul the wedding. Zoe was sure of it. The fear crystallized, scraping inside her until she didn't think she could stand straight. Zoe kept her gaze on the Persian rugs as she considered her getaway.

But there was nowhere to run or hide. She'd last less than a day in the desert that surrounded the village. The only thing she could do was stand before everyone.

The music ended abruptly and the guests fell silent. Zoe went from cold to numb as she heard the familiar shuffle of the chief elder getting closer. It would only be a few moments before Nadir either claimed her as his wife or disposed of her.

Nadir needed this marriage. No, it was more than that, Zoe decided as she remembered the earnest look in his eyes. They needed to rely on each other.

Zoe's heart pounded. She wasn't sure if she was brave enough to take that kind of risk. She wasn't very good at relying on someone else.

The elder stood before them. Zoe struggled for her next breath as black dots formed around the corners of her eyes. She tightened her grip on Nadir's arm. She found it strange that she was relying on the very man whose strength could destroy her.

Her hands were ice-cold as Nadir and the elder exchanged pleasantries. When they turned their attention to Zoe, she felt as if she was going to shatter.

"Allow me to introduce my wife," Nadir said to the older man.

Her breath was suspended in her throat. She was afraid to sag against Nadir in case she'd dreamed those words. It was only when the guests exploded with cheers that Zoe knew she was no longer under her uncle's heartless power.

Now she belonged to the Sheikh.

# CHAPTER SEVEN

ZOE dismissed her curious maids for the night and gave one final glance at the clock. It had been hours since the ceremony concluded. Instead of returning to the honeymoon suite with Zoe, Nadir had been invited to a private meeting with the tribe's elders. He had sent her upstairs without a backward glance.

Now that she had risked everything to stand beside him, Nadir had no use for her anymore. Good, Zoe decided as she flicked the hem of her short emerald-green negligee and walked over to the bed. She was happy with the development. Thrilled. She was tired and she didn't have to be on her best behavior anymore.

Slipping between the sheets and turning off the lamp, Zoe rested her head on the pillow and tried to get comfortable. If only she could forget the pleasure Nadir had given her last night. She needed to keep a safe distance. She knew better than to get close to a man. Rely on him. Want him. It only brought trouble.

Zoe frowned as images of Nadir and Uncle Tareef tumbled across her mind. They had spoken like friends at the ceremony, and that hurt because Nadir knew how the man had treated her. Maybe Nadir didn't believe her. After all, what man would take the word of a woman over that of another man? The word of an outcast over a respected citizen?

She needed to be cautious with Nadir. If she had problems with her uncle, Nadir would side with Tareef. She still wasn't safe or free while living in this ultra-conservative desert kingdom, but she would safer under the Sheikh's protection.

His protection was all she would get from Nadir. She was fine with that. Ecstatic. If she was lucky, he would barely pay attention to her. He had consummated the marriage and no longer needed to associate with his wife. He was probably in the second hotel suite right now, while she was aching for his touch.

Zoe moved restlessly. So what if she was in a loveless marriage? So what if she longed for a man who didn't want to share a bed with her? It was better this way. She'd get over the rejection. And once she got back to Texas she would be embraced by her old friends and wouldn't feel so alone.

She gave her pillow a punch and settled down. At least she wouldn't throw herself at Nadir out of loneliness. She wouldn't make the mistake of equating love with sex. It was a good thing she had learned her lesson with Musad, because if Nadir tried to seduce her again she wouldn't be able to resist.

She didn't have anything to worry about because he wouldn't lower himself again. She was an outcast. A bride no man wanted. She wasn't a perfect Jazaari woman. She hadn't come to him as a virgin. He wouldn't return to this bed.

Zoe curled into herself, determined to dream about a better tomorrow. It took a long time for her to relax.

Just as she started to fall asleep she felt the sheets lifted from her warm skin and the mattress sink underneath her. She blinked groggily and saw Nadir lying beside her.

Heat rushed through her veins and her heart leapt. She hated how energized she felt when she was with Nadir, but at the same time she found the sensation addictive. "What are you doing here?"

"It's my bed."

Were the shadows creating an optical illusion, or was he moving closer to her? She could have sworn he hadn't moved. "It was your bed last night but you didn't sleep in it."

"Last night I didn't know your ulterior motive for marrying The Beast."

Her breath hitched in her throat. He sounded so confident, but he didn't know everything. He couldn't. "And now you know?" she asked, hiding her vulnerability with aggression. "Or have you suddenly gotten over your raging paranoia?"

"You agreed to an arranged marriage because you needed to get out of your uncle's house before he found out about your...ill-advised romantic liaison."

If she hadn't been so nervous she would have smiled at his attempt to soften what was her biggest mistake. "Nothing gets past you. But how does this change last night? You were furious that I wasn't a virgin."

"You took me by surprise, but it doesn't matter to me if you were a virgin or not when entering this marriage."

"How modern of you," she drawled.

"You could have warned me."

"No, I couldn't."

"Last night I thought you were hiding something else. Something more serious. But your only fear was being sent back to your family. That concern is gone. Tonight you have nothing to hide."

He had no idea that she had even more reasons to hide tonight. The more she revealed herself to him, the sooner he'd learn all her secrets.

"You are in a very forgiving mood," she said. "What's really going on?"

"Honestly?" He reached for her and drew her close. "I couldn't stay away from you."

"Stop teasing. It's not funny." She pressed her hands against his bare chest. As her legs collided against his she discovered that he was naked. Dark excitement pierced her.

"You don't believe me?" he asked in a husky voice. "Let me show you."

Zoe knew she should protest and avoid him. When he touched her she didn't think about anything else. The way he made her feel was so intense that every goal and dream she had was momentarily forgotten.

Nadir covered her mouth with his. Pleasure, hot and tingly, washed over her. She softened the moment his lips touched hers. She wanted to melt into him as his kisses became urgent and demanding.

She shouldn't yield so quickly. She needed to create an emotional distance and not reveal her deepest fears and desires. It was safer that way. She must never give Nadir that much power over her.

She pulled away. "There is no need for us to sleep in the same bed. We are officially married."

"I know one way to celebrate an official marriage." Nadir pulled her against his chest and she felt the heat pouring off him. "And it requires a bed."

When he pressed his hands against the small of her back she couldn't resist tilting her hips. He murmured his delight as she slid her bare leg over his.

"This is a bad idea," she whispered as she immediately straightened her leg. "We don't have to have sex. The marriage has been consummated. It's legal. It's done. There's no going back."

"Think of this as added insurance," he suggested, his hand caressing the length of her spine.

Zoe arched, her breasts thrusting against his chest, her tight nipples rasping against the thin silk. She discovered that she really wanted to accept the flimsy excuse. She wanted to have one more night with the Sheikh.

Nadir plucked the strap of her negligee with impatience. "Take this off," he said against her mouth.

Zoe hesitated and shook her head. The more barriers they had between them, the better it was for her.

Nadir's kisses became less demanding and more persuasive. Zoe sighed as his lips lingered on hers. "You don't need to be shy with me," he whispered.

Shyness had nothing to do with it. Her first instinct was to strip off the emerald silk. But she couldn't capitulate so quickly. She wouldn't let him take over. If only she had as much power over him as he did over her.

"What if I let you set the pace?" he asked.

Zoe bit her lip as heat washed over her. "*Let* me?" she asked. "I can take control anytime I want."

"Then what's stopping you?" he challenged.

"Because you'll snatch the control away from me." It wasn't the full truth but just one of the reasons.

"Try me."

She'd love to, but she shouldn't. She wanted Nadir, but she didn't want to get too close. But it would be just one more time. How could she possibly get too attached, knowing that this would be the last time? Especially if she was setting the pace.

Zoe skimmed her hands over his broad shoulders and muscular back. She felt the strength and power under his warm skin. As she trailed her fingertips over his hip bone he jerked. Zoe smiled against his mouth at the telltale sign. She had just discovered he was ticklish. She was inordinately pleased that he had a weak spot.

She drew her hand lower, but Nadir encircled her wrist with his strong fingers. She groaned with disappointment as he moved her hand to his shoulder.

"Don't you want me to touch you?" she asked.

"I don't want this to end before it begins," he said as he skimmed the strap down her shoulder.

"We have all night," she reminded him as rubbed her fingertips along his chest. She would need all night to wrestle control from him. It would take a lifetime to hold any sexual spell over him.

Nadir looked intently into her face. Zoe held her breath. She wasn't sure what he hoped to find. The darkness was a veil, and he wouldn't be able to read her eyes among the shadows.

To Zoe's surprise, Nadir gathered her close and rolled onto his back. She was sprawled on top of him as she stared at him in confusion.

"Touch me as much as you want," he offered.

Zoe's heart started to pump hard. Her skin felt hot and taut. She wanted to explore and taste all of him, but that would reveal just how much she wanted him, how much she couldn't keep her hands off him. He would use that to his advantage.

Unless she drove him wild first. She wasn't sure if she could. She slowly straddled his legs and placed her hands on his shoulders.

"Put your hands behind your head," she ordered softly. She sensed his curiosity and added, "I don't want you to stop me."

"I wouldn't dream of it," he drawled as he laced his hands underneath his head.

She couldn't read his eyes, but she saw the arrogant smile and felt the male confidence coming off him in waves.

She wanted to rattle his confidence. She dipped her head, her long hair cascading onto his shoulders. She darted her tongue at the center of his collarbone. He tasted warm and male. She dragged the tip of her tongue from the base of his throat to the cleft of his chin. She dared a glance at his face as she deliberately licked her lips. His features were stiff, his jaw clenched.

"Do you want to stop me now?" she taunted.

His eyes glittered. "No," he answered gruffly.

A reckless fire coursed through her veins. He didn't want to show his weakness any more than she did. Zoe leisurely stroked his chest before licking and teasing his flat brown nipples with her teeth. As she caressed his abdomen she listened to the way his breath hitched in his throat and felt his muscles bunch under her touch.

She gently wrapped her hand around the base of his hard length. Nadir bucked. She pumped her hand and watched him arch his back, listened to his choppy breathing. When Zoe took him in her mouth he tangled his fingers into her silky hair.

Suddenly he pulled her up. She barely had time to protest as he grabbed her by the waist. She looked down at him, her tousled hair in her face as Nadir positioned her. She straddled his hips and he guided her down.

"I thought I was in charge," she murmured.

"I changed my mind," he said through clenched teeth. She felt the sexual energy pulsing from him. He was through indulging her.

"I knew it wouldn't last," she said in a husky voice as her breath caught in her throat.

A relentless heat flushed through her as she sank onto

his length. He slowly stretched and filled her. Zoe struggled for her next breath. She rocked her hips and a shower of pleasure sparked inside her.

Wild need lashed inside her. She wanted to close her eyes to hide how she felt, but she couldn't pull her gaze away from his.

She reached for the hem of her short negligee. Slowly she bunched the silk higher. She teased Nadir, enjoying the rise and fall of his chest as she rolled and tilted her hips. She allowed the silk to fall back down before she bunched it up higher still. As she finally stripped and tossed the negligee to the side she no longer felt vulnerable under his hot gaze. Instead she felt beautiful. Sexy. Powerful.

When his hands tightened on her hips she knew the teasing was over. He had indulged her long enough and he was taking over. She saw the primal male look in his eye before he led her into a wild, intense rhythm.

The pleasure Nadir gave overwhelmed her. Overpowered her senses. She was out of control, mindlessly following him. It was as if her body was not her own. She desperately needed to pull back even though her body begged for release.

She wanted to submit to the excruciating pleasure, but she knew the moment would change her. If she surrendered now, she would be bound to him in the most elemental way.

Nadir slid his hand against the damp curls between her legs and pressed his fingertip against her clitoris. White hot pleasure ripped through her like a bolt of lightning.

Zoe cried out as sensations tore across her mind. She couldn't hide her response. She rode the wave of pleasure as she felt Nadir find his own thundering release.

Moments later she slumped against him. Her body still pulsed, her skin was slick with sweat and she nestled her head against his shoulder. She knew it would be better, safer, if she went back to her side of the bed. But she needed to sustain the connection a little longer.

She squeezed her eyes shut as she listened to the erratic beat of Nadir's heart. If she wasn't careful she might become infatuated with her arranged husband.

That would the biggest mistake she could make. She wasn't going to trust this feeling. Nothing would keep her in Jazaar.

# CHAPTER EIGHT

SUNSHINE streamed into the bedroom windows. Nadir propped his arm and rested his chin against his hand as he watched Zoe sleep. She was curled up in a ball, her fists under her pillow, her legs drawn up.

Even in sleep she wouldn't let anyone get close. He knew that wasn't always true. She had allowed one man into her heart. A man who hadn't been worthy of her trust.

Soon Zoe would learn to trust and rely solely on him. It was his right to expect complete loyalty and honor from his wife. Perhaps he would need to visit her in the mountains from time to time to reinforce her commitment. It wouldn't be a hardship to share her bed whenever he visited.

But she could never live in the Sultan's palace. She was too American, too improper to be his wife. He would have to hide her away if he wanted the political support of the Jazaari men.

Nadir brushed a wayward piece of hair from her cheek. He was amazed that someone with her harsh upbringing had such a soft exterior. Zoe's forehead wrinkled in a frown and she curled into herself even tighter.

He was tempted to stroke her gently. Coax her into opening up to him. She had last night, giving him a glimpse of the passion and fire inside her. He imagined how wild and intense the sex would be if she trusted him completely.

Nadir shifted restlessly as anticipation coursed through his veins. He wanted her again. He was becoming insatiable. Throughout the night he had reached for her. Even as they slept he had had to touch her. He couldn't remember the last time he'd felt like this about a woman. He didn't want to inspect this need too closely, certain the fierce lust would burn out once the honeymoon was over.

He had decided that Zoe had had enough time to sleep when he heard the familiar buzz of his cell phone. He hesitated for a moment, wanting to ignore his duty. He was tempted to tune out the rest of the world so he could enjoy a leisurely morning of pleasure with Zoe.

The persistent buzz of the phone reminded him that the demands of business would continue to intrude. He got out of bed quietly so he didn't waken Zoe. With the hope that he could conclude business quickly and return to bed, he strode naked to the sitting room to find his cell phone.

He grabbed it from a low table and answered with a harsh growl. His mood didn't improve as he listened to his assistant.

"I will go to Singapore and deal with it myself," he said. "Make the arrangements for me to leave tonight."

Nadir ended the call, wrestling with an unfamiliar sense of reluctance and disappointment. He didn't want to leave Jazaar. He stared out the window that overlooked the desert. These days it felt as if he was away from his beloved land more than he was home.

"You're going somewhere?"

Nadir turned when he heard Zoe's voice, husky with sleep. He saw her leaning against the bedroom door. Her tousled long hair fell in waves, hiding most of her face. She held a rumpled bedsheet against her.

"I am in charge of a business deal that's important to the future of Jazaar," he explained slowly as his gaze traveled down the sheet that barely hid her curves. His body stirred in response. "Negotiations have broken down. I have to go to Singapore."

"What about me?"

He dragged his gaze up to her face. "What about you?"

"Where am I going? You can't leave me," she said as she casually brushed her hair from her eyes. "It will look bad if the honeymoon ends abruptly."

She said it lightly, but Nadir understood her concern. Even though he had announced Zoe was his wife, it *would* look bad if he left her immediately after the wedding ceremony. It wouldn't strengthen his fragile relationship with the tribe.

Nadir knew he could quietly send Zoe to Omaira or to his mountain palace. No one in the tribe would know that they weren't together. But Zoe was still keeping secrets. What if she tried to run away again? That would shame him in the eyes of his people.

"The honeymoon hasn't ended," Nadir said as he walked towards her. "You are coming to Singapore with me."

Zoe went completely still as a tension invaded her body. "Are you serious?" she whispered.

"Of course." He rested his arm against the doorframe and looked down at her. "Why do you ask?"

She bit her lip. "You said you wouldn't take your wife on business trips."

It was true, but it was in his best interests to take Zoe with him. As he had investigated her family over the last few days he had found several reports of her defiance and disobedience. He got the feeling she would not accept being sent away quietly.

Nadir had also seen in the reports that Zoe had attempted to run away countless times. What if she was running toward something? Or someone—like her lover?

"This isn't just a business trip," he announced. "We are relocating the honeymoon."

No matter how hard Zoe tried to hide it, Nadir saw the excitement building up inside her. He didn't know why she felt the need to keep her enthusiasm hidden. The idea of traveling seemed incredibly important to her.

"This way I can keep an eye on you," he said as he tucked a long curl of her hair behind her ear.

The excitement in her eyes dimmed and she scowled. "I don't need a babysitter."

"I will be the judge of that." He trailed his hand down her throat. His fingertips rested on her pulsepoint. "Something tells me that you'll make a run for it the moment my back is turned."

Zoe lowered her gaze. "You're paranoid. Anyway, I don't have a passport," she said, her chest rising and falling rapidly. "I don't even have luggage."

"Mere details." He lightly caressed her collarbone.

"But we're leaving tonight," Zoe pointed out.

"That's for one of my assistants to worry about."

"But—"

He curled his fingers along the edge of her sheet and pulled it from her loose grasp. It fell to the floor and he kicked it to the side. "There are many other things on your to-do list before we leave," he said as his gaze roamed her body. "Returning to bed is at the top of that list."

Nadir curled his arms around her waist and lifted her up. Zoe didn't protest. She wrapped her legs around his waist and speared her hands in his hair before she kissed him.

As he rushed blindly for the bed Nadir knew relocating the honeymoon had nothing to do with the tribe's opinion. He wanted Zoe with him for a little longer. And it wasn't just because of the incredible sex. At this rate he would gain her complete trust and loyalty before the honeymoon ended.

The black sedan purred to a stop a few feet away from a sleek private jet. Zoe closed her eyes and ordered herself to remain calm. She had to play it cool or she would raise suspicion. There was no excuse to mess up when she was so close to escaping.

She opened her eyes and reached for Nadir's hand as he helped her out of the car. She moved with precision, although her limbs were weak with nerves. She stood on the tarmac at Omaira International airport and looked around.

She couldn't believe she was just a few steps away from leaving Jazaar. Forever. There had been times when she hadn't thought this moment would come, but now after all these years she was about to leave. In style, she thought with wicked amusement as she glanced at the red carpet rolled out for them.

She should feel relieved. Unencumbered. Zoe slowly exhaled as she walked onto the carpet. She wasn't sure exactly what she was feeling. Excited. Overwhelmed. Scared.

The desert wind pulled at her hair and her designer dress. The high heels she wore felt strange. Gone were the threadbare hand-me-downs and ill-fitting sandals. She was about to cast off that part of her life and go after her dreams.

She wrapped her hand around the stair railing and made her way to the door of the private plane. *Just a couple more steps...* Her chest was tight with apprehension. What if Nadir changed his mind at the last minute? What if there was a delay?

Even if the plane took off on time she wasn't exactly

home free. Singapore was far away from Houston, Texas. And she didn't have access to her new passport. Zoe worried her bottom lip. One of Nadir's many assistants had it for safekeeping.

She wasn't going to think about that right now. Today she was closer to her goal than she had been the day before. She was going to create a wonderful life and make something of herself. She had to remain focused and not get distracted by the sexual chemistry she shared with Nadir.

As she reached the plane's door Zoe greeted the flight attendant with a polite smile. She was about to cross the threshold when she froze. She felt a curious pull that made her turn around and take one last look at the deserts of Jazaar.

She stared in the direction of her old village. It was miles away, and she couldn't see it, but she had the awful feeling that the place would remain a part of her. Would this new world, this new life, be any better than the one she was leaving behind?

"It's beautiful, isn't it?" Nadir said at her side. She glanced up and saw him looking at the majestic sand dunes. "I've been all over the world and nothing compares."

Zoe pressed her lips together. She knew better than to argue, but it made her wonder how she could have anything in common with Nadir. How could she have a kinship with someone who adored her prison? He might have good memories and be tethered to his desert kingdom, but she wanted to forget everything that had happened to her here. Pretend that this place had never existed.

She turned abruptly and entered the plane. She halted and stared at the sleek lines and modern decor. It was like walking into a luxury home. The cream leather seats promised the ultimate comfort and the soft green sofas beckoned for travelers to kick back with a drink and chat. A door at the rear offered a glimpse of an elegant dining room and a curving staircase that led to another floor. She'd never seen anything like this and was tempted to explore.

It was also a surprise to see men in business suits typing away on their laptop computers and speaking quietly on their cell phones.

"These are a few of my employees working on the negotiations," Nadir said after he'd greeted the flight attendant. "I'll introduce you once we are in flight."

Zoe gave a nod and went for a leather chair at the back of the room. Maybe it was a habit to find the quietest, farthest corner, but she did not want to be in the way of the hardworking team. She buckled up and grabbed her e-reader from her bag.

As she turned on the device, eager to delve into a new story, she felt compelled to look out the window. She didn't move as the sun began to set. She watched the vibrant colors streak across the sky as Nadir sat down next to her.

"Why are you sitting all the way back here?" he asked.

"I didn't want to intrude on your business." She felt the plane begin to move and glanced over at Nadir as he buckled his seat belt. "I don't need to be entertained. I have my e-reader."

The plane picked up speed. This was it. She was leaving Jazaar. Her heart started to beat hard against her chest. She curled her hands around her seat belt.

"You don't like flying?" Nadir reached for her hand and laced his fingers with hers.

It wasn't that. After six years of planning and praying, she was out of Jazaar. It was too good to be true. As the plane lifted into the air Zoe closed her eyes and emotion clawed her throat. She was free. She gripped Nadir's hand. She was finally free.

She fought for composure. She didn't want Nadir to see how important this flight was for her. She slowly opened her eyes and glanced out the window. The tightness in her chest loosened and she exhaled shakily. The sun glowed against the sand dunes.

"You keep glancing back," Nadir mused. "Are you already getting homesick?"

She'd been homesick for six years, the longing so strong and thick that it almost suffocated her. "I don't have the same affection for Jazaar as you do," she said hoarsely as she removed her hand from his. "If I were a powerful sheikh I might feel homesick for the one place where I reign supreme."

"Your opinion may change now that you're a sheikha."

It was unlikely. A cage was a cage, no matter how gilded it might be. "I think I'd need to do a lot of traveling before I would miss Jazaar."

"You'll have to make the most of this trip." Nadir leaned his head back on the soft leather seat. "After our honeymoon, my plan is to delegate most of my traveling."

Her heart lurched. "Really? Why?"

"The initiatives I'm making for Jazaar's future are demanding more of my time and attention. I need to be here."

Zoe glanced back at the desert through the window as shock reverberated in her chest. She'd had no idea that he was ending his jet-setting ways. She had married him at the right time. If he planned to curtail his traveling this was her one chance to escape.

"You're surprised by my decision?" Nadir asked. "I don't understand why. My obligation is to Jazaar."

"Um…" She tried to keep her expression blank as she faced him. "You don't strike me as a stay-at-home kind of guy."

"Is that right?" His gaze ensnared hers and she saw the

amusement in his dark eyes. "What kind of man *do* you think I am?"

Zoe grimaced. She'd kind of walked right into that one. She wouldn't dare tell Nadir that she found him a man of sophistication and glamour. He was a sensual man, a sexy man who could easily seduce her.

He smiled and her heart skipped a beat. She couldn't quite look away from the breathtaking sight. It transformed him as the harsh features and deep grooves softened. She wished he would smile more often.

"Your eyes are very expressive," he said.

Her face burned bright. She wanted to squeeze her eyes shut but she refrained. "You have no idea what I'm thinking."

His smile slanted with knowing. "If we were alone," he said in a low, husky voice, "I would grant your wish and seduce you right now."

Her body jumped to attention as he made the husky promise. A warm ache twisted low in her belly. She needed to break the spell he had woven between them. She hectically looked around and saw one of Nadir's employees hovering nearby.

She dipped her head and stared at her e-reader, although she couldn't focus on the screen. "I believe you are needed up-front," she muttered under her breath.

"I believe I'm needed right here." He rubbed his thumb against her wrist. She knew he could feel her erratic pulse.

Zoe cleared her throat. "Anticipation makes it sweeter. Haven't you heard?"

"It doesn't make *you* sweeter," Nadir murmured, his thumb drawing circles on the inside of her wrist. "It makes you more demanding, more aggressive, even—"

She sharply turned her head and met his gaze. "If you don't know what to do with a strong woman in bed…"

"Oh, I know exactly what to do." He lifted her stiff hand and brushed his lips against her knuckles. "And you'll find out once we're alone in our hotel room."

Her body clenched as heat stung her skin.

He lowered her hand and moved away. "But now I have to attend to business." He released his seat belt. "Think of all the possibilities while I'm gone."

The pulsating energy evaporated the moment Nadir left. As she watched him approach his waiting employee Zoe wanted to sag against her seat. She pressed her hand against her flushed face, knowing she would spend the entire flight imagining what they would do once they arrived at their hotel.

What was she doing, teasing this man? Did she think the moment she was out of Jazaari rule she could regain her boldness? Nadir was a powerful man, a fearsome sheikh.

Not to mention a bold and audacious lover. Red-hot memories tumbled through her mind. The night before he had taken her countless times and—

*Oh, my God.* Zoe clutched the armrests and pitched forward as panic ripped through her. They hadn't been using protection. Not once.

Why hadn't she thought about this before? She had taught family planning to the women in her tribe. She knew better!

Zoe frantically worked out the dates in her sluggish mind. She worked them out again. It wasn't the right time of the month for her to become pregnant, but it was still a risk.

She turned to look out the window. Dread weighed heavily on her shoulders. She caught a last glimpse of the desert before her view was shrouded by the clouds.

She clapped her hand over her mouth as her stomach twisted cruelly. There was only one thing that could trap her in Jazaar. Having Nadir's baby.

# CHAPTER NINE

SINGAPORE wasn't what she had expected, Zoe decided as she rode the hotel's private elevator with Nadir. She had imagined the scent of tropical flowers permeating thick, humid air. She had thought she would be greeted by a young, vibrant atmosphere and an explosion of color.

The elevator doors quietly slid open and revealed the dramatic entrance to the penthouse suite. The dark wood lattice walls flanked a wide window that provided a stunning view of a glittery skyline. An enormous round table sat in the middle of the room. In the center of the table was a slender glass vase with a deceptively simple arrangement of bright red orchids.

A crack of lightning forked through the dark sky and illuminated the fierce tropical storm that had greeted her the moment she'd stepped out of the airplane. Zoe flinched as a deafening clap of thunder boomed over their heads. Nadir placed a firm hand on her spine and escorted her out of the elevator.

She was very aware that she didn't jump when Nadir touched her. Was he aware of the significance? Did he realize that after years of dodging, evading and instinctively protecting her back, she now accepted his casual touch with just a moment's hesitation?

They were met by the penthouse butler, a formally

dressed older man. He bowed low with a respectful greeting and guided them into an opulent drawing room.

*A butler?* Zoe bit her bottom lip as she followed, acutely aware of Nadir's hand resting possessively on her hip. She didn't know penthouse suites had a servant on-call. That was going to make it more difficult to slip away unnoticed.

Another jagged bolt of lightning sliced through the sky and Zoe braced herself for the thunder. The immediate rumble sounded ominous, and she instinctively curled against Nadir's side.

"The storm will pass soon," he murmured in her ear as he tightened his hold. "They don't last very long."

Zoe wasn't so sure about that. The storm howled in growing fury and the rain lashed against the windows, but she wasn't going to tremble or slink into a corner. She had learned never to show her vulnerabilities in front of anyone and she wasn't going to start now. She was embarrassed that Nadir noticed her moment of cowardice and grateful that he didn't tease her.

As the butler offered tea, Zoe was pleased that her hands were steady when she took the fragile china cup. She stepped away from Nadir's hold and sat on a sleek black sofa.

She didn't know what was wrong with her. She had to snap out of it. She had dealt with plenty of thunderstorms when she was growing up in Texas, but it had been a while since she'd seen one.

Zoe hoped she hadn't lost her steely nerve along with everything else. She needed it now more than ever if she was going to grab her chance for freedom.

Once the butler departed lightning flashed again, casting the room with an eerie glow. Zoe cautiously placed her teacup on a low table before the thunder rumbled.

Her spine straightened as she felt the sizzling tension in the room.

She was alone with Nadir. She couldn't help but glance in his direction. He watched her with intensity. The naked desire in his eyes made her shiver with anticipation.

Zoe bit her lip and dragged her gaze away. She would have to ward him off. No way could she risk a pregnancy— not when she was inching closer to her goal.

She didn't want to avoid Nadir. She was eager for his company…for his attention. It was definitely a sign that she needed to move on before she got in too deep with him.

"They are waiting for me at the office," Nadir said with a hint of regret.

"I'll find something to occupy my time," Zoe promised briskly as she rose from her seat. She wanted him to leave, but at the same time she wanted him to stay.

"No need." Nadir flicked his sleeve and looked at his watch. "Your assistant will be here in a few moments to go over your itinerary."

"My assistant?" Why did she need an assistant? Or was that code for babysitter? "Hold on. Did you say I have an itinerary?"

"Yes." Nadir set down his drink. "Rehana will take you shopping, to the spa and sightseeing."

She was right. The assistant was really a nanny, a minder. That would ruin all her plans. She had to think fast and get rid of the assistant without making Nadir suspicious.

Zoe slowly approached him. "That's very thoughtful of you, but I—"

"And your Arabic tutor will arrive later this afternoon."

She stumbled to a halt and stared at him. "You arranged lessons for me?"

"I told you I would." He frowned. "Why are you surprised?"

"I…" She had prepared herself for disappointment, assuming he wouldn't remember his promise. "Most of the men in my family are against educating women."

Nadir's eyebrow arched. "And you thought I shared the same views as your uncle?"

"No! No, of course not." She had been trying so hard not to say that, but Nadir had clearly read her mind. "The tutor is a wonderful surprise. Thank you."

Zoe brushed her lips against his cheek. She felt the muscle bunch in his jaw. Tension radiated from him. She knew Nadir was exerting his willpower and holding back. The gesture of thanks was a mistake. She knew better. One kiss was all it took for them to wind up in bed.

"I should go," he said gruffly, his gaze on her mouth. He swallowed hard. "If you need anything let the butler know. He will always be here."

At this rate she'd have an entire entourage with her when she tried to leave. "Nadir, I appreciate everything you've done for me, but it's not necessary. I'm looking forward to exploring on my own."

Nadir's eyes narrowed. "You will not go out alone."

Zoe folded her hands and fought to control her temper. Why must he say it like that? She was smart and capable. "English is spoken here," she reminded him. "I can navigate."

Nadir shook his head. "Your guide and a driver will be with you at all times."

Zoe squeezed her fingers together. She kept perfectly still as her mind raced. How was she going to look for the American embassy or hop on a plane to Texas when everyone was keeping an eye on her?

She reached out and cupped her hand against his angular jaw. She enjoyed seeing his eyes darken. She knew this was the last time she would have a chance to touch him. Once he left the suite she would disappear from his life.

"You don't have to feel guilty about leaving me alone on our honeymoon," she said earnestly. "I know how to take care of myself. I'm used to it."

"And your family were quite used to the trouble you caused when you were by yourself," Nadir murmured. He turned his head and placed a kiss in the center of her palm.

Another bolt of lightning ricocheted across the dawn sky. Zoe's breath hitched in her throat as she watched the brilliant light flash across the dramatic features of Nadir's face. He looked rough and dangerous. Sexy.

She felt her skin flush and tighten. Her hand tingled under his mouth. She wanted more of this. More of *him*.

Maybe it wasn't smart to make a run for it within minutes of arriving in Singapore. She held his gaze as the electric tension shimmered between them. Perhaps she should get familiar with Singapore and create a strategy. She could leave any time within the next few days.

Nadir reached for his cell phone and punched a button. "Rehana? Change of plans. You won't be needed today," he said as he pressed his lips against the inside of Zoe's wrist. "Let them know I won't make it to the office for a couple more hours."

"You're not going to the office?" Zoe asked as she watched him turn off his phone. "I thought you were needed for intense negotiations. It's the whole reason we're in Singapore."

He tossed the phone on the table. "I'm delegating because I have more important things to do."

She frowned. "Such as?"

A smile tugged at the corner of his mouth. "Spending the morning with my wife."

Zoe slowly blinked. That was the last thing she'd expected him to say. He wanted to be with her, too. A warm, tingly feeling washed over her. "You don't need to," she said softly.

"I want to." His dark eyes sparkled. "And you want me to as well."

He thought this was all to get more attention from him? What arrogance! If only he knew she was trying to get some time alone. "I didn't say that."

"You didn't have to," Nadir said. He slid his hand over hers and laced their fingers.

And at that moment she wanted to be with him. Spend time together. She wanted to act like newlyweds, even if it was pretend. This was an arranged marriage, not a love match.

"What if I ask you to cancel my itinerary?" she asked hopefully.

"I will for the morning," he compromised as he pressed his mouth against her temple. "But you *will* meet your tutor."

Zoe made a face. "This is supposed to be my honeymoon, not a special brand of torture. It took me forever to learn how to speak Arabic."

"You need to learn how to read it," Nadir said. He pressed another kiss against her cheek. "How else are you going to read bedtime stories to our babies?"

*"Babies?"* Her heart lurched. Where had *that* idea come from?

"Yes, babies," Nadir said smoothly, although he seemed as surprised as she was by his comment. "I expect more than one."

Of course he would. He was the heir to the throne. She should have thought about this! "We have never spoken about having children." Now was the time to tell him she wasn't ready for a baby.

"What is there to talk about?" he murmured.

"Plenty." Zoe closed her eyes, her mind whirling, as he caught her earlobe between his teeth. She shivered as the hot sensation sparked just under her skin. She wanted to forget everything and indulge in the pleasure.

She knew what she couldn't say. That the only time she would become pregnant was when she was in a solid and loving relationship. That she needed to feel safe and free before she brought a child into the world.

"I need an heir," Nadir said softly. "Jazaar is already on baby watch. There's hope that we will have a baby boy nine months from now."

"Jazaar can wait."

"But can I? I like the idea of you carrying my baby." She heard the male satisfaction in his husky voice.

Of course he would, Zoe decided. She shouldn't read anything in what he said. A pregnant sheikha was a sign of the Sheikh's strength and virility. It had nothing to do with how he felt about her.

"You want me to have your baby? *Me?*" She didn't fit any requirement for a good Jazaari bride. Why would he think she could make a good Jazaari mother?

"You are the Sheikha. My only wife. Who else can give me a legitimate heir?"

Ah, *that* was how she met the qualifications. Zoe struggled to collect her thoughts. "Nadir, I'm not ready to have children."

He went still and slowly lifted his head. "What are you saying?"

"I think we should use birth control," she said carefully, but she couldn't bring herself to meet his gaze. "I'll take care of everything. In fact I'll meet with a doctor today."

There was a long pause and Nadir took a step back. "You don't want my baby?"

She winced. "I—I didn't say that. I'm saying—"

"That you don't want my baby right now?" he said in a low, restrained tone.

She was making this worse. Zoe knew she had to explain, but she was hesitant to bring up her dreams. She had never talked about her goals much because the only way she could protect them from her family was to keep them secret.

Nadir was different from anyone she had met in Jazaar. If he understood why those goals were important to her he wouldn't get in her way. He might actually show her support.

"You may not know this, but I have a few goals," she said, looking down at the ground as her pulse quickened. "I want to accomplish some things before I have a family."

"What are your goals?"

She dared a glance in Nadir's direction. He seemed genuinely interested. No, it was more than that, Zoe realized as the hope swelled in her chest. He was pleased that she was sharing something about herself.

She nervously swiped her tongue across her bottom lip. "I want to complete my education."

"I also want that for you," he said with a shrug. "That's not a problem. Your Arabic tutor is just the beginning."

"I want more than a basic education," Zoe explained, her words coming out in an excited rush. "I want to become a doctor."

"A doctor?" Nadir repeated dully. What had he started? He had no idea why he had mentioned babies earlier. Though he was warming up to the idea of Zoe being pregnant with his child, especially after she'd displayed courage and loyalty at their last wedding ceremony.

And a moment ago he had been pleased that she was finally opening up to him. It was a sign of her trust in him. Now he had to deny her that dream.

"Honestly, I don't know if I have what it takes to become a doctor," she said. Her face was aglow with enthusiasm as she gestured with her hands to emphasize her point. "But I want to continue the work of my parents."

His gut twisted. He'd had no idea she had ambitious plans for her future. Plans that interfered with her new role.

"No."

His voice was soft but it affected Zoe like the lash of a whip.

Her eyes widened and her hands froze in midair. "Did you just say no?"

"Having a career outside the palace is not practical. As much as I want to modernize Jazaar, they would not understand a working sheikha."

"They'll get used to it," she promised.

Nadir shook his head. "My detractors already think I am too Western. Having an American wife with career ambitions would give them too much ammunition."

Zoe dropped her hands to her sides. "I see. You need to show that you have tamed your American bride."

He wouldn't have put it that bluntly, but it was the truth. He needed to show every tribal lord that he embraced their culture while dragging them into this century. "I need a sheikha who will honor tradition," he said. "A woman who symbolizes all of Jazaar's values."

"Beauty, refinement and obedience." She spat out the words with disgust. "Have you considered that becoming a doctor would *enhance* my role as sheikha?"

"No. The sheikha's role is to support her husband. Nothing else can take priority."

He saw the impotent anger in Zoe's eyes. The determined set of her jaw. She was willing to fight for her dreams even if it meant going against him. It was clear that she saw him as the enemy.

Nadir swallowed a sigh. She would never see that he was protecting her, not destroying her. The draconian palace officials would fight her every step of the way, and they wouldn't stop there. The officials had outdated views about women. They would quash her spirit so she would remain obedient.

It would be best for her if she didn't cling to her dreams. She needed to pick her battles carefully.

He wondered why Zoe's family hadn't warned her about the sacrifices she would have to make to become Sheikha. They probably didn't care. They were only concerned about the bridal price and their connection to the royal family.

Zoe never should have married him. She didn't fit any of the requirements to be a royal bride. Not only had she given up her lover to be at his side, but she had future ambitions that she was not allowed to pursue. And she wasn't the type to surrender her dreams. He was going to have a fight on his hands.

Nadir crossed his arms and braced his legs. "Zoe, there are some things you can't do because you're the Sheikha. The logistics and security measures would be impossible. A doctor's duties would challenge a sheikha's rules of conduct. A career is just not feasible. You can be a patron or president of a medical charity, but you can't work as a doctor."

Zoe's eyes narrowed and her lush mouth drew into a firm line. "Taking care of the women in my tribe was the only thing that got me through the days."

"And now you have a new tribe and a new role."

She closed her eyes and exhaled sharply. "This is unfair. I never wanted to be a princess or a sheikha. I've always wanted to be a doctor."

"You have already made your choice, Zoe."

"I didn't make the choice," she said bitterly. "The choice was made for me."

"I'm not going to change my mind," Nadir warned her, his voice soft and lethal. "This conversation is over."

She clenched her hands and thrust out her chin. She wasn't going to let him see her crushing disappointment. It was her only protection. This was why she'd kept her dreams a secret.

Why had she even thought the Sheikh would be an ally? Because of his progressive ideas? Or had she mistaken his amazing lovemaking skills for actual caring? Nadir could pretend to be a thoughtful husband, but he made it very clear that he saw her as an interchangeable accessory.

She wanted to fight harder. Fight dirty. But she would run the risk of revealing too much, and Nadir could use that against her. Zoe slowly unclenched her fists and fought for composure. Why bother fighting? She was going to leave him and go back to Texas. He could make plans for her. She wouldn't be here to follow through.

"Fine," she bit out. She couldn't look at him, knowing her eyes flashed with defiance. She felt his surprise and suspicion at her quick capitulation. "But I'm still going to a doctor about birth control," she said as she turned on her heel and headed for the doorway.

"You still don't want my baby?" he drawled.

"Maybe I want the honeymoon to last a little longer," she said sarcastically over her shoulder.

"If that's what you want," Nadir said, "we won't try to have children until after our first wedding anniversary."

She whirled around. She was stunned that he'd agreed to one of her wishes. What was he up to? She studied his expression and he appeared sincere. "Do you really mean that?"

Nadir slowly approached her. "But you might already be pregnant."

Zoe shook her head. "It's the wrong time of the month for me, but I'll have the doctor verify that today."

"Good." He cupped her elbow. "And I meant what I said about the medical charities. You could do great work without being a doctor."

Zoe stared at his hand and gave a sharp nod. She didn't trust herself to speak. He thought he was being magnanimous. He didn't understand that what he was offering was a transfer from a small cage to a slighter bigger one.

She was not going to get the support she needed from Nadir. It didn't matter that she was becoming addicted to his touch or that she felt closer to him than anyone else. She had to leave him or she would lose everything again.

# CHAPTER TEN

Zoe's polite smile was about to fall off as she said goodbye to her assistant and stepped into the penthouse the next afternoon. The moment she heard the elevator doors slide shut her shoulders sagged with relief.

"I swear, that woman is going to drive me crazy," she muttered under her breath. She heard footsteps and saw the butler approach. Would she ever get a moment to herself? All she needed was one minute to disappear. Just one minute. Was that too much to ask?

"Your Highness," the butler greeted her as he gave a bow and took her packages. "The Sheikh is in the drawing room."

That surprised her. Zoe glanced at her wristwatch, but she still had plenty of time to prepare for the charity gala they had to attend. Why was Nadir here? Perhaps her question should be what rule had she broken this time to warrant Nadir's early arrival?

She strode into the drawing room with her head held high. She knew she looked like a polished princess from head to toe, thanks to a day at the spa and salon. She had been on edge and impatient, waiting for a chance to run away, but that tenacious assistant had never allowed her a moment alone.

She halted when she saw Nadir stretched out on the

long sofa. His jacket had been discarded and his tie was askew. A whisky tumbler sat on the ornate carpet by the sofa. His eyes were closed.

Now, her mind screamed as she stared at him. *This is the minute you've been searching for. You will never see Nadir this unguarded again. Disappear!*

She'd rolled back on her heel, prepared to make a dash for the elevator, when she studied his face. He looked exhausted and pale. The lines in his face were etched deep. Was he ill?

She pressed her lips together as she was swamped by indecision. Should she stay or should she go? She clenched her fists and sighed. She'd better not regret this choice, but if Nadir was unwell she needed to help him. She could find a different time to disappear. Hopefully.

"Is there something that you want?" Nadir asked. He didn't move and he kept his eyes closed.

Zoe dipped her head. She should have known he'd been aware of her the moment she'd stepped into the room. Nothing got past him.

She slowly walked to the sofa, finding it strange to look down at him. "Are you feeling all right?" she asked. She placed a hand on his forehead. His skin was cool to the touch.

He caught her wrist in his firm grasp without opening his eyes. It was only then that she realized this was the first time in their marriage that she had reached out and touched him outside their bed. Zoe hoped Nadir didn't read anything into that gesture. No, she decided. It would be beneath his notice.

"I'm fine," he said. "I'm thinking about the next move in my negotiation strategy."

"If you say so, but in Texas we call this a nap." She

gave a tug, but he didn't release her. "I'm going to get ready for the gala."

"I'm at stalemate," he confessed wearily. "I can't get them to accept my terms. And do you know why?"

She looked around the room. Was he talking to *her*? A Jazaari man didn't discuss business with a woman. Everyone knew that. "Uh…no…?" she said tentatively as she checked for signs of delirium.

"They think that I hold the same antiquated beliefs as the Sultan. No one is willing to invest in Jazaar because they think nothing will change when I rule." His eyes opened suddenly and his gaze held hers. "Do you think I'm a modern man?"

She felt his strong fingers around her wrist. She could lie, but he genuinely wanted her answer. "No."

Nadir's eyes narrowed. "No?"

Zoe gave another tug but couldn't break free. Maybe she should have lied. "I think you are more forward-thinking than the men in Jazaar. But compared to the men in other countries, no, you aren't modern."

He stared at her and heavy silence pulsed in the room. He slowly uncurled his fingers from her wrist. "Thank you for your honesty," he said coldly.

She drew her hand away from him. "I didn't mean to insult you."

"You didn't." He sat up and rested his elbows on his legs.

She had a feeling that she had offended him. Zoe sat down on the edge of the coffee table. "What company are you negotiating with? How modern are they?"

"They are a telecommunications company. My goal is for everyone in Jazaar to have access."

"Really?" She leaned back in surprise. Nadir was more aware of his countrymen's needs than she had first realized. His goal would bring a positive impact to the remote areas, and providing instant information to everyone would also reshape the tribal hierarchy. Zoe smiled at the possibilities. "So, what's the problem?"

Nadir ran his hands through his dark, thick hair. "The company is owned by a socially conscious widow."

"Ah." And Jazaar was not known for its women's rights. "Are you negotiating directly with the widow?"

"No," he said tightly, and Zoe knew it was a blow to his pride that he was dealing with an underling. "But she is very involved with the negotiations."

How could Nadir prove his modern approach? Whatever he said or did would be influenced by their preconceived ideas. Unless...

"Will she be at the charity ball?"

Nadir looked at Zoe with growing suspicion. "Yes, her company is sponsoring it."

Zoe began to rub her hands together as she formed a plan. "Then it's time to reveal your secret weapon."

Nadir tilted his head as if he was bracing himself for bad news. "And that would be...?"

Zoe spread her arms out wide. "Me."

He stared at her with disbelief. "You?"

"Yes, me. Your thoroughly modern American bride." She shimmied her shoulders. "Come on—you know I would knock all their preconceived notions on their asses."

He groaned and covered his eyes with his hands. "Zoe, you are not ready to represent Jazaar."

"I may not represent Jazaar to the people of Jazaar, but what about representing the new and improved Jazaar to other countries?"

Nadir slowly leaned back and studied her intently. He was seriously considering what she had said. Zoe was glad she was looking her finest.

She saw his gaze harden. "What are you really up to?" he asked.

She frowned and lowered her arms. "Nothing."

He slowly shook his head, as if that couldn't possibly be the right answer. "Why do you suddenly want to help me?"

Good question. This guy was keeping her from what she wanted most. He had too much power over her life and her future. It would be better to sabotage him, but she didn't want to. "Maybe I'm trying to do something nice."

Nadir's eyebrows went up.

She scowled at him. "It's been known to happen."

"I'm sure it has, but you're unpredictable." He shook his finger at her. "You could start an international incident without trying."

She folded her arms. "Do you want my help or not?"

"Okay, Zoe, I would like you to represent Jazaar." He reluctantly accepted her help. "But if you go too far…"

"Trust me, Nadir." She rose to her feet. "By the end of the night you are going to see me in a whole new light."

Nadir heard the orchestra play a final note with a flourish as they left the charity gala. He held Zoe's hand firmly while he led her down the steps to the waiting limousine.

"I look forward to meeting you tomorrow," he said to the vice-president of the telecommunications company. He felt triumph rolling through Zoe and gently squeezed her hand in warning.

"I'm sure we can negotiate terms that will satisfy all parties," Mr. Lee said. "Also, Mrs. Tan invites you and your wife to her home later this week to celebrate the deal."

"We would be honored," Zoe replied.

Nadir helped her into the limousine, fighting the urge to bolt before she caught him by surprise again. He said goodbye to Mr. Lee and unhurriedly got into the limo himself. As the car pulled away from the curb he slowly exhaled. He had never considered galas exciting, but tonight had been a rollercoaster thanks to his wife.

"I think that went well," Zoe said, resting her head against the leather seat. "I didn't want to leave."

"Why? Did you want one more victory lap around the ballroom?"

She laughed. It was unbridled and earthy. Very unprincess-like. The Sheikha didn't know protocol or diplomacy, but it didn't matter. Zoe had proved she was a brazen and modern woman. A new breed of royalty.

"I told you I was your secret weapon. You didn't believe me, did you? But you let me go after it because you had nothing to lose."

It was true. He hadn't had high hopes of getting back to the negotiating table, but Zoe knew how to present them as a modern couple. Most of the time. "I should have brought a muzzle for you," he said on a low growl.

Zoe laughed again. "It would have clashed with my gown."

His gaze traveled down the lilac gown. It was a modest design but the delicate fabric hugged her body. She'd been the sexiest woman at the event, overshadowing those who wore barely-there dresses.

He shook his head and tore his gaze from her body. He would not get distracted. "You just couldn't help yourself, could you?"

Zoe's smile grew wide. "I'm sorry."

No, she wasn't. She had planned the surprise attack to test her power and his patience. It was strange he wasn't angry about it. He only wished he had had a little more warning. "I'm creating a domestic violence program?" he said. "Since when?"

"It kind of slipped out when I spoke to Mrs. Tan," she

said with a shrug. "And it sounded really good so I just went with it."

"It was a very detailed lie. A twenty-four-hour crisis line? Group counseling? Emergency shelter? You came up with all that on the spot?"

"Those are some of the services my mother volunteered at back home. We could use them in the village," she explained. "I guess you could tell Mrs. Tan that you can't push your program through the bureaucracy."

"I don't think so." It was a good idea, and he wished Zoe had had those resources when she'd needed them.

"What are you going to do?"

"Make it happen." Warmth spread through his chest when he saw Zoe's eyes light up. "It will be your project."

Her jaw dropped. "My project?"

"It's your lie," he reminded her as he held her hand. "Anyway, you know what the program needs."

"I don't know if that's a good idea. I might mess up."

"I doubt that."

She looked out the window. Nadir studied her, wondering why he'd never considered that Zoe would be an asset to him. She was fearless in telling him the truth and could become a powerful ally.

She had already created an opportunity that had been denied to him. She could recreate the image of Jazaar and improve business and diplomatic relations if he had her at his side.

But she was still a liability when they were in Jazaar. It would be safer for her if he hid her in the mountain palace, yet he was no longer considering that an option. Until he had to make a decision about her future he would show his modern sheikha to the world.

The music pulsed in synch with the lights and Zoe felt the primitive beat vibrating under the dance floor. The people around her swayed their arms and hips to the sensual beat. Zoe curled her arms over Nadir's shoulders and moved even closer to him. She was rewarded by the gleam of his eyes.

A sense of joy and promise flooded her body. The week in Singapore had been the happiest she had known in a long time. Even the Arabic tutorials hadn't dimmed her spirits. She had dreaded the lessons, remembering the struggle she had had learning the language when she'd first arrived in Jazaar. But this time it wasn't as frustrating or as painful because no one was expecting immediate results. She felt as if her world was expanding each day, each hour.

She had shed the caftans and robes of Jazaar for younger, brighter clothes. Clothes that reflected who she was, not who people wanted her to be. During the week she had met interesting people and explored Singapore. Yet her favorite moments had been the ones she'd shared alone with Nadir.

She hadn't expected someone as sophisticated as Nadir to accompany her to all the tourist attractions. She knew he was extremely busy, but all his attention was on her when they were together. Whether it was sharing a kiss on the cable car ride to Sentosa Island, or discovering Singapore's glittering nightlife, Nadir seemed more fascinated by her than his surroundings.

But it was time to go, Zoe thought with a hint of sadness. Nadir's business negotiations were finalized. She had an escape plan ready. She shivered as she thought about the risky maneuver. She had to go now if she didn't want to be carted back to Jazaar.

She had to leave if she wanted to give her dreams a chance, but she was strangely reluctant to go.

"Thank you for bringing me to this nightclub, Nadir.

I've never been to one." Even if she had been invited to dance at a wedding or festival she wouldn't have participated. She hadn't felt like dancing until now.

"Your wish is my command," he murmured in her ear.

*If only.* "It's going to be hard leaving Singapore." *Hard to leave him.* "I've had the time of my life."

Nadir raised his head and looked into her eyes. "You're not feeling homesick for Jazaar?"

She controlled her expression in case he saw her true feelings about Jazaar. "No, not at all."

Anticipation flickered in Nadir's dark eyes. "Then you will accompany me to Athens."

"Athens? As in Greece?" The cautious excitement hummed inside her. "Seriously?"

"I have some business there I need to attend to." Nadir's hands slid sensuously down the length of her spine and rested low on her hips. "I'm not sure how long it will take me."

"I would love to go," she said. "Did you know that Greece is the birthplace of western medicine?"

"Zoe..."

The soft warning in his voice punctured her enthusiasm. She knew better than to discuss that forbidden topic with him. She drew back until they were barely touching. "Sorry." She forced the word from her throat. "When do we go?"

Nadir gathered her close until she felt his strong heartbeat against her chest. "Tomorrow."

She wasn't sure if Greece was closer or farther away from America. It would be better to execute her plan tonight. But she wanted to be with Nadir. She wanted to pretend just a little longer.

He must have seen the need in her eyes. She felt the air around them spark as his harsh features darkened. Zoe's breath hitched in her throat as her skin tingled with anticipation.

"Let's go back to the hotel," he said abruptly, capturing her hand in his and leading her off the dance floor.

She stared at their joined hands as she followed him. His dark hand was large as it engulfed hers. She felt safe. Wanted. No longer alone.

It wasn't real, Zoe reminded herself. It felt incredibly genuine, but she was falling under the spell of a honeymoon. She should leave now, before she could no longer tell the difference between fantasy and reality. She should escape now in case she didn't get another chance.

She enjoyed being with Nadir. She had been so lonely before she met him, and she would be alone again once she left. She wanted to make the most of this moment. But when was the right time to leave?

Zoe continued to stare at her hand twined with Nadir's. She felt his urgency and her legs wobbled. Her gaze fastened on the deep brown and festive henna design that still decorated her hand. It reminded her of the young brides from the tribe.

Those brides never went on a trip for a honeymoon. It simply wasn't part of tradition. Instead the brides were treated like princesses, doing no housework or cooking until the henna wore off.

Zoe knew her decision was made when she focused on the floral design at the base of her thumb. In a week or two her honeymoon would be over. Once the henna faded, that would be her sign to walk away from Nadir and start her new life.

## CHAPTER ELEVEN

"ARE you sure you want to know?" Zoe asked hesitantly.

Nadir's curious expression didn't change. "I asked, didn't I?"

She wondered why he'd chosen this moment to ask. They were curled up together in bed, naked and spent. She was lying on her stomach and facing him, her hands tucked under a goosedown pillow. Nadir was sprawled on his back, his face close to hers.

She suddenly knew the answer to her question. Her stomach twisted as she fought off the sinking feeling. Nadir had asked because she had finally lowered her guard.

They'd been traveling throughout Europe for the past week and a half, acting like newlyweds. Nadir had successfully wooed her into gradually opening up to him. It had been a determined, aggressive campaign and she had fallen for it.

She should be furious at herself for believing in the fantasy, for sharing too much. But it was strange; she didn't regret it. Zoe had come to the startling realization that she had never felt as close to anyone as she felt to Nadir.

At some time during the honeymoon that had started in Jazaar and had now moved to London she had started to trust Nadir. Just a little. She wasn't going to repeat her mistake and discuss her dreams, and she knew better than to reveal all of her deepest, darkest secrets.

"You don't have to tell me," Nadir said softly, and turned his head to look at the ceiling.

She hadn't realized she had allowed the pause to stretch for so long. "Sorry, I was trying to decide which mistake was the worst," Zoe said lightly. "I have so many to choose from."

She never should have started this ritual of sharing something about themselves right before they fell asleep. It was one thing to share a favorite color or a childhood memory. It was another thing to expose your weaknesses, mistakes and fears. Especially to someone who had the power to use that information against you.

"My worst mistake..." Zoe suddenly felt jittery and cold washed over her skin. She looked away and took a steady breath. "My worst mistake was probably Musad Ali. He was the son of our neighbor."

She felt the mood shift in the luxurious bedroom. She didn't have to spell it out that Musad had been her lover. Nadir slowly turned to face her.

Maybe it was wrong to share this part of her past. It was risky, but she wanted Nadir to understand her.

She focused on his broad shoulders. She had never told anyone about Musad. It was her secret, her shame. Maybe it wasn't a good idea to tell Nadir. Their intimate relationship could change from this moment on.

"Musad was the wrong man to get close to," she admitted hoarsely. "He was the wrong man to trust." She'd used to think all men were untrustworthy. Now she wasn't so sure.

"How long did it last?"

She blinked when she heard his calm question. Her gaze flickered across his face. He showed no judgment or anger. Was that really how he felt, or was he holding back so she would reveal more?

"About six months," she answered tentatively. "He promised to marry me before he went to college in Chicago. But he always intended to leave me behind."

"If your uncle had discovered the affair…" Nadir murmured.

Zoe shivered at the thought. "It was stupid. Reckless."

He reached out and rubbed his hand along her bare arm. "You were in love."

She hadn't been in love with Musad, but she was ashamed to admit it. Love could make a careless action seem noble. She, however, had made one bad decision after another.

"I was trapped in my uncle's house. Terrified and miserable," she explained. "When I was with Musad I could forget for a while. Musad promised he would take me away from it all, and I was so desperate to believe him I didn't see that it was just a line to get me into bed."

"How did your cousin find out?"

"I'm not sure." When Fatimah had taunted her with the information, it had blindsided Zoe. "I wonder if she saw us together. At the end, Musad was taking a lot risks. So was I. I wanted to rebel."

Nadir frowned. "He exposed you to danger."

"I don't think that was his intention," Zoe said. She didn't think very highly of Musad, but she also didn't believe that he was calculated or cruel. "Musad was selfish, and he used me, but he would also have been punished if our relationship had been discovered."

"But you would have been punished more," Nadir pointed out, his eyes narrowing with anger. "And you had to get out of your uncle's house before Tareef found out. Marriage was your only way out."

"Yes." Out of her uncle's home. Out of Jazaar. Out of hell.

"You were even willing to marry The Beast."

Zoe made a face. "I hate that nickname of yours. You are not a beast."

"Are you sure about that?"

His dark voice sent a shiver down her spine. Was she sure about him? Could he hide a violent nature until it was too late for her? He was different from her uncle and the men in the tribe, but he was also more powerful and dangerous.

"Now it's your turn," she whispered. She remained still but she was tempted to curl up in a protective ball. "What was *your* biggest mistake?"

A long pause hung between them. Zoe wanted to cringe because she knew she had crossed a forbidden boundary. He could ask personal questions, but it was impertinent for her to do the same.

"Yusra," Nadir answered. "She was my biggest mistake."

Zoe was surprised that he had spoken Yusra's name. He never talked about that night or the scandal that had tarnished his reputation. "Why?" she dared to ask.

"I should have exerted more self-control."

Zoe froze as her heart stopped. Her skin prickled with warning. What was he saying? That he deserved the nickname? That he had the potential to be wild and untamed as a beast?

Nadir suddenly rolled on top of her. Her heart beat hard against her ribs as she felt his erection against her skin. Should she be afraid of her husband?

"I will never allow my emotions get the better of me again," he promised hoarsely.

He wrapped his hands around her wrists and held her

arms above her head. He lowered his head and claimed her mouth with his. Her pulse skipped wildly as she responded to his determined touch.

When he broke the kiss, she stared into his dark eyes. She didn't speak but she wanted to shatter this moment. She saw the desire in Nadir's eyes, but she saw something else. Something dark and unreachable.

Whatever had happened on his wedding night with Yusra, he wouldn't tell her. He saw no need to explain his past actions or his cryptic words.

What was wrong with her? She should fight him off and escape. She should be afraid of him. Instead she lay underneath him, naked and vulnerable. Wildly excited and drawn to his darkness.

He kissed, licked and nibbled down the length of her body. The sound of her gasps and his murmurs of appreciation echoed in the room. She dug her fingers into his shoulders when he worshipped her breasts with his hands and mouth. She twisted the bedsheets in her fists as he darted his tongue into her navel.

Zoe bucked her hips as Nadir dipped his head between her legs. A shower of sparks tingled under her skin as he pleasured her with his mouth. Ribbons of desire danced through her blood. She tangled her fingers in his hair as need flashed hot. A moan was torn from her throat as she climaxed.

Pleasure still rippled through her as Nadir hooked her trembling legs around his lean hips. He surged into her, groaning as her body eagerly welcomed him. His powerful thrusts quickly became uneven and wild. Zoe clung to him, her legs wrapped tightly around him, as another climax tore through her.

She heard his harsh cry as he found his release. He slumped against her, his body slick with sweat. Her arms and legs felt weak, but she held him close, unwilling to let this moment go.

He rolled onto his back and she watched his chest rise and fall with each breath. Their arms were touching, his hand covering hers, but it wasn't enough for her. She must trust him on some level if she needed to be in his arms.

But if she asked it would show too much of how she felt. Zoe nervously curled against him and shivered. "It's freezing."

Nadir's chuckle sounded drowsy and he gathered her against his solid chest. "Hardly. September in London is glorious. You are simply used to the desert."

"You're probably right." She didn't like the idea that she was more comfortable in the desert than in a cosmopolitan city.

"Admit it," he said sleepily as his arms wrapped around her, "you miss Jazaar."

Zoe wanted to scoff at the suggestion when a memory assailed her. She remembered the quiet hush and the tantalizing spices. She had enjoyed looking out into the desert and watching the sun dip below the sand dunes. She had learned to appreciate the natural and harsh beauty of the arid region. "I miss some things." *But not deeply enough to go back.* "Like the heat."

Nadir's eyes gradually closed. "Then you will be happy to know that we will be somewhere warm this time tomorrow."

She went on the alert and her heart skipped a beat. Was he already planning to return to Jazaar? "Where are we going?" she asked cautiously.

"Mexico City."

Zoe's eyes widened. "Mexico...?" she said in a whispery breath. Mexico shared a border with Texas. She would be incredibly close to home.

"But until then I'm prepared to keep you warm." His words were slurred with sleep.

"That sounds like a good plan," she said. She cupped her hand against his cheek and stroked the dark stubble.

Zoe noticed that her henna had almost disappeared. Only a few stubborn swirls remained. It still counted, she decided, as she tilted her head to kiss Nadir. Her honeymoon would officially end in Mexico.

The decision should have filled her with hope and determination. Instead it made her want to make the most of the honeymoon before she walked away from her husband forever.

# CHAPTER TWELVE

NADIR gratefully stepped into the hotel lobby and found the hushed surroundings were a peaceful oasis from the dynamic city. The soft cream sofas and the warm brown walls reminded him of the desert. Even the peasant art framed in gold made him think of Jazaar. He was working hard and traveling now so that afterward he could return home for good and take care of his country.

The meetings with his Mexico City office were becoming more difficult. As he walked past the elegant front desk Nadir admitted that it didn't help that he had been distracted. He had left Zoe, warm and willing, in their bed. The sex they had shared that morning had been nothing short of mind-blowing.

It had not been his best idea to mix his honeymoon with business trips. He'd thought he could get his fill of Zoe before he ensconced her in his mountain palace. Instead he had become insatiable for his wife. He couldn't imagine being away from her for more than a day.

Worse, he was starting to rely on her. On more than one occasion he had sought her opinion or her point of view. She was very knowledgeable, and provided him with a look into tribal life he could not get from any of his advisors.

Anticipation twanged in his blood as he headed for the elevators. When he saw the hotel manager hurrying to greet him he wanted to growl with frustration. He didn't want any more delays in returning to Zoe.

Nadir frowned. When had his every waking moment started to revolve around her? He didn't just want to bed her. He wanted to be with her. Spend every waking minute together. Shock reverberated through him. This was more than desire and lust. Was he falling for his arranged bride?

As he wrestled with that inconvenient thought, the hotel manager intercepted his path to the elevators. "Your Highness, I hope your stay has been pleasant," the man said with a slight bow. "I understand you are leaving us tomorrow?"

"Yes, we enjoyed our stay here, Señor Lopez."

"We are very fortunate that you have chosen our hotel." His smile suddenly brightened. "And may I say that your wife is an amazing woman?"

"Yes, she is." Zoe was a fighter, with survival instincts. She had the heart of warrior, the mind of a scientist, and the beauty of a goddess. He was proud to have her as his wife.

"So beautiful," Señor Lopez waved his hand to emphasize his point. "So brilliant, so curious."

Nadir went still. "Curious?"

The hotel manager bobbed his head. "Yes, she has taken great interest in the public health conference here at the hotel. The Sheikha has attended a few panels after meeting with the guest of honor. She fits right in."

Dark frustration spun inside him. Nadir struggled to keep a mildly interested expression. "Is that right?"

"She has quite a few ideas about maternal health. The debates can get…intense."

"I can imagine." He had forbidden her from medicine. He had trusted her. "The Sheikha never backs down."

Señor Lopez gave another small bow. "I hope the Sheikha enjoyed her stay?"

"I'm sure she did." He bade the hotel manager goodbye

and walked into the elevator on numb legs. Anger whipped through him as he gave a vicious swipe of his key card to activate the elevator.

It was time to go home. He had placed too much trust in Zoe. Given her too many liberties. Nadir knew he was beginning to sound like his father, but he didn't care. He had made those rules to help her assimilate into royal life and she had ignored them.

He'd managed to get his temper under control by the time he stepped into the penthouse suite. This time the soothing décor was invisible to him. All he noticed was that Zoe was not there to greet him. For some reason that made him angrier.

As the butler approached him with a wary smile, Nadir tersely asked for Zoe. He was informed that she was sunbathing. Nadir stalked to the private pool that was just off their bedroom.

His steps faltered when he saw her. She was lounging by the pool and reading an e-book. Her sunglasses were perched on her head and the modest blue swimsuit she wore skimmed her curves.

His stomach clenched as he silently watched her. Her dark hair was piled on top of her head. He didn't have to sink his fingers into it to know it would feel like warm silk. Her sun-kissed skin would be soft and fragrant. And her lips...Nadir's body hardened and his skin began to tingle. Zoe knew how to drive him wild with just her mouth.

She wasn't what he had expected in a wife. She was no Jazaari bride. She was sexy, opinionated and exciting. And disobedient. Nadir clenched his teeth. Extraordinarily disobedient.

When Nadir slid the door open, Zoe glanced up from her e-reader. The joy in her eyes and the wide, inviting smile surprised him. She was genuinely happy to see him.

Her smile dimmed when she caught his expression. "Bad day at the office?" she asked as she sat up.

"I understand you attended the public health conference?" he replied with icy calm.

As if a heavy curtain had fallen, Zoe's expression went blank. She looked down and turned off the e-book reader before setting it on the small table at her side. "I'm not sure who gave you that idea."

Nadir knew he was in for a battle. Zoe wasn't going to share any details. It was one more secret to hide from him.

"Should I call the assistant assigned to you and ask for details about your day?" He loosened his necktie with a vicious tug.

Zoe's mouth tightened. "No, there's no need for that. I attended a few events at the conference."

The vein in his forehead began to throb. He thrust his hands in his pockets. "After I told you to stay away from anything related to medicine?" he asked with lethal softness.

"The guest of honor invited me. He's a respected authority on newborn health!" Zoe insisted, jumping up from her lounge chair. "It would have been rude to decline."

"I'm sure you could have come up with an excuse."

Her jaw shifted to one side. "Why should I have made an excuse? I wanted to go. Those people understand me. I felt like I finally belonged somewhere."

"Don't disobey me again," he said in a fierce whisper.

Zoe went rigid, her body slightly shaking with tension. "It's not like I planned it!"

Her outburst surprised him. No one talked back when he gave a command. "I mean it, Zoe."

She didn't back down. She thrust her jaw out and her dark eyes glittered with defiance. "You are unreasonable.

There is nothing wrong with having opinions about medicine or having basic first aid skills."

"You won't need to use them."

"You don't know that. What if you collapse this very minute?" she asked, planting her hands on her hips. "Do you want me to stand back and hope someone else can help you?"

"Yes."

Zoe blinked. "Are you serious? You really wouldn't want my help?"

Nadir saw the hurt in her eyes. He wanted to erase the pain and tell her his decision had nothing to do with her abilities. But he needed to stay firm. Zoe needed to understand that she couldn't resurrect her old dreams. Those dreams had died the moment she married him. He hated the fact as much as she did, but it was time to move forward and not look back.

"My security detail is trained for any type of emergency," he explained. "If I found out you'd interfered with their jobs I would be furious."

"Well, I don't *have* a security detail."

"Yes, you do." Nadir frowned. How could she not know? Did she honestly think he wouldn't keep her safe?

She narrowed her eyes and tilted her head as she stared at him in confusion. "What are you talking about?"

"You have had a full security team following you since our wedding day. How else would I have found you when you wandered off into the bookstore in Omaira?"

*She had a security detail.* Her heart stopped as shock rippled through her body. There was a team of professionals who tracked her every move. She had had no idea.

She looked down and clasped her hands together in front of her. She couldn't let Nadir see the horror in her face. All this time she had been angry at herself for not taking any opportunity to escape. She had hesitated in Athens, procrastinated in Europe, and held back in Mexico. Yet had she tried to leave she would have failed spectacularly.

"Who? How many?" Zoe asked. She had no idea who was following her. She didn't recognize anyone as they traveled from one place to the next.

"That doesn't matter." Nadir dismissed the questions with a wave of his hand. "You are not playing doctor. I don't want to hear that you gave so much as a vitamin to someone."

She remained silent. How could she possibly make a promise like that? Didn't he know her at all?

"Zoe," he warned, "you need to learn how to obey."

She looked up at him from beneath her lashes. "Or what?"

Nadir's eyes darkened. "Don't push me."

"I know how *you* feel about the idea of me studying medicine. But do you know how I feel about it?" she asked bitterly. She lifted her head and met his gaze. "Do you know that I've always wanted to follow in my father's footsteps? That medicine fascinates me? Do you know? Do you care?"

Nadir slowly folded his arms. "I know that you have been fascinated by medicine since you were a candy striper when you were thirteen years old. You found the hospital atmosphere exciting, but what you really wanted to do was continue the work of your parents."

His answer astonished her. She hadn't thought he understood, but he knew exactly what drove her. And he would still keep her from her dream rather than support it.

She shouldn't be surprised, but she felt as if Nadir had betrayed her. She should have known better than to reveal what was important to her.

"I also suspect you're hiding a few medical thrillers on that e-reader."

She cast a guilty glance at her e-reader. "Oh." He was fine with her having a passing interest in medicine as long as she didn't use it.

"I'm protecting you from a battle you can't win."

"But you are keeping me away from something that I love."

"I know." Nadir thrust his fingers into his hair and exhaled sharply. "I will create a role for you in the medical community," he said slowly. "You can take a small part in our health ministry."

She drew her head back as her heart began to pump hard. Was Nadir truly bestowing an honor? She was almost afraid to believe there were no strings attached, no bait and switch. She hated being cynical, but it was her only armor. "There are no women in that ministry."

"There will be resistance," he said, and she could tell it was major understatement. "But it's nothing I can't handle. I know that the women's health system in our country is lacking, but I didn't understand how bad it was until I listened to your experiences."

"I'm not qualified," she was quick to point out. It was a prestigious position, but she was young, uneducated and female. "I don't think I would be very effective."

"You're the Sheikha. My wife. They will listen," he answered confidently.

"Thank you for the offer, Nadir. It's very generous." It wasn't her dream, but it was something. There was no guarantee that she could become a doctor, but with Nadir's proposition, she could change the way they practiced medicine in Jazaar. "I'll think about it."

Nadir reached out and cupped her face with his hands.

He tilted her face up and looked intently into her eyes. "That's the best offer you're going to get."

"I know." She was beginning to understand that. But she wanted to live her life on her own terms, and she didn't think she could do that if she was with him. She couldn't have everything and she needed to make a decision fast.

Nadir studied her expression for a moment. He sighed and dropped his hands. "You should get ready for dinner."

Zoe gave a nod and stepped away. The sun had dipped and it was getting cooler. "Where are we going?" she asked.

"On the jet."

She froze. They were leaving Mexico City earlier than planned. Zoe's gaze zoomed to her hands. The henna had disappeared days ago, but she hadn't made an attempt to leave. She took small, choppy breaths as regret almost suffocated her. Now she was trapped and she didn't know when she would get another chance to leave.

"Are we returning to Jazaar?" she asked huskily, her throat tight as panic pounded through her.

"Not yet," he said as he watched her carefully. "We're going to America."

Zoe gasped and she raised her hands to her mouth. *America.* Unshed tears burned her eyes and her heart swelled in her chest. After all these years she was returning home.

"Are you all right?" He grasped her elbow.

"Yes." She lowered her hands and noticed they were shaky. "I...I thought we weren't going to America because you didn't have any business there at the moment."

"I have to attend a few meetings," he said as he slowly released her arm. "I thought you'd be pleased. You keep suggesting a quick trip to the United States."

Alarm shot through her. Had she been that obvious?

She cast a quick glance at Nadir. He was alert. Watchful. Suspicion lurked in his dark eyes.

"Thank you," she said with a gracious smile as her heart thumped wildly. She stood on her tiptoes and grazed her lips against his cheek. "It's a wonderful surprise."

"Apparently."

She blushed at his dry tone. She wished she had controlled her response. She needed to be more careful. No way would she mess up right before she reached her goal. "What part of America?"

"New York City," he replied, his eyes never leaving her face. "We'll stay for a couple of days."

"I can't wait," she said, and she tenaciously held on to her gracious smile while she thought her heart was going to burst with relief. "I'll get dressed right away."

She hurried inside before Nadir could say a word or change his mind. A wild energy pulsed in her veins. She was going to be in America in a few hours. After all these years of wishing, dreaming and planning, it felt as if her mind was caught in a chaotic whirlwind.

Zoe looked over her shoulder and saw Nadir. His head was bent down as he punched something into his phone. She was ready to leave Jazaar, to abandon her old life. But was she prepared to abandon everything she had with him?

She didn't know. All these years she had thought she could walk away without a backward glance, but that was before she'd fallen in love with her husband.

He was a fool. Nadir gritted his teeth as he punched out a number on his phone. He'd seen the truth on her face. She wasn't able to hide it. Why hadn't he seen it sooner? Now he knew the real reason Zoe wanted so desperately to go to America.

He rubbed his forehead with tense fingers as he placed

the phone to his ear. He'd known something was up when Zoe, oh, so casually, kept suggesting a quick trip to the United States. It was more than a passing curiosity about the country where she had once lived. She was determined—no, *driven* to get to America.

But he had not quite figured out what she wanted in America. It turned out that she had given him all the evidence throughout their honeymoon. He had been too infatuated, too enamored with her, to put the clues together.

"Grayson?" he said when his head of security picked up the line. "I need you to track down someone in the United States and keep surveillance on him. His name? Musad Ali. He lives in Chicago."

Nadir disconnected the call and stared unseeingly into the blue water of the pool. He was tempted to cancel the trip to New York, but she would yearn for it even more. He'd take her and show her that there was nothing and no one waiting for her in America.

Once and for all, he would prove that all Zoe needed was him.

# CHAPTER THIRTEEN

TIMES SQUARE was exactly what she'd expected. It was late at night, but the streets were bright and shining from all the lights. Zoe glanced at the large-screen television billboards that were several stories high. Lights of every color flashed before her eyes. Crowds of people choked the sidewalk. Vivid yellow New York cabs fought for an inch on Broadway. The scent of street vendors' salty pretzels wafted in the air.

The city was energizing. Loud. Big, bold and very American. And yet for some reason she didn't feel at home. She missed the peace and tranquility of the Jazaari desert.

*It's only because you're not used to it,* Zoe told herself as she and Nadir left the opulent theater where they had attended the opening night for a Broadway play. She had grown up in a quiet Houston suburb and spent the past several years in a much smaller village. She was simply out of practice. She would adapt quickly.

A limousine was waiting for them at the exit. Zoe paused and looked at Nadir. He was stunning in his black tuxedo and wore it with enviable ease. The suit emphasized his athletic physique and hinted at his glamorous life.

"Let's walk back to the hotel," she suggested. "It's not that far away."

Nadir gave her an indulgent look. "You can't get enough of this city."

She smiled in response as he dismissed the limo driver. She liked New York City, but she wouldn't have enjoyed it without him. Nadir was the perfect guide. He was entertaining, attentive and fascinating. When she was with him her day was full and exciting. It was going to be difficult giving all this up for a life of narrow focus and solitude.

Nadir rested his hand on her back as he guided her along the sidewalk. The front of the theater was packed with women dripping in diamonds and men in white scarves and black ties. None of the men could compare to the elegance and masculine beauty of her husband.

She walked through the crowd, inhaling the mingled perfumes and brushing up against fur coats and sequined jackets. Celebrities, politicians and titans of industry hustled to get a chance to speak to Nadir. It suddenly dawned on Zoe that this would be the perfect time to disappear. She slowed her step as she considered the opportunity.

It was nighttime and there was a big crowd. Most of the people were focused on Nadir. She started to breathe faster, her hands growing cold as she contemplated her next move. She was in the middle of a jostling crowd and that was a security team's nightmare. She knew from sightseeing earlier that a subway station was nearby. What was stopping her?

But as the thought crossed her mind she rejected the idea. She wasn't prepared. The blood kept pumping hard through her veins as she looked around, noticing all the escape options. She couldn't do it. She couldn't walk away from Nadir like this.

She knew he would be sick with worry. He would tear this city apart looking for her, believing she was lost or in danger in this overwhelming place. His protective streak was often an obstacle, but it felt good to have someone strong and powerful looking out for her best interests.

Zoe reached out at her side and immediately found Nadir's hand. He slid his large, warm palm against hers before lacing their fingers together. With a simple touch Zoe felt safe and cared for. She didn't have to look for him to know he was there, ready to take her hand.

Would she ever be ready to leave him?

Zoe bit her lip as the thought flickered in her mind. She had no answer, and that worried her. Sensing Nadir's gaze on her, she glanced up and found him watching her. His harsh features were softened, his dark eyes gleaming, and there was a hint of a smile on his hard mouth.

"Thank you for taking me to the play," she said.

"It was my pleasure." His voice was a sexy rumble.

A slow heat suffused her body. She was acutely aware of how her red evening gown hugged her curves and the way her soft wrap brushed her skin. The past week had been all about pleasure.

"What did you think of it?" she asked.

"I enjoyed watching you the most." He leaned forward and whispered in her ear. "I find your enthusiasm very sexy. And you find everything in this city exciting."

"You can't blame me," she said with a laugh. Everything she did with Nadir was brighter and sweeter. Better. There was only one explanation for it. "I'm still on my honeymoon."

They had spent most of their time exploring Manhattan, walking hand-in-hand through Central Park and strolling through shops and museums. Leisurely lunches had a tendency to last for hours as they talked and laughed. Their evenings had been filled with the theater, sporting events and the most exclusive lounges.

And the nights they shared were magical. Nadir made

love to her with an intensity that blew away all her inhibitions. She couldn't deny him anything.

She wondered if their married life would continue this way, or if the connection she felt with him was just a little honeymoon enchantment. Would Nadir continue to make their time together a priority? Right now he didn't want any interruptions or distractions, but how long would that last? This week Nadir had gone so far as to turn off his phone when they were together. That simple gesture was more important to her than their trip to a famous jewelry store after-hours.

"Are you sure you're able to take all this time off from work?" she asked as they waited at a crosswalk for the light to change. "I don't want to wake up in the middle of the night and find you working."

Nadir gave a slanted smile. "Why would I spend the night with my laptop when I have you in my bed?"

"Why indeed?" she replied as a blush warmed her face. She shyly ducked her head as they crossed the street. It was only when they were in bed that she could express her love and trust in Nadir.

Each day she fell a little more in love with him, but she wasn't confident about expressing it. They had an arranged marriage, after all. Emotions and love weren't part of the deal.

That was the real reason why she hadn't disappeared from his life the moment they arrived at the JFK airport. Zoe's mind clung to that thought as they passed by a ruby-red glass staircase. It wasn't because there had been no right time to escape, or because she was afraid of the unknown. It was because her love for Nadir was growing so strong that she was willing to risk her freedom to stay with him.

She shivered as the truth hit her. He pulled his hand

away from hers, only to wrap his arm around her shoulders. She sighed when he drew her close to him, inhaling the crisp autumn night and the faint sandalwood of his cologne.

"Cold?" Nadir murmured as they walked in tandem, hip to hip. "We're almost at the hotel."

Zoe leaned her head against his broad shoulder. What if she stayed with him? Would that be so bad? Her chest tightened as the forbidden thought floated through her mind. She had never allowed herself to think of the possibility, yet it had drifted around her like a shadow for the past week.

As they entered the stunning lobby of the luxury hotel Zoe allowed herself to consider the question. Nadir wasn't like the men she knew. She could get an education and she could travel with him. She wouldn't live with the relatives who were the main source of her misery in Jazaar.

But she couldn't give up her dreams of practicing medicine now. Not after such a long struggle. Not when she had finally set foot on American soil.

If she went back to Jazaar with Nadir she'd have to give up the future she'd planned. She wouldn't get the chance to fulfill her dream of becoming a doctor.

Was she willing to throw away what she had for something that might come true? What she had with Nadir would develop into something strong and everlasting. She would never meet another man like him, and could never love anyone as she loved him.

And what were her chances of becoming a doctor? Zoe frowned as she entered the private elevator with her husband. She hated to ponder the possibility of failure. There were many people who pursued a medical career and didn't make it. What made her any different? She didn't even know if she could get into a university.

Nadir, on the other hand, had offered her a great opportunity to work with the health ministry. She knew that if she worked hard she could make a difference. It wasn't her dream, but it was something. It was close enough.

He was also offering her something she had always thought out of reach: a family. There was no family waiting for her in Houston, and she had always known that she would be alone there, trying to survive and follow her dream. After living with her relatives, after her relationship with Musad, she had thought she wanted to be alone.

As the elevator doors closed she stared blindly at the floor numbers flashing on the screen. Was she really considering changing her goals this late in the game? Could she stay with a man known as The Beast?

"You've grown very quiet," Nadir said as he raised her hand to his mouth and brushed his lips against her fingertips. "What are you thinking about?"

His question snapped her out of her reverie. "Actually, I was wondering about your nickname."

Nadir went very still. "What about it?"

"What really happened on your wedding night with Yusra?" Zoe wasn't sure if she was ready for the answer. She might have built an image of Nadir up in her mind. Maybe he *was* The Beast and she refused to see it.

Nadir pushed a button to pause the elevator. "Why do you want to know?"

She shrugged. "It doesn't make sense to me. You use the reputation to intimidate your opponents, but I know you're not a violent man."

Nadir looked steadily into her eyes. He showed no expression, but she sensed he was on guard. "Yusra miscarried after the ceremony."

"Oh." Her chest tightened. He'd had a relationship with Yusra. Of course he had. Yusra was gorgeous and the perfect Jazaari woman. Jealousy twisted inside her. Not only had they had a love-match, but Yusra had been carrying his child. "I thought you'd had an arranged marriage."

"It *was* an arranged marriage," he explained slowly. "The baby wasn't mine."

Zoe's mouth dropped open. "No way. Yusra? I can't wrap my mind around that. Who was the father?"

"I don't know. She wasn't going to confide in me."

"All that blood and the pain. A miscarriage would explain it. I'm surprised no one considered that possibility. They were far too willing to believe Yusra's side of the story."

"I should have handled the situation better," Nadir admitted as he looked away. "I could have annulled the wedding in a less spectacular fashion. I was angry, and during that time I allowed my emotions to rule my head."

"But you had to sever the relationship?" She knew Nadir could never stay with a woman who betrayed him. "You couldn't trust her after that?"

He nodded slowly. "I never told anyone outside my family."

And now he was sharing the secret with her. Zoe understood the significance in that and wasn't going to take it lightly. She squeezed his hand. "You should have defended yourself when the gossip started."

"No, that would have placed Yusra in a dangerous position. I was furious with her, but she would have been punished for sex outside of marriage. It was difficult enough to keep her hospital information a secret."

"I should have known that was what happened." She had instinctively known that Nadir hadn't hurt his first wife, but she could have put the medical clues together.

"How would you?"

"Give me some credit. I've been your wife for over a

month. I've seen you at your best and at your worst. I know you could never hurt a woman."

Nadir rested his forehead on hers and sighed. "Thank you, Zoe."

"But you didn't need to adopt The Beast reputation," she said softly. "I'm sure there are some people who would have believed in you."

"You believe in me." He brushed his lips against hers. "That's all I need."

And she had believed in him for a while. Zoe wasn't sure when she'd started to see past his reputation. She wouldn't have lain in bed with Nadir if she'd suspected he was abusive. She wouldn't have considered staying married to him if she'd thought he had the potential to be violent.

And she *was* going to stay with him, she decided as the nervousness bubbled up inside her. She could be married to a man known as The Beast because she knew the truth.

She needed to be with him. They were a team. A couple. She easily imagined building a future together and eventually creating a family. She wanted this dream even if it meant giving up the idea of becoming a doctor.

"No more talk about Yusra," Nadir said. "Instead, I want to take you dancing. We can go to the nightclub you mentioned."

"It will only take me a few minutes to change." Zoe leaned into him, absorbing his heat and strength. "And what shall we do tomorrow?"

"Whatever you want," he promised as he slid his hand along the length of her arm. "Tomorrow is our last day here."

The idea suddenly made her jumpy. Her pulse began to accelerate and she pulled away from him. "And then we return to Jazaar?" She'd meant to sound casual, but her voice came out high and reedy.

"Yes."

She felt a bead of sweat on her forehead and her stomach cramped with anxiety. She felt trapped, caged in the elevator. What was wrong with her? She had made up her mind, but her instincts hadn't gotten the message.

Was it a good idea to return to the place she had tried so hard to escape? She brushed her forehead with a shaky hand. Was she thinking this through enough?

Nadir turned and cradled her face in his hand. When he caressed her mouth with a kiss she closed her eyes and melted into him. The panic blurred and the anxious questions faded away as she returned the kiss.

Yes, she was making the right decision. She was going to survive in Jazaar. This time she had Nadir at her side. This time she would thrive.

She barely heard the chime and reluctantly broke the kiss the moment the private elevator opened into the penthouse suite. She saw the sensual promise in his eyes and felt the curl of excitement low in her belly.

As they crossed the threshold to the entry room, she saw the butler approach.

"Good evening, Your Highnesses," the tall young man said. "I trust you enjoyed the play?"

"Yes, we did," Zoe answered with a bright smile as Nadir helped remove her wrap. "Thank you."

"You have a visitor," the butler informed Nadir as he accepted their coats.

Zoe saw a movement in the corner of her eye. She turned to see Nadir's brother Rashid step out of the balcony that overlooked Times Square and into the room. While he wore a T-shirt, jeans and sneakers, his mood was anything but casual. He appeared just as unfriendly as when she'd met him briefly at her wedding ceremony.

As she greeted him with a polite smile, she saw a disapproving look in his eyes before he ignored her completely. Zoe wasn't sure why, but she sensed that her honeymoon was officially over.

"Rashid, your manners need to improve," Nadir said as he watched Zoe enter the bedroom to change for the nightclub. He waited until she'd closed the door before he turned his attention on his brother. "Not only have you crashed my honeymoon, but you were bordering on rude to Zoe."

Rashid shrugged off the reprimand. Nadir frowned at his brother's attitude. His brother should make an attempt to welcome his bride into the family. What did he have against Zoe?

"There'd better be a good reason why you're here," he said as he invited Rashid to sit down. Under normal circumstances he would be happy to see his brother, but he didn't want the world to intrude on his relationship with his wife. He wanted to focus on his marriage and build a solid foundation.

"Your honeymoon has lasted for over a month." Rashid leaned back and spread his arms on the back of the sofa.

"I have also conducted business." Nadir silently admitted to himself that he hadn't kept to his usual brutal schedule. He did his duty, but Zoe was his priority.

"I'm just relaying a message from our father." Rashid hooked one foot over his knee. "You are a sheikh and you are needed to deal with matters of the state."

"And I will return the day after tomorrow." Nadir strolled over to the window and looked out at the iconic view. "Couldn't this have waited?"

"I wanted to give you an idea of what you are facing." Rashid rose from his seat and walked over to stand next to his brother. "Many people have declared that The Beast has been tamed by his American bride."

Tamed? Nadir scoffed at the suggestion. When it came to Zoe, he didn't feel very civilized. Just the thought of her made him passionate and territorial. "Soon they will forget that nickname."

"Because they think you've become soft," Rashid argued. "Many of your progressive ideas are now under attack because you aren't perceived as ruthless anymore."

"Ridiculous. I will show them not to underestimate me." And once his country got to know Zoe they would admire and love her as their future Sultana. "That reminds me I want to add Zoe to the health ministry. She is very interested in medicine and she has worked in women's health for years."

Rashid reared back. His mouth sagged open as he stared at Nadir. "You can't be serious," he whispered in horror.

"Why would you say that?"

"You married for political reasons." Rashid swept his arm out and pointed at the bedroom door. "Zoe Martin is a means to an end."

Nadir's jaw tightened as he controlled his temper. He didn't like Rashid's tone. His brother would soon learn that what had started out as an arranged marriage was proving to be his most important relationship.

"And now you've taken her on a lavish trip." He gestured at the penthouse suite. "Rumor has it that you take her advice. That you seek her counsel. And now all of sudden she's getting a powerful position in the kingdom? She must be very good in bed."

Nadir grabbed his brother by the shirt and pinned him against the window. "Be very careful how you speak about Zoe," he said in a low growl. "She is my wife."

"She is your blind spot," Rashid countered. "Marrying her was supposed to solve your problem with that tribe. Instead she has Westernized you."

"You think someone could dictate how I act?"

"I didn't think so until you met Zoe." Rashid pulled his shirt from Nadir's grasp. "But talk in the business world says otherwise. They say you are so besotted with her that you can't think straight."

Nadir arched an eyebrow. "The businessmen in Athens may not agree with you." Mexico City was another matter, but after discussing his strategy with Zoe he had miraculously triumphed.

"You're not as focused," Rashid insisted. "Not as driven. Your wife is becoming a dangerous distraction."

"So what if I'm not at every meeting or if I can't be reached every second of the day?" Nadir asked, his irritation sharpening his tone. "I don't have to explain my actions."

"I think you're acting like a fool with your wife. Giving her a place on the health ministry?" Rashid groaned at the thought. "What is *wrong* with you?"

He was falling for Zoe. Hard. That didn't mean that his decision-making was faulty. If anything, his eyes had been opened. Zoe was the wife he needed when he became Sultan.

"What happened to your plans?" his brother complained. "You were going to send her to the palace in the mountains. She was going to stay there out of the way so you could get back to your life in Omaira."

"So?" He had made those plans when he didn't know Zoe. Now he knew he couldn't live without her.

"Zoe is a liability. You need to stop stalling and follow your plan. The sooner the better."

Zoe slowly closed the bedroom door and staggered back. Her heart was racing, her stomach curling. She felt sick as Rashid's words spun in her head.

Nadir was going to pack her off to the mountains. The room whirled and slanted and she grabbed onto the back of a chair. He wanted to send her somewhere isolated and forget her while he returned to his life. It would be business as usual for him, purgatory for her.

The stinging news cut through her. Zoe's knees slowly buckled and she clumsily sat down. She couldn't believe it. She slowly shook her head as she stared at the closed door. Nadir had played her well.

She didn't trust anyone but she had believed in him. She had thought he cared for her, maybe even felt something like affection. But she had been mistaken. Nadir was only enjoying the sexual chemistry they shared.

She placed her head in her hands and drew in shallow breaths as she fought back nausea. She felt as if she had just dodged a bullet. She had almost given up her dream for Nadir. For a *man,* she thought bitterly.

It was sickening. Horrifying. She had been so close to her goal and had almost turned her back on it for the promise of something stronger. Deeper. Imaginary.

Zoe winced at her stupidity. Had the ministry offer been a lie? Had the caresses and late-night talks been pretend? She wanted to believe that Nadir had meant all that, but now she wasn't sure.

Her arms and legs started to shake. She wanted to run. Hide. Weep. She couldn't...not yet. Not until she had disappeared for good.

She had to behave as if her world hadn't turned upside down. That meant she couldn't hide in her room and lick her wounds. Zoe slowly rose from her chair on unsteady feet.

Now she needed to act as if she was a happy bride on her honeymoon. It hurt to think of the way she'd felt just a few minutes ago. How blissful, how incredibly ignorant she had been of Nadir's plans.

She blinked back tears and took a deep breath. She had to try. If she could successfully pretend to be a shy, virginal bride on her wedding night, then she could do this. Nadir expected to see a wildly naïve woman, Zoe decided with a spurt of anger. She wouldn't have to put up the act for long before she disappeared into the night.

She straightened her shoulders and flipped back her hair. The anger inside her started to grow, flaring hot and bitter, eating away at her. She took a deep breath and pasted on a smile. It was showtime.

She swung the door open and strode into the sitting room. She looked in the direction of the men, careful not to make eye contact with Nadir as they turned to her. She sashayed her hips as if she was ready to party.

"I'm sorry I took so long," she said to Nadir without looking in his direction. "Rashid, are you going night-clubbing with us?"

Rashid chose not to answer. Somehow she had expected that. What was the point of communicating with a sister-in-law when she was going to be thrown into a prison for the rest of her life?

"Nightclubbing?" Nadir stared at her light blue bandage dress and skyscraper heels.

She saw the sexual heat in his eyes. Her traitorous body responded eagerly, her nipples rasping against her bra. Zoe was tempted to tease him before declaring he could never touch her again. *Never again.*

"I'm sorry, Zoe," Nadir said with what sounded like true regret. "We won't be able to go tonight. Something came up."

"Oh, that's a shame." She gave a pout and saw Nadir's

gaze settle on her lips. She'd rather he watch her mouth than read her eyes. "Well, I can go by myself."

"Go...by yourself?" Nadir repeated dully as Rashid's jaw dropped.

"I'll be all right." She brushed off his concern with an ebullient wave of her hand. Wild emotions churned inside her as she hurried for the elevator. The click of her heels echoed the fast beat of her heart. "I have a security team. Nothing will happen to me."

"You are *not* going to a club."

Nadir's harsh tone would make anyone obey, but Zoe was beyond listening. She needed to escape before they returned to Jazaar. She needed to get away from Nadir before she talked herself into staying with him.

"But you'll be busy." She didn't look back and pressed the elevator button. *Open... Open... Please open...*

"Zoe, you will stay here." He was at her side just as the elevator doors opened. He cupped her elbow and turned her to face him. "In fact, the urgent work I have won't take too long. Rashid and I will work here."

Damn, she had played it all wrong. Despair clawed at her chest. She had to get out of here, had to disappear, but Nadir wasn't letting her out of his sight. So much for slipping out of his life while he wasn't looking.

"Download an e-book," he suggested as he guided her away from the elevator. "I'll be in soon."

"If you insist." She wasn't going to get out tonight. She'd have to bide her time. "Goodnight, Rashid," she said with a smile.

Rashid didn't say a word and turned away. Yeah, that guy didn't like her at all, Zoe decided as she kept her smile steady.

"Goodnight, Nadir." She brushed her lips against his

cheek and stepped back before he could deepen the kiss. She hurried to the bedroom as tears threatened to fall.

She should have known better. The scent, the feel, the heat of him had brought on a cascade of emotions. She never should have gotten close to him. She should have left when she had a chance. But she was going to make up for the mistake now.

## CHAPTER FOURTEEN

"Gone?" Nadir's head snapped up as panic blazed through his veins. He stared at Grayson, his head of security, standing in the center of his office. "What do you mean that Zoe is gone? Gone where?"

Nadir remained very still as dark emotions burned through him like acid. He restrained himself from jumping into action. He wanted to go out into the city and tear it apart. He needed to find her and bring her back safe.

"We don't know, Your Highness," Grayson admitted.

The man showed no expression, but Nadir could tell that he was shaken by the security breach.

"We lost her around the Rockefeller Plaza."

Zoe was gone.

The words rippled in head. He had spent all night going over business with Rashid. When he'd looked in on her this morning Zoe had still been fast asleep. He had been tempted to wake her up, but he'd had a breakfast meeting he couldn't afford to miss.

He rubbed his hand over his face. *Gone.* He should have kept a closer eye, but he had grown too arrogant. Too complacent.

"The best-case scenario is that Zoe has got lost, but it's unlikely. We would have spotted her."

"She's been gone for an hour?" Nadir dropped his hands

and sprang from his chair. He began to pace behind his desk. He should have been contacted immediately. "Zoe's not lost. She would have returned to the hotel."

"We have all systems in place," Grayson assured him. "If it's a kidnapping the phones are—"

"It's not a kidnapping," Nadir said, and stopped in front of the window that overlooked the Hudson River. Zoe had wanted to come to America from the moment they were married. There was only one thing that had driven her here. Nadir's eyes narrowed into slits as jealousy roared to life. One person.

"We contacted the butler at your hotel suite," Grayson informed him. "The Sheikha didn't pack a bag. Nothing is missing."

Nadir's mouth twisted. Even his security detail had considered the possibility that Zoe had left him. He had not seen it coming. He had done everything to make her happy and satisfied. Where had he failed?

"Check on the whereabouts of Musad Ali," Nadir said in a low growl. He glanced up at the gray skies. "If you find him, you'll find Zoe."

He had to admit the truth: Musad was the real reason why Zoe had married The Beast. It hadn't just been to get out of her uncle's house or out of Jazaar. She wanted to be with her lover.

Nadir closed his eyes as he fought off a wave of dizziness. The blood roared in his ears. He slowly opened his eyes. He wasn't going to let her go without a fight.

*Zoe* was his wife. Every action he made was to protect and care for his woman. Their relationship would always be his top priority. He had thought this honeymoon would demonstrate his commitment to her.

"She can't have gotten far," Grayson said, his voice

sounding far away, although he hadn't moved. "I'll check the airlines, car rentals, bus and train depots."

Zoe had been acting differently since they came to America. She'd been quieter and often lost in thought. Many times he had caught her staring out the window or staring at her hands. Had she spent those moments daydreaming about her lover and planning her rendezvous?

"It's a damn shame she doesn't have a cell phone," Grayson muttered. "We could have tracked her GPS."

Nadir froze as a glimmer of hope flickered inside him. He slowly lifted his head and turned to Grayson. "There *is* a way we can track her."

"Good. How do you want me to retrieve her?"

Nadir slowly exhaled. "We don't." He barely got the words out. "We let her go."

*A few months later*

"Are you sure you want to go home, Zoe?" Cathy asked as they stood in front of Zoe's apartment building. "It's not even midnight."

"Thanks, but tomorrow is my first day of work," Zoe said to the small group of friends. "I can't waltz in there after partying all night."

"All right, all right," Cathy conceded. "We understand."

"Goodnight!" Zoe said with a wave. She enjoyed hanging out with the group of college students. They didn't have a lot in common, but she wasn't so lonely when she was with them.

She had been in Houston, Texas, for only a few months, and thanks to a few pawn shops and the haggling talent she'd picked up in Jazaar she had managed to finance a few things on her dream list. She had passed her high school equivalency test and would soon go to night classes at the community college. Tomorrow she would be a receptionist at a doctor's office. It was nowhere close to her dream of becoming a doctor, but it was a step in the right direction.

Returning to Houston hadn't been the homecoming she had envisioned during her dark, lonely days in Jazaar. Once she had gained her freedom Zoe had been compelled to return to her hometown. She had thought she would feel peace or relief once she stepped onto Texas soil. Instead she had felt lost and disoriented.

Her childhood home had been torn down for new housing. Friends had moved away. The hospital that had been a second home to her had changed so much that it was barely recognizable. There was very little to remind her of her parents. She only had their graves to visit.

When she stood at the cemetery and stared at their simple gravestones Zoe knew she had to push on and continue her family's work. She had no pictures or heirlooms to keep the memories alive, but she had always felt close to her parents when she practiced medicine.

Zoe was slowly rebuilding her life and had even got a place of her own. She glanced up at the large, nondescript building. The small studio apartment barely fit a table and a sofabed. That was all she needed for now, and it was all hers.

As she opened the security door she realized her friend Timothy was at her side.

"I'll walk you up," he offered, and held the door for her.

"That's very sweet of you, but I can manage." All her new friends were protective of her. They could tell she wasn't familiar with city life.

"I insist." He grasped her elbow and led her into the building.

Zoe held her tongue as they walked through the corridor. Timothy would find out soon enough that she could take care of herself. He didn't know much about her life. None of her new friends did. She was still a little reserved with them and hadn't shared much of her past. They probably wouldn't believe her. What sheikha wore clothes from a charity thrift shop?

If she *was* still a sheikha... She had had no contact with her husband. Nadir had never found her. Had he even looked for her? Or was he looking for another wife? Someone more suitable?

She pushed the thought away when she reached her door, Zoe grabbed her keys. "I should be fine, now," Zoe said. "Thanks, Timothy."

"No problem." He rested his arm against the doorframe and leaned in. "Good luck on your first day of work."

"Thanks. I'm a little nervous," she admitted. She had worked so hard to get to this point. What if it wasn't worth it?

"You'll do great," he said, before placing his hand on her shoulder. "We should celebrate tomorrow night."

"I would love to, but most of the gang has class tomorrow."

"I meant just the two of us." He squeezed her shoulder. "Like a date."

She dropped her keys. Zoe bent down quickly to retrieve them as her mind whirled. She'd had no idea Timothy was interested in her.

She wished she was interested in him. He was a nice guy. He was supportive, kind and hard-working. He was also handsome and fun to be around. He was safe.

But he was no Nadir.

And that was the problem. Zoe closed her eyes shut as grief and regret slammed through her. She was still in love with her husband. Missed him so much that it hurt. She couldn't imagine being with another man.

"Thanks, Timothy, but I can't," she replied as she rose to her full height, clenching the keys in her hand. "I just got out of a relationship and…"

He held up his hands in surrender. "Say no more. I understand. The time isn't right."

"Exactly." She was grateful that she didn't have to deal with any drama. That was another thing she liked about Timothy. There were no highs or lows. Life was calm around him.

"So I'll wait."

Zoe gritted her teeth. Waiting wasn't going to change anything. She could never feel for Timothy what she felt for Nadir. There was no spark, no passion. She couldn't imagine sacrificing all her dreams for Timothy.

And that was probably a good thing.

"I'll text you tomorrow to see how the job went," Timothy promised. He kissed her cheek, letting his lips linger on her cool skin. "Sweet dreams."

"Goodnight," she replied softly, and watched him leave. She wasn't sure what had brought that on. She had never shown any romantic interest in him. Or in any man for that matter. She had had tunnel vision from the moment she'd disappeared in Rockefeller Plaza.

She shook her head and entered her apartment. She flipped on the lights and gasped. Her heart lurched when saw Nadir sitting on her sofabed. Hot, swirling energy roared between them.

He had come to reclaim his bride.

"Nadir!" She stared into his eyes, unable to look away, to move. He looked menacing in a black designer suit. He sat quietly, but there was nothing casual about him. He was alert. Watchful. Ready to pounce.

"Who's loverboy?" he asked in a low growl.

"What are you doing here?" All of her nerve-endings

had sparked to life. Emotions swirled inside her, threatening to burst. One moment she felt comatose, and now she felt violently alive. "How did you get in?"

"I've come to take you home."

Home? No—more like prison. He wanted to send her to the remote regions of Jazaar. She knew she should dash outside and get away as fast as she could. But it would be of no use. Nadir wouldn't lose her twice.

"How did you find me?" Her voice croaked.

Nadir slowly stood. "Your e-book reader has Wi-Fi. My security team was able to triangulate your coordinates the first day you disappeared."

A humorless smile tugged at the corner of her mouth. She had left all of Nadir's gifts behind but she had forgotten that the e-reader was in her purse. She had eventually hocked it, along with everything else she had. It had hurt giving up that one gift.

"You've always known where I've been?" Her eyes narrowed with suspicion. "I don't believe you."

"I let you go because I thought I finally knew the real reason you married The Beast," Nadir said softly, almost nonchalantly. "Getting out of your uncle's house was only the first phase in your plans."

She didn't say anything. There was no point; it was true. Nadir had figured it all out.

"But you couldn't leave Jazaar unless you were accompanied by a male relative," he continued as he took a step closer. "Your Uncle Tareef wanted to keep you under lock and key. You didn't have anyone in your family who would cross your uncle. Fortunately, a husband would do."

Zoe gritted her teeth. She would not feel guilty. She would *not*. Nadir had had his reasons for marrying her. It pushed along his goals. She had the same right to go after her dreams.

"I thought you wanted to go to America for sentimental reasons." A muscle bunched in his jaw. "It was only while we were in Mexico City that I suspected the truth."

Of course. That was when she had attended the medical conference. Nadir had realized she wouldn't give up her dreams. "And yet we still traveled to America?"

Nadir shrugged his shoulder but she saw a glimpse of stark pain in his eyes. "I guess I was arrogant enough to believe that you would choose me."

She *had* chosen him—up to the moment when she'd heard of his plans. But she did not want to let him know she had been so weak. Zoe pressed her lips together. She wouldn't give him the satisfaction.

Nadir gave a deep sigh. "But my sacrifice was for nothing. You didn't meet with him. You didn't make any contact, didn't even try."

Zoe frowned. "Meet with whom?"

"Musad Ali," he said in an angry hiss. "Your first love."

Zoe stared at him and comprehension slowly dawned on her. "You think I did all this to get out of the country so I could rendezvous with...Musad?"

He nodded sharply.

"This is unbelievable. You think I went through all this to reunite with a man who treated me like dirt?" Zoe placed her hands on her hips. "What kind of woman do you think I am? Do you really believe that I would want to be with someone who abandoned me and exposed me to dangerous gossip?"

"What was I supposed to think?"

She glared at Nadir. "The only reason I would hunt Musad down is to kick his ass. But, honestly, he isn't worth the effort."

"You say that now because he stood you up."

"Let me make it clear," she said as anger flushed her

cheeks. "Musad is my ex-lover. Emphasis on *ex*. I am not in love with him and I was never in love with him."

"Then why did you escape from your security detail that day?" Nadir asked. "Why did you leave me?"

"Because I was ready to sacrifice every dream I had to be with you." She had been too caught up in the make-believe. It had felt real. Strong. Lasting. But it had been just a fantasy that had almost cost her her dreams. Her freedom. "I didn't know about your plans," she accused. "You had no intention of having a relationship with me once the honeymoon was over."

Nadir took a step back. "I never said that."

Zoe's mouth twisted with disgust. He was still lying to her. "I heard you, Nadir. I heard you talking to Rashid on our last night together. You planned on dumping me in the mountains of Jazaar."

Nadir muttered a savage oath and speared his fingers into his hair. "That was before I met you."

"You mean that was before you discovered there was sexual chemistry between us." Zoe crossed her arms. "That's why you allowed me to go on your business trip. Otherwise I would be trapped."

Nadir clenched his jaw. "I'd like to think that what we have is more than sexual chemistry."

"It *was*. It was a lot more for me," she confessed, and she felt tears threatening to spill over her lashes. "I learned how to trust you even when I was risking everything to be at your side. I was ready to give up my dreams for you. I was prepared to follow you back to Jazaar because I love you."

Shock chased across his face. Hadn't he known how she felt? How could he not have known? Wasn't it obvious in the way she lit up when he entered a room or in the way she kissed him? She had placed her trust in him again and again. She didn't do that for just anyone.

"I actually thought I could return to Jazaar, the one place I swore I would never visit again." She felt a teardrop trail down her cheek and angrily brushed it away. "I knew that you didn't love me back, but when I was with you I felt loved and cared for. And it all turned out to be a lie."

"It's not a lie." Nadir reached for her, but she backed away, her spine hitting the door. "I love you, Zoe. I want you to come back."

Her breath hitched in her throat. He loved her? No, she wouldn't believe it. He was up to something. "I'm never coming back. Do you really think I can trust you after I found out about your plans?"

"I want to be with you. Every day. Every night." He took another step closer. "I want you at my side."

She shook her head. "Why? Why now after all these months?"

"I thought I was doing what was best for you. Letting you go was the hardest thing I've ever done," he confessed.

"But you didn't let go. Not really. You were tracking me all this time."

"I had to make sure you were safe. I stayed away so you could live the way you wanted. But I can't let you go," he said rawly. "I need you in my life."

"No, you don't. You need to find another wife. I'm the worst sheikha in history. I'm not a proper Jazaari woman." Her voice rose as he kept advancing. "I'm a liability."

"That's not true." He placed his hands against the door, effectively caging her. He surrounded her but was careful not to touch her. As if he didn't trust his restraint. "You are the wife I want. You are the advisor I need. We make a great team."

"No." She didn't want to remember those times. The

moments when she had felt connected with Nadir. When she had believed they belonged together.

"Zoe," he said in a low, pleading tone. He rested his forehead against hers. "I make sacrifices every day to perform my duty. I've given up a lot to fulfill my destiny. But I won't give up *you*."

He brushed his lips against hers. The faint touch sent shockwaves through her body. It took all of Zoe's willpower to remain still.

"Please, Zoe," Nadir's voice cracked with emotion. "Please give our marriage a chance. I can't live without you."

"And I can't live *with* you," Zoe whispered. She flattened her hands against his chest and tried to push him away. "Not in Jazaar. Not in a royal life that keeps me from what I'm meant to do."

"I will do everything in my power to protect you and your dreams," he promised, clasping his hands around hers.

She noticed how his hands shook.

"You will have the best tutors so you can get your medical degree."

She froze. "The palace won't allow that."

"The two of us will fight for it. As a team. And we'll fight for your right to practice medicine."

"That's going to be a battle." An ugly, bitter fight that could weaken his position in the kingdom.

"It'll be worth the fight." He lifted her hand and pressed his mouth against her palm. "And you can travel whenever you want. Without a male relative's permission."

Hope flared inside her. "Wouldn't you worry that I would run away?"

"I trust you."

She looked in his eyes and knew he spoke the truth.

Even if she ran away, he trusted that she would return to him again and again.

Zoe wished she was brave. She wanted to go with him, but she was too afraid. "Nadir…I just don't know if I can return to Jazaar. I always felt trapped there."

"I know."

"I want to be with you," she admitted, "but I don't know if I can take that risk."

"Which is why we'll stay here."

Zoe's eyes widened. Had she heard him correctly? "Here? In Texas? But you have to be in Jazaar. You said so yourself."

"We will have a home here and one in Jazaar. I will make trips to my homeland when it's necessary. You can return to Jazaar when you're ready."

His homeland was important to him. She couldn't allow him to give that up. As cosmopolitan as Nadir was, he thrived in the desert. "But Jazaar…"

"Is going through many changes," Nadir insisted. "When I returned to Jazaar I saw the kingdom through your eyes. I've been making it a place where you can feel safe and free."

"You did all that? For me?" She cupped his face with her hands and stared at him in wonder. "But what if I'm never ready to return?"

"Then we will make our home elsewhere," he promised. "I will live where you want. Tell me you're willing to give us another chance."

She stared into his eyes, her heart pounding fiercely as she took the leap of faith. "Yes, Nadir. I want to share my life with you. I want another chance."

Triumph shone in his dark eyes. "You won't regret it, Zoe. I promise."

"I believe you," she said with a tremulous smile, before Nadir captured her mouth with his in a hard kiss.

# EPILOGUE

*Two years later*

ZOE sat in front of Nadir on his powerful Arabian horse as they watched the sun dip behind the sand dunes of Jazaar. A cooling breeze tugged against her caftan, but she felt warm and secure in his arms. She smiled as the colors of saffron and gold streaked the sky.

"You're right," she said softly as she leaned her head against Nadir's shoulder. "A Jazaari sunset is one of the most beautiful sights of the world."

"I believe I said nothing can compare with it," Nadir murmured as he stroked her hair.

Zoe's skin tingled from his gentle touch. "I don't know if that's true. I haven't traveled as much as you. *Yet*," she clarified.

She had made several international trips alone in the past year to attend public health conferences. As much as she enjoyed the trips, and learned valuable information, she didn't like staying away from home for too long.

The gold streaks faded and the sky turned to sapphire. A sigh of satisfaction rumbled in Nadir's chest. "Jazaar is becoming more and more beautiful."

"I agree." He was the reason for that. He wasn't the Sultan, but through his power and connections her husband was slowly modernizing the kingdom. Zoe no longer saw Jazaar as a prison but rather as a burgeoning paradise. The desert was her home, her haven.

Nadir looked down at her. "You do?"

"Yes, I thought the dedication for the women's clinic today was a sight to behold." It had been a struggle getting the health ministry to listen to her, but she had made her voice heard.

"Your parents would have been honored at having the clinic named after them."

She nodded. "I can't wait to open more around the kingdom."

"And one day you'll work in those clinics."

Zoe heard the pride in his voice. "One day," she agreed. "It's probably a good thing I'm not going to any more conferences," she said as she patted her rounded stomach hidden under the folds of her caftan. "I'm staying close to home for the next year or two."

"Good idea." Nadir covered her hands with his. Zoe swallowed the lump in her throat at the sight of them cradling her pregnant belly. "Sure you won't get bored?"

She scoffed at the idea. "Are you kidding? My schedule is packed before this baby arrives."

She had so many dreams, and Nadir was making sure she had every opportunity to make them come true. Her life was so full that her world was only limited by her imagination.

"We should get back to the camp," Nadir said with a tinge of regret as he lightly tugged the horse's reins. "Your Arabic tutor will be waiting."

Okay, she loved *almost* every minute of her life. Reading and writing Arabic was more difficult than she had ever imagined. "Can I skip the lesson tonight?" she asked.

"Don't you want to read Jazaari folk tales to our baby?"

"At this rate our baby will have to read them to me."

He chuckled. "Perhaps you need another incentive. Wouldn't you like to read our marriage contract? Don't you want to know what I had to promise you?"

"No need." He supported her with her studies and encouraged her to make changes in the health ministry. He protected her and made sure she felt safe and loved. She had more than she had dared to dream. "You've given me everything I need."

Nadir curled his fingers under her chin and tilted her head so she could see his face. Her pulse quickened when she saw the love and devotion in his eyes.

"I love you, Zoe," he said as he reverently brushed his lips against hers.

Zoe reached up and cupped her hand against his cheek as she deepened the kiss. She knew he loved her, but she liked hearing it every day. Nadir wasn't going to let her down. He was the man she could trust and love. He was the man she could rely on.

"I love you, Nadir," Zoe said. "Let's go home."

\* \* \* \* \*

# MILLS & BOON®

## Why not subscribe?

Never miss a title and save money too!

Here's what's available to you if you join the
exclusive **Mills & Boon Book Club** today:

✦ *Titles up to a month ahead of the shops*
✦ *Amazing discounts*
✦ *Free P&P*
✦ *Earn Bonus Book points that can be redeemed
  against other titles and gifts*
✦ *Choose from monthly or pre-paid plans*

### Still want more?

Well, if you join today we'll even give you
*50% OFF your first parcel!*

So visit **www.millsandboon.co.uk/subs**
**or call Customer Relations on 020 8288 2888**
to be a part of this exclusive Book Club!

SUBS_2014

# The World of Mills & Boon

There's a Mills & Boon® series that's perfect for you. There are ten different series to choose from and new titles every month, so whether you're looking for glamorous seduction, Regency rakes, homespun heroes or sizzling erotica, we'll give you plenty of inspiration for your next read.

## By Request
*Relive the romance with the best of the best*
12 stories every month

## Cherish™
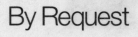
*Experience the ultimate rush of falling in love.*
12 new stories every month

## INTRIGUE...
*A seductive combination of danger and desire...*
7 new stories every month

## Desire™
*Passionate and dramatic love stories*
6 new stories every month

## nocturne™
*An exhilarating underworld of dark desires*
3 new stories every month

For exclusive member offers go to
**millsandboon.co.uk/subscribe**

WORLD_ M&Ba

# Which series will you try next?

*Awaken the romance of the past...*
6 new stories every month

*The ultimate in romantic medical drama*
6 new stories every month

# MODERN™

*Power, passion and irresistible temptation*
8 new stories every month

## MODERN
# tempted™

*True love and temptation!*
4 new stories every month

You can also buy Mills & Boon® eBooks at
**www.millsandboon.co.uk**

WORLD_ M&Bb

# MILLS & BOON®

## Why shop at millsandboon.co.uk?

Each year, thousands of romance readers find their perfect read at millsandboon.co.uk. That's because we're passionate about bringing you the very best romantic fiction. Here are some of the advantages of shopping at www.millsandboon.co.uk:

* **Get new books first**—you'll be able to buy your favourite books one month before they hit the shops

* **Get exclusive discounts**—you'll also be able to buy our specially created monthly collections, with up to 50% off the RRP

* **Find your favourite authors**—latest news, interviews and new releases for all your favourite authors and series on our website, plus ideas for what to try next

* **Join in**—once you've bought your favourite books, don't forget to register with us to rate, review and join in the discussions

Visit **www.millsandboon.co.uk** for all this and more today!

MILLS_WEB